THE SYDNEY CIRCLE

A NOVEL BY

Alice Ekert-Rotholz

Translated from the German by
Catherine Hutter

POPULAR LIBRARY

An Imprint of Warner Books, Inc.

A Warner Communications Company

THE SYDNEY CIRCLE

From the master storyteller who gave us the international bestseller *Rice in Silver Bowls*, THE SYDNEY CIRCLE was originally published in 1964 in Germany. Newly translated by Catherine Hutter, this is its first American paperback publication.

*   *   *

"COMPELLING...a story about present-day Australia, its society still in the making, with new immigrants working like yeast upon the old, its landscape, like Rigby, only half-tamed." —*Publishers Weekly*

"Anyone intrigued with 'strange, disorderly, magnificent' Sydney will want to read THE SYDNEY CIRCLE." —*St. Louis Globe-Democrat*

"Intriguing and stylishly written...holds just the right combination of suspense and interesting characterization to make it good entertainment." —*Booklist*

"Sprawling...teeming...the plot is compelling—sex, murder, ambition." —*Library Journal*

"Her characters are full and rich with meaning and her story contains depth." —*Ocala Star-Banner*

"This excellent novel grabs the reader from the very beginning and it is so interesting one is likely to forget work, duty, and even fun, to continue turning page after page. How it all ends is quite, quite satisfying." —*Wichita Falls Times*

Also by Alice Ekert-Rotholz

Checkpoint Orinoco*
Rice in Silver Bowls

PUBLISHED BY
POPULAR LIBRARY

*Forthcoming

For
Julia in Sydney
Robert in Melbourne
Margaret and Frances in Queensland
Patrick in Queensland

1

A Marriage in Sydney

I think often of what's wrong with my marriage. I'm a first-rate brooder. Father always said, "Don't worry. You have only one head." Mother would look at me thoughtfully and then say to Miss Jennings, "With a sour expression like that, Anne will never find a husband." Miss Jennings agreed.

Unlike me, Mother was lively, witty, and always busy. Understandably she wanted to get rid of me by marrying me off, but felt that I would turn out to be a dud in the London marriage market. She wrote thrillers that sold well, and Miss Jennings did the typing. After I was sixteen I didn't read Mother's thrillers any more. The hunt for the unknown perpetrator bored me and seemed somehow dated. Who on earth wants to know today who committed the murder in the hunting lodge? The only interesting thing is *why* anyone should prefer to shoot human beings rather than foxes or hares. But Mother went on working with her gaggle of suspects, and her bank account proved her right. Miss Jennings thought Mother was right too. Miss Jennings also had a bank account.

When Father wasn't practicing in Harley Street, he felt just as expendable as I did. We knew that Mother loved us in her way, but we would rather have been loved in our way. There's nothing new under the sun about that.

Our family home behind Avenue Road was old, rather dingy, and angular, but we liked it there. I crept daily into one or the other of its corners, and brooded to my heart's content. Father spent the little free time he had in the garden. He never pondered about our family life. He went to his club where everything was as it should be.

Mother enjoyed a happy marriage with her secretary. I couldn't stand Miss Jennings, and she reciprocated my feelings. When I was sixteen, I wrote my first poems. Mother wanted to know who on earth would want to publish anything like that. Poems were only another disgusting form of brooding. Of course she was right, but I had my pride and went on writing poetry. Our cat watched me. The poor thing had to listen to it too. Miss Jennings shook her head, with its thin, dyed curls, as she held my lyrical productions at a safe distance and read them through her glasses. Then she laid my old notebook on a side table with her long, pointed fingers. It was as if she thought my outbursts of lyricism might be catching. "How about a nice little novel, Anne?" she asked, stressing a friendly tone, and poured our sixth cup of tea.

We were sitting in Mother's twilit studio with its view of the autumnal garden. All the windows and doors were drafty, and the approaching darkness painted grotesque shadows on the walls. A true London October day, ideal for planning family matters with a disastrous outcome. October to February was Mother's best time. Miss Jennings could barely keep up with Mother's arrangement of corpses, named or nameless. Even though she always used the same formula, she thought up a different variation every time. "What nonsense!" I said sullenly. "I can't write novels."

Miss Jennings didn't like to be told by a sixteen-year-old girl that her ideas were nonsense. At Mother's request, I had to apologize. Mother treated her secretary like fragile Chelsea porcelain; she wasn't a member of the family and could therefore give notice. I sat there brooding silently, but Mother brought me back to reality fast. "Of course you can write novels! There's nothing simpler. but you do have to keep your eyes open and observe people."

"You certainly do," Miss Jennings said, quite superfluously. "Where would we be if all of us spent our time daydreaming?" She closed the curtains and turned on the desk lamp. Our family life was over for the day.

I disappeared to my attic room with my poems. I loved every piece of furniture in it, from the creaky couch with its faded Turkish cover from Manchester, to the antique bureau and two wobbly armchairs. Later I was sad when Alexander labeled my old furniture junk, and only my great-grandmother's bureau was allowed to accompany us to Sydney. It stands in some corner or other of our house in Vaucluse and still brings back family memories. Alexander fixed up my bedroom according to his own ideas. He was right. The bright Australian sun would have exposed the tired wood and scratches mercilessly.

I tore up my poems. Mother was right again. All of them were right. My poems were lousy. Beautiful emotions were not enough. Form and style were everything. That was the only point on which Mother and Alexander agreed.

Since I had no chance of winning laurels with my poetry, Father got me a job in a travel bureau in Piccadilly. In the evenings I sometimes went to lectures on topical subjects in a club on Avenue Road, not far from us. They were fairly simple lectures. There were a lot of gray-haired members in the club, with scholarly backgrounds and acute arthritis. There was tea and a discussion period. Since I had nothing exceptional to say, I said nothing. Anyway, I was the youngest member. Here life began at seventy.

Mother had given up long ago trying to make an attractive young lady of me. Miss Jennings had always known what a futile effort it was. Father had got the job in the travel bureau for me shortly before he died, so now we three women were living alone in the old house on Avenue Road. What I liked to do best was lie on my couch and read general psychology for home use. If I had been a more active person I would

probably have studied psychology. Mother could have taught
me quite a lot in this respect, but she had no time for my
hobbies. She had to concentrate on her plots. At meals she and
Miss Jennings conversed mainly about murder by poison, hidden wills and bank robbery. On Sunday she clipped scandal
articles from the paper. Miss Jennings had been keeping useful
crimes on file for years, and could come up any time with
scandalous, sensational material. If one took a look at this
alphabetically listed raw material one got the impression that
the London population was interested mainly in doing away
with their nearest and dearest. My aversion to newspaper scandals and sensational crimes must date from that day.

Gradually I learned to hate the sight of all the newspapers
lying around the house. The headlines wriggled like fat black
worms on tables and chairs. I would have loved to leave home,
but where was I to go? Since I didn't know, I stayed. Mother
had resigned herself to my unavoidable presence at tea time
long ago. She was even quite fond of me, although I had
disappointed her in every conceivable way. Shortly before my
engagement she sacrificed a little of her precious time and
bought a small Chelsea vase for me at an auction. It brought
tears to my eyes; my voice was choked when I thanked her.
She asked sharply if I had a cold and sent hot milk and honey
up to my room that night. Then she dictated to Miss Jennings
for three more hours. She was never tired. Or perhaps she was
just harder on herself than most people. Perhaps one has to be
like that if one wants to be successful.

One day Alexander Rigby turned up at our travel bureau in
Piccadilly: an architect from Sydney on a grand tour of Europe,
very tall, very sympathetic, and with an aura of Australian sea
air about him. He was forty years old, and his blond hair was
attractively gray at the temples. He was planning a trip to the
European continent. I was to arrange the itinerary for him.
What he liked and wanted to see was rivers, or the ocean, and
it was his intention to have a look at the architecture of various
periods. He told me all this very casually in his Australian
accent. It sounded as if his wishes weren't at all important,

yet he expected them to be fulfilled. I could tell this by his nose, which was long and narrow, and was hooked imperiously. In his long, ascetic face, his lips were surprisingly sensual, but when he pressed them together he suddenly looked cautious and slightly cruel. Anyway, he gave me this impression once, but then it was quickly dispelled. Mr. Rigby was exceptionally pleasant and could laugh like a boy. He had been to Scotland to look up some relatives, but had found none left. His mother had married a man in New South Wales when she had been very young, and never left Australia again. The remark about his mother was the only biographical bit of information he gave me. Did he avoid speaking about himself out of modesty?

He wanted to discuss his trip over a good meal and for this purpose invited me, by phone, to come to his West End hotel. "This is Rigby again. I want to know more about Paris." He paused for a moment before he invited me. That I might turn him down evidently never entered his mind. Nor mine! I was very rarely invited out because I had so little to offer in the way of conversation. In spite of the fact that I was twenty-eight years old, I still reddened when I was asked to express an opinion in front of a lot of people.

Mr. Rigby was waiting for me in the lobby. He came up to me walking lithely and with a carefree air. He was taller than all the other people around us, and his nose jutted out of his face like the prow of a ship. The women looked at him surreptitiously and curiously; he didn't seem to notice it. Much later I found out that every glance cast at him by women registered with Alexander Rigby, and that he couldn't live without their admiration. But he hid this need just as carefully as he hid his whole private life. He was an amusing conversationalist, but not communicative. As long as I was in love with him, I appreciated the fact that he didn't confide any dissonances of his soul to me.

Besides Paris and Brussels, he wanted to see the old cities in Switzerland and South Germany, and the modern buildings in Stockholm. I had been to several of these places with my father, and answered his questions to the best of my ability, but I had an oppressive feeling in the pit of my stomach when Mr. Rigby said, "What a pity that you don't have a graphic memory."

I didn't know exactly what he meant by that, but I realized that Mother had had every reason to tell me I should be more alert. Mr. Rigby was looking at me out of the corner of his eyes—had he noticed how the wind had gone out of my sails for a moment? "Forget it," he said cheerfully. "I like you just the same."

He could afford to be generous. He had enough graphic memory for three architects. Form and color were realities for him. Of course he also had a mathematical memory which bordered on the miraculous, but about that he was tactfully silent. I could sense that architecture was a passion with him. I knew nothing about any of his other passions. Out of politeness I asked him about Sydney. He immediately took out some photographs and explained the views—radiant colors, deep blue water, a luminous sky, snow-white yachts in the sun, many green islands, a huge silver bridge in the background. "Port Jackson," he murmured. "Sydney's harbor."

I stared at the photographs. "Are the colors really like that?" I asked shyly.

"Of course! We have the most beautiful harbor in the world— San Francisco excepted." After a while he added, "And the best life."

It could have sounded boastful, but it was a simple statement of fact. I asked him what he thought Europe had to offer him. He laughed loudly. "Oh . . . a lot!" he said, and looked at me suddenly in the eye. I reddened and swallowed my red wine the wrong way. He patted me on the back until I stopped coughing, then he looked calmly around the room again. "That woman should only wear gray-blue," he said unexpectedly. I hadn't even noticed her.

I found him extraordinary, and of course he lived on an exciting, sparsely populated continent. Sparsely populated? Mr. Rigby said that from Potts Point to King's Cross, Sydney was so densely populated, a kangaroo couldn't get through. Then he showed me a picture of his house in Vaucluse. It faced the water, in the background lay the bush, and it looked strangely uninhabited. "A beautiful house," I murmured. Mr. Rigby admitted that there were worse houses in Sydney. "We have a funny conglomeration of styles," he said. "All different, yet thrown together. And so much ornamentation."

I was silent as I thought that Alexander Rigby would probably fall flat on his face at the sight of our house with its gables, columns, and balconies, but fortunately he'd never get to see it. I would have liked to know if he was married, but didn't dare to ask. It was none of my business.

He spoke about hobbies, and raised his eyebrows in amusement when I told him about my evenings at the club. He probably hated all indoor activities. When he wasn't setting houses with glass frontage into the rocky walls around Sydney, he was painting bush birds with strange names, or spending weekends in his summer home in Manly. He was apparently a bachelor. I found it unbelievable that he lived alone, but he apparently went in for a lot of activities suited to a loner: he fished and sailed, surfed in the Pacific when he was in Manly, and designed bold, stark buildings which evidently sprang out of his strong protest against Victorian, Spanish, and just plain ugly suburban villas. At least that's the impression I got after our sixth dinner in the West End. I still didn't know if he was married, but I didn't tell myself any more that it was none of my business. I had gathered from the discussions in the club that one should not drive the art of self-delusion too far. I did not like to think of Mr. Rigby's pending departure.

At our farewell dinner, the lobster didn't taste good to me, although I was seldom treated to such delicacies. Every bite stuck in my throat. Perhaps Alexander's radiant mood depressed me. He was looking forward too much to the trip. In three days he would be in Paris. He said you couldn't show your face in Sydney if you'd missed "gay Paree" on your European tour. Then he tried to lift my spirits by telling me a lot of Australian stories which at first didn't sound funny but afterwards made me laugh. Mr. Rigby's humor was discreet and dry. I always noticed a few seconds too late that the story had been meant as a joke; then, when I laughed, he winked and asked what was so funny.

Now and then his eyes dimmed, as if he had discovered unpleasant memories at the bottom of his wine glass. Then something seemed to be torturing him, but he kept whatever it was to himself. He did everything he could to play the dinkum, the honest-to-God Aussie, the Australian as he is supposed to be in Europe—a nice, simple fellow who knew the bush inside out. He really did know the bush in New South Wales and Queensland very well, but that wasn't what mattered most to him, which was to be an Australian like every other Australian. I couldn't pass judgment on that. After all, Alexander Rigby was the first dinkum Aussie I had ever known.

He invited me to go to Paris with him.

I told them at home that I was going with a friend from the travel bureau. Mother was happy about it. After all, I was twenty-eight years old, and since Father's death had seen nothing more of the continent. Mother and Miss Jennings were busy right then with reports on the dealers in dope in Soho and Notting Hill, and as usual I was superfluous. My Aussie had only invited me because traveling in a foreign country left him little choice—that was perfectly clear to me—but I was happy just the same, and very grateful to him. He had no idea of how monotonous my life was, and I had taken good care not to let him know it. Mother did what she could for me. In spite of the royalties on her books, we never had enough money. We missed Father's income. The tax bureau seemed to be especially greedy to take a big bite out of the authors of thrillers. I looked in my closet and frowned. Oh well ... Rigby knew my restaurant wardrobe, and my good black dress had even elicited a compliment. It was simple, but very well tailored, and the back was practically nonexistent. I sang as I pressed it, "Anne Carrington!" I called myself to order. "You must be crazy!" What I really wanted to do after finishing my ironing was write a poem, but then I had given up writing poetry. I stretched out on the couch and read Shakespeare's sonnets. Shakespeare had said everything much better.

Alexander and I became engaged in Paris...

He saved me from an uneventful life. I am not one of those people who can take the bull by the horns. I am shy, and was born with no initiative. Oddly enough, I hadn't even been unhappy in my little rut. I love the familiar things of life. Alexander tore me abruptly into a totally strange, new world where dreamlike beauty and the dross of a big city appear in a brazen light without transition. Contrasts have always startled me. How was I ever to get used to these surroundings? Instinctively I had avoided the extravagant thing, and from the photographs, Sydney had looked pretty extravagant to me. High-rise houses, their glass eyes trained on the Harbour Bridge, towered into the tropical sky like architectural exclamation marks over dark streets and Victorian business buildings. The pictures showed forlorn barracks, all the same shape, in the old quarters of the city, and the arrogant crystal facade of Alexander's villa in the eastern suburb. There was also a small replica of Hyde Park which had to appeal to any Londoner. After all that, Alexander showed me his pictures of the Taronga Zoo, a vast natural park in which animals of every period and zone lived in their own widespread preserves. "I spend every free minute I have in Taronga," Alexander said.

He may have been right, he probably was, but it irritated me that everything in Sydney had to be more grandiose than anywhere else. Even the filth and desolation in the old harbor area was a painterly achievement in his eyes. He was a local patriot and made no efforts to hide it. And he told all this so softly and casually that it didn't sound boastful. But I sensed that he would resent even the mildest criticism of Sydney in particular, and of Australia in general. Once he showed me an aquarelle sketch of an Australian bird. "You can paint too?" I asked, astonished. "Nonsense!" he said at once. "I just daub for my pleasure. But our birds are magnificent."

He was fifteen years older than I. This I found wonderful. I had a weakness for father figures because my own father had understood and respected me. I had missed him very much, and my psychology books provided no information as to how a girl was to get along without a father. The other fatherless girls I knew seemed to manage very well.

It was actually ridiculous that I looked upon Alexander Rigby as fatherly in those London weeks, but I saw in him what I wanted to see. I was probably very naive for my twenty-eight years. Anyway, Alexander called me "the innocent of Hampstead." And how should I have gotten any experience since I had accepted the meager portion fate had handed out to me without any resistance? I have undergone quite a change in Australia. Alexander doesn't like it. He married a grateful girl with no contrariness in her nature. To his dismay, I know now, after seven years of married life, exactly what I *don't* want! Like any Australian woman. Alexander Rigby's older sister, for instance, Miss Grace Rigby.

Naturally I didn't show Alexander that love was a foreign word in my vocabulary. In London I kissed him to the best of my ability. My awkwardness and reserve seemed to please him. He treated me with absurd caution. Mother said he came from a new country with old puritan morals. Although he could be lively enough, I considered him lacking in temperament, a dyed-in-the-wool bachelor who conversed with exotic birds in his free time. I am sure the whole Taronga Zoo couldn't have come up with such a prize sheep as myself!

I never gave a thought as to why Alexander Rigby transported such an insignificant creature as myself to his dream villa in Vaucluse to be his wife. Mother wondered about it right away. Surely this Aussie, with his appearance and position, had to have the choice of innumerable desirable girls in his hometown. Why did he choose a wallflower like Anne Carrington? Of course Mother didn't express what she was thinking; my happy face seemed to stop her. Miss Jennings evidently also wondered what possible snag there could be in my engagement to the Australian. Mother of course made all sorts of inquiries, but to Miss Jennings's disappointment, all Alexander's information turned out to be correct. He really was a famous architect in Sydney, partner in a prestigious firm, very wealthy, and the villa in Vaucluse belonged to him. Where was the snag? Both ladies considered unlikely the fact that he had fallen in love with me.

I told myself that Mother and Miss Jennings were suspicious for professional reasons. Alexander had fallen in love with me whether it suited Miss Jennings or not. After all, I wasn't bad-looking, especially when I wore my black dress. I had good posture, and could be alert when I wanted to. Even Mother had to admit, after some hesitation, that "this Mr. Rigby" was not going to provide any material for a new thriller, but that he was just what he professed to be: a true-blue Australian! Moreover he converted Miss Jennings effortlessly to the same conclusion simply by smiling at her pleasantly. From that moment on she looked upon him as an attractive, albeit somewhat primitive, nature man, an oceanic miracle from the fifth continent!

Mother asked Alexander what a dinkum Aussie really was. "Nothing exceptional, Lady Carrington. Just a fellow who won't take orders from anyone and is a good comrade." Mother found this touching but too good to be altogether true. But none of us really knew Rigby. How could we? We knew nothing of his uncontrollable and irrational devotion to his mob, as he called his friends and co-workers. I have meanwhile found out that the mob plays the main role in the life of the Australian male, whether he be a farmer in the bush, a veteran of both world wars, a member of the yacht club, harbor worker, cattle herder, wool shearer, ice dealer or a doctor on Sydney's famous Macquarie Street. The mob cements friendships with collective memories and seals the whole thing—with the rigorous exemption of the wives—with an enormous consumption of beer. The second thing he kept from me was his housekeeper, a gem, a jewel, who will never leave.

I still believe that Alexander really did fall in love with me in London. You can't quarrel about taste. He even found me beautiful. He is certainly not the man to say anything like that and not mean it. When he looked at me in London I grew more and more beautiful from minute to minute. My dull hair grew shiny, my too-light eyes gained depth, and the blood shot up

to my pale face. In his presence I wasn't long and thin any
more, but tall and slender. During the period of my engagement
in London I was young for the first time in my life.

Mother looked upon Alexander naturally as the man who
had saved me from a mundane life in an office and would be
a splendid provider, but at the same time she felt an inexplicable
dislike for him which she never lost. Miss Jennings suddenly
respected me. I was of course the same person I had been
before the great event, but I had, so-to-speak, in my sleep
gained a certain aura. I am sure she felt that she would have
been able to cope with the unknown duties awaiting me in
Sydney much better than I would. Perhaps she asked herself
for the first time in her life, faced with this triumph of indolence, whether indefatigable diligence and iron energy didn't
perhaps frighten men off. They never knew what was good for
them. She looked at Alexander's photographs with great interest. The idyllic beach at Balmoral evoked an outcry of delight. Alexander's father had spent his old age there, on the
sun porch of a white house with a view of the harbor. Jonathan
Rigby had lived and built in Parramatta, in New South Wales.
Alexander had gone to school there. He told us that Parramatta
was the oldest country town in New South Wales.

I asked him if he went there often. He drew an imaginary
circle with his long, sinewy arms. "That's how big Parramatta
is." After a pause he added, "There's a very nice old jail there,
otherwise nothing but a lot of sheep, dairies, and a little industry."

We couldn't see enough of the beach pictures. "Australia!
Land of the sun! How I would love to live there," Miss Jennings
murmured. She wiped her glasses and ignored Mother's astonished look. Alex smiled at her enchantingly. He had discovered the unconscious worship in Miss Jennings's nearsighted
eyes, and was very pleased. "You will have to visit us in
Sydney, Miss Jennings," he said. Miss Jennings coughed happily, although she knew very well that nothing would ever
come of the visit. She was no fool, and realized that her place
was in the London fog, but for a moment the Australian sun

had blinded her. "It must be wonderful," she said. "Such an exciting climate."

Why do people say that time heals all wounds? In seven years of married life, time has done little for me. Together with the Australian sun, it put wrinkles in my face. Wherever time may have distributed its healing medicines in Sydney and surroundings, it overlooked me. I am thirty-five years old and dead tired. Alex says that comes from brooding. Every day he reminds me more and more of Miss Jennings.

My husband finds my despondency repulsive, and I can't blame him. After all, I am living under the finest sun in Sydney. A spectacular waterfront and a dizzyingly high standard of living should satisfy anyone. Who do I think I am? I live with a background as depicted in the colorful travel bureau brochures in Martin Place. I must have remained a tourist. I have never penetrated the reality of this turbulent, young, enthusiastic city. They say there aren't any old people in Sydney. They're all young, wonderful—or dead!

Wherever I go everybody thinks Alexander is wonderful— I mean, as an architect. He grows higher into the sky daily, like the new skyscrapers in the city, with their constantly modernized facades. Alex is an exponent of cloud techniques.

The other day I overheard a conversation in the restaurant of the Chevron Hilton Hotel.

"Who built your house, Jim?"

"Rigby, of course. From Marchmont, Rigby & French. We chose him because he falls between two generations. Always the safest thing to do."

"Is he very expensive? We're expecting our fifth child."

"Well, yes. Rigby's best isn't cheap. He works with Bridgeford and Briggs in Hunter Street. If you'd like to talk to him . . . he's coming to dinner tomorrow. Lucy's crazy about him."

"How about his young wife?"

"She's a pommy import." Pommy . . . the Australian nickname for the English, with their cheeks as red as pomegranates.

"So?"

"Mrs. Rigby is a loner."

"She is? But then she can't be right for Alex. He didn't come down with the last shower. I saw him water-skiing in Manly the other day. I'm telling you—remarkable! Why, he could have had any girl he wanted in New South Wales."

"How long have you been living in Sydney, Buddy?"

"Let me see . . . four years. We were stuck in the bush."

"Then you can't talk about Rigby. There was something . . . it didn't go down very well. But that's water over the dam today. Only after that Alex couldn't find a suitable wife so easily, not in Sydney, not Rigby status. We're a great big democracy, to be sure, but you've still got to have the right wife."

"That's what I say, Jim. Cheers for your Lucy. She was born on a bed of sheep's wool, wasn't she?"

"The best you can find in the country. Cheers!"

"Which reminds me . . . I don't like the wool prices lately. They're not really bad yet, but where are we heading? The immigrants . . . thinking they can interfere with us old-timers on the wool exchange! Should be thankful that we let them in! What did they have in starvation Europe? Sure there are decent fellows among them who ought to be given a chance. But they should be thankful if we give them work in Darling Harbour. And they're perfectly happy at first, but then, on the wool exchange, at the races, on the beach, we could do without the Naussies. Cheers!" He was referring to the new Australians. "The beer isn't what it used to be either. What were we talking about? Oh yes, Rigby. The guy's unlucky. I think he paints, as a hobby. Portraits. Did you know that, Buddy?"

"No. But as long as he doesn't paint my daughter, I don't care. Girls go for that man, although he'll soon be out of the running. Must be pushing fifty. Then he must have been thirty-three or thereabouts when it took place. What really happened?"

"Strange that you didn't read about it in the papers. After all, Sydney doesn't come up with a scandal like that every day. And we're accustomed to a thing or two."

"I'm too tired to read in the evening. What did he do?"

"They never really found out. Nobody was in the Blue Mountains with him when it happened. But something always sticks, even when there's no conviction..."

And then whispers ... whispers ...

What I was eating stuck in my throat. I had invited my friend Shirley to have lunch with me. She lives with her family in a cheerful, old-fashioned house on the other side of Harbour Bridge. Shirley is my only friend in Sydney and New South Wales. I met her quite by chance—just as I met Alexander quite by chance—in a travel bureau. She was working with Qantas, Empire Airways, in Hunter Street. I wanted to go back to London at the time, but then I stayed after all. Mother was busy, and Miss Jennings would have known all along...

Shirley Cox drives twice daily over the bridge to the Qantas offices, a building Alex approves of. It shoves its bold swung-glass facade triumphantly into the narrow streets of the inner city. A small building, still in Victorian mothballs, is hunched beside the glass giant. It knows that its days are numbered. Shirley was sitting in the reception room of the glass palace: tall, blond, with thoughtful blue eyes and the most beautiful teeth in all five continents. She was a product of the Australian sun. In her too the simple friendliness and hospitality of the suburbs beyond the Pacific Highway sparkled.

Shirley listened to the conversation about Alex without batting an eyelash. I have no secrets from her, and she knew anyway what had happened in the Blue Mountains ten years before Alexander's jaunt to London. All water over the dam. Everybody knew about it except me. Everybody in Sydney knows all about the Rigbys. Alex's only sister is the publisher of a famous Australian women's magazine. Miss Rigby is a regular guest at the Chevron Hilton. But on that day, she wasn't there.

I rose abruptly. "Don't go, Anne!" Shirley said firmly. She is five years younger than I but much more experienced, and a delightful realist. Of course Shirley never wrote poetry in her youth, but spent her free time in the fresh air on Bondi

Beach. Bondi is more popular than Manly, where Alex and the yacht club swim. Shirley's mother broils wonderful steaks, and her brother, Douglas, is a police officer. They call him Curl because of his curly hair.

Once a week I drive to the Coxes in my little red sports car, and once a week Shirley has supper with me in Vaucluse. Alexander is hardly ever there, and his "jewel," in her black dress, sits on her own balcony with its view of the street. From our big terrace you see the ocean. The harbor lights are mirrored in the water and in the strangely fluctuating darkness. Two white hanging lamps burn in the unreal night, and the tropical air shivers with Alexander's secrets.

At nine Mrs. Andrews appears in her ridiculous black dress with a batiste apron, and serves iced pineapple or red melon. Our housekeeper has an unpronounceable Hungarian name, and Alexander engaged her shortly after "the tragedy." Like me, she knew no one in Sydney. She is thin, unbearable, and cooks marvelously. A jewel. A type that is constantly washed up on the Australian coast. I don't know to this day why Alexander preferred not to let me know of her existence, nor why Mrs. Andrews hates me. In seven years she has never once smiled at me. She worships Alexander, but isn't very much in evidence when he's around. Then she rolls out her paper-thin strudel in the kitchen and thinks her own dark thoughts. The two of us sit alone in paradise and never know when Alexander may bring twelve members of his mob to dinner, and when or if he's going to turn up at all. When he does, he of course wants dinner right away. Mrs. Andrews produces a meal as if by magic and serves the master. She is hungry for praise, and if Alex is in a good mood he says casually, "Very good, very tasty, Mary." Mary gives him a blissful look, medium-strength, and glides around with the goulash platter as if walking on air. Her evening is made. Ridiculous how this gray, gaunt person humbly scatters her incense around him, but Alexander accepts even incense with paprika.

I think he hates me because I see what he's like and not as

he would like me to see him, as he was in London. He would prefer jealous scenes, stupid reproaches and cheap tears. Alexander can cope with anything like that with amiable brutality, but unfortunately I can't play along. I can't be jealous of women I don't know, and I am not interested in marital snooping. We have remained strangers. Alexander has no tenderness in his makeup. All he has is an uncontrollable thirst for beauty, and a peculiar avidity for admiration. If I could admire him, everything would be all right. He would forgive my so-called frigidity, my inability to enjoy the Aussies, or at least pretend to, and my slowness in conceiving children.

After I have brought Shirley home, late in the evening, I drive back in the moonlight, over the Pacific Highway to the Harbour Bridge, a gigantic silver span which prevents this strange, disorderly, magnificent city from falling apart. Shirley, amused by big figures, told me that the bridge was made of fifty-two thousand tons of steel, and that fifty million people crossed it every year.

For years now I have been one of those fifty million. I know about ten people in Sydney, counting Alexander, Miss Rigby, and Alex's jewel. Some of those fifty thousand tons of steel must have entered into me. One day Alexander appeared unexpectedly for tea. A young girl got out of his big white sports car with him, a blond girl, about seventeen, I thought. I looked into her sly dark eyes. They reminded me of someone, but I'm slow. It didn't occur to me who it was.

"Daisy is going to live with us," said Alex.

The housekeeper, with a stony expression, served his favorite pastry and open sandwiches. I poured tea and saw to it that my hand didn't tremble.

"What are you talking about, Alex? You can't just pick up a young girl somewhere and . . ."

I stopped in the middle of the sentence. I could feel the housekeeper's hot eyes on my neck.

Alex asked, "What makes you think I pick up young girls somewhere? Really, Anne!" He was all hurt innocence, the great Rigby from Marchmont, Rigby & French. I said hesitantly that I had never seen this girl. I raised my voice, and Alexander's eyebrows went up. "My dear Anne, how are you ever going to get to know people if you sit at home all the time? Your friend Shirley Cox, and old John seem to be the only people in Sydney you approve of."

Professor John Darling was a friend of Alexander's student days. I liked him. I have never seen two such different people as Alexander Rigby and John Darling, a bachelor by inclination. But of course he knew Alexander's mob, and they knew him. There weren't many people who didn't know Professor Darling from the Sydney university. John came to see me sometimes. It was always a treat for me.

"I don't want any strange teenagers around, Alexander, and that's final!" I was behaving very badly. Mother would have shaken her head. Alexander looked at me with polite disgust. During every marital quarrel he was smooth as marble and just as hard.

"I know Daisy," he said finally, "and that's enough." He passed the cake plate to the girl. "Here, eat, little girl. You want to win at the swim meet, don't you? Are you training hard?"

"And how! Do you think I'll win a prize, Uncle Alex?"

I could feel a headache coming on.

"I think it would be best if Daisy moved into the room with the flowered drapes," Alexander said calmly. "She's in the flower stage."

The young girl giggled. Mrs. Andrews gave a good imitation of a forced smile. Daisy watched her Uncle Alex out of her sly, dark eyes. They were slightly slanted. At last it dawned on me—they were Mrs. Andrews's eyes, only narrower.

"The young girl will *not* move into that room!"

"Why not?" Alexander was still smiling amiably. He was the stronger in every one of our disputes, and he knew it. He was part of this alien, sunnily smiling continent, with the dark bush in the background.

"Why not?" I asked too loudly. "Because I don't want it. And I hope you'll respect my wishes, Alexander." My voice sounded like a stranger's. When had I ever addressed anyone so sharply? Was this thin, tense person with the shrill voice still Anne Carrington?

"I always respect your wishes," Alexander said, even more pleasantly. "Come along, Daisy. I'll take you back to your digs."

I didn't know where her digs were. Why hadn't Alexander told me about the girl?

A few weeks after this conversation, Daisy moved into the room with the flowered drapes. But she only stayed weekends. The big house stood empty. I couldn't prevent an indigent Australian like Mrs. Andrews from spending a weekend with her daughter. Sometimes I heard Daisy chattering and laughing with her mother. They sat on the little back veranda in front of Mrs. Andrews's bedroom. Often I could hear loud, male laughter: Alexander's.

I didn't know what to make of it. All I knew was that Alexander's housekeeper hated me. I don't know to this day what the young creature thought of me. I ignored her and she ignored me with the insouciance of youth. I couldn't blame her. I did nothing to make a good impression on the girl. Why should I have? She was an intruder. In the end I talked to John Darling about it.

John is of medium height, much too thin, has a long narrow face, and his hair is almost white. His eyes behind his rectangular glasses are keen. There is something of the pedigreed dog about him. He looks taller than he is, perhaps because he holds himself so straight, perhaps also because of his quiet air of authority. He moves slowly, thinks fast, and always has time for his friends. He comes from a family of famous old settlers near Camden. Once he took me with him to Darling Farm. One could believe one was in England there. In New South Wales a rural British idyll is the only tangible realization of the free English settler's dream. There were more oaks and elms than eucalyptus trees and Australian mimosa. I saw meadows like the ones in Surrey, rows of light trees. "John!" I cried. "You have poplars!" He smiled and led me into what he called the park. The main house, overgrown with ivy, stood in the middle. I had to swallow hard. I was in New South Wales, yet here I felt at home. In a corner of the park stood the little stone house of the first Darlings, built by convicts. But again, the church could have stood in England. John's brother supervises the farm with modern methods. Their cattle are famous. And the little stone house of John's ancestors watches . . .

The convicts came from England. Under the blue Australian sky they must have dreamt of the foggy moors and their pubs in London harbor streets, soggy with rain. I tasted the milk in the huge wainscotted hall of the main house. John's family were silent people, but they were friendly. Nobody asked about "the old lady"—England. They had never seen the land of their ancestors. They were dinkum Aussies.

I didn't open my mouth while John drove me back to Sydney. He didn't say anything either, but watched the road. Alexander was waiting for us in John's Spanish villa in Rose Bay. As far as he is concerned, John's house is a nightmare. Style, with no consideration for the landscape. The yellow stucco villa had thin, modest Baroque columns, arches, colonnaded walks and ornamental chimneys. Alexander would rather have drowned in the Pacific than live in John's Spanish villa. The fact that he never made a remark about the wrought-iron embellishments was testimony of his friendship for John. Alexander had recommended a Georgian-style house, but John liked the ambience of a Spanish mission. The influence of "depressing columns," as Alexander termed this pseudo-Baroque element, is evident in all Sydney suburbs. "John doesn't need to have good taste. John is first class." With which Alexander confirmed his loyalty to John and his columns once and for all.

So my husband could be a friend. Secretly he admired John, possibly because of John's kindness. And he loved John. Perhaps he didn't love me any more because, on a closer look, he had found nothing to admire in me. I suppose marriage is the cold shower after a feast of illusions. At any rate, this applies to our marriage in Sydney. In London, Alexander had been quite different. He had only shown me his facade. That was his right. I had shown myself in my black dress and had tried to be entertaining.

I thought of the friendship between Alexander and John Darling. I noticed much too late that John—who liked to remain in the background—protected Alexander, as only the unpretentious person can protect the glamorous one. He saved Alexander from himself as long as he could. He was the only one who could contradict Alexander without creating an icy atmosphere in the blazing sun.

John is professor of anthropology at the University of Sydney, and works in an honorary capacity for the welfare bureau, for education, and for the integration of the native population of New South Wales. He sometimes brought me the magazine *Dawn*. I put it away in my antique bureau and never read it. I was so distracted by my backache that I hadn't let the black Australians enter my consciousness yet, although John said once, "The aborigines should have a place in your new experience, Anne."

One evening I was sitting with John on the terrace of our house. He had come because I needed him. He sensed it. I don't know how he was able to take the time and try and make an Australian of me. I must have seemed hopeless to him, more hopeless than the blackest of his black sheep. "What's the matter, Anne?"

I told him about Mrs. Andrews's daughter. "Alexander's interest in her is unnatural," I said, with unusual vehemence.

"Take it easy, Anne." John was looking at the red eucalyptus in our garden as if he had never seen it before. The red eucalyptus is a variation of the national original. "I find it quite natural that Alex wants to help. You surprise me, Anne."

I blushed, but then I told myself at once that John was one of those idealists produced by every country that is too practically oriented. As far as I could see, Alexander showed this friend of his only two of his many faces. Finally I said brusquely that I thought Daisy was Alexander's illegitimate daughter. Mother and daughter couldn't possibly be clinging to him like ivy otherwise.

John didn't laugh often, but now he laughed loud and long, and couldn't seem to stop. "Are you laughing at me, John?"

John shook his head. "You have read too many of your mother's thrillers, girl." And he was one of my mother's fans! "Let me reassure you—Mrs. Andrews brought Daisy with her from Hungary when she was a baby. Her husband didn't survive a dispute with a communist functionary. She left the child for a while with some people in Surry Hills. It cost her the last piece of jewelry she had been able to smuggle out, but she was worried about getting the position Alex was offering if she applied for it with a screaming baby. And she was right. Alex is not patient."

"So why didn't he tell me anything about it? He's paying for the girl's education, you know. That's very decent of him."

"You're in a young country, Anne. Here people help each other without any musical accompaniment."

I said nothing. I realized how little I knew my husband.

"We are a nation of immigrants," said John. "Unfortunately not always with understanding for the newcomer. Yes, yes . . . Mrs. Andrews came here two centuries too late, and from the wrong country, I mean as far as language and tradition are concerned."

"It is always difficult to be in a strange country, John."

"Certainly. But our new Australians after the Second World War are having a harder time than our English ancestors. An historic abyss separates the immigrants from Italy, Hungary, Greece, Poland, from our satisfied settlers who take our high standard of living for granted. Oh dear heaven, all it is, really, is a conflict of manners and morals. We do much too little for these new arrivals, Anne. We're too easily satisfied with ourselves. That's the trouble."

"I admire you, John. You're so patient with me."

"I like you, you little idiot! You'll be all right. Just be a little more tolerant."

"Do you think I'm impossible?"

"I think you're young and—forgive me—inexperienced."

"I'm living on a dead-end street, John."

He smiled. "A funny expression for such a sprawling city. Tell me, Anne, is it really so difficult to get accustomed to living in Australia? It's the best country in the world."

"But it's all so strange! And the contrasts are so ... so ... harsh."

"It's a young country, Anne. You see too much civilization in Sydney. We find the city very Americanized. You should see the vast flatlands, experience the loneliness of the bush! Why don't you and Alex ever travel into the bush? Why don't you ever go with him to Taronga Park? Or to water-ski in Manly."

"He hasn't asked me to."

"The next thing you'll expect Alex and me to be introduced to you!" John said amiably. "Good heavens, girl! Alex didn't build that bleak glass house in Vaucluse for you to sit in for the rest of your life. Don't you swim?"

"I have a weak back. It hurts all the time. I'm always tired, John."

"Have a massage! Do something, Anne! Stand on your head! What are you interested in, anyway?"

What was I interested in? I had even put my lay psychology books away in the antique bureau. I said nothing. I felt as I had felt in school when I had been too shy to answer.

"I'll find out." John was smiling. "You'll see. Everything's going to be all right. After all, you didn't land yesterday!"

"If only Alex would help me! But he doesn't need me. He has the mob."

"He needs you, all right, but you don't make it easy for him. Alex wrote me such a happy letter from London."

"We were happy then."

"You'll get used to it, my dear. Alex ..." He hesitated. I didn't move. "Alex may not be very easy to understand, Anne. He doesn't have much use for the safe or intimate thing. He lives with his esthetic vision. And he can't show his feelings. In this country the monologue is the most popular form of conversation. With whom were the fellows to talk when they moved through the bush alone? Even when there were two of them, each one was lost in his own thoughts. They had told each other everything they had to say long ago."

"But that's all ages ago, John. I do find the bush legend sentimental."

"It is not a legend." John's voice was sharper than usual. "The bush plays a part in our lives . . . as a eucalyptus forest, as an idea. Just as the old bush men talked to their waltzing Matildas, we in the city still like to talk to ourselves."

I knew that the waltzing Matilda was the lonely wanderer's knapsack. But we lived in Sydney, an Americanized island of happy materialism, with the bush and its monologues in the background. I had no idea what Alexander's conversations with himself were about. I saw the closed faces of John, Betty West, and Miss Rigby before me, and among them the pinched face of Alexander's housekeeper. What did they talk about when nobody else was listening? The floor seemed to be swaying under my feet. Mother and Miss Jennings had always expressed themselves clearly, especially over my and other people's deficiencies. I had known where I was at. But was John my friend? Had Alexander told him about his disappointment in his marriage? Or was everything a monologue?

"Alex doesn't care a thing about me," I said harshly.

"Nonsense! Then why did he marry you?"

"That's what I'd like to know. Perhaps he'll tell you."

"How about a nice cold glass of beer, Anne? It's very hot tonight, isn't it?"

I was cold. I felt it in my bones that John Darling and old Marchmont of Marchmont, Rigby & French, knew every detail of the scandal. And I would be damned if they didn't know whether the rumors were founded or not. But I didn't ask John. Even if Alexander rejected the dialogue of marriage, even if he neglected me—he was my husband. He gave me a life for which I was envied. You could read in the Sydney *Morning Herald* about our parties and trips. I sat crouched on the top of the social ladder and could pick the big tropical stars. Naturally one falls harder when one sits on top, but there wasn't a shadow of scandal. I saw to that. I appeared with my husband whenever necessary. Sometimes he asked me to leave my martyr's face at home. I didn't know that I looked so dismal. I only noticed to my dismay that now I liked to nag almost as much as Mother or Miss Jennings. My housekeeper, who, after all, took all the everyday burdens off my shoulders, was my victim because, unlike Alexander, she was always there. I was unfriendly to young Daisy when I saw her in the garden during our weekends. I had nothing against the girl since I knew all about her, but after my conversation with John Darling, she was for a long time a symbol of my defeat. Alexander didn't respect my wishes in any way at all. I couldn't nag him. Either he laughed, or walked off silently to his shed in the garden. His distaste for dialogue left me high and dry and drove me slowly into the desert. For Alexander there was only the mob or the monologue. Gradually I got the hang of the monologue. It was my only distraction, and after all, I've always been a first-rate brooder. I knew exactly what I lacked. I didn't need analysis for that, as Miss Rigby advised. She was as friendly as ever, but she was about as comforting as the New South Wales Public Library. Alexander gave me everything, only not himself. But there was nothing new under the sun about that.

John looked up silently at the rising moon. The contrast between the beauty of my surroundings and the meagerness of my life was almost funny. I would have to be hellishly careful not to lose my respect for life. Vaucluse gradually became a void . . .

"Will you be at Miss Rigby's tomorrow night, too?"

John started. I had torn him out of his monologue. Then he said gently, "I am always at Miss Rigby's. I am part of the inventory."

"If you weren't going to be there, I'd stay home."

John looked at me, so astonished, that I reddened. The cold moonlight washed over us. Beautiful, merciless Australian night. "I was joking," I said apologetically.

"Then let's laugh," said John.

2

Among Us Old Australians

They say you haven't been in New South Wales if you haven't admired Harbour Bridge sufficiently, or the post office on Martin Place. You also have to have seen Mrs. Macquarie's Chair, and of course the Blue Mountains, where the scandal had taken place about which the Rigby family preserved a deathly silence. There is so much you have to see in this city. Sydney by night. The endless chain of lights that stretches across hills, shines on bays and waterways, and how fifty-two thousand tons of steel transform Harbour Bridge into a work of art. And one has to see the "sheilas," the girls sauntering along King's Cross, that little Soho of nostalgia. And no one should leave Australia without having seen the sheep fair in Sydney. Then it's winter in this hemisphere. At home it is June, and we wear summer dresses whether it's raining, hailing, or snowing.

There is almost too much to see. I found the millions of sheep in their dry, functional stalls remarkable, also the many people, wet from the rain, standing in awe around this wealth of their land. One should also visit hotels out in the country where, in white tiled bars, the men, joking and singing, order countless rounds of beer for each other. Alexander was never more of a stranger to me than when he came out of a bar. Then he seemed taller, more brutish, and was in a state of excitement I never saw him in at home. Are we women different too when we are among ourselves? Don't our men recognize us then either? Anyway, my friends and I were not allowed to drink beer in the men's sacred tap room, but in a stuffy ladies' salon. For me, however, the most remarkable sight was Miss Rigby,

Alexander's older sister, publisher of a popular magazine called *Insight*.

I shall never forget the party Miss Rigby gave in her house in Bellevue Hill. Miss Rigby isn't exactly enthusiastic about Alexander because two incessant talkers have to be rivals. No sooner has Alexander collected a group of people around him, than he becomes a great talker. Miss Rigby, seven years older than her brother, and, like him, someone you can't overlook, can be turned on any time, day or night. She is the Cicero of Sydney. Australian women, young and old, and from every walk of life, have been hanging on her lips for years, swallowing the nectar of her wisdom. *Insight*—an elegantly caparisoned parade horse of journalism, illuminates not only the reception rooms and verandas of the old colonial houses in the city, but also casts a sharp and universal eye on the farm women in the bush, and on the borderline bigwigs at the edge of the great desert. Nurses, models, students, masseuses, salesgirls, waitresses, and I—all of us read *Insight*, look at the glossy color illustrations and the fashions, modeled by a beautiful girl called Candy. Some us skip Miss Rigby's stern but forthright editorials, but all of us read the unabridged novels of the Australian author, Elizabeth West. This lady has evidently tried out everything in the way of male love of which the readers of *Insight*, especially the lonely creatures in no-man's-land, hadn't even dared to dream. Naturally Miss West takes the puritan morality of the continent into consideration, in spite of several pretty hot episodes. Sex is cautiously and subtly rationed.

Every inch of an old Australian, Elizabeth West knows exactly how far she can go. Of course she was present at Miss Rigby's party. She is her bosom friend, insofar as one can speak of bosom where Miss Rigby is concerned. To be precise, Miss West inhabits several rooms in Miss Rigby's house in Bellevue Hill. Alexander can't stand her. Miss West has innumerable imaginary illnesses. In his eyes that is a deadly sin. When, a few years back, I began to need treatment for headaches and backache, he treated me like a criminal. He is disgustingly robust.

I had been in Sydney only four days when Miss Rigby's invitation made me panic. Actually it was a polite order. I sensed on the phone that Miss Rigby would never accept a refusal. Alexander had already prepared me in London for his only sister. He addressed her in the soft ironic tone she hates as "Miss Rigby." I found out from Alex that not only did his sister know everything, but that she could also ferret out every foible and weakness known to mankind! Later she told me that Alex unfortunately wrapped himself up in the cocoon of his sleeping bag in order not to have to face the truth about himself. What that truth was, she didn't say.

When Miss Rigby walked up to me in her huge reception room in Bellevue Hill, I felt like a student who was not going to get anywhere near the top of the class. And I was right. On that first evening Miss Rigby asked me if I wouldn't like to contribute something to the magazine on the subject of career women in London. All I could have offered her were my torn-up poems. I had never paid any attention to career women. Perhaps Mother and Miss Jennings had been enough. Of course we girls in the Piccadilly travel bureau had worked, but mostly we had been waiting for elevensies—tea with raisin bread. Instead of discussing social problems, most of the girls had talked about their beaux, and I can't deny that we found this topic quite interesting. Of course Miss Rigby would have approved highly of Mother, because she too preferred thrillers and detective stories to Miss West's romances.

I must admit that Miss Rigby was very nice to me, right from the start. She would never have wasted her time being unfriendly to an unimportant young woman. But she was really interested only in women with careers, if possible with university degrees, or in responsible positions. She was one of those amazons who were propagandizing for women in the Sydney war of social prestige. Naturally Miss Rigby also dealt in her magazine with the Australian housewife and mother's considerable problems, but these were relegated to the back of the magazine, and her editorials and the general tone of the paper was directed at the career woman, like Miss Rigby her-

self. A woman's magazine of course has to have recipes and
fashion reports, and deal with questions of child behavior. But
Miss Rigby dealt with such boring themes in her own way.
The fashions were suited to women in the public limelight,
and the recipes were for dishes that could be prepared in no
time flat, with frozen and precooked foods, but they were so
subtly described that you didn't notice it right away. The steaks
served at the party resembled sacrificial lambs with vegetable
garnish, all trembling under a layer of aspic. Alexander had
eaten an honest-to-God steak at home. On the way back to
Vaucluse, he compared his sister's garnished dishes with the
contemporary architecture that ornamented honest walls with
fake columns, treated fine wood to make it look like a different
material, and offered practical items in grotesque packaging.
After this party, contrary to his usual behavior, he talked his
head off because he wanted to bridge an abyss. It was a deep
abyss, and I fell into it in spite of his life belt. Namely, when
Miss Rigby, Miss West, Alexander and I were drinking our
last demitasse on the big veranda, Miss Rigby happened to
mention the "tragedy" in the Blue Mountains. She had of course
taken for granted that I knew all about it. But I didn't. On the
way home I was still very upset, and Alexander's remarks
about steak in aspic and fake columns fell on deaf ears. Finally
I asked him how he had managed to keep such an important
event from me. He replied that he had wanted a fresh start and
the whole thing lay years back anyway. That was all. I don't
know how I got to my ultra-modern bedroom that night. I
groped through the house like a blind man. I still remember
sitting for half an hour beside my old bureau in the spare back
room. It was ridiculous, of course, but I had to hang onto
something familiar.

In all these years I never became really close to Miss Rigby.
Her nonchalant yet superior attitude, her enormous intelli-
gence, and amazing energy prevented any intimate relationship. Compared to her my mother was a warm hearth, even
though thousands read Miss Rigby's books, and she was well
known because of her many television appearances. But Mother

was unobtrusive, whereas Miss Rigby was someone who couldn't be overlooked, if only for her size: endlessly tall, much too thin, and with an Australian eagle profile. Her short straight hair looked as if it had just been styled by a hairdresser; she was smartly dressed and immaculately groomed. She exhorted her readers to always dress as befitted the occasion and not to sit around on their verandas in old housedresses out of slovenliness, or in cowardly flight from the sun. That Miss West sat around just like that on all the verandas of Bellevue Hill was a well-kept secret. Miss West's heroines of course kept up appearances in city or bush.

Without having to do any research on it, I knew Miss Rigby's opinion of me. This was funny because usually I am a poor judge of the reactions of strange people. I had really believed that Alexander was in love with me. I don't know if the heat gave me a sixth sense, but I often heard in my mind what Miss Rigby was probably telling her friends about me.

"My dear . . . my brother has brought a young wife back with him from London. I like Anne, but the pommies are conservative and slow, no denying that. Anne will get used to things here. It isn't all that hard in Sydney. Of course she must try to acquire our habits and share our viewpoints; mechanical efforts to adjust don't suffice. I wonder often why Anne isn't more cheerful, but after all, she is married to my brother . . . On the other hand, she has nothing to worry about, and Vaucluse isn't the worst place in the world. In our set nearly all of us come from pioneer families. When I think what our ancestors had to put up with compared with Anne! Desert heat, loneliness, flies, mosquitos, drought, natives, bush fires, and whatever else. And of course with the hunger and sickness of our animals and children! But did our old Marchmonts and Darlings, or, pardon me, Rigbys, make sour faces like our immigrants today? No, my dear, they held their heads high and sang!

"Perhaps Alexander's young wife has it too good. Granted that she had a job before she married Alex. She ran a big travel bureau in London. But she's become as slipshod here as one of my problem children from the Outback. Naturally I answer every one of their letters. The poor things depend on me. I tell my readers in Queensland and West Australia: when do I get your articles about gold prospectors? Think of your forefathers! The heat is perfectly bearable when you live accordingly. Do your duty with a smile. The kookaburra in the bush laughs too. Girls, I say, tell your men what you think of their beer consumption. You women and mothers are more important than the mob with whom your man spends his Saturdays. Insist that he participate in your family life whether he wants to or not.

"Young Anne often has backache. I have recommended Molly Fleet, a very good masseuse. Unfortunately she has a disfiguring birthmark on her face, but I told Miss Fleet exterior beauty wasn't important. She wrote to the Mailbox, asking what she could do about her depression. I told her to throw away every mirror in her house. What I don't know doesn't hurt me. I invited her to tea at the office. We Rigbys come from Parramatta too. The Fleets are also real Australians. Molly's ancestors—female side—began life here in New South Wales as deportees. A very interesting criminal record from old Parramatta. Miss Fleet has bourgeois inhibitions because her ancestor was a convict, but I told her at once, 'Don't be silly, Molly! The largest and finest families in the country often started out like your matriarch. Mostly the poor souls hadn't done a thing, perhaps only looked at their masters the wrong way or drunk a gin or two too many. Just between us old Australians, you can be proud of your great-grandmother! Best British import!' Not to be compared with the odd people settling in New South Wales nowadays. They land here and expect us to learn Italian or Polish. They stick together and are interested only in their own families. Especially the new Australians from the unsettled countries in Europe. Always insulted when they're supposed to speak English! Yes, Alexander still has his Hungarian jewel.

"How about his marriage? My dear, you know my brother! The less said about it, the better. Just between us, he didn't tell Anne . . . oh, forget it. The tragedy's gathering dust, and Alex wanted a new start. A little naive, no? No, I don't know Anne's mother, but Lady Carrington must be considerably more energetic than her daughter. She writes excellent thrillers. But I can't tell Betty that. Our dear Miss West will tolerate no best sellers beside hers! Where is Betty from? From Adelaide. But she has only developed in Sydney under my influence. Nice young person. I've grown very accustomed to her. If only she weren't so untidy! She can make a total mess of any room in a matter of minutes. But then, all of us have our little weaknesses. Yes, my dear, I do too!

"But I *would* like to do more for Alexander's wife. A very decent girl—clean, reliable, good background. But can you tell me where to find the time? No, Anne doesn't complain, but all of us know that Alexander is not a talented husband. Why does he keep on marrying? I thought he'd gone crazy when he cabled me from London that he was engaged. After his experience with Flora Pratt, I would have thought he'd had enough of marriage once and for all. But that's his problem. Young Anne will have to make the best of her life. I wonder what she would have thought of our Flora. The first thing I think I'll do is send Anne this masseuse from Parramatta. It is incomprehensible that such a young woman should have such a lot of ailments. I don't take them seriously because our dear Betty West has all sorts of imaginary illnesses too. We Rigbys are always well."

Alexander has told me nothing about his first marriage. His wife was a bar girl and considerably older than he. The scandal concerned her sudden death in the Blue Mountains. Miss Rigby calls the scandal a "tragedy." That sounds better.

It seems that the poor soul, the widow of a wealthy sheep farmer in New South Wales, fell off a precipice as she was looking over it. Alexander was unpacking the picnic basket when it happened. The poor old thing—bad luck! She had apparently been all dressed up in a ridiculous flowered hat and high-heeled shoes, as if going for a stroll in King's Cross. Miss

West stared at Alexander unflinchingly while his sister tact-lessly mentioned the first Mrs. Rigby. Miss West's fluttering eyelashes behind her fashionable glasses betrayed an earlier intimacy which Alexander chose to ignore. In Vaucluse, hours after the party, he explained impatiently that the first Mrs. Rigby had been just as nearsighted as she had been fun loving, but out of vanity she'd refused to take her glasses along on the outing. In her eagerness to see the grandiose view, she had walked too far across the rocky plateau and fallen into the abyss below. "Horrible mess," Alexander murmured, which I took was to cover the whole business. Because of her immense fortune, his friends had considered him an opportunist and a murderer, but Alexander shrugged and said, "One's friends always like to think the worst," Marchmont and John Darling excepted, of course. The two hadn't thought anything, while the damned cobbers had pestered the life out of poor Alex, until Mrs. Andrews had come to Vaucluse. Yes, her Hungarian cuisine had cheered him up considerably. *That* I could believe! He likes it when women spend hours thinking up what he is going to eat, and prepare his meals in this infernal heat. He lunches with Marchmont and French somewhere near his of-fice.

In the end Alexander assured me that his friends had always meant well. He *could* of course have pushed the first Mrs. Rigby off the rocky prominence, but whatever I might be thinking, he had *not* done so. In short—he didn't hold it against his friends that they had chosen to question his morality. After all, all Sydney had been talking of nothing else. Yes, today he was again enjoying happy hours with the old devils at the yacht club. A nice mob . . .

Over lunch at her women's club in Elizabeth Street, Miss Rigby assured me that I should not brood over an embarrassing event that happened so long ago. With her psychological acu-men she had noticed that brooding was my great talent. Alex had won out over the police at the time; as for the police— what did the fools know anyway? Miss Rigby shared the Aus-tralian disregard for authority in general and the police in particular. I looked at her long, fine face with its eagle-beak nose and her remarkable hairdo—every lock in place—and decided she must have suffered terribly over the scandal, but she betrayed as little emotion as every dinkum Aussie. In spite of which I got the feeling that she was not heartless. She had fine qualities, but she hid them carefully, according to the best Australian traditions. Like Alex in London, Miss Rigby wanted to demonstrate to the world that she was gloriously average. Suddenly I wished we could be friends, but I was too shy to make the overtures.

Grace Rigby also told me that the first Mrs. Rigby had fallen down the cellar stairs once. That was when she had been a bar girl, just before her marriage to a fabulously rich Merino farmer. "And now let's speak of more important things, Anne," with which Alexander's sister closed the book on the past. Controlled impatience made her voice sharper. Flora had simply been stupid. Glasses were there to be worn. For the rest of this intimate conversation, Miss Rigby discussed capital investments, television programming, her honorary activities in immigration centers, and John Darling's cultural efforts on behalf of the native Australian population.

"Have you and John Darling been friends for a long time, Miss Rigby?" I asked.

"Of course," she replied, with increasing impatience. "The old kangaroo is part of the inventory. Why aren't you eating anything?"

There isn't a picture of the first Mrs. Rigby in the whole house in Vaucluse. I have the feeling that Alexander didn't need the first Mrs. Rigby, and he doesn't need me either. He needs his friends, and occasionally the bees that make honey for him. But I can't be sure of anything. He is constantly being transformed in front of my very eyes into completely different men. It makes me feel queasy. Today I am sure of only one thing: all the gold and silver of Broken Hill can't bring back the man I knew in London.

In the evening I usually sit on the big terrace. The lanterns

cast a ghostly light on the harbor. The moon is dreamy, a moon
for beginners. It makes no impression on me any more. The
wooded spits of land, speckled with houses that look like toys,
stretch out into the water like giant crocodiles. Next week
Alexander will be fifty. I think he dreads it. Just the same, or
perhaps just because—he is giving a party for his mob.

My back aches all the time, but the girl from Parramatta is
a good masseuse. Poor thing! In her case inner beauty has to
do everything. Not easy when one is only twenty-two years
old. By the way, in spite of the invigorating air up there, I
haven't been alone with Alexander in the Blue Mountains in
all these seven years. He might get ideas...

3

Elizabeth West, Author.
Sydney, N.S.W.

I was born in Adelaide some years ago. South Australia has
an unfavorable climate for authors who write about romance.
My home town has very straight streets; even the trees on our
avenues look formal and severe. As a child I used to love the
mountains behind our city; they were friendly and green. And
then I loved my cat, Lake Torrens in the evening, and my
friend Gretchen. Her parents had immigrated to Adelaide from
Germany. Gretchen told me grim fairy tales. The names of the
authors were Grimm too, and I found that hilarious. "What are
you laughing at?" Gretchen asked, offended.

We quarreled only once. That was when she declared that
German settlers had founded Adelaide. But I knew from my
grandfather that Captain William Light had beaten Gretchen's

ancestors to it. I heard my grandfather screaming the information across the garden fence to Mr. Breitschneider, his oldest German friend. My grandfather Withers was very old; he spat sometimes when he spoke and complained often about how many German names there were in the city. Of course Captain Light founded Adelaide. After a lot of back and forth Gretchen couldn't deny this historical fact any more, but then she insisted that it had been the Germans who had got Adelaide going economically. I had nothing to say against that. We did only what was necessary, and that was why we got some mileage out of our beaches and mountains and our weekends.

Later Gretchen and I lost track of each other. One can never say when childhood friendships end, but more often than not it happens from one day to the next. I cried because I missed her and because I didn't want to see her any more—very illogical of me, but I have never been able to break this behavior pattern with people I love. There was a time when I didn't want to see Alexander Rigby any more; still I missed him wherever I went. I tried to tell myself that I could get along beautifully without him, but that only made things worse. Especially in the moonlight. When one is alone, the moon is an infamous invention.

When Gretchen disappeared from my circle of friends—we told our other friends that we were bored with each other—it was also the end of fairy tales for me. I didn't hear any more until I met architect Rigby in Sydney. He really is a good raconteur of fairy tales. The moonlight went so well with what he told, but unfortunately I nearly always closed my eyes. Today all I can say is that what I experienced with Alexander Rigby was just as grim as the tales of the Brothers Grimm. Only no blood was shed. And Alexander didn't do me in in a German fir forest but in the Hungarian Restaurant Szabo, in King's Cross.

That all happened over ten years ago. I have learned to live without Rigby. When I met him at Miss Rigby's with his second wife, I had to think of the times in George Street. It was about a hundred years ago, and the moon over Sydney was much brighter than it is today. I was still a stranger in the big city, and twenty years old. I knew nothing about men. In Adelaide the sexes didn't have their fun together, and little has changed in that respect. Even in cosmopolitan, worldly-wise Sydney an abyss yawns at every party between the men and the women. After conventional greetings, the men drink beer on "their" veranda, and we women gaze at the moon. Today I don't mind. Alexander Rigby has spoiled all personal romance for me. All I'd have to do is write down the opposite of what took place between us, and I'd have a nice love story, ready to go to press.

Perhaps I should have stayed in Adelaide. Then I would be sitting today in the botanical gardens with my children, and when the youngest boy would fall into the lake, my oldest would jump in after him. And we would go home happily to a white house with a garden. On the weekends my husband and the boys and I would drive to the mountains behind the city, away from the heat of the streets. Enormous red and white flowers bloom in our mountains. There, with wine and olives, I could have dreamt safely of men like Alexander Rigby, but no . . . I had to travel to relatives in Sydney to learn all about life.

When I think that in Sydney I was never able to get away from the Rigby family I have to laugh, as I did over the Brothers Grimm. And by the way—Alexander and Anne Carrington are about as suited to each other as a Tasmanian tiger and a koala bear. But that, thank God, isn't my problem. I only ask myself how long the whole thing will last. They've been married seven years, but strictly separate. You can sense that. Rigby doesn't know the meaning of love. Lucky man!

I began my famous career in Sydney as Alexander's secretary at Marchmont & Rigby in George Street. The first Mrs. Rigby had just died, and he had bought his way into the firm of the famous architect, Marchmont. French was probably still in diapers at the time, or playing with blocks. Marchmont & Rigby didn't have the ultramodern office then that they have

today. They worked in smaller rooms in the shabbier section
of George Street, where there were all sorts of junk shops,
second-rate restaurants and sleazy apartments; in short, it was
not the George Street of the Queen Victoria Building or Saint
Andrew's Cathedral. That's the only section of Sydney's oldest
street that's good enough for Alexander Rigby today. I fitted
in with his beginnings in George Street.

Of course in those days I wasn't called Elizabeth. I was little
Betty Withers, private secretary. Alexander has changed a lot
in the course of the years, but at thirty-three he was just as
ambitious and fanatical a worker, and in his spare time he had
an eye for the ladies. Many visitors to Australia say that we
don't have enough ambition, and that "Fair enough" is our
slogan. That may be true in certain cases, but in what country
isn't the average person satisfied with the average thing? And
there are people like Rigby everywhere. Unfortunately, as a
lover he spoiled me for the fair-enough boys. One can reject
Rigby, but one can't forget him. His designs are just as remarkable as he is. He introduced the vertical line to Marchmont
& Rigby. His houses reach high into the sky, like his dominant
hooked nose. But it's no concern of mine any more.

When I gazed at the moon with Rigby ten years ago, I wasn't
particularly attractive. My hair, instead of being shiny red, was
dull brown and stringy. I had a round face—no powder—and
wore dresses and lipstick in all the wrong colors. In order to
do something to enhance my appearance, I was also wearing
some pretty awful costume jewelry. Mother Nature hadn't treated
me lavishly, and I didn't know yet how to improve on her.
Young Mr. Rigby looked at me thoughtfully and hired me. He
had noticed the servile admiration in my eyes behind my unbecoming glasses.

I was eager to learn and wanted to achieve something in
Sydney. I at once decided to stay with Rigby until nothing
short of death tore me away from my desk in the small anteroom. I was much too shy to look my young boss in the eye.
I listened to his dictation, eyes lowered, had boundless respect
for him, and stood in the doorway trembling when he was

developing his plans for Marchmont & Rigby. Even then he
scarcely raised his voice when he was excited but proposed
new ideas casually, then waited with iron nerves to see how
they turned out. I found him as beautiful as the Apollo on the
Archibald Monument, and he had the advantage of not being
bronze. Sometimes I dreamt about him, the way one dreams
when one is barely twenty and has had a stern upbringing in
Adelaide. Then I would wake up bathed in sweat in my furnished room in Paddington. Today I know that Rigby prefers
stone, bold lines and glass to little girls. Perhaps one has to
be like that if one wants to give the most powerful city in New
South Wales the boldest silhouette in all Australia. Just the
same, at thirty-three he still had a healthy appetite for moonlight, and he was still living in the poorer section of George
Street.

He was very nice to me, which made me deliriously happy.
When he smiled at me, I melted. "Do you never go out, Betty?"
asked the grieving widower after six months of my chaste
admiration.

"Where should I go? I don't know anybody in Sydney."

"Well, now—you know me."

I couldn't have heard right! *He* wanted to go out with *me*?
I stammered that I had nothing to wear.

"Your dress is nice enough," he said, knowing better.

It was the only friendly thing he ever did for me. He came
over and cleverly removed my fake coral necklace. "You must
never wear red," he said. I was crushed. I had thought red was
my best color. I asked him shyly what he thought I should
wear. He said, quick as a flash, "Blue. Every shade of blue.
That would be right for you. So tomorrow evening, when we're
through here, we'll have dinner together. Where is the letter
from Farrell & Sons? Please write: Dear Sirs ... etc. etc."

I bought myself a blue dress with a month's salary. That
was how it all began.

Of course my boss didn't take me to any of the elegant
restaurants to which he invited Mrs. Trent. Mrs. Trent was a
pretty, well-dressed client who rarely laughed. Rigby must have

summed up her vapid solemnity as depth. His first wife, a bar girl, had been known in Sydney as kookaburra, the laughing bird. Evidently right now Rigby needed a serious redhead from Sydney's best and wealthiest circles. Patrick Trent was a well-known real estate agent, and Marchmont & Rigby was building him a house. Mrs. Trent appeared in George Street in elegant summer dresses and always wanted to speak to Mr. Rigby. Once I heard her sob, but when she left the private office of her architect, she ignored me just as arrogantly as ever. It always gave me a stab in the region of my heart that a wonderful man like my boss should have fallen into the clutches of a woman like Mrs. Trent. What wouldn't Rigby do in order to be able to build according to his ideas?

He took me to a restaurant in Pitt Street. There he could be sure that his friends from Vaucluse wouldn't see him with me. The place had a lot of colored marble and carved walnut furniture, and tried to demonstrate how the Italians had lived in the Renaissance. Rigby must have hated it. I thought the place was wonderful, especially the carved head of an angel over the bar. It reminded me of Gretchen. We had been such good friends. Sydney was so big and impersonal.

Alexander Rigby made no declarations of love. He wasn't that simple. He told me about a lady called Lola Montez who had appeared at the Royal Victoria Theatre in Pitt Street. The theatre and Lola were gone long ago. Pitt Street was very narrow, a gorge: women with market bags, girls with illusions, shops, a smell of gasoline, coffee shops, bars, whining radios, tooting horns, and anonymous sighs. When Rigby was already treating other secretaries to ice cream and kisses, I sometimes wandered down to Circular Quai where I could catch a whiff of seaweed, and crept around Pitt Street again. Perhaps Rigby would turn up suddenly where Lola Montez had delighted earlier Rigbys at the Victoria Theatre. But I imagined they liked to gamble just as much as Alexander, and met with bookies and the mob at the Hotel Tattersall, with the marble bar. After Gretchen and the Brothers Grimm, Rigby and Lola Montez were my murky stars. Once I lost my way and ended

up at the Salvation Army by mistake, the folk place for tee-
totalers. It was during my meager time, two long years after
Rigby had written me off.

My first manuscript was a historical romance eight years
after the Rigby episode. Lola Montez in Pitt Street. Of course
not a soul was interested in it. It was naive and written without
any elegance of style. One cliché after the other from beginning
to end. I sent it to *Insight*, and Miss Rigby wrote me that the
novel was so bad, things could only get better. By now I was
twenty-eight.

Miss Rigby took me in hand. I was not to write any more
novels, only short articles about Sydney today. Occasionally
a short story in which people met on Harbour Bridge and told
each other strange experiences that had taken place on Sydney's
narrow streets or in the suburbs. That suited me better than an
office desk, and Miss Rigby paid well. My first *Insight* novel
was a sensation, and I was thirty. Grace Rigby had introduced
me to her friends long ago, and I met her brother, Alexander,
frequently at her villa in Bellevue Hill.

When I saw Rigby again in his sister's reception room he
had been making a point of avoiding me for several years. I
had gone back to Adelaide for a while. Gretchen was married
and already had children. I worked in her husband's office and
sometimes spent an evening with her when her husband was
drinking beer with his friends. I saw how other people lived—
not excitingly, not especially happily, but not especially un-
happily either. Gretchen and her husband ate the bread of life
in peaceful harmony—fair enough. She treated me with a note
of condescension since I had come back from my excursion
to fabulous Sydney somewhat the worse for wear, taciturn,
and resigned. Defeats aren't easier to take in Adelaide than
they are in Sydney. When I had had enough of my mother's
complaints that I wasn't married yet, and when Gretchen's
condescension suddenly became unbearable, I packed my suitcase and went back to Sydney. I made a mediocre impression
in various offices and in the evening wrote in my diary in my
new room in Bathurst, only to kill time. But it suited me that
nobody knew me. I didn't know myself either.

Meeting Rigby again on Bellevue Hill was amusing. He's so smooth—love and hatred roll right off him. Miss Rigby was very proud of her "young talent." There was an illustrated article about my career and my best seller in the Sydney *Morning Herald* (Miss Rigby was related to the owner), and of course in the *Advertiser* and the *Adelaide News*. My friends at home could therefore read about me mornings and evenings. One of my finest moments was when I imagined Gretchen's face. We always want to prove to just one person that we're worth something. I was able to study Rigby's face after my triumph. I did so in Miss Rigby's reception room, and discovered only sincere pleasure at seeing me again. He was happy about my success, perhaps also about my red hair which went so well with my blue-green dress. *Who* was Rigby? I thought all night of the times he had once spent with me. Had he seen a second Lola Montez in Betty Withers? Years ago I had loved him naively and with exhausting passion. We lived together for six months. My provincial devotion must have bored him to death.

At the time Rigby let me go with two weeks notice because he sensed that I wanted to marry him. It's only fair to say that he had just recently been widowed and the scandal had to be lived down. Who would want to marry again when one's first wife had just died so tragically? I of course had the usual wish to get married. It had little to do with love but everything to do with the need for protection and security. I was in my third month. And the doctors in Macquarie Street don't make mistakes. I never tried to save money on doctors. Today Miss Rigby says I'm a hypochondriac and laughs herself silly over my various ailments. But at thirty things begin to go downhill.

After I had left the office with a sizable check, Rigby hired an older secretary with practical views and shoes. I sold costume jewelry, gloves, and cosmetics in a little shop on Pitt Street until shortly before the birth of the child. I didn't touch Rigby's check; the hospital was going to cost money. Once I saw Rigby's tall figure in front of the shop window of the little store. I was just selling a perfume for magical evenings and held up the small bottle like a fanfare as I found myself looking straight into Rigby's eyes. He stared back. Then he turned around and hurried away, and disappeared in one of the exotic little arcades. Was he afraid I'd run after him? In the whole episode, nothing seemed as unseemly to me as Rigby's hurry. He had been my hero; suddenly he was a man like any other. That this offended me beyond anything else was a result of my youthful innocence. Today, at cautious intervals, I pick up somebody on Bondi Beach, but my partners are temporary. After the first performance, they don't feel right. They want to be valued and praised for their favors. Fair enough, but still not good enough. Yet one can't live for *Insight* all the time. I wonder if Miss Rigby ever had a weak moment? Unthinkable!

Until his marriage to Anne Carrington, Rigby visited me twice a week in Bellevue Hill. He got his tea and his favorite pastries, and we talked. That's how I happen to know two or three of his faces. The wheel of time sometimes stood still in moments like those; sometimes it flew. I am writing my real novel, nothing saccharine. It will probably never be published. Rigby read the first ten chapters, then he got married in London. For *Insight* I write realistic stories with happy endings. The realism shows up only in the background material: Adelaide, Sydney, the bush in New South Wales and Queensland. Our subscribers want to feel firm Australian ground under their feet when they wander off into the land of beautiful dreams. I couldn't present them with a no-man's-land. They want to travel to where people are so much more attractive than on our sheep stations or in their shops or on their beaches. We are a rather monogamous and unromantic mob, but that doesn't mean that our girls and women don't dream just like their smarter and more skeptical sisters in other parts of the world. Yes, yes, I'll do the right thing by you! Hero and heroine get each other in the end, and the seducer or adventurer has to retire with his tail between his legs. The marriage is saved! Our readers can go on happily with their housework.

Miss Rigby doesn't know that years ago her brother and I conversed about Lola Montez in Pitt Street. And Alexander doesn't know that his child died soon after birth. He doesn't know anything at all about the brief existence of his son. I gave birth to his son without his knowledge, and buried the child without his assistance. If Miss Rigby knows anything about it, she doesn't say so. Apart from her unnerving love of order and superior knowledge, she is still the salt of the earth.

I never saw a brother and sister more unlike each other. She doesn't think much of Alexander, except for his talent. Of course we don't live in one of his houses; Miss Rigby would never spend that much money. We live in an old-fashioned villa with turrets and eaves, and a conventional reception room with many souvenirs from pioneer days. Our kitchen is American, and the bathrooms have a Roman luxury. The furnishings are up-to-date and lacquered. In our garden everything grows wildly, ivy climbs up the walls, and from the big veranda we have a view of the harbor. Rigby no doubt finds the house good enough, especially since the wide, shady verandas are in Colonial style, but he despises our esthetic indifference, and the stucco ornamentation on the roof and front door gives him cramps.

Do I hate Rigby? Why should I? He introduced me to pain, pushed me into deep waters and didn't throw me a life preserver. But through him I experienced the primeval night and the wild noon hour of nature. Sometimes he drew me gently into the magic circle of twilight in which homesteads and feelings dissolve and the Harbour Bridge is nothing but a gigantic steel ring, vibrant with music. I was with him on the wide, open plains, and under a deep blue sky looked at the faraway horizon, or we watched the moonlit flight of the bush birds in our lonely, violent woods.

Rigby prevented me from ever again living out of intellectual tin cans or looking through rose-colored spectacles. Without him my novels wouldn't have had a core of truth hidden under their obligatory icing. They would have ended in the wastepaper baskets of Adelaide and Alice Springs. Rigby forced me to see with my own eyes and to use my own words, not because he was particularly interested in me, but because he hated clichés. "Don't talk like a wooden parrot, Betty! Find your own damned words!" He was thirteen years older than I and had found his own lifestyle long ago. And his eyes weren't dimmed by love. Yet young, stupid and giddy as I was during that time in George Street, I could sense a silent conflict in Rigby. His taste and his need to be alone with mute material or with his birds conflicted with the Australian wish to simply be a good fellow among other good fellows. Not to be conspicuous. Not to be isolated from his cobbers by more talent or sensitivity. Today Rigby's dilemma is evident. He hurls himself with enthusiasm into the paradise of the average. Our Rigby is a rather difficult Australian...

It looks as if he still frequents the short-order kitchens of love. Things like that aren't important to him. He only needs a woman when he's completed a plan, and existence is suddenly as empty as the desert. And there always has to be a new woman. He mirrors himself in their eyes. He lives alone, a married bachelor, or spends his time with the mob. Australia was discovered for men. They feel best when they are among themselves. After we women have produced children, all we do is spoil the poor devils' fun. As soon as I had grasped that, I wouldn't have married Rigby, even if he'd given me a sack of black opals. To marry him meant to lose him, because he had all sorts of crazy ideas about freedom. He thinks that any marital consideration leads to slavery. In my opinion, with the right partner, it leads to freedom. But I didn't know that years ago when I gazed at the moon with Rigby. Beginners have such a hard time with love because they think it's so easy.

If I had married Rigby, I would have fallen into some sort of abyss, although not geographically as definable as, let's say, the Blue Mountains. I wonder if Alexander pushed the first Mrs. Rigby over the precipice because he needed her money, or was it because he couldn't stand her? Perhaps she stumbled and he only helped a little. I can easily imagine Alexander doing dark things when he just happens to have lost his moral balance. Rigby always was a gentle shocker.

Oddly enough, seven years ago, before he flew to London, he proposed to me. Evidently Betty Withers had changed to her advantage. But I wasn't a beginner any more. I knew a little something about the chasm between the sexes. I no longer expected love to be reciprocated. I knew better, whether the moon was shining or not. When Rigby proposed, I thought carefully of how I could turn him down and hurt him least. I didn't want to lose him as a friend. He meant too much to me. But I didn't want to jump in just because Rigby was suddenly sick of being alone. Otherwise why did he suddenly and so unexpectedly want to marry again? Was he getting old? But he was only forty-three at the time and even today is still much younger than I. Why did he suddenly, out of the blue, see happiness and rainbows over a hearth of one's own? I told him I had turned into an odd person and was afraid of marriage. He laughed. I asked him to forgive me for not appreciating the honor sufficiently. "Forget it," he mumbled sullenly. That was something I couldn't do on order. I can't forget good or bad things. His offer of marriage of course remained strictly between us two old Australians.

When Rigby brought his young English wife to Bellevue Hill for the first time, I had recovered from the surprise. His marriage had shocked me somewhat: again he had comforted himself with repulsive haste. I looked him straight in the eye for a second or two—he hadn't forgiven me. I don't know why he can't stand rejections of any kind; after all, nobody is spared them. In the next moment Rigby beamed at me and I beamed back, dutifully. Suddenly he seemed to me like someone seen in a dream. He stood before me, living, yet without substance. I knew that when I looked again, there'd be nothing but air. Anne Rigby was very pale, very beautiful, but she was frowning with tension, her eyes were lifeless, and her lips were closed tight. What was Rigby doing to her? Anne was a refined, unsuspecting girl from another world. Miss Rigby quite obviously intimidated her dreadfully, although she was very friendly to Rigby's new wife. You have to know Miss Rigby very well not to be intimidated by her. But she's a great old war horse!

Next week Alexander will be fifty! All the best...

I never met Flora Rigby, née Pratt. During those years I was witnessing Gretchen's marital happiness in Adelaide. When I came back to Sydney, Flora was already dust. Miss Rigby had lined a drawer with old newspaper that showed the first Mrs. Rigby before the accident. I looked at the picture for a long time. She was ridiculously overdressed; she looked sly, vulgar, and somehow so tragic, it could make you weep. Somewhere under that flowered summer dress, which was much too youthful for her, a heart must have been beating. What had Alexander done to her?

A while ago Miss Rigby had a visitor, a girl from Parramatta. I don't like Molly Fleet. She is too busy minding other people's business. She is twenty-two, and in spite of her good figure and beautiful hair, she doesn't have a young man to invite her for ice cream or the movies. Unfortunately, with her birthmark, she doesn't exactly look appetizing. That is tragic in a city like Sydney where there are so many beautiful girls, the model Candy, for instance, who poses for fashions for city and bush in *Insight*. She is appetizing, all right.

Isn't it funny that Rigby has no idea that this girl from Parramatta knows him? I find it weird. She reminds me of a nightmare I had days ago in which I was being followed down Pitt Street by a lurking eye. When I turned around, the eye was gone.

Rigby doesn't know how often lately Molly Fleet has had her eyes on him. Miss Rigby doesn't like it. She told Molly Fleet that it couldn't possibly be her brother, it had to be someone who looked like him. Her brother had nothing to do in that section of Sydney. Miss Rigby also advised Molly to keep her mouth shut.

I don't know if I should warn Rigby. If the girl from Parramatta has mistaken him for someone else, how would Rigby take it? If there's anything he hates it's someone mixing in his affairs. And what concern is it of mine anyway? None at all.

4

Stanley F. Marchmont—Architect

"When Menelaus and his companions captured Proteus, he transformed himself in their hands into a lion, a leopard, a bear and a serpent. Then suddenly Proteus became a fountain, and after that a tree. Yet to those courageous men who held him captive throughout all his transformation, he finally had to confess the truth about himself."

CLASSIC TALES AND LEGENDS

After the Second World War, my old friend, Jonathan Rigby, brought his son Alexander to my office in George Street. Every word spoken by Jonathan was worth one Australian pound. He said, "There he is, Stan. Make something of him!" with which he shoved his bean pole of a son in my direction. It was the rainy season in New South Wales and the lights were on in our dark anteroom where later our famous Elizabeth West— at that time Betty Withers—worshiped Alex idiotically. He was very patient with her. He didn't fire her until she wept on the sketches and mixed up letters to contractors. We called little Betty "Sparrow." She must have gotten terribly on Alex's nerves. He was never a patient man, but he didn't fire her until none of us could stand her. Let's ring down the curtain on it. Alex is the best man in the world, a little difficult, perhaps, but only on holidays.

I looked at the young man. I liked what I saw. Young Rigby had graduated from the University of Sydney; his old man still lived in Parramatta.

Alex bowed almost imperceptibly. His eyes expressed a genial stubbornness, the Scottish dreams of his mother, and the burning wish to make a good impression on me. In this first hour he was determined to win my approval, come hell or high water. I pretended not to notice it, but somehow the young fellow touched me. He held his head, with its rebellious blond hair, lowered slightly, as if in this way he could better hide his thoughts. "Will you take me on, Mr. Marchmont?" My appraisal was already taking too long to suit him.

He stood like a tree planted in my small office. When he stretched up full-length, his head touched the chandelier I had inherited. I nodded to Jonathan, he nodded back. Okay. Alex looked at the sketches and plans on the table with glowing eyes. We had a drink, and the matter was settled.

The first Rigby came to Australia as a stonemason, from some starvation area or other in Yorkshire. In Parramatta he built a little shack for his Scottish girl. Alex inherited his feeling for material from him. His long, strong fingers could sense the specific possibilities of glass, stone, iron, cement.

"What was it like at the university, young man?"

Alex threw back his head and laughed. "Boring! But you've got to go through with it. Now I know exactly what I *don't* want." He jumped up and stuck his long nose with the arrogant Rigby hook into my building plans.

"The young whippersnapper should be thankful that he could go to university," Jonathan growled. "*We* didn't have things that easy."

Alex pushed his tall old man aside, respectlessly but amiably. He had always loved his father, and later built the house in Balmoral for him. "I'm happy as a lark, Father." Suddenly he was silent. Then he stretched tall and said, "I will . . . I must . . ."

"Watch out for that chandelier, boy!" I cried, and both of us laughed. Alex found the electrified grapes very funny. The chandelier came from the old country. It had belonged to my grandmother. She had been very funny too.

I had all sorts of differences with young Rigby. In his wild soul the rascal nurtured the customary distaste for authority, and I happened to be the boss and pointed this out to him as

gently as I could. I fired him four times. Four times he came
back. I had no idea how he spent his time during his absence;
probably in Taronga Park with the birds or in King's Cross
with a sheila. That's what they called the young girls. Or he
simply ran around studying the building styles in our city, the
whole bit, from classic colonial, past Victorian Gothic to modern.

When Alex turned up again several weeks later with a long
face, and had his demon so far in control that he could at least
show a respect he probably didn't feel, I didn't make things
easy for him. No. I let him sweat blood. He had to apologize
in one way or another, or he could look at the office from the
outside. When he came back for a fourth time, a cool wind
was blowing in the office in spite of the November heat. Before
his last exodus, the young man had thrown my English porcelain teapot against the wall. I was attached to my teapot, and
I hated broken china as a form of argument.

Alex put a silver teapot down on my desk. "This one can
take a bounce or two, Boss," he said, grinning, embarrassed,
and careful not to bump against the chandelier. I grimaced,
but the hell with it, I was glad that the blond pup would be
around again.

"I am waiting for an apology," I said stonily, ignoring the
teapot for the moment. It happened to be just the sort of thing
I liked.

Alex mumbled something—a lip reader might have been
able to read an apology into it—then he laid down three sketches
in front of me. I didn't look up so as not to have to look into
his imploring eyes. So . . . I silently accepted his garbled apology. After all, you couldn't expect chicken meat from an ox!

The plans for a high-rise house in Potts Point and two villas
for the bays were bold and precise. Even as a green lad, Alex
was already a visionary. His designs reflected the two aspects
of our city—the industrial landscape and the timeless, idyllic
waterfront. I looked at the boy surreptitiously. No doubt about
it, he had the secret of creativity. Like Proteus, he could change
his shape. He became the tower he was building, the wide

windows facing the sea, the stairs, the garden that was to frame the house. I pushed the teapot aside. "Why is the gate on this side?"

Alex reddened right up to the roots of his hair, but he swallowed my objection like a lamb. He stared at his sketch sullenly but intently. Finally he entered the change I had suggested with a red pencil. "Thank you, Boss. You're quite right." I didn't want any thanks. All we two wanted was good buildings for Sydney and New South Wales. We drank our reconciliatory beer. Alex beamed. Not a care in the world. He was back in his stable. I thanked him for the teapot.

Alex a woman chaser? Ridiculous! Where would he find the time for such amorous nonsense? Even during his brief marriage to Flora Pratt he spent most of his weekends and evenings with me. We sailed on his yacht around the sprawling harbor; we spent hours in Botany Bay where James Cook started the history of our land in the eighteenth century. I knew a lot about the first colony. The Marchmonts came to New South Wales with the Rigbys. Alex listened. They were happy hours for me. And during our excursions, Alex saw the architectural development of our city as if in a gigantic picture book. That was necessary for his development. He who wants to build the houses of the future must know the stones of the past.

On our trips we never mentioned Alex's marriage, but a young man who always has time for his friends can't be enjoying a fulfilled marital relationship. Alex strode through the streets—a race horse that had shaken off all reins, I thought sometimes. He looked at buildings and parks with mute, consuming participation. His love for the pure, unadorned line originated in these hours. He absorbed everything that bore the signature of Francis Greenway, our famous Colonial architect: churches, hospitals, the Hyde Park barracks. Alex loved the lyrical grace of Greenway's best buildings and the noble Georgian lines. But he was striving for a new classicism of the future. He admired Greenway as an example of his period. Ah yes, a convict like that, who had so quickly become government architect under Governor Macquarie, didn't land in

Sydney cove every day! Greenway was a Bristol man. Like the Rigbys, his ancestors had been English stonemasons and architects. It was a lucky day for Sydney when Francis Greenway had been caught forging promissory notes.

Alex wandered past Victorian buildings and statues. There was a house in Pitt Street overloaded with Victorian ornamentation. Alex called it "the wedding kitchen." Sometimes he would stop dead during our walks or travels through the suburbs, and take notes, stretched up tall in the sun, staring across the harbor and the bridge. He had a very personal relationship to the Harbour Bridge. He never spoke of his love for Sydney, but nodded contentedly, like a lover who can see his beloved over and over again without ever tiring of her.

He wanted to transform the city, but he didn't know yet that Sydney was transforming him. All of us became a part of this centipede on the sea.

I lived through the scandal with Rigby. He continued to come to the office, but he wasn't really there. For the first time he laid his plans aside with indifference and stared down at George Street. "She is dead." That was all he said.

Evening after evening John Darling and I sat with him on the wide, empty terrace in Vaucluse. Sometimes Robbie French joined us. The Blue Mountains, where Flora had met her death, were all around us, a harsh memorial wall. We kept Alex company, not because he was so disconsolate but because the scandal had washed over him like a tidal wave. From one day to the next, the darling of the yacht club was isolated in a way that happens usually only among schoolboys. The press pounced on him and the police interrogations were no help. He was stubbornly silent, and we said only what was necessary. What was there to say?

Granted, I hadn't cared much for the aging bar girl with her tinny laugh. Alex never admitted to more than fifteen years difference in their age, but Miss Rigby told me that Flora Pratt was twenty-two years older than Alex. It was nobody's business. If Alex wanted a mama, why not? He wasn't the only one looking for a mother in marriage. But all the time the glowing fire of our continent was raging in him. In the open-air cage of Vaucluse, his eyes must have been following the flight of the bush birds . . . How had he been able to stand this marriage? Or . . . hadn't he been able to stand it? All my feelings, my knowledge of Rigby's creative powers, protested against this uncivilized suspicion. But hadn't Greenway, the forger, also created immortal monuments in this city?

I don't know if Alex knew what I was thinking. We were closer than most colleagues. I loved the fellow, goddammit! And I knew he was fond of me.

He stared out at the woods and the bays. His eyes were strangely empty. There had always been something of the restlessness of the wild black bush cockatoo in him. When the wilderness rose up in him, he always spoke softly. Then his voice crept like a tiger around the room. Once Alex appeared in George Street with a black eye. He had walked into something . . . Alex, who had the agility of the lifeguards on the beach? Then he had laughed suddenly, just as on the first day, when Jonathan Rigby had shoved him over to me. "I had a little difference of opinion with Flora." So *she* had given him the black eye. But what had he done to her? He didn't say and I didn't ask. Miss Rigby had already told me that the two were constantly having little "differences." Had they had a little difference in the Blue Mountains on the edge of a precipice? This in spite of the fact that I despised the virtuous mob in the yacht club because they thought it might have been murder, and talked about it in all the bars in the city. If he ever wanted to marry again, he wouldn't find a girl in Sydney. Not in all New South Wales! News travels fast in our gigantic nest.

I shall never forget those evenings in Vaucluse. We three could just as well have been traveling through the bush at night, a hundred years ago, with our blankets and our billy. Nothing but sky, eucalyptus trees, and three cobbers. We knew that one is born alone and dies alone, and we carried this stern wisdom together.

The harbor ferries plied slowly back and forth. The traces

of their lights were swallowed up by the water. The Macquarie light tower cast its white beams from the foothills thirty miles into the night. Our young widower looked dark and stubborn. "Poor old thing," he murmured. "She did her best. Who wants some more beer?"

These few words in memory of the first Mrs. Rigby were sparse enough, but Alex had managed to get them out. After that he was silent again, until he gave me a sardonic look. "Do you think I'm glad she's dead? Go ahead. Think I'm a stinking murderer. I don't give a damn what you think, you old kangaroo."

Of course I ignored the look and what he said, as I always ignored Rigby's shamelessness. That brought him to his senses quicker than anything else. Right then he looked as if he'd like to smash something.

I never doubted that young Rigby had found Flora's money attractive. As long as I've known him, he's always been able to make wonderful use of any kind of capital. Not for his own needs—he has none—but for his plans and constructions. At the time his friends from the yacht club had been astonished when Alexander Rigby had married a shopworn bar girl with varicose veins, flowered hats, and a juicy vocabulary, since he was known for his esthetic commitment. But the mob didn't fuss about it for long and soon enjoyed playing cards with Mrs. Rigby now and then, exchanging dirty jokes and drinking beer with her. Alexander's presence wasn't necessary. Flora stood behind the counter, fat, rouged, and good-humored, as she was accustomed to. The villa in Vaucluse began to look like a tavern.

Miss Rigby was very decent to Flora, but these two Sydney exhibits were about as suited to each other as a falcon and a kookaburra. It was ridiculous, particularly because it was generally agreed that most old Australians got along well together. Without the aborigines and the immigrants of all colors and creeds, there would be no friction.

Miss Rigby knew her duty to the new family member and

doggedly tried to think of it when plagued by dark thoughts. Too bad that the dialogue between Miss Rigby and Flora Pratt never made the stage.

Flora's visits to the *Insight* offices in Philip Street were a farce. *That* was a street she knew well. That was where the stupid, unfair police, who begrudged every dinkum Aussie his bit of beer and gambling, had their headquarters. Flora was a good poker player, and she could drink like a fish. But she held her fat fingers so tightly around her purse that Alex reddened whenever Flora mentioned money at any parties on the north shore. He also often had to pour her into the car in an inebriated condition, and take her home.

When Flora began to appear more and more often in the *Insight* offices, chattering with anyone waiting there for an interview—sometimes the waiting room rocked with laughter—Miss Rigby finally had to ask her to discontinue her visits. Miss Rigby would visit her once a week in Vaucluse, and she was as good as her word. She visited "Alexander's aunt," as the mob called the first Mrs. Rigby, every week, not without affection, and let the endless flow of Flora's words pass over her for exactly one hour, after which Grace Rigby drove to her club in Elizabeth Street, satisfied with her good deed. She never discussed Flora with anybody, not even with Alexander. But when the young man turned up at the office looking green, I'd ask Miss Rigby what in God's name was wrong in Vaucluse again. Then she'd tell me what a sobbing Flora had told her. Miss Rigby didn't feel sorry for Alex; the fool had paid no attention to her warnings. Miss Rigby hated it when her advice was ignored. Thousands of her readers obeyed her—why not Alex? If she felt sorry for him in spite of this, she probably stifled her feelings alone on her Bellevue Hill veranda.

Only once did she interfere. Alex had beaten Flora up so badly that she had been immobilized for days. She told Miss Rigby during her weekly visit that the "pig" had tried to kill her. And then he'd have her money! The poor woman was in a state of panic and seemed deathly afraid of her young husband. She disappeared from Vaucluse for several weeks and took up residence in her old quarters in Redfern. Alex went and brought her back. I implored him to treat his wife more gently, but he said a good beating was the only argument that made any impression on the old bitch. And laughed mirthlessly. If I hadn't been so horrified over his brutality, I would have felt sorry for him. He walked out of my office whistling and proceeded to make life hell for French. All with his mean, soft speech and tiger eyes. French had had just about enough of Alex that day, although ordinarily he admired him with youthful enthusiasm. Alex liked the young man. A pity he couldn't beat him up too.

After Flora's death, Miss Rigby said compassionately, "She did so enjoy life. And what's left of it? A sackful of bones." The Rigby family expressed themselves emotionally about any tragedy. But Miss Rigby also told her younger brother not to give a damn about the scandal, and that was very decent of her, especially since no one knew what she was really thinking.

The old "aunt" had left Alexander, for better or for worse, such a fortune that, after a fitting lapse of time, we had to order a new sign: Marchmont & Rigby, and we moved to a better section of George Street. Alex could spend money freely for the first time. He is lavish, and had already visualized the new office while he was beating up his old wife.

Robbie French is our new partner, an exceptionally nice young man, just as old as Alex was when Jonathan brought him to my office. Now Alex is making an architect of him. Robbie is the nephew of S. W. French, the General Motors-Holden people. So he has a golden background, round astonished eyes, and his own stubbornness. He likes statues for gardens and terraces.

He started out in life as a sculptor. Alex gave one of his statues the name *Weeping Susie*. She had two tiny heads, and unlike the statue of Queen Victoria in front of the post office, no clothes on at all. French wanted to send *Weeping Susie* off to a park in Rose Bay, where we had built a villa, but Alex went wild. Robbie hates to work for nothing, and besides, he needed the money. He still had quite a few homeless nudes from his sculpture period. Principally we had nothing against ladies with more than one head, and would have tolerated any gyrations in clay or stone if they had grown on Robbie's own stamping ground. But anyone could see that *Weeping Susie* and all the others were the result of the undigested life of an artist in Paris. Alex almost gave in as his favorite pupil wiped the sweat off his smooth, innocent forehead. The west wind was blowing, and it was infernally hot in the office without the struggle over *Weeping Susie.* "*You* ask your client if he wants your *Weeping Susie* whimpering here." Alex pointed to a secluded area on his sketch. "Of course we'll plant a lot of shrubs around her. And that's that, Robbie. I don't want to hear another word about *Susie!*" French swallowed happily. "And now may I get back to my work?"

Weeping Susie stands to this day in the park in Rose Bay, behind bushes and flower beds. The unsuspecting owners are even proud of her. And Alex said young French was going to be A-okay, and *Weeping Susie* could have been worse.

It has been a great joy to me to see Rigby training our new employees. These young men are to go on building when we have to leave our drawing boards. Alex has built a shed at home where he discusses ideas and ground plans with anyone who wants to, and he does it patiently and amiably. Today his dynamic ambition is a socially oriented power. Only the very best is good enough for the Sydney of the future he pounds into his young pupils. I consider it a privilege to have witnessed Alex's development. I did little for him. It is he who has the ability to make a vision technically useful.

Nowadays I mostly watch. The firm has grown, there are a lot of employees. The apprentices sweat on the third floor. I am seventy-four, an old bird perched contentedly on my terrace in Mosman Bay. One of my ancestors knew Archibald Mosman and told me about his whaling days. As a boy I would have liked above everything else to roam the South Pacific like Mosman and come home to our bay with oil and whalebone. Of course Mosman wasn't only an adventurer but also a very smart businessman. That he had from his Scottish ancestors, but doing business was easier in 1829 than it is today. Still, in 1840, everybody went broke because of the depression. We did too. My father had to start all over again. That's not unusual in our country. All water over the dam now. But I think of a lot of things when I look out at the bay and see the ferryboats plying toward Circular Quay.

Today I like nothing better than to watch my flowers. Wouldn't mind doing it until I'm ninety-five. I think Alex would too. We have done splendidly together. Alex still asks my advice when any important problems come up. Nobody would believe how much delicate feeling hides in that robust man. Once a week I go to the office. My doctor on Macquarie Street won't let me do more. Bertie grumbles—he wants to do something for his money. Splendid young man! We built a house in Avalon for James Dobson—he's Bertie's old man.

Miss Rigby likes young Anne. Of course she comes from quite another drawer than fat, funny Flora, but something's wrong in that marriage too. It can't be Alex's fault. To be sure he is restless, and the women always were after him. That's not his fault. No, no, I won't have anything said against Alex. And I said so to his dear sister the other day, just between us, at our weekly dinner together.

I'd like to know what she has against her brother. A good thing I swallowed my proposal that time in Windsor when Grace Rigby was showing me the historical houses there. Don't know what came over me. We would have quarreled constantly over Alex. I was too old for her anyway. Forget it! And *Insight* would have been a blight on our marriage. Not that Grace isn't a nice, reliable person even if she does know everything better than anyone else. When she keeps her mouth shut, she's still almost beautiful today. She always reminds me of French's *Diana* statue. I mean the figure, of course. French's *Diana* squints and her nose is crooked. But if he likes her, what do I care? Miss Rigby is fifty-seven now, and Alex will be fifty next week. Hard to believe when you see him surfing.

When I occasionally eat in Bellevue, Miss Rigby serves a good solid meal. No esoteric decorations for me! But I find the steep steps in her garden a bit difficult lately. Grace and young Betty West, née Withers, come running to meet me when Charles drives me there. Then we walk up the steps slowly. One gets the feeling that one's moving between walls of flowers. Nice girls, both of them. Very friendly to the old man.

I brought my chauffeur from Hobart with me when I was visiting friends. Charles Preston's real name is Carlo Pressolini, but he gets furious when you remind him of it. New Australians are more Australian than our kangaroos and emus. Charles drives well; one has to in today's traffic. His moods are no concern of mine. He can't dish them up to me. His people come from Genoa. He has relatives in Tasmania. The Italians are terribly family conscious, cling to each other like leeches. Not like us, thank God!

Miss Rigby told me something funny, and she knows what she's talking about. This girl from Parramatta is supposed to have told her something about Alex. She is Anne Rigby's masseuse. If she makes any trouble there, I'll have it out with this goddamned Sheila personally. All of us have had more than enough of gossip about Alexander. What does this girl with the birthmark want in Sydney anyway? Of what concern is the birthmark to Miss Rigby? The girl should go back to Parramatta. Sydney is overpopulated as it is. It *must* be a mistake. What could Alex possibly want in *that* neighborhood? When he isn't with me, he's conversing with his birds in Taronga Park. He can sketch birds wonderfully—he has almost too many talents.

I must *not* listen to women's gossip. How right I was not to propose that time. Who can stand living with the same woman all his life? Alex seems to have had enough of married life again. At the time I thought he was crazy when he wired his engagement to Anne. But I will ask Alex if there's an element of truth in this bit of gossip. The boy was always rash. He'll probably laugh and I'll forget it. He's done a lot of crazy things over the years, but he's never lied to me. Alex wouldn't do anything like that to this old man.

5

Monologues of Some New Australians

Hungarian Rhapsody
Mary Andrews, née Margit Berzsenyi, housekeeper.
Sydney.

In a few days Mr. Rigby will be fifty years old and we are giving a party. The new Mrs. Rigby is giving me a lot of superfluous advice in her pommy voice. Of course I don't obey a single one of her orders, or what would become of us?

She was a stenographer in London before she married my master. She knows neither our land nor her husband, and she ignores my daughter and me. For that God will punish her. My, Mr. Rigby does his best to cheer up this morose woman. What a wonderful man he is! But what was he thinking of when he married her? I almost fell flat on my face when he wrote from London that he had become engaged. At once I prayed to the Holy Mother to stand by my poor master. If he didn't have iron nerves—in spite of the fact that he is so gentle, and at least in my kitchen is a little cheerful—what would we do? My daughter Daisy—actually her name is Julika—worships Mr. Rigby. She is still only a child, but she knows when she's treated well. I would kiss the hand of our benefactor, but in this country that isn't done.

I have only been in Australia seventeen years and am therefore a very new Australian, but the second Mrs. Rigby is even newer. Yet she has my master, his house, his money, and his social position. She might also have his love if she tried harder.

I suppose she thinks that would be beneath her—the fool! My poor master sometimes looks terribly worried. All of us suffer from her nagging. "Why didn't you put fresh flowers in my room, Mrs. Andrews?" or the fruit juice is too warm, or too cold, or too sweet, or too sour. If I didn't love my fellow man, I could gladly poison the second Mrs. Rigby. Then all of us would have peace, and eventually Mr. Rigby would marry my daughter. But perhaps heaven will have mercy and remove the second Mrs. Rigby in a natural way. Her backache and headaches must mean a weak constitution unless she's trying to attract my master's attention with them. But if she is, she's on the wrong track. Rigby hates invalids. I asked Molly Fleet today if Mrs. Rigby's back pains were worse. The girl from Parramatta said, with a very fresh glance at me, "Would you like that, Mrs. Andrews?" I turned my back on her. I hope she noticed that I consider it beneath me to react to such suspicions. But in this country they all think they can do whatever they like with us new Australians. Molly Fleet probably didn't even notice how insulted I was. The people here have no sensitivity. That fresh masseuse has already been punished by heaven with a birthmark. In Hungary people used to be very suspicious of anything like that. Good Christians don't have the fiery hand of Satan on their faces!

I wouldn't be surprised if the second Mrs. Rigby didn't end up in a wheelchair. She already walks quite stooped, a young woman of thirty-five! At that age I could uproot trees. Unfortunately I had to get out of Hungary just at that time. First we had the Nazis, then the Communists. That was a bit too much for my poor fatherland. It doesn't look as if Julika and I could ever go home again. So I've got to be satisfied with Vaucluse.

Once, before his English marriage, I asked Mr. Rigby if he wouldn't like to live in Europe, in Paris, for instance, where I once studied for two semesters. At that time my parents still had their estate, and every well-brought-up Hungarian learned French. Rigby laughed as if I'd made a huge joke. "Away from Australia? Are you crazy, Mary? This is the best land in the world!" I said nothing. He gave me a sharp look and said,

"Aren't you happy here, old girl?" In the evening he brought me a box of chocolates. As the tears of gratitude welled up in my eyes he hurried out to the veranda. He can't abide tears. The box of chocolates was packaged in quilted silk. It's faded today, but it still stands on my bedside table, beside my prayer book.

Why does such a wonderful man have such bad luck in marriage? I must admit, he's rather naive. How can one be happy in this country if one has lived in Hungary? Of course Mr. Rigby was in Paris shortly before he became engaged to this Anne Carrington. That's where he must have gone off his head, the poor man. What would he do without me?

I noticed right after landing that Australia was too bright. I don't nag like Mrs. Rigby; I've always been known for my good-naturedness. "You are a too soft and generous soul," the father of my child said, shortly before the Russian occupation of Budapest. Of course it was sheer good-naturedness on my part that in the general rush I still let this doomed man give me a child. Yet I did not complain. The second Mrs. Rigby should take me as an example. But then she would have to pay more attention to me, and that would be too much trouble. She is the laziest woman I have ever known. In these seven years she hasn't even produced a son and heir for Marchmont, Rigby & French. I know that my benefactor is deeply disappointed in her. But he hasn't even complained about it to me, his old confidante. I can't understand it. The poor man needs someone to comfort him. But men never know what's good for them. There's nothing new about that. My student's name, by the way, was Ando. That's why I called myself Andrews when all Australia refused to pronounce my family name.

Without wanting to find fault, Australia is not only too bright, but the contours are too sharp. They stab like daggers. And I don't like Mr. Rigby's buildings. He may be a genius, but I prefer a real Hungarian castle with turrets and gables. The whole mishmash of Sydney is held together by Harbour Bridge, a not-very-pleasing sight. Sometimes I think if only the bridge would collapse and Mrs. Rigby would just be . . .

But I must not think like that! I wish her all the best. She needs it.

To mention a very small objection I have to my new home: I miss all the talk in Budapest. Here I am reduced to holding monologues. Of course I could get together with my compatriots over here, but most of them are uneducated animals, and the few intellectuals are so critical of Sydney that their crass lack of gratitude vexes me. In the home where they settled us at first I cried every night over the miserable behavior of my compatriots. The home was of course wretched, but good enough for us. "Immigrants who make demands are ridiculous," I said to my grumbling fellow Hungarians, and Mr. Szabo threw a ripe tomato in my face. I sought and found solace in prayer, and in the botanical gardens, which are really beautiful. Mrs. Szabo and the others complained that they didn't have any money for shopping; their dear children would starve here. That was scandalous! We had enough to eat to keep us from starving, and I told my compatriots that immigrants couldn't expect chicken with wine sauce. And I prefer to draw the curtain of Christian love over what Mr. Szabo had to say to that. For weeks I couldn't bring myself to pray for the Szabo family, but then I told myself there had to be pigs in God's farmyard too, and I begged the Blessed Virgin to stand by these dreadful people. And my prayers were heard. Today Mr. Szabo has a big Hungarian restaurant in King's Cross and is loaded with money. Although everything he has, he has thanks to my prayers, I still have to pay for every meal when I feel like eating Hungarian food on my day off. Although the Szabos tell everybody what good Australians they are, they are just as inhospitable as they were in the immigration station. They had money at the time from relatives in America, who were quite right in wishing the Szabos at the other end of the world. Mrs. Szabo used to buy all sorts of goodies which the family ate with satisfaction in our presence. Not that I would ever have accepted anything from them, but they certainly should have offered us something. When I think how generously my parents treated even unwelcome guests! And the Szabos had come over with their passage paid in part by the Australian government! I had too, but I am grateful and satisfied with everything.

Unfortunately there is a great lack of intellectual activity in New South Wales. There are no animated conversations here as there were in Budapest, except about the price of wool and sports events, and no discussion at all about the eternal values of life. My daughter's father was studying philosophy in Budapest, and over our coffee we used to have discussions in which our intellects embraced. *That* you won't find here! The Aussies lack elegance when it comes to pairing in bed, and that's that. The men here have a primitive aversion to talking to their female partners. Their inherited collective ideal is the sheep in feminine form.

No wonder Miss Rigby and Miss West decided they could do without such partners. I admire both ladies, although with all due respect I have a few things to say against them. They pay too little attention to metaphysics. When I mentioned this to Miss Rigby, she said that first things came first, for instance the problem of men finding work, and the women and children learning English. But Mrs. Laszlo and Miss Karasz came back to the home weeping from the English classes the government had arranged for them. They had been treated like ignoramuses! And Miss Karasz can write poems, and Mrs. Laszlo is clairvoyant and can do invisible mending! Why does Miss Rigby complain all the time about the lack of skilled workers among the Hungarians in Sydney? Aren't poems anything? Is a look into the obscure future worth nothing? Miss West gave the hopeless ones private lessons in English, but she didn't seem to be very patient, because the children often came running to me in tears. I taught them Hungarian, and all about Hungarian literature, so that they wouldn't forget our beautiful country. Poor children! After class the Misses Rigby and West often had tea with us, and once Miss Karasz recited a poem, in our language, of course. Whereupon the Misses Rigby and West left rather hurriedly. But they are really very kind to our little ones, and twice a week Miss West goes swimming with them.

I wonder when she writes her novels? This author swims too much!

In Sydney they simply have no neighborly feelings. Nobody asks anybody how they are, what their ideas are, or about their love life. Mr. Rigby never asked me with whom I lived in Hungary and what I had done there. What a paradise his married life could have been if he had conquered his specific needs and married me years ago! But he couldn't make up his mind to do so, and I was very careful not to bring up the subject.

At the time, seventeen years ago, his first wife had just died. He needed someone to look after him, and I needed someone to protect me against the unknown perils of Australia. Sometimes the good spirits of this youthful widower astounded me, but I noticed right away that he was conforming to the customary aversion to emotional demonstrations. But today I am again sometimes astonished over how cheerful my benefactor is, in spite of his dreadful marriage. When the mob meets in Vaucluse, they laugh and joke until late into the night. The second Mrs. Rigby goes to bed instead of looking after her guests. All that falls upon me. But what wouldn't I do for my Mr. Rigby! I would serve beer and make sandwiches until late into the night even if I was dead tired, which I usually am. After all, I'm over fifty now. But when the housewife sleeps, the housekeeper has to be up!

Actually Mr. Rigby must be feeling desperate. The second Mrs. Rigby makes life hell for him. She is always tired, something is always wrong, she sits on the veranda all the time with Miss Cox or Professor Darling. In Hungary there would have been something going on between those two long ago, but Professor Darling has ice water in his veins. With Mrs. Rigby I'm not so sure. The pale silent ones usually run deep. She's very young and would be very pretty if she didn't have such a sour expression. Mr. Rigby ignores it, just as he ignores the other tragic aspects of his marriage. Like all Australians, he doesn't want to suffer. I very soon noticed that in this country everybody flees from the pangs of the soul. It's a collective flight, and I consider it quite possible that one day a mass nervous breakdown will attack these cheerful people. But let's hope for the best.

My English is very good, still sometimes shopkeepers and uneducated people find it funny. English is a horrible, unmusical language. What would the Aussies do in Hungary? Or if Australia became an Asiatic colony? Nobody knows today where he'll have to emigrate to some day. Let's hope my master stays here, since he thinks this country is the best in the world.

When we immigrants came to Sydney seventeen years ago, we were received with friendliness. The Australians got on my nerves right away, but I must admit that my nerves weren't perhaps in the best shape any more. Anyway, I found the Australians too rough and unnaturally cheerful, but they did try to make us feel at home on the fifth continent. We were even served tea in some city hall or other, with perfectly terrible cookies. As I said, the Aussies did their best.

Later Miss Rigby spoke to us in a club for European immigrants, looking down on us a little perhaps, but that may have had something to do with her extraordinary height. She had brought along copies of *Insight*, a new magazine in those days, and like every native Australian, a sackful of good advice. We should try to change our way of thinking and former habits as quickly as possible. (Just try it! I thought.) In that way we would become real Australians all the more quickly, she said sternly. The inhabitants of this fifth continent wanted to help us to do so. It sounded as if the Australians were the crowning achievement of creation. When compared with our poor, confused heap of humanity, they could feel that way. Miss Rigby then said at the tea table, where I had the honor of sitting next to her, something I shall never forget. Very cautiously she made it clear to us that we could not live in a new country under protest, and that we could only achieve the social recognition everybody needed if we grew to be part of the country. I said shyly, in my broken English, that this was easier said than done, and Miss Rigby agreed. I found this so wonderful of her, I could have kissed her hand.

Perhaps it is part of my nature that I always anticipate insults,

but this trait of mine has taken on extraordinary proportions
in Australia. Perhaps every immigrant is too thin-skinned but
I must have lost six skins on my way over. I became suspicious.
I had guilt feelings toward my hosts. Perhaps I hated accepting
things from others; in my homeland I would have treated the
Aussies royally.

Miss Rigby got me the job with her brother. At first I was
so confused and exhausted by the heat that I broke Rigby's
teacups, one after the other. He was very friendly and considerate. When I said, "Punish me, sir," he laughed and said, "I
wouldn't dream of it, or you'll punish me with your cooking!"
He never treated me like a slave. An intellectual housekeeper
from Budapest with a fatherless child, or the wife of a minister
from Canberra—they were all the same to him.

At the time Alexander Rigby was thirty-three. His youth
probably helped him over the death of his first wife; anyway
he seemed rather offensively genial to me. After all, the first
Mrs. Rigby had fallen off a precipice before his very eyes.
Miss Rigby had told me about it before introducing me to her
brother. She brought me to Vaucluse herself. She didn't want
me to spend the few shillings I had on a taxi. It was very
friendly of her, but *when* did she work?

At first I couldn't find my way around this chaotic city.
Harbour Bridge grinned at me from every direction. When I
think of our Elizabeth Bridge! How intimate, how old, how
noble! Well of course, Budapest wasn't built in a hurry.

Perhaps, deep down in his heart and in spite of his good
humor, Mr. Rigby was grieving for his first wife. Perhaps
people grieve differently in this sunny land. In the entire house
in Vaucluse there wasn't a single picture of Flora Rigby. Probably my benefactor had loved his wife so much that a picture
of her would have magnified his sorrow unbearably. After all,
it was only years later that he married again. Poor man! He
deserved a better wife.

Shortly after I had begun my employment in Vaucluse and
Alexander Rigby began to eat my food with great enjoyment,
a conversation took place between us. I was about to remove

the empty platter of Szegediner goulash when, to my astonishment, he grabbed my arm. "Very nice, Mary."

"Thank you, sir. I do my best. I wasn't born a cook."

"I didn't mean the goulash; I meant you!"

My sense of refinement balks when I try to recapitulate what happened next, but without further ado, Mr. Rigby pinched my behind. I screamed and drew back, and the goulash platter fell at his feet. I stood up very straight. "Excuse me, sir, but you have no right to insult me just because I had to immigrate to this country!"

"What's the matter with you, woman? I was just paying you a compliment."

I was speechless. I wasn't accustomed yet to Australian jokes. Rigby leaned down and wanted to pick up the platter; I lunged forward and our heads collided. He thought this was very funny and laughed. I put the platter back on the table without saying a word.

"Why so funereal, Mary? What have I done this time?"

"I am in deep mourning, sir."

"So am I. And I need cheering up."

I had to think of my daughter's father, whom the communists had murdered. Granted, he had sometimes driven me crazy because he'd say his favorite sayings to me over and over again, but the dead are right because they are dead.

"Good night, sir."

"Where did you get your beautiful blond hair from anyway?"

"Good night, sir."

Mr. Rigby jumped up and took me roughly in his arms. In Hungary when one wants to seduce a woman one tells her first that one is interested only in her mind and soul. The rest then follows quite naturally. Nothing makes a woman so acquiescent to the physical side of love as a conversation about mind and soul. Naturally Rigby couldn't be interested in my mind since he didn't know that I did occasionally think. He believed only in what he saw. I didn't defend myself in his arms; I was much too run-down in spirits. He kissed me, not without passion, and unfortunately, after a proper moment of hesitation, I kissed him back.

"That's better, girl. Much better."

He let go of me abruptly. "Breakfast tomorrow morning at 7:00 on the dot. Good night."

He walked off into his studio. I stared at his broad back and his rebellious shock of hair. My knees were trembling. I crept off to my veranda and stared at the acacia tree. That night he came to me.

He was so experienced that even his routine seemed spontaneous. That a man and a woman sleep together and call it love is nothing new, but Alexander Rigby gave me an absolutely oceanic feeling, and this ocean carried me away from my mundane life. I don't know if he gives other women this feeling; anyway, that's none of my business. Perhaps ecstasy can be just as repetitious as cleaning vegetables.

Our affair lasted four months, three weeks, two days and one hour. This last hour, which he kept from me, seemed longer than the four months. The ocean is an infamous invention; when it spits us out, we're in no-man's-land again. I had been through difficult times before Alexander Rigby admired my hair, but now I learned what it meant to have absolutely nothing. Rigby once showed me some pictures of the Northern Territory—they call it the dead heart of Australia. Now I didn't have to travel to the Outback any more. No desert could be more deserted than my everyday life. I lived from one day to the next in a shabby landscape where everybody looked alike. Yes, I lived in the Outback. That was my big Australian experience: endless monotony, dried up riverbeds, unslaked thirst and crippled trees under a merciless sky. I prayed like the early settlers in biblical territory, but the desert wind blew sand into my throat.

Of course women were embraced and deserted in Budapest, too. When we bored our men they sought other pastures. We didn't behave differently when we wanted another man or to be left in peace. But in the old Europe such ugly separations were accompanied by beautiful farewell speeches and a few final, tactful words. The men of course didn't mean a word they were saying, and we certainly didn't believe we were suddenly too good for the joys of the flesh. In love one believes only a yes or a no, yet this old-fashioned ceremony saves the self-respect of both parties. It is certainly just as important as pinching behinds and kissing.

Alexander didn't desire me any more. Perhaps I had been too intense. Perhaps not. Anyway, the fun was over. I waited for him night after night, idiot that I was! Once I even crept into his bedroom, but it was empty. Next day, in silent fury, I threw a bottle of his after-shave lotion on the kitchen floor. Rigby happened to come into the kitchen to tell me that he was going to dine at home, but I'd just taken his apple strudel out of the oven and he ate it like a little boy, straight from the wooden board. "What's stinking of musk here?" he asked. I got red with fury. He picked up the broken bottle and looked at it thoughtfully while I washed the dishes. Then he passed his hand across my hair and said, "Forgive me, but we couldn't go on like that." Then he got into his car and raced off to the city.

I wallowed rapturously in my wounds. I told myself a) Rigby hadn't deserved my love, b) he had a heart of stone, and c) he loved someone else. And then of course, d) he'd come back to me. The latter couldn't have been more foolish, but it gave me great pleasure to dream, in my kitchen, how Alexander Rigby would crawl on his knees before me and beg for my love. After a year had gone by I realized that this satisfactory scene would never come to pass. So gradually I became "Rigby's jewel." I needed money and a roof over my head. Miss Rigby would have considered me ungrateful if I had given notice, and where could I find refuge in this alien city? The real reason why I stayed, of course, was deeper: life with Alexander wasn't simple, but life without him was unthinkable! The daily sight of him was pleasant torture. Once, in a foul mood, I burnt his sacred dinner. He threw his napkin on the table, drove to King's Cross in a rage, and ate at the restaurant of my enemy, Szabo. He was crazy about Hungarian food, no doubt about it. The following week Mr. Szabo winked and asked me if the famous architect didn't like my cooking any more. That's my good compatriot for you!

When Rigby turned away from me, I tried going on a hunger strike. I arranged it so that I fainted in his presence. He stretched me out on a chaise longue, shoved a pillow under my head, and poured so much water over my face that I preferred to wake up. "What's the matter?" he asked impatiently when he saw my tears. "Are you pregnant?" I shook my head. His sigh of relief didn't escape me. As a consolation prize he gave me a large opal. I never wear it.

Until his second marriage, Alexander talked a lot of things over with me. Since his brain was no longer befogged by passion, he noticed that I could think too. But since he has married again, he doesn't need me anymore. The second Mrs. Rigby can't stand me. That amuses me.

A while ago the masseuse from Parramatta looked at a photo of Rigby and began to laugh. Mrs. Rigby was on the phone in the next room. I watched Molly Fleet from behind the door, which was half-open. She picked up the photo and laughed again. How did she happen to know Rigby? He's always in George Street when his wife is getting her massage. I walked into the room on tiptoe. Miss Fleet turned around fast. She got so red, the birthmark on her cheek was as if on fire. In her fright, she dropped the picture and I picked it up without saying a word. That evening, when Rigby was sitting on the terrace alone, I asked him if he knew the masseuse. He looked surprised and asked, what about her? No, he didn't know her, had never seen her. I told him he hadn't missed anything, and he said he considered himself lucky to know one woman less. He laughed at my hurt expression.

Mrs. Laszlo has to give up her fortune-telling because her Australian clients already know everything. Miss Karasz helped her for a while. Then Mr. Laszlo made a lot of money with his tailoring and Mrs. Laszlo bought a delicatessen store. Since Miss Karasz couldn't live on her unpublished poems until she got married—nobody in this country takes the trouble to learn Hungarian—she helped Mrs. Laszlo in the store. Salami and cheese instead of lilies and larks. Then Miss Karasz got a job through Miss Rigby as a housekeeper for a Mr. Patrick Trent, a very rich real-estate agent for whom Mr. Rigby had built a house years before. Incidentally, the first Mrs. Trent had died a natural death, but I never mentioned it in Rigby's presence. In the house of a hanged man, one doesn't talk about rope. . . . Then something happened that day the whole Hungarian colony hasn't gotten over to this day. . . . Miss Karasz, the hope of good Hungarian literature—caught this stinkingly rich Mr. Trent and actually married him five months ago! A female shark in the guise of a wallflower! All of us were horrified! Even Mr. and Mrs. Szabo admitted that they had never seen Miss Karasz as a siren. "With that bosom!" said Mr. Szabo. He is just as vulgar in Sydney as he was in Budapest. If I had wanted to, I told him, I could have been Mrs. Rigby today, but I did my duty without grumbling and for thanks I was now being insulted constantly by Mr. and Mrs. Rigby.

Patrick Trent and Alexander drink together. For me Mrs. Trent is and remains Miss Karasz, no matter how expensive her bras are, and the fact that she pretends to have forgotten her mother tongue. She had the nerve to answer me, her former protector in the immigration station, in English, when she called on the Rigbys together with her fat, unsympathetic husband. I had prepared a cold buffet supper and then went to bed with a headache. The second Mrs. Rigby was furious, but I have no intention of ever waiting on Miss Karasz. Alexander didn't seem to care. He even brought me one of his wife's headache pills and seemed worried about me. Because of the dinner, of course. But I'd prepared everything and set it up in the dining room before I'd gone to lie down. "Don't do anything foolish, old thing," said Alexander, and slapped me so heartily on the shoulder, I nearly collapsed. I replied that I was the only person in the house blessed with common sense, whereupon he said he'd welcome it if it were a little more noticeable!

When the Trents had left and Mrs. Rigby was taking a shower, I tottered into the dining room to put the dishes away. Alexander was standing happily at the long table, eating leftovers. How he manages to stay so thin and eat so much is beyond me. Then he helped me wash up. He has his good sides. I tried not to ask what he thought of the second Mrs. Trent, but in the end I did. "I like her just about as much as the girl with the birthmark." When is this man ever serious? I said that I thought Miss Karasz was more Australian now than the Australians. Rigby said I should let it be an example to me. The tears welled up in my eyes and Rigby dried them with a paper towel. What's so wonderful about the Aussies that everybody's supposed to emulate them?

Yesterday, when I cleaned Mrs. Rigby's bedroom—I haven't been able to find a single love letter from Professor Darling—I couldn't find Alexander's picture which the girl with the birthmark had looked at so intently. *What* was going on in this house? Later I found out that Mrs. Rigby was getting a new frame for it. For his fiftieth birthday. Perhaps so that he can see what he looked like seven years ago when he was her fiancé. But I thought of course that the girl from Parramatta had stolen it for some dark reason or other. Why had she looked at it for such a long time? Why did she drop it when I came into the room quietly? And why had she laughed?

Ligurian Solo

Charles Preston, formerly Carlo Pressolini. Various professions, Sydney.

The first girl I met in Sydney was Molly Fleet. She came from Parramatta, wherever that is. After giving her a good looking-over, I crossed Parramatta off my map.

I met Miss Fleet in a coffeehouse in King's Cross. When the electric lights are turned on in the evening in this oasis of Sydney, one can imagine oneself back in Genoa. For a moment. The magic doesn't last. In Sydney I am a new Australian; at home I was a child of the land.

I studied law in Genoa. The university was housed in a palazzo, and that appealed to me. Beside my work at the university, I studied to be an opera singer, learned to chauffeur the automobile of the old signora through the streets at high speed, and had a few other professions. The usual intrigues at the Verdi Institute prevented my engagement at La Scala in Milan. In my country there are as many intrigues as fruit and tenors.

In Sydney I work as a waiter in the Restaurant Rosso in King's Cross. Nobody here appreciates my talents. The old Signora Pasolini in Genoa recognized the moment she laid eyes on me that there was something special about me. At home, unlike Australia, this is considered something desirable. I have been living in Australia for quite a few years now, but I still find it difficult to be like everybody else. By the way, my first job here was for old Marchmont, the architect, but he was rude to me, and we parted with mutual dislike. We Genoese are renowned for our difficult temperament and our pride. When we fly into a rage, the words stick in our throats. I often tried to explain the Genoese temperament to Mr. Marchmont, but he said he knew as much about it as he wanted to know. A furious devil deep down inside me, together with the grief over the arrogance of my new compatriots, forced me to leave. Marchmont and I gave each other notice at exactly the same time. It was the only moment of complete agreement between us. As I carried out my trunk I sang the grand aria from *Il Trovatore*. The old devil should have noticed what he had lost in me, but he went right on reading the Sunday *Morning Herald* without changing his expression for a moment. Still feeling very bitter about it, I applied for the position of waiter at the Restaurant Rosso in King's Cross. That was the best I could do because Mr. Marchmont had given me a useless recommendation. He hadn't even mentioned my extraordinary skill in maneuvering my way through the heaviest traffic in Sydney's business streets.

Raffaele Rosso also comes from Genoa, but his wife is a real Australian in every sense of the word. She calls him Raff, and all she can do is broil steaks. But she's okay. Raffaele embraced me with tears in his eyes when he heard that I came from his home town. He has never hired a Neapolitan. That gang lives five coffeehouses away from us, but as far as the Aussies are concerned, we all come out of the same pot.

Why did I stare at Molly Fleet's profile in the bar? Because she reminded me of Ginetta, my first girl friend. The same red-blond hair, the same long, narrow neck that stamps young girls as the victims of passion, the same full breasts and narrow waistline. Miss Fleet sat at the bar like a statue, with her profile to me. And how beautiful this profile was in the dimly lighted bar! It could have come from Liguria. In Genoa, as is well known, we have a surplus of beautiful profiles, the Campo Santo with angels and cypresses, the magnificent palaces and banks, Christopher Columbus, and the best artichoke torte in the world. Not to mention our famous pesto sauce. Shortly before I left Mr. Marchmont, I told him about this sauce, which is the very spice of life. I quoted with pride, "Once a foreigner has tasted our pesto sauce, he will never leave Genoa." And what did my Australian reply? Steak was good enough for him! I stuck my fists in my pockets and prayed to my guardian angel for help in this crisis. I would have liked to roast this steak eater on a grill!

Steak or no steak, at home we have girls with the most beautiful profiles, and since I was still homesick, I gazed at Miss Fleet's profile with nostalgia. Unfortunately she paid no attention to me. Her round forehead and the meekness of her neck would have inspired Fra Filippo Lippi to a Madonna portrait. No doubt about it, Miss Fleet was more beautiful than Ginetta!

She was wearing a light-blue dress and gold sandals. Her legs, with their slim ankles, were remarkable. Poor Gina couldn't compete with them. I sat there for a while and dreamed. Ginetta and I had parted company years ago, but I still thought sometimes of our nights together. Molly Fleet's profile aroused memories in me. The grand passion, the feeling that flowers, earth, oceans, and fire were alive in my blood, overwhelmed me for the first time in these surroundings.

At home I had had the possibilities for a brilliant future, but my turbulent inner life made an adjustment to the outside world difficult. It had to be conquered brutally, and I was a dreamer, yes, I'd like to say a poet, who produced too much to ever

write it all down. My father was a civil servant of no conse-
quence, with a sickly wife and eight children. During the Second World War, I celebrated my tenth birthday. My father was
a fascist like everybody else. Unfortunately this totalitarian
deviation made life very difficult for us after the war, because
my father, unlike most other men, could not deceive. And that
was his misfortune. I couldn't go to university, which my father
had planned for me because I was so brilliant; instead I started
to work as a waiter in the Restaurant Pasolini in the old city.
What a comedown! Signora Pasolini may not have been as old
as she seemed to a young boy like me, but when I saw her I
had a foretaste of what lay ahead. I can't deny that I was an
extraordinarily handsome young man. The signora looked me
over for a while with her glowing dark eyes under their heavy,
bluish lids. She had black, smoothly parted hair, a bold, manly
nose, thin lips, and very big ears. She always wore black, with
a valuable cameo at her neckline. The help trembled before
this big, heavy woman, and the scornful way she smiled when
something didn't please her. I noticed after a while that her
attitude toward me changed, but I couldn't say exactly how. I
could only feel her glowing eyes looking at me strangely, but
since she still spoke coldly and scornfully to me, I decided I'd
just imagined it. I was even a little afraid of her. She was like
a gigantic wave that could break my back. One evening she
asked me what my plans for the future were, and from then
on things began to look up. I had explained, modestly, that I
wasn't born to be a waiter. She sent me to the university where
I was to study law, to driving school, where I passed my test
with honors, and she saw to it that I took singing lessons; she
was a real mother to me. Anyway, that's the way I saw her
for a long time. The frames of the mirrors in the restaurant
were gilded, and sometimes I looked at myself in them pleased
with what I saw, when the old signora and I ate a festive meal
together in a corner reserved for us.

Around this time my father's youngest brother emigrated to
Tasmania and asked me if I wanted to come along. But I
laughed at him. I had so many brilliant careers ahead of me

and would one day be Signora Pasolini's heir. My Uncle Fabio said I was a fool, and how much longer did I think the old witch was going to coddle me? He laughed suggestively, we punched each other around a bit, but then we embraced amid loud laughter, and Uncle Fabio went off to Tasmania. Yes, he said, when things in Genoa weren't going so well for me any more, there would always be a spare bed in Hobart for his favorite nephew. That was really nice of him because thanks to our little differences of opinion, he had a black eye and a broken rib. But I wouldn't hear a word against the old signora at that time. I called her "Mama" once, whereupon she slapped my face. She was forty-five years old and a young woman! She got out of her plush armchair laboriously, and that evening dined alone.

Uncle Fabio was right. She was a man-eater and devoured me skin and bone, but what could I do? I didn't go far at the university—unfortunately there were intrigues against me there too, but my voice was my treasure. Sometimes I drove the signora to a village near Genoa where she had spent her childhood. The village was built on a rocky hillside. Life must have been hard there. The signora was hard too, but when I sang for her, she softened. I had to sing a lot.

When Ginetta came to the Restaurant Pasolini as a waitress, everything ended fast. Ginetta was seventeen, gentle, intelligent, and beautiful. I was twenty-four. We went for outings together until the old signora found out that I was taking Ginetta to the seashore instead of studying. She rampaged like a grotesque goddess of vengeance in her black dress, which had two grease spots on the collar and was too tight across her bosom; then she threw us out.

I could write off my future and was miles away from riches and fame. The signora slandered me everywhere. I didn't mind giving up my law studies, which had bored me to death, but unfortunately nobody wanted my golden voice either. At first I tried to get a job as a chauffeur, but the owners of elegant cars who could afford a chauffeur wanted references. They did not hire anonymous vagabonds. Perhaps I did look a little wild in my misfortune; anyway the car owners behaved as if they thought I might cut their throats during an outing. The signora had done a good job on me. I finally did try to get a reference from her, but she laughed in my face like a Fury.

Gina couldn't get work anywhere as a waitress; the signora saw to that too. The poor girl hadn't learned anything practical. Her mother was a laundress and there was never any mention of a father. On my advice she tried to get a job as a nursemaid, since she didn't know how to cook, but all the married women in Genoa assured poor Gina that she was too young to look after children. She was of course only too beautiful for their husbands. I was desperate when my little Ginetta—so young, so devoted, so willing to work—had to provide the food we ate and the roof over our heads with the oldest profession in the world. I swore that I would repay her doubly and triply just as soon as I triumphed at La Scala. Unfortunately things turned out differently. First of all I couldn't vocalize because of the hot steam coming from the laundry, and then my music teacher refused to give me free lessons. The wretched man declared that the gold in my throat sounded tinny!

I hadn't been to see my parents for a long time because my brothers had made fun of my humiliation. They had always said I was a braggart, but that had been pure envy. To make a long story short, I had to make do with the proximity of the laundry. Our attic room on the harbor was devoid of any of the comforts of home. When Gina came home, tired and teary, I didn't feel like any love play either. The steam from the laundry was slowly affecting my brain.

One day Gina came back from walking the streets of Genoa with a disease. That did it! I finished the braised squid which Gina's mother had prepared marvelously, and naturally withdrew from both women. I had to live with my parents—not easy—until I could emigrate. Under the circumstances I had to consider Australia.

When I met Gina at a café a few weeks later, she begged me to marry her and take her with me to the fifth continent. She would do any kind of work here until I became famous and wealthy. The poor thing must have gone out of her mind! The idea of marriage was ridiculous! How could I introduce a sick prostitute to my venerable mother as her daughter-in-law? Since Gina couldn't make any money right now, I sold my watch and gave her some of the money, also five percent from the sale of the gold bracelet Signora Pasolini had given me. Hard to believe, but Gina threw the money at my feet! With which she proved that she really had gone crazy. I picked up the money from the floor, enraged, and added another bill to it, but she tore it up and threw the pieces all over the kitchen. I was furious over having been parted so carelessly from my money, and decided to curb my generosity in the future. I left the kitchen without saying goodbye.

Until my Uncle Fabio sent me the travel money from Australia, I helped my mother at home. The past excitement had made me hoarse, and I had to give up my plans for the opera for a while. My Uncle Fabio had a gas station in Tasmania, and seemed to be doing very well. I couldn't get over it, because Uncle Fabio had never distinguished himself by any exceptional capabilities. At any rate, he seemed to be having better luck than I. He also wrote about the high standard of living in the workers' paradise of Australia. All of us had to laugh. With Uncle Fabio, every sparrow was a peacock. How could we in Genoa know that this time he was not exaggerating? I asked if there was an opera company in Hobart, but Uncle Fabio didn't reply to that. Did he still quarrel with his wife in Tasmania and celebrate tearful reconciliations? He had always been slightly secretive, but after all we were blood relations, and you can't choose your uncles.

When I was ready to leave for Australia, my youngest brother said he thought dry macaroni was better at home than roast chicken in a strange land. The little idiot was just envious, but I had no intention of having him follow me to Australia, and intended to advise Uncle Fabio not to send him money for the trip. We Italians have a family life that is perhaps too intense, and too many petitioners and intriguers on our own doorsteps. In Australia they say, "Mind your own business!" I never heard wiser words.

Uncle Fabio has been an Australian for a long time, but in a typical Italian way he sticks his nose into everything that doesn't concern him. When I told him later in Hobart that as Australians, we should stop this eternal spying on our neighbors, he laughed. Nothing seemed funnier to him than to conform to Australian customs. So why in the world hadn't he stayed in Genoa? Recently I have had to ask my compatriots to please stop addressing me as Carlo or Pressolini. My name is Charles Preston now, whether the people at home like it or not. When I told Uncle Fabio of my intention to change my name shortly before I moved to Sydney, he puffed himself up like a turkey and spat in my face. As far as he was concerned, I was still a Pressolini. We happened to be at his gas station, and I'd have liked to pour a can of gasoline over his head, but I'd have had to pay for it. I found breathing difficult, although actually the air in Tasmania feels quite European. I hated Uncle and Aunt Pressolini and their chattering daughter. The whole beautiful island was spoiled for me. I would have liked to throw myself into the Derwent River, but that would have given my brothers Guido, Felice, Roberto, Michele, Filippo, and my sister Angela, too much satisfaction.

In order to get my mind on other things, I sometimes went for an outing to the botanical gardens, or to Saint Mary's Cathedral in Patrick Street. Or I went down to the harbor where the Tasmanians throw colored ribbons to their friends from the shore. The natives paid no attention to me—that would have been unthinkable at home. In the shortest time everybody knows everybody in Genoa, but not even the Australian girls gave me a look. They don't know how to show a handsome young man their approval. Slowly I lost the ground under my feet. I betted like every native Australian. I tried everything I could to become an Australian, even if only a new one. In vain.

I would probably still be sitting staring at the ships in the harbor of Hobart, if Mr. Marchmont hadn't seen me in the garage and taken a fancy to me. Of course he never admitted it, everybody here is tongue-tied, but would he have taken me along to Sydney with him if he hadn't taken a liking to me?

His old chauffeur had just died. That may have played a part. He needed a new one. We did a trial run around Hobart— what a sleepy nest it is!—and I was hired. For the first time in his life, Uncle Fabio was speechless. Sydney! A metropolis! And an opera house was going to be built there soon! He paid my gambling debts—as a blood relative I had that coming to me—my aunt fried and baked Italian delicacies, insofar as she could get the necessary ingredients. My cousin, Claudia Pressolini, followed me everywhere. I imagine she hoped to get to faraway, exciting Sydney through me. All the time—calculations, intrigues, and secret ambitions! I smiled at Claudia. She was sixteen years old and pretty, with shiny black hair, but nobody in Hobart paid any attention to this pint-size Venus. And they didn't even know that Claudia was sly, brash, and insanely curious. She reminded me of Perugino's *Maria Magdelena* when she lowered her eyes and was silent. We embraced after the festive meal, I sang a long opera aria, Claudia coughed and stared at me enviously, and Uncle Fabio, with tears in his eyes, handed me a quite handsome sum of money.

We kissed on both cheeks. After all, I was his favorite nephew, and there would always be a bed for me in Hobart. I didn't say anything about how ridiculous his offer was; Uncle Fabio didn't know any better. Before I turned my back on Hobart and left with old Marchmont, I prayed in the cathedral for the soul of the unfortunate prostitute, Ginetta. She didn't deserve it, but one should forgive those who have treated one unjustly. Shortly before my emigration I had walked past Gina's house by chance. I wondered how she was doing, if she was cured of her illness, and had found a modest, honest job. I felt the pain of parting, and stared up at the dirty windows, lost in thought. Just then somebody opened the window. It was Ginetta, but how neglected she looked, her hair undone, her skin yellow. No sooner had she spotted me—unfortunately I stood rooted to the spot, I was so startled over her transformation as I stared up at her—then she grabbed a pail and poured the dismal contents over me and my new suit. At the same time she used such language to upbraid me—any jailbird

could have learned a thing or two from her. How could such
foul language pass beyond the lips of my gentle beloved? As
soon as I came to, I of course screamed back at her, but in
more civilized tones. After all, I had been to university, my
father was a civil servant, and I had taken singing lessons from
a professional. Our dispute might have ended peacefully if a
crowd hadn't collected, as if by magic, around Gina's whore-
house, and encouraged my former sweetheart to give me hell.
I had to beat up three men before I could get away. And for
this creature I had prayed to heaven! I thought of the earlier
Ginetta, who had worshipped me shyly and devotedly. Dreadful, how women change! I still see red today under Sydney's
blazing sun when I think of her. In the time of our Ligurian
moonlit nights, I had idealized her. That is always one of the
errors of love.

And now, years later, a young and beautiful version of Ginetta was sitting beside me at the coffee bar. Somebody called
out, "Hello, Molly Fleet!" But beautiful Molly didn't turn
around, and I could go on looking at her profile. How reserved
she was! I hadn't forgotten how readily Gina had embraced
me. I had dreamt of intimacies, but the fulfillment came much
too fast. It should never follow hard upon the dream.

The stranger in the coffeehouse seemed made of different
stuff. Marble! Very pleasant in the heat. I imagined how mild,
how refreshing such an Australian girl had to be: a crystal bird
in the cool blue air. Molly Fleet. The name told me nothing.
Lucia would have suited her better. She didn't turn to look at
me, although she must have felt my burning eyes. After all,
even an Australian was a woman. The full breasts, the narrow
waistline, were made to be embraced. And her long, red-gold
hair! Still I hesitated to accost her. In Genoa I wouldn't have
wasted a second, but on this continent you never knew where
you were at. Besides, who can seduce a woman with words
when he's been drinking ice-cold beer for hours? Should I
speak to Lucia?

Not long ago, on the beach, an Australian girl had been very
rude when I had admired her bathing suit in my perfect English.

The Aussies won't learn Italian, although it is the international language, daughter of Latin, the language of Dante! Should I address Lucia?

A year before I had got a punch in the jaw from a huge Australian with a red face and a bald head because I had smiled at his little lady in a Greek bar. Actually I had only been responding to *her* smile, but the idiot didn't know that because he was reading the paper all the time, and only looked up suddenly. I struck back, with pleasure, but who got thrown out by the manager? I did! The new Australian! The old Aussie, with his bald head and beefsteak neck was of course right. I'd like to meet *him* in Genoa! As I left he yelled something snide about my homeland, but I ignored it. He was too big and strong for me, a bush brigand who had somehow found his way to Sydney. His raucous, scornful laughter rang in my ears for days. He laughed as melodiously as a wombat! But it must be nice to always be right when pitted against a respectable immigrant.

It was high time to stop this monologue and to address Lucia Fleet. If only I hadn't done so! She got up indignantly and, head held high, left the bar. She even left her iced drink unfinished. She had to be an Australian because they are born extravagant. I exchanged glasses surreptitiously and drank Molly's drink to the end. After all, it was paid for. Then I paid for my drink hurriedly and rushed after Miss Fleet.

The evening lighting effects in King's Cross confused me somewhat, and all around me people were talking in different languages. Miss Fleet was walking slowly down Sydney Boulevard. From whatever angle you looked at her, she had a gorgeous figure. That's what sports do for you. They finally did go in for sports at home, but the figures of the girls are not yet as Australian as they should be. In Genoa the girls remain more interested in men than in sports. You can't accuse Australian girls of that!

Molly-Lucia Fleet stopped under a street lamp and looked for something in her handbag. She still had her back turned to me, and I looked at her slim, naked legs with the narrow ankles.

Her golden sandals were high-heeled. They made her as tall as I. I would have to look out that she didn't grow over my head.

At last I had caught up with her. Anyway, we were now standing side by side under the street light, in Genoa an explosive situation. Miss Fleet continued to turn her back on me and rummage around in her handbag. Was she looking for a handkerchief? I took a new lace handkerchief out of my pocket which I always carry with me for such occasions.

"Excuse me, miss. Did you leave this in the bar?"

Molly turned around abruptly and stared at me. The light fell full on her face. She seemed to have escaped hellfire, but she still bore the scars of the flames on her face. A birthmark covered her left cheek like a fiery hand—the eyelid, the earlobe—and ran down to her jaw. Nature had created a beautiful body and then, in a dark mood, had ruined it. The handkerchief fell out of my hand. I looked at the ruined beauty with fascination and horror. Molly Fleet stood motionless, only her lips trembled. Suddenly she pushed her long, red-gold hair across the disfigured half of her face like a curtain. I wanted to rush away, but couldn't move. I looked into her eyes and saw her despair. This girl was just as isolated as I was, in a world of naive self-satisfaction. Molly Fleet, too, had to be satisfied with the monologue.

I felt dizzy. Time passed. Was I experiencing an adventure that Odysseus had missed? But perhaps I was just suffering from too much sun, the result of shopping that morning in the market without a hat. Anyway, the European facade of King's Cross disintegrated into its individual parts before my eyes. The Restaurant Rosso whirled through the air, the pavement crumbled, a huge shark sailed up to me, its jaws wide-open. I teetered between attraction and disgust in the void of a nightmare.

A few seconds later, everything was in its rightful place again. As if in a trance, I raised my hand and pushed the curtain of hair aside and touched her cheek in a horrified caress. I had the curious feeling that I would never be the same again.

I had taken a trip to Hades. Perhaps all this was nonsense. The hot wind in Sydney must have driven me crazy. What was so dreadful about a birthmark? I had touched it. The color hadn't come off. But my touch had awakened Miss Fleet out of her torpor, and she slapped my face. Not surprising. What right had I to stroke her face? She murmured something which, in my excitement, I didn't understand, but it didn't sound flattering. "Bloody foreigner," or something like that, suitable flattery for a new Australian.

Anyway, the veil that had isolated us for a few seconds from the rest of humanity had torn abruptly. The sweat was running down my forehead, although I was freezing. I probably had a fever. I wanted to run away from this person, but I stood as if paralyzed. The slap in the face burned like a fiery scar. I had wanted to console this unhappy Australian, that was the truth, but only I knew it.

Miss Fleet had walked away long ago. Why did I have the feeling that I would never sing again? Wasn't one punished for offering a sacrifice at the altar of horror? I shook my head. All over the world there was ugliness and despair, but Ligurian grief contains an element of poetry. Miss Fleet's sorrow was as dry as the Australian desert.

Mrs. Rosso came running up to me. She had on her apron, and her wispy, gray-blond hair waved around her thin, intelligent face with its long Australian nose. She looked like a tamed bird of prey. She had flown from the Northern Territory of Sydney one day and had captured my landsman, Rosso, forever and a day. Muriel Rosso was angry. I could see that. The first guests were arriving, and here was her waiter making an ass of himself. But when she took a closer look at me, she asked, "Are you all right, Charles? Come and lie down for a moment. I'll bring you a nice cold beer."

Beer is the universal remedy from Hobart to Sydney. Muriel Rosso meant well. I picked up the lace handkerchief for gallant introductions, carefully brushed the dust off it and handed it to Mrs. Rosso. She raised her sandy-colored eyebrows and thanked me, astonished. Muriel was very bright. For the first time I was glad that the Aussies preferred silence to talk. She led me back to the restaurant and gave me a beer without saying a word. She would have been a wonderful mother, but she was too old when she married Raffaele Rosso, restaurant owner in Sydney. "Take it easy, young man," she said, disappearing into the kitchen, and was at once in the midst of an endless dispute with Raffaele. They quarreled all the time and were very fond of each other. Raffaele obeyed Muriel in spite of all his noisy protest. He needed someone to tell him what to do. She protected him unobtrusively in his new fatherland. And me. She was a good old girl—faithful and solid, if lacking in imagination. Raffaele, the stupid fellow, could have done worse.

I hoped that I would never meet the girl with the birthmark again. I avoided the bar where I had admired her profile. I hid from her during the day and at night she poisoned my dreams. That was the thanks I got for compassion. She was taboo for any man. In my thoughts I laid a stone in front of her unknown door.

Three weeks later I saw her again. It was the hottest November I had ever experienced in Sydney. The sky was dusty and the grass in Hyde Park was dead. Molly Fleet was standing under a lamppost in Darlinghurst. She nodded as if we were old friends. And we were, in a sense. When one has seen pain in the eyes of a woman, one knows her intimately. The Italian is born with this knowledge and leaves the world with it.

Why didn't I run away from this fatal intimacy? Again I felt feverish and depressed. Nothing good could come of it. I stepped closer. Instead of running away, I asked, "Are you waiting for anyone?"

"No," said Miss Fleet. "Nobody waits for me."

6

Monologue of a Girl from Parramatta

Whenever I burst in on a group, there is a pause. People stop talking, stare at me, and a slimy silence rises in my gorge. Or those present suddenly start speaking so fast, I am sure they have been talking about me. But perhaps they've only been talking about the Anzac Monument, or about their experiences in the bush, or the latest newspaper scandal in Sydney. In any case, at times like this my birthmark is flaming red. Then somebody says. "Do sit down, Molly. You confuse me when you stand around like that."

It must be wonderful to have nobody staring at you. What I'd really like to do in Sydney is swim, underwater all day, because the sun sheds its bright light on everything. As a child I looked forward to the night because it erased all faces. Every morning I looked in the mirror to see if the night had erased my birthmark. My older sister, April, grinned. "There's no earthly reason for you to look in the mirror, little one," she'd say, and I'd go for her with my fists. She would have been pretty as a picture if her chronic meanness hadn't spoiled everything. April didn't have much imagination and not much love for her fellow man, but she was very pleased with herself. She hated anything ugly. She forbade me to wear her earrings. Evidently the idea that they might touch my face made her shudder.

When I had finished my training as a masseuse, I moved to Sydney. In Parramatta everybody knew everybody else, and I hoped that in Sydney I would pass unnoticed. In Parramatta, the streets crept up on me and threatened to crush me. Our city had been modernized, true, but it was still the oldest settlement in New South Wales. I looked forward to Sydney especially because my sister was staying home. April would never leave Parramatta, and why should she? She helped Father in the brewery he had inherited from his uncle, and then there was my grandparents' farm near Parramatta. My brother, Stephen, ran it since grandfather's death. That's where I felt at home. As a child I had been happy with my grandparents and the cows. The cows never stuck their heads together when I came to milk them. I loved them, and I think they loved me.

In Sydney I sometimes long for Parramatta. For instance when Mrs. Doody, my landlady in Darlinghurst, gets into one of her rages, or when her niece, Candy, doesn't choose to listen when I'm talking about myself. Then, from a distance, Parramatta seems damned friendly. Even if at home things were sometimes horrible, I was safe in the old city where I knew every street, and all the paths and obelisks in the park. And the people at home were used to the sight of me. I hadn't thought of that when I left. On the other hand, nobody would have spent a penny on massage in Parramatta. The farmers and merchants would have laughed in my face. In Sydney Miss Rigby got me top-drawer clients, for instance her sister-in-law, Anne. A while ago I saw a photograph of Alexander Rigby in his wife's room, but then the Hungarian housekeeper came in on tiptoe and startled me. If she knew why I laughed! Mama Doody says a married man is like the weather or a pimple on the nose—only stupid girls get excited over him. But the weather stays with us and our old men disappear. She should know. Nobody in Sydney has ever seen Mr. Doody. Did he remain stuck in Ireland? I haven't been able to find out. I find it great fun to snoop around in the secrets of the people here, otherwise I have very little distraction, and besides, I often find out while I'm about it that other people aren't as happy as they pretend to be. I thought Mrs. Rigby lived in paradise, but then I found out a lot of things about her husband. *Very* funny!

The Rigbys' Hungarian housekeeper, who speaks such curious English, wanted to kill me the other day. Why are the new Australians constantly in such a state of excitement? For the least reason, the bush is burning. I think the Hungarian woman, whose name I can't pronounce, is madly in love with Mr. Rigby. How can she be? He's going to be fifty next week, and seems to be an unpleasant fellow. His nose is turned up all the time, even in the photo. I daren't think of it, or I laugh myself silly!

He *is* handsome, has a good figure, no stomach, although he's so old already. If I wasn't afraid of Miss Rigby, I could have some fun. But she's a tiger in a silk suit. I'm sure she has pots of money. She says I must have got her brother mixed up with somebody else; he was never in Darlinghurst. What does this arrogant old woman know about her brother? I said at once that, yes, I'd probably been mistaken.

My clients with the chronic backaches come from Miss Rigby. There they sit in their fine houses, and I don't like any of them. They think Sydney belongs to them, and they're probably right. My grandmother on the farm said you could never have a conversation with Sydney people because they always had twenty answers for the simplest question. Grandmother Fleet was in Sydney once, but never again! She thanked her heavenly maker when she got back to the Parramatta River, and the cows, and the cupboards with her preserves. She threw up her hands when I moved to Sydney. My brother was just milking the cows, automatic milking. All of us found milking by hand much more satisfactory, but Stephen runs with the times and wants to get the last drop of milk out of our cows. He mumbled that it was all the same to him if I wanted to move to Sydney or not, but on the farm there'd always be a place for me. That was the longest speech Stephen Fleet ever made. He was so startled about it himself, that he turned purple-red and teetered home from the tavern late that night. He's not a bad brother, only satisfied with everything. But perhaps I would be too, if I had the farm and a decent face, and the cows belonged to me. A short while ago Stephen bought some new, more efficient stanchion barns. For that Grandmother had the money, but when I needed new clothes for Sydney, they both said the machinery had cost too much. We have sixty cows. What Grandmother really meant was that with my face it didn't matter if I had a new dress or not. But for a goodbye present she gave me a sweet white dress that she'd sewn herself, and some of her best preserves. So she's a good soul, but grumpy. *Only* the cows do the right thing!

But where Lily II is concerned, I have to agree with her. She is the successor of Lily I, and just as sensitive. Sometimes I kiss her and she kisses me too, especially when I milk her by hand. Stephen won't admit that milking by machine has to confuse a sensitive cow. I heard a lecture about it not long ago in Sydney. Sometimes Lily looked at me quietly and sadly when I told her all sorts of things in her stall. If only I had her here in Sydney! But what would Mrs. Doody say to that? Yet her boardinghouse in Darlinghurst is a pigsty! The plaster is peeling off the walls, in the kitchen the tap drips, it stinks of rancid fat, and "Mama Doody," as her tenants call her, likes to run around in a slovenly housecoat with a towel over her shoulders and curlers in her hair. But I can save money here; she doesn't charge much rent. When I've earned enough with my massaging, we can enlarge the herd. Stephen and Grandmother Fleet have nothing against it, and the cows would belong to me, says Stephen. I can name them too. The farm lies in a sheltered area, and the pasturage is fine, a little limited if we enlarge the herd. But perhaps we could buy some more land from a neighbor. I'm reading a lot here about cattle disease, and hormones, and the chemical composition of milk, and so on. Grandmother Fleet advises me not to collect a lot of that sort of nonsense in my head: cows have always given milk without such knowledge. Grandmother has her own system and lives according to her own rules. She also has her own face. Her skin is stretched taut, sunburnt and sere over her massive cheekbones, and her blue eyes are still blue and keen. In the evenings she sits on the wooden veranda and watches the trees and the stars.

Sometimes she tells Stephen and me about the big droughts she experienced. The land looked like an endless strip of parchment and the riverbeds were dry. Grandmother Fleet belongs to South Australia. Once she showed me a picture of her family home, a medium-sized wooden shack standing lost between red eucalyptus trees. A few hens were visible on the fenced-in piece of land, and there were fruit trees, and Grandmother as a young girl with a basket of fruit on her arm. In the background were the Flinders Mountains, wild and forbidding. I have never seen anything as lonely as the three hens behind that fence. Grandmother said her parents were dissatisfied because the earth was unfruitful, but then the government or whoever put copper in the ground, and after that it was first-rate and everything began to bloom. Today the Tiger Moth planes spray the earth with fertilizers and chemicals, but Granny doesn't want to hear about that. She says the earth should nourish the earth. This in spite of the fact that as a young girl she had to drag every drop of water into the house in pails. On the other hand, she could already ride a horse before she knew her *ABC*'s.

Mostly she says nothing in the evenings. She's usually a little tired from preserving and cleaning, things like that, but of course she'd rather die than admit it. She is as rough and unapproachable as the Flinders Mountains, but just as in the mountains, there are gaps and narrow paths that at some time or other lead into an inhabited valley. I hope Grandmother Fleet will live forever. I don't mind how much she scolds me, I just want her to be there when I come to the farm. She will never understand why I moved to Sydney. Sometimes I think a swarm of mosquitoes must have bitten me. But I wanted to see the world. Until now all I've really seen is Darlinghurst. The villas of my clients are like the ones in the movies—everything so unbelievably beautiful and clean. I would like to see a toothbrush with worn-out bristles, like Stephen's, in one of the bathrooms. An old toothbrush like that is *real*, is used, and in my opinion, belongs to the household.

What I find funny and have still not been able to get used

to is the noise in Sydney. Apart from the traffic, Mama Doody
and her niece, Candy, talk all the time. My ears buzz. Or they
sing, both of them, with raucous voices, that some idiot or
other should stir the wallaby stew:

> So stir the wallaby stew,
> Make soup of the kangaroo tail,
> I tell you things is pretty tough
> Since Dad got put in jail!

In this way I found out that Mr. Doody is a jailbird. The
whiskey tears run down Mrs. Doody's face when she sings the
last two lines of the old bush song. Irish dreams are usually
mixed with whiskey; that's why they burn so. Mrs. Doody is
as Irish as if she had landed in Sydney yesterday. Her old man
ended up in jail quite by chance, says she. She had tried her
best to explain everything to the police, but had the dogs
listened to her? Then she shrugged her fat shoulders and asked
me who in Sydney ever listened to the Irish? No one! she yelled
furiously, not one stinking soul from Darlinghurst to Vaucluse,
where the moneybags were. Whoever has money may even
come from Dublin!

Candy sometimes has a visitor, a huge Irish sugar daddy.
He has a fat stomach and a villa somewhere in the finest district.
He really may come from Dublin. Candy doesn't favor any of
her admirers. Any of the bank accounts in New South Wales
are all right with her. She is so beautiful, it could make you
weep! Now she models in *Insight*, all through my influence.
But the money slips through her fingers, and Mama Doody
and Uncle Doody need a lot for their drinking. Candy gives
Mama Doody much too much because the Irish are terribly
family-conscious. Like the Italians. That waiter from Genoa
bores me to death with dramas about his clan in Tasmania and
Liguria. But I don't show him that I don't enjoy listening to
it. He is the first and only man I have to go out with.

Why I really left Parramatta is my secret. I miss Lily terribly,
and sometimes I'd like to be with Stephen again. If he were
in a good mood, he'd talk about milk production and the va-

garies of the cows. Hard to believe, but some animals have no social sense. They want to dominate the other cows, and always be first out on the field. Lily, of course, never pushes. When I tell Mama Doody or Candy about our Lily, they put their hands over their ears, or Mama Doody sings a dirty song in her rough voice. What good air there was in Parramatta! After all, it's a rural town; even if a lot of cars tear across Church Street today, Parramatta doesn't smell *only* of gasoline, like Sydney. My city isn't called "Origin of the River" for nothing. The early natives called it that before the convicts from England landed. One of my ancestors on my mother's side was a convict and lived in the Women's Factory, as the jail was called, until she got married. She had to weave, and later was a maid on an estate in Parramatta. I was ashamed for years because of Great-Grandmother Cocker, but Miss Rigby says that our old Cocker was a good British import, not to be compared with the weird people landing in New South Wales today. When I think of Carlo Pressolini at the Restaurant Rosso, how he boasts and the act he puts on, I have to agree with her. But the Fleets are a clan of a different color. My mother and grandmother Cocker, née Bradley, always go around with their eyes lowered and have nothing to say. Father is a beast, of course, and weathered like an old eucalyptus tree. A grim man! But Mother had no choice. How big is Parramatta anyway? And after I turned up with a birthmark over half my face, Father looked at everything that was Cocker or Bradley with a scowl. But my birth was just as much his fault as my poor, shy mum's. But that I had to happen too, after she had turned out to be useless in the brewery because she was too weak physically, that was the last straw!

Stephen sometimes took me along to Parramatta Lake, but even if he didn't say a word to me, at least he brought me. We swam and sat under giant trees, and Stephen always had food and his billy with him. He is three years older than our sister, April. I'm the youngest, and what a sight! When Father saw me and drew his thick eyebrows together, I froze in the blazing sun. I couldn't help it; I was devastated about the flaming hand on my face. I tried even then to cover the thing with my hair, but once, when April and I were quarreling, she cut off my hair. Now I was naked, and hid in Parramatta Park. April laughed. After that I was sent to my grandparents on the farm for a while.

I tried to bite April on the cheek while she was sleeping, so that she would have something to suffer over too, but the bitch woke and beat me up. I screamed so loudly that Father came running. He thrashed us both and swore. But when April cried, he gave her beer. April was the only creature beside his dog that he loved. I couldn't sit down for three days, he'd beaten me that hard. Then Stephen took me to the farm, where I stayed for quite a while. I was five at the time, April was ten and Stephen thirteen. I was happy on the farm. I yelled bloody murder when I was supposed to go home again, but it didn't help. I learned at a very early age how ridiculous tears were, and in the future swallowed them.

My hair had grown again, but now I hated April. She had really done me in. Mother was never the least bit tender to me, and Grandmother Cocker kept to herself. She always said she was a burden in the house, and I think she was. She never contradicted anybody, which made Father and Stephen furious. She had a long, dolorous sheep's face with human eyes. Her mouth was thin, and drooped. Sometimes a drop that didn't want to fall hung from her long, sharp nose. Father hated the sight of it. Then Grandmother Cocker buried her face in a huge handkerchief and coughed humbly. Her hair hung down her forehead, thin, white, and stringy hair. Grandmother Cocker looked as if she had been born old, and begged everybody's pardon for being there. She was wonderful with flowers, and sometimes I heard her talking to them and the bushes in the garden. When Father came home from the brewery and caught Grandmother Cocker having her weird conversations, he started fearfully. If he had trampled on her flower beds, she wouldn't have objected. She was broken and finished and superfluous, and didn't even know how to die! She only died last year. Stephen said she had apologized constantly because she was bringing so much confusion into the house with her dying. Nobody had time for the funeral—I mean, not really. I would have been sad about her death if she had once dared to be nice to me. But she wanted to please Father, and pursued this hopeless undertaking for years. Grandmother Cocker would certainly have been happier in the Parramatta jail, but she never had the guts to do anything wrong. Father sometimes joked about her, but his jokes were grim, and only Grandmother Cocker laughed fearfully. She left no gap in our home. That is perhaps the saddest thing one can say about a good, honest creature. Grandmother Fleet on the farm would be missed terribly. All of us know that. But she is as indestructible as the bush. She loves life and life loves her. People like that have a lot of strength.

So why did I really leave Parramatta a few years ago? I wouldn't admit it to anybody, because it's pretty foolish. One day April didn't call me Molly anymore, but Mole. That means birthmark, as well as the little animal, and it was the worst thing that could have happened to me. The children in school also soon called me Mole, and one day I jumped into the Parramatta River and didn't want to come up again. But Stephen saw me and fished me out, cursing. He brewed tea and wrapped me in a blanket, and didn't tell anyone at home about it. He didn't know why I had wanted to drown myself, and I didn't tell him. But after that he kept an eye on me. April was a pretty girl. She was popular and often invited places. Father was proud of her nice little face and jolly talk. She wore mostly green because it went well with her red-gold hair and white skin. She had green glass earrings. Nothing seemed as wonderful to me as those earrings. Once I crept into her room and tried them on. I held my hair like a curtain over my left cheek. The green earrings sparkled. Just then April burst into the room and tore them off me with an expression of revulsion. Like Father, she hated anything ugly. That wasn't right, Grandmother Fleet told him. Although she sometimes gave me a good thrashing, Granny knew her way around the Bible very well, and sometimes I surprised her saying the rosary with a cross face and in a great hurry. But she sent me to confession and was furious when Stephen swore. She could swear pretty well, too, but *she* was allowed to. For years I thought that Grandmother Fleet had a very special arrangement with heaven. I was too young to realize what Grandfather's sudden death had meant to her. But the next day she was already preserving fruit. I happened to walk by and could see her tears falling into the pot. She screamed for me to get out, and what did I want in the kitchen anyway? Then she went on cooking and weeping. I picked her a big bunch of mimosa. She loved mimosa. She put it in a clay bowl that had a crack and couldn't be used for cooking any more. She stroked my hair fleetingly, and pushed me out of the pantry. "Clean the shed, and make it fast!" she said. That evening my mimosa stood in front of Grandfather's picture.

April hardly ever came to the farm. Grandmother couldn't stand her, although she would rather have bitten her tongue off than admit it. She had created a cozy home for herself, Stephen and me, and that was that. She treated April with caution because she didn't like her. To Mother she was always compassionate and nice. This daughter-in-law naturally didn't suit her at all. Mother had the soul of a hen. She was so timid and parched and dry, like a piece of sunburnt Australian earth. She had been a milkmaid on the farm. Father had married her when she was expecting Stephen. I found a letter from Father in a drawer on the farm. There it was, in black and white . . . Mother sometimes opened her mouth when Father was angry with me, as if she wanted to say something. I always hoped she'd stand up for me, but not a single word passed her lips. I think I despised her, but a child isn't aware of anything like that. It is horrible when mothers won't say yes or no. Mother didn't even show her anger. She never punished me. I simply couldn't arouse her interest in anything I did. Sometimes I was dreadfully naughty and did silly things at the brewery, only to attract Father's attention. When he beat me black and blue I knew I was at least there for him. I tried in every possible way to please him, but all he did was look at me somberly. As if it were my fault that I had to run around with a fiery birthmark. And the children copied April, and called me Mole.

April grew up to be a beautiful, voluptuous cow and wanted to get married. In the evening she strolled along the river with young boys. I often followed her and knew that they necked, and how she squealed when the boys got fresh. She tried to catch the son of a rich sheep farmer near Parramatta, and she actually got him to the point where they became engaged. The two sat on the veranda, and Father treated to beer. I wrote April's fiancé an anonymous letter about what she was up to on the banks of the Parramatta River, and that was the end of that fine engagement. April is still at home, helping in the brewery. Nobody ever found out why the young farmer didn't come back. Soon after that he married another girl. His name was Robert Donahue. He was a big solid man and deserved something better than April anyway. As a small child I had loved and admired April. Why had she called me Mole? Why had she torn her earrings off my ears so that they bled? She had cooked her own goose.

When Mother died a year ago, April and I scarcely spoke to each other. After the funeral I drove to Grandmother Fleet at the farm. I noticed to my astonishment that Stephen must have loved our mother. His eyes were red, and he spoke even less than usual. In the evening he sat with his glasses on his nose near a hurricane lamp on the big wooden veranda. His beer and his dog, a very young dog, were waiting for him on the wooden table beside him. She was crouched there obediently. Stephen had a book on the control of disease in the cow barn in his hands, but he wasn't reading it, he was just staring straight ahead. He must have been thinking of Mother because he sighed twice and lunged furiously with the book against the flies. Then he drank his beer down in one gulp, and picked up his dog. He still had his glasses on. I followed him. He sat down on the shore. I asked if I could stay with him. He took off his glasses and said the shore was big enough for two. I cuddled up to him and he didn't seem to mind. He sat between the dog and me. It was very quiet. I asked him if he didn't know of any man for April; the brewery bored her, and after all she was a pretty, strong young girl. But Stephen said he didn't know anybody stupid enough for April. Suddenly I was terribly afraid of hell, although April had no idea who had spoiled things for her. But now I wanted her to get married and stop standing around like a bare eucalyptus tree after a bush fire. I hadn't confessed my sin yet. God knew all about it anyway, and I didn't think Father Kelly could do anything about it. Where could we get a man for April? Parramatta isn't a small town any more. There's a lot of industry along Parramatta Road all the way to Sydney, and good farm land around us, and the nice jail and shops and everything. But a country town like that can be monotonous when compared with Sydney. And people have very good memories. They didn't forget that April had been jilted, and the men in their pubs and the women over their tea still asked each other what could have been wrong with her. Where were we going to find a suitable man for her? The gossip was actually as old as the olive tree John MacArthur planted on the lawn of Elizabeth Farm in 1805. The story of the olive tree lives on in Parramatta too. And the olives are as hard and dry as April is today. One could throw stones at the crows—it's that dreary at home now.

On the farm too, things were different. My only girl friend wasn't there any more. She was a native aborigine and as brown-black as roasted coffee. Her name was Goonur. She had snow-white teeth and a sweet, friendly face, beautiful eyes, a flat nose, and full lips always ready to laugh. Goonur had been at a mission in New South Wales for four years, and helped on our farm with the cows. I saw her for the first time after I had tried to bite April on the cheek. I told Goonur what I had done, and she said she would pray for me. At the mission, religion had got into her system. She was very understanding where my Lily was concerned; she knew that Lily was my special cow and left me alone with her.

Goonur always wore brightly-checked cotton dresses and jewelry made of all sorts of little berries and dried fruit, and Grandmother Fleet let her be. She understood the animals and helped with the preserving of the fruit. She sang in a high, monotonous voice songs she had learned as a child with her tribe in the bush. They were always the same few songs about the stone frog or the two "wi-oombeen" brothers and the emu, about Eerin, the gray owl, or about the whirlwind and the rainbird. I wanted to teach Goonur our bush songs, but she shook her head with its black, wooly hair, and said her songs were good enough for her. She knew everything about trees and flowers, and spoke to them in a cooing voice. When anybody came, she giggled and ran away. Altogether, she often ran away, and then I would look for her, and weep when I couldn't find her. I'd stand at the lakeshore and cry, "Goonur, where are you?" and suddenly she would spring out of the bushes like a kangaroo and hop around me. I liked her a lot, and she never said anything about my face. She stroked my long red-gold hair and wove little wreaths for me out of wild flowers.

One day Goonur was gone. We looked for her everywhere, and Stephen even tried to find her in the bush. Grandmother Fleet made inquiries at the mission, but she hadn't turned up there. Her bible lay on the kitchen table, wrapped in leaves. Either she was looking for her tribe or she had set out for Sydney. Grandmother was furious because I wept, and said nomads were nomads, and Goonur wasn't worth weeping over. But I could see Grandmother looking around surreptitiously for days, when she was with the cows or cooking or sewing a cotton dress for me. She had liked Goonur very much, but again didn't want to admit it.

Strange things happen in this world of ours. I would never have moved to Sydney if I hadn't seen a copy of Miss Rigby's magazine on a table at my teacher's house in Parramatta. I was still going to school, and Miss Conroy was sweet to me. I asked her if I could take the magazine back to the farm with me, and she said of course, but I was to please keep it clean; that would only be polite. Miss Conroy had a thing about politeness, but she was the best of the lot, Grandmother Fleet excepted. I read *Insight* from cover to cover in Lily's stall, and it did get a bit dirty. After the holidays I gave it back to Miss Conroy. I was somewhat upset, when she asked if the cows had read *Insight* too. It was true in a way. Grandmother was furious, but Miss Conroy remained calm. But she didn't give me a book or a magazine to take home again for a whole year. I let me read, though, on her veranda. This was a great honor, because Miss Conroy was something special, like Lily, and only she could teach me things.

She was incredibly patient and unbelievably good. On those afternoons, over tea, she told me that what counted was the inner beauty of a human being. I would have liked to believe her, but experience spoke against it. Possibly I haven't succeeded in achieving this inner beauty.

Miss Conroy was born an old maid and lived contentedly in a world without men. She came from a fine old family where I am sure nobody ever swore or yelled so that the eucalyptus trees shuddered. The Conroys owned a lot of property near Camden, and their family history was very interesting, dating back to the free settlers in New South Wales. She talked about it sometimes, and she sent the Conroy saga to Miss Rigby for *Insight*. I read it later in Sydney, and got a lump in my throat. Miss Conroy was a good egg. She was pretty as a picture, but untouchable. Ash-blond curls, pink-white skin, and a pleasant smile. She adorned her pleasant, well-meaning self with simple lace, and collars that she had inherited. It gave her a sexless and enchantingly old-fashioned charm. She was clever and polite and compassionate, and for years did what she could for me. But she came from such a silent, pleasant and secure world, that she no longer could console me when school and my childhood were over. It was she who arranged that I study massage. Our pharmacist had had his daughter learn it in Sydney, and she taught it to me. Later, in Sydney, I took an examination. Miss Conroy gave me a letter of introduction to Miss Rigby. The Rigbys had lived in Parramatta once. My teacher was worried about me because I was having a hard time, and sometimes misbehaved. She loved people, she really was unbelievably good, but then nobody had ever caused her any trouble. And somehow she managed to drag politeness out of anybody or everybody with whom she came in contact. It bordered on magic!

Two years ago, when I went to say goodbye to her in Parramatta, she was already lying quietly and contentedly on her flower-laden veranda. We had our last tea together, with delicate pastries and the fine English bone china teacups from "the homeland." Every bite stuck in my throat. I spared her my confession to the trick I'd played on April. She was much too ill for any excitement. Her heart was tired, and I think Miss Conroy was tired too. She gave me her blessing in a toneless voice, and again whispered something about "inner beauty," which was all-important. And then she said that a button was missing on my blouse, and that I should always dress nicely in the city. As a memento she gave me an opal ring, a family heirloom

I never saw her again. She died three weeks after I moved to Sydney. I went to Camden for the funeral and her family stared at me. Who was I, and what did I want with their clan? I was sad because I knew that my "inner beauty" wasn't anything to brag about. On the farm I wept until I couldn't weep any more, then I went back to Mama Doody and Candy in Darlinghurst. What would Miss Conroy have said to the Doodys' manners? And to the boardinghouse and Candy's men? But probably she would have imposed some sort of politeness even on Mama and Uncle Doody. Nothing was impossible for Miss Conroy. She was sorry for bad or coarse or ruined types, but who wants to be pitied? I would never have played a trick on her. She would have overlooked it, and that's no fun . . . She was perfect.

I had been living just about a week with Mrs. Doody in Darlinghurst, not far from the King's Cross places of amusement, when Candy arrived. She comes from a gold-prospecting family in Kalgoorlie, and what could she be but a gold digger? She is, moreover, the most beautiful girl I have ever seen, and it is hard to believe that she is Mama Doody's niece. Candy is a natural blond. Her broad smile is naive, yet calculating, and she thinks the life of a model and occasional call girl wonderful. The latter profession is supervised by Mama Doody.

If Candy were not so lethargic and totally lacking in ambition, with her looks she could be a film star in Hollywood. Or marry some minor prince in retirement. She laughed heartily when I told her that. "Forget it, Molly," she said. "Australia's good enough for me." She is perfectly satisfied with her rich clients. Funny, in a way, that such a beautiful person should not have been repelled by my face. But perhaps she liked to look at her reflection in a dark pond.

As a model much in demand, she could already have been living in style, on her own, but with her indolence and good nature, she stuck to her Aunt Doody. The venetian blinds were broken, the plaster was peeling off the kitchen walls, but it didn't bother anybody. Candy's room though had been redecorated and painted, her couch upholstered with pink material. I washed and ironed the slipcovers when they were soiled. Then Candy lay like a bonbon in a silk-covered box. When I looked at her I felt hot and cold. She was almost too beautiful.

Candy didn't like me very much. Who did? But since she was pleasant and lethargic by nature, she let me fuss over her. I did her shopping, washed her beautiful gold-blond hair, and massaged her, because she was afraid she might grow fat, like Mama Doody. Her fear was not entirely unjustified because she ate sweets all the time, and when it was hot, didn't like to move around. Soon she found me indispensable, even if I was nothing much more than a piece of furniture to her. I typed her letters for her too, and sometimes I wrote them for her, which Candy found terribly funny. I liked her because she wasn't cruel and never called me Mole. I had told her about it, without mentioning my crime and April's misfortune, and Candy's big baby-blue eyes had filled with tears. Later I found out that she cried easily. Her tears were meaningless.

She had the Irish temperament that flared up easily. She could rage or weep over the littlest things, but afterwards she always asked me to forgive her. From the start she treated me like an old factotum whom one would never fire. Once she cried when a chair collapsed, and in the movies she sobbed her heart out. But anybody could have dropped dead beside her, she'd never have noticed it. Miss Conroy had wept for me too, but she had only been thinking of what she could make of me. Had she had the feeling that the big city wouldn't be good for me?

For a few months I was hoping that Candy would be my friend. She was so pleasant, and thanked me for every little thing I did for her. I don't know from where she got her nice manners, certainly not from her Aunt Doody, but all my efforts to become her friend failed. Sometimes she reminded me of the Pacific Ocean in Manly: what you threw into it eddied around for a minute or two and then sank.

How startled the Italian in King's Cross was when he suddenly saw my face under the lamppost. I could have killed him, but of course all I did was slap his face when he touched my birthmark. I'm not a carnival puppet, and he should keep his dirty hands to himself.

Charles Preston's real name is Carlo Pressolini, and he works as a waiter in the Restaurant Rosso. I never wanted to see him again, but I did. And we went and had a drink in the bar where he had admired my profile. I sat down again exactly as I had sat before, and that made him feel better. Just the same I had the feeling that he would have preferred to run away, but I asked him questions about Genoa, and that kept him with me.

Today I told Candy about my first honest-to-goodness admirer, if one can call Carlo Pressolini that. Until now I'd had to dream my men up. Candy seemed to believe me, but she wasn't particularly interested. However, she did ask, "What does your Carlo look like?"

"You wouldn't like him," I said hastily. "He's a wop with oily hair."

"I'll have to take a look at him in the restaurant."

"No, you won't!" I said.

Candy's eyes opened wide. "What's the matter with you? Sunstroke?" I had gone too far. At once I was humble and willing, like Grandmother Cocker, God rest her soul.

Carlo was quite good-looking in his way, and he had a soft, gentle manner, whether he meant it or not. I think it must be quite nice in Italy. According to Carlo they drink wine there instead of beer. I think wine makes men gentle and hungry for love; with beer they growl like radios turned on too loud, and it makes them sleepy before things even get started. At least that's what I think. Carlo never kisses me, much less anything more than that. But I don't expect it. "There are always mavericks," Stephen would say, when one strayed from the herd and stood alone in the meadow. I am twenty-two years old. April lost her virginity and her fiancé long before that. I wonder what it would be like to be with a man. I would so like to have a baby, then he could disappear. A little one that depends on you—that must be beautiful! A baby like that must think, at least for a few years, that every mother has a thing like that on her cheek. My baby would have only me, and wouldn't turn its face away when I was feeding it. If Carlo would give me a baby—there'd be room on the farm. And it would be something new for Grandmother. That would be perfect. But I can't ask him . . . no . . . I don't have that much courage. Father never comes to the farm. He doesn't get along very well with his mother, and if he tried to beat me because of the baby, now I'd hit back. I've grown big and strong. But it's nonsense to even think of Father being furious about my son. And April sits there with nothing. Why doesn't she find a man? She's still good looking at twenty-seven, and there's cash in the brewery. When she was seventeen she ran after everything in pants; what's the matter with her now? I shouldn't have done it . . .

I know so little about myself. I love Granny Fleet and Stephen; I'd do almost anything for them. And they deserve it. And then again, I have such dark thoughts and think up awful things and snoop around and hate people. Isn't that odd? If Carlo would love me and leave me like any other girl, then at least I'd have experienced something, and wouldn't be empty and sour, like an unripe lemon. I pray, of course, and sometimes I go to confession, but I don't carry anything through. If I looked like Candy, or like myself without the birthmark, I think I would be so grateful. I'd do a lot of good deeds. Then Father O'Brien wouldn't have to worry about me. He's got enough to worry about anyway, here in Darlinghurst.

If Carlo wasn't such a stranger, everything would be easier. But just sitting around in a coffee bar doesn't make for greater intimacy. He's just as much of a stranger to me as the second Mrs. Rigby and their Hungarian housekeeper. I think the new Australians laugh over different things than we do, and perhaps they cry over different things too. And then such a lot of them find something wrong in our country. Why don't they stay home when nothing here is good enough? This is the best country in the world; everybody knows that. But Grandmother says the Naussies know why they came here. Father is hiring a German in the brewery. But most of them want to live in the big cities, in Sydney, or Melbourne, or Brisbane. Carlo said the other day, "Sydney is a melting pot." He uses such fancy language because allegedly he went to the university in Genoa. I don't believe it, but in his free time he is always reading serious books, and I guess learns the stuff by heart. Why didn't he become a lawyer if his parents really sent him to university? And he says they live in a big villa and have a car in Genoa. So why is he a waiter at Rosso's? But if I were to ask him, that would be the end of it, I know.

Candy really does have rich clients. Mr. Trent is supposed to be great fun, but rich men like that can be damned nasty when something doesn't suit them. I see how arrogant they are in the city. The way they get out of their cars. But Mr. Trent, the Irish giant, handles Candy like gold. You can't say that about Mr. Rigby. In Darlinghurst we call him "Albert Ritter, traveling salesman." We believed him. Why not? I always watch him in the hall when he visits Candy on Wednesdays. Mr. Trent comes on Mondays. Ritter doesn't know me. I always stand half-behind the door.

When I saw the picture of her husband at Mrs. Rigby's the other day, I burst out laughing. So Albert Ritter is really Alexander Rigby! I haven't told Candy yet. Even in his picture,

Rigby-Ritter looked arrogant. A hooked nose, a narrow mouth, but his eyes ... no sheila should look too deeply into them. But Candy is stupid. I mean, emotionally she's a dope. But she takes good care of herself. She even got a few quite nice pieces of jewelry out of Rigby. Apparently she's a better gold digger than her ancestors in Kalgoorlie. None of them were able to make a go of it in western Australia, and Candy sits pretty right here. Models have it made these days. When Candy, with her long false eyelashes, strides along, hips swaying, and that scornful expression on her little doll face—the photographers have taught her that—then no queen or Hollywood star could look more disdainfully at us miserable creatures. Candy has the last word at *Insight* and other magazines. When she wants to go to a shop, she drives up in a limousine. There are no buses in the advertising world, says Carlo. Goonur told me that her tribe believes in the medicine man, and that's how the white Australians believe in Candy's soap, or the refrigerators, or the wrinkle cream which she is supposed to use, and which will restore any shattered marriage. You can read it in the letters Candy gets from *Insight*. The men want to know more about the perfume, "Blue Night," and suggest a dinner à deux. Rigby and Trent do the same thing, and both of them are married. The married men seem to be the craziest. Of course they pay double or triple. Mama Doody says they have to give their wives lots of presents because of their guilty consciences. Why do they get married when they'd rather be free? When the fine gentlemen come to see Candy—their cars always wait for them at a discreet distance—I have to think of the older men who sometimes came to the farm. They had big torn felt hats and weathered faces: cattle drovers with no herds in the dry season. Grandmother Fleet gave them tea in the dusty twilight, and damper, our flat Australian cake baked in ashes; then they moved on like long question marks on our endless country roads. Every now and then, when the wind whirled the dry earth in the air, the wanderers would disappear in a yellow cloud of dust. Funny how often I have to think of these vagabonds when Candy's johns come stalking up to Mama

Doody's hovel. These gentlemen have left the herd too. Why do they take Candy's alms while their decent wives hold supper for them at home? Why are old married men as restless as bush runners?

It's none of my business. I don't have a husband and never will. But a young man would be well-off with me, in every way. Rigby has a nice, pretty wife, much more reliable than Candy...

Yes, I had to laugh when I saw Rigby's picture in Vaucluse. If he knew how intimately I know him! Candy tells me all about him, what he says, his jokes, and what he's like in bed. That may not exactly be decent, but it has to be. If I didn't know all about him, it wouldn't work. Because I write Candy's love letters to him for her.

7

It Is Hot in November

On the morning of his fiftieth birthday, Alexander Rigby felt at least a hundred years old. He wasn't a brooder, but on this hot November morning he was inexplicably depressed. "I must have caught it from Anne," he thought as he shaved. His wife beat every sulking record from England to New South Wales.

Unfortunately Rigby hadn't been aware of this seven years ago. He had found Anne a shy but jolly young girl who would give him strapping sons and a little daughter for his leisure hours. A single daughter would have suited Rigby fine. Young women in numbers bored or frightened him.

He had proposed to Anne in Paris. She had been sweet there. "Paris—never again!" he thought as he lathered his face. Yes. And now there was still no hope for a successor to the architectural firm. And he was fifty. When was he going to begin to raise sons?

But the worst thing was that Anne had changed so much. It was as if in the course of time a cute little koala bear had been transformed into a porcupine that burrowed down into the earth whenever a human being showed up. Dammit! thought Rigby. Why was Anne so shy? And why did she complain constantly about backaches? She had a masseuse, didn't she? At fifty, he could still outdo all the greenhorns around. Last week—the spume had flown high—he had beaten French at water-skiing! Age just didn't count, he thought with satisfaction.

He hadn't changed in the last seven years. And if Anne would keep her eyes open, she'd soon find out that there were much worse and more boring husbands than he. But Anne didn't keep her eyes open. She was not all that interested in her husband.

Rigby shrugged. Marriage was a lottery, and you could pick a dud. Of course Anne wasn't exactly a dud. First of all, she was beautiful, and she was so well-mannered that she could fire the most unpleasant things at him quietly, almost amiably. When he thought of the uproar to which his first wife had treated him, differences with the second Mrs. Rigby were almost a pleasure.

Rigby stopped shaving, and out of the blue asked himself why Betty West, née Withers, had turned him down seven years ago. For years she hadn't looked at anybody but him. Her success must have gone to her head. He had been an idiot to teach her how to write, years ago, by kissing every cliché from her naive lips. Thanks to that, Withers now found him beneath her. But only figuratively speaking, because he was still taller than any woman around. He wasn't so old yet that he walked stooped and couldn't straighten up. The idea made Rigby laugh out loud.

Yesterday he had wanted to begin a new life with his wife. He tried every few years to overcome a dead point in his marriage and was hurt when his attempts were ignored. With that in mind he had taken the trip to the Blue Mountains with

Flora. Was it his fault that this new beginning had been the end of the first Mrs. Rigby? All the world loves a newspaper murder, but no one had been able to prove anything. Maddening that on this festive day he had to think of his first wife! For years now he had banished Flora Pratt into one of the farthest corners of his mind. He had to think of something else at once.

The nicest thing that came to his mind in a hurry was the model, Candy. He had always had a weakness for anything lovely. It could be girls, or flowers, or a perfect line on a piece of paper. The girl, Candy, was, as her name implied, a sweet-meat. He didn't expect her to also be a Madame de Staël or even an Elizabeth West. Candy had a career in the illustrated world as a sight for sore eyes. She was the golden bird in a jungle of houses in the city. Besides, she wrote him darling letters, hardly to be expected from her, because her conversation was below average. Candy was probably shy, and he liked that. Anne, and her predecessor, Betty, had been shy at first too, but less expensive. Candy's letters went to a cover address. Rigby knew enough bachelors glad to do him the favor. One helped oneself as best one could. Nothing to worry about. The moment would come when he could repay. He was a good correspondent, and answered every letter Candy wrote. But, seen by the light of day, Rigby tore them up. Albert Ritter, traveling salesman, wasn't balmy enough to write the most intimate things, even under a false name, to a sleazy boarding-house in Darlinghurst, where the police could find them some day. And since the police, in spite of their stupidity, still came across far too many things, they could eventually find out who Albert Ritter really was. And the scandal of the Blue Mountains had been quite enough for him.

If Rigby was perfectly honest with himself, he would have given up these excursions to Darlinghurst long ago—if Anne had paid more attention to him. But he couldn't just sit every evening on the terrace with this taciturn, aloof wife, and more often than not with John Darling there too. Rigby knew he could trust the old fellow completely, but he just couldn't stand the number three. Even worse was Anne's sudden conviviality as soon as John turned up in Vaucluse. And his housekeeper had noticed how his wife came to life in John's presence. Of course he didn't discuss his wife with Mrs. Andrews. He still had all his marbles! Actually, right now he would have preferred a pleasant married life to haring after models. That was really more French's style, but that young man was interested in nothing but sports, beer, and architecture. Today's youth was funny.

And he, with his new beginning? Anne should have realized that one could love him only on *his* conditions. A young person had to adapt herself. He was the older, unfortunately, and the wiser. Anne was slow, but surely one didn't need seven years to know one's way around with such a simple fellow as himself! Anne still didn't have the faintest idea how to handle him. Yesterday he had tried, as patiently as he could, to instruct her. Possibly he had been a little ironic in the course of the discussion. Anne hated irony. And metaphor. Perhaps she hated him, or had her love soured? In short, last night on the terrace, he had been at special pains to be nice to his wife, although it should have been the other way around. He had almost been tender. That hadn't happened for quite a while. The atmosphere had been right, too: soft lighting on the big terrace and the water shimmering like mother-of-pearl on the floodlights. Steamers and boats were painted in fluorescent colors, and the black woods stood watch in the background There was nothing on earth to compare with Sydney at night; there was also nothing on earth to compare with Mrs. Rigby's icy inflexibility. After a pause, Anne had informed him that she didn't need charity. What on earth did she mean by such nonsense?

Rigby cut his chin as he thought about it. God was his witness: he spent a fortune on his wife. Always the best of everything; he even paid for her massages. It was enough to drive one crazy! If there was anything he hated, it was ingratitude. He had brought Anne from a hideous suburban home to paradise, and he never once complained about what he spent on her.

Rigby wiped the last drop of blood off his chin and wiped

the perspiration from his forehead. Although it was early, the sweat was already pouring down his naked torso. That was the west wind. When it blew through the city in the spring, Sydney was an oven. Tonight he would swim in the ocean with his guests in Manly. Anne didn't swim.

He combed his thick hair back from his forehead. It was graying at the temples. What did he demand from his marriage anyway? A nice friendly creature at the breakfast table, not too soft, not too loud, not too stupid, and not . . . oh, the devil take it!

Rigby stepped through the open French window onto his private veranda. The sun glittered on the water and gave the harbor panorama a sharp clarity. It was the finest panorama in the world, but today Rigby longed for a solid fog. He had experienced it three years ago in London. Without Anne. She hadn't felt any desire to see her mother and her nice old secretary again—what was her name? Jennings—right. Even he, who frankly could do without seeing his family for years, had been astonished by Anne's lack of feeling.

Rigby held his hand up to his eyes, the morning sun was so blinding. In London's pea-soup fog, all human beings and the towers of Westminster had suddenly become indefinable. You could give the city content and dreams according to your imagination. Lady Carrington had been in the midst of writing a thriller, and Rigby had been able to give her a few tips about accidents. Hmm . . . it was ridiculous, but even the London fog, which Flora had never experienced, reminded him of her. If things went on like this, he could hang himself at the end of his festive day!

"Am I really getting old?" he asked himself astonished. What was it like, anyway, to grow old? He fastened his belt absentmindedly. It was an old belt and still fitted perfectly. Not an ounce of fat. When he thought of Paddy Trent, how heavy he was, and his Hungarian wife who could also lose a few pounds, he could be satisfied. And Trent was younger. In the sea he looked like a walrus. But otherwise he was a very decent cobber. From Ireland. His ancestors had come to Queensland from Dublin. Trent and he had become fast friends right away. Too bad that Paddy's first wife, the serious redhead, had driven him, Rigby, crazy with her so-called love. Today, seventeen years later, he had no idea whether Trent had suspected anything. All he knew was that dear old Paddy would have been happy if his wife hadn't bawled him out whenever he wanted to have some fun with his mob. The young woman, whose reputation wasn't all that snowy either, had been so bold as to spy on poor Paddy, like a policeman. Anyway . . . the police . . .

Why did his friends also have such bad luck in their marriages? It couldn't be the fault of the men or the climate. Except for the west wind, Sydney had the best climate in the world.

Rigby picked up a sketch from his bedside table and looked at it. The new house for the Trents in Avalon. Trent made a small fortune in his real estate business. They were building like crazy in Sydney. Trent & Company and Marchmont, Rigby & French got along like turtle doves, and shoveled in the money. Paddy was an honest cobber, even if he didn't understand anything about architecture. He would get a flat roof, however much he wanted a gabled, red tile one. Of course the flat roof was more expensive; it would have to be carefully insulated against the heat. But that wasn't what mattered. Trent was old-fashioned and you couldn't give in to that. A flat roof with a cleverly concealed water tank fitted in with the times. Horribly romantic gables and things like that were prehistoric. The next thing somebody would be asking for was Tudor windows! Not from architect Rigby!

After Rigby had condemned his friend Paddy to modern functionalism, he put the sketch in his portfolio, satisfied. Trent always built a new house when he married, after an appropriate amount of time had elapsed; an amusing little thing this time around—Klari Trent, née Karasz. She was no Venus, but Rigby had seen considerably less prepossessing females in his time. Unfortunately one had to give Paddy, who knew more about beer than women, a few pointers. Well, that was what he was doing. He was a good fellow and loyal to his mob.

How was that again about growing old? Even if Rigby had

felt a hundred early this morning, he already felt better as he thought of his breakfast with Anne. It was nice to have his young wife with him when he was eating. Anne looked just as fresh in the morning as she did in the evenings. The English complexion was indestructible. Rigby hoped that on his birthday his wife would be charitable and smile at him. One could have anything one wanted from him with a little good behavior and tenderness.

Did one change after fifty? Rigby frowned. Would nothing more exciting happen? Would erotic desires and naive delight with one's own existence diminish? Did the demanding extravagances of one's earthly realm lose their charm? Old Marchmont probably knew all the answers to these questions, but he was a churchgoer. Rigby had no use for anything like that. Anne called him a heathen, but she'd better forget about that. First she should remember her duties as a loving wife. She was too well-off with him, that was the trouble. He had always been proud of his ability to face reality. Why did he have such grotesque thoughts today? Nobody really knew the truth about life after death. One had to be satisfied with letting it surprise one. There was time enough for that. When he looked back at the past years, he could in all modesty be satisfied. At any rate, insofar as his profession was concerned. But now a considerable portion of his life lay behind him. Beside the monotony of everyday life and little pleasures, would nothing be left eventually but work? Was aging mainly a physical experience or primarily one of the mind? Did it come as a treacherous shock or as a last roll call to one's conscience? Would he be the same Rigby ten years from now, or only a worshiper of the era of technology in a repulsively objective world?

Rigby looked at himself in his long built-in mirror, and what he saw didn't please him. If he went on brooding like this, the legendary girl with the birthmark would have to massage *his* back too. Until now he had fortunately not seen Miss Fleet face-to-face.

Where was Anne?

Was she going to oversleep on his birthday? "All the better," Rigby mumbled, but he didn't mean it. Birthdays, weddings and funerals were important events for the Rigbys. A birthday morning with nothing special going on was not his idea of a birthday. Before his marriage, the mob had arrived at dawn; they had all celebrated vociferously and breakfasted on the big terrace. And that was as it should be. But a breakfast with noise and song was unthinkable where the second Mrs. Rigby was concerned. My God, Flora had caroled like a lyre bird and a kookaburra in unions on his birthday. "Alexander's 'Aunt' wasn't the worst of wives," even Miss Rigby had admitted on several occasions. In the evening Miss Rigby and the *Insight* crowd had given him a rousing party. And during the brief period of his widowhood, Betty West had wished him luck, almost lovingly. Those were the days! But not good enough for idiot Rigby. He'd had to marry again!

And now, the hell with it—he wanted his breakfast! Had Andrews overslept too? She had never forgotten his birthday, but if it came down to it, he could celebrate solo! He didn't need a woman to sing his praises in the November heat. But Mrs. Andrews was standing on the terrace like a sentinel, and had already opened the parasol over the flower-bedecked table. There were worse women than Andrews, he had often said. "Devilishly hot this morning," he mumbled.

Mrs. Andrews coughed her agreement and held a bunch of flowers under Rigby's nose. Absolutely superfluous with everything blooming wildly in the garden. And what was this? Rigby was holding a small package in his hands. Andrews shouldn't spend money on him. He'd told her so often enough. He looked slightly bewildered at a volume of poems by Judith Wright. She wrote excellent postwar poetry, but he couldn't take poems on an empty stomach. Nor at other times. Arrangements in glass, metal, and cement satisfied his poetic needs completely. Certainly the language of modern architecture was not as articulate yet as the lyricism of New South Wales, Victoria and Queensland, but it had also developed, with vision and experimentation, to an ever-bolder expressionism, especially in this wide-open water citadel that welcomed the architectural experience. Sydney's inhabitants were a visual lot. Mrs. Andrews couldn't grasp that, but he wasn't interested in her grasp of things. He had every reason to be cautious. His jewel had a built-in explosive device. Beside Miss Rigby he didn't know one practical woman. Oh, Andrews meant well. This evening she would be his guest. He was having the whole thing catered by a restaurant so that Andrews might enjoy herself too. Right now she looked as if she wanted to run away. Were all females in their early fifties so sour?

"Thanks for the book." Rigby laid the little volume down beside the flowers with a stony expression. What he needed was a new angel; Andrews knew it only too well. "I would like to be excused from tonight's party, please," she said formally.

"Why?"

"I don't fit in with the guests."

"Neither do I. We have fun on birthdays whether we like it or not. Is that clear?"

Rigby's jewel gave him a look of remembrance which he chose to ignore. Years ago, when he had let himself in for this foolish business with Andrews it had been a hot November too. The same west wind. Well, yes—only an arrant fool sought his fun in his own house. In the course of the years, Rigby had tried frequently to marry his jewel off to one of her former compatriots in Sydney. All of them had done very well. Restaurant-owner Szabo in King's Cross had tried very hard to find a husband for Andrews, if only to please his steady client Rigby, because personally he couldn't stand Mrs. Andrews, but she stuck to Rigby, and right now she was driving his wife quietly crazy. Were all jewels so complex? He must try to find out. Why the hell was Andrews constantly offended? After all, he hadn't robbed her of her virginity. She had arrived in Sydney with a baby. He had been wondering for quite some time whether he shouldn't adopt Daisy, since he had no children, but until now he had been afraid of Anne's reaction. Women were a problem. If only they would love him less, everybody would live happily ever after. When he recalled the scenes Andrews had made—why did he have to think of them today?—he had to admit that he preferred her in her present, half-frozen condition.

"All the best to your half-century," said Andrews.

"Shut up!" Rigby looked irritably around his festively decorated table. "Where's my food?"

Andrews held up a letter. "For Mrs. Rigby." After a pause she said glumly, "A man's handwriting."

"It's none of my business," Rigby said loyally.

Mrs. Andrews left satisfied. The letter had vexed him, even if he had pretended that it didn't concern him.

Rigby leafed through the volume of Judith Wright's poems, frowning. Who was writing letters to his wife? *His* wife? Rigby turned the pages angrily. What was that supposed to be? Sculpture?

The shape that waited there was future, fate . . .

How did this sheila from Armidale know such things? Rigby came across the famous bird poems. Not bad. Rigby himself couldn't have done better than the one about the lyre bird. Once, in Queensland, he had had the patience and luck to listen to the arias of this rare Australian bird in the bush. The lyre bird's own specific melody blended with the mysterious imitation of all sorts of sounds, from the noise of a motorboat to the laughter of the kookaburra. The male could raise his magnificent tail in the shape of a Greek lyre. The female was nothing to look at, as it should be.

> I'll never see the lyre birds—
> The few, the shy, the fabulous,
> The dying poets . . .

Rigby closed the book abruptly just before Andrews appeared with the covered dishes that gave forth an aroma of eggs, bacon, grilled tomatoes, and steak. His jewel was not to catch him reading poetry in this infernal heat. But it would do no harm if he were to read what Judith Wright had written about the black cockatoos and currawangs when he got to his

office. After the office he would take the ferry from Circular
Quay and visit the birdhouse in the Taronga Zoo. The bird
world calmed him. The thought made his face light up for a
moment. But where was Anne? Did he have a birthday every
day, and the fiftieth one at that? And what bastard was writing
his wife long letters?

Anne Rigby knew that she should have set the alarm. She
knew that Alexander was expecting her to appear for breakfast.
She knew everything. But she lay in bed as if paralyzed, and
the November heat crept slowly under her skin. The fuss Alex
was making was ridiculous. The calendar meant nothing. Besides, they weren't two love birds any more, and a fiftieth
birthday was no occasion for jubilation, not in her opinion. At
that moment she couldn't remember when she had last laughed
heartily. Perhaps with John Darling or Shirley Cox. Anne
yawned and turned on her other side. She had a half hour or
so, then she would have to get up. At any rate, she was going
to try to, to please Alex, although she felt she was no means
in duty bound to do anything to please him.

When Andrews knocked on the door three times, Anne sat
up, startled. She didn't need the alarm any more. Andrews's
expression was malicious. It didn't make Anne feel good.

"Mr. Rigby has almost finished his breakfast."

"But it's only six-thirty!"

Andrews looked at her wrist watch although she knew exactly what time it was. "Half-past seven, Mrs. Rigby."

"Thank you." Anne was so furious that she reddened.

Mary Andrews stood indecisively for a moment. Should she
help Mrs. Rigby into her housecoat? Comb her hair? Impossible! Let Rigby see what he had married. But Andrews hadn't
been able to stand the sight any more of Rigby waiting patiently
for his wife to appear. Andrews closed the screen door quietly.
Should she be an absolute angel and suggest to Rigby that he
wait a little longer?

Anne got up laboriously. In spite of the massage her back
ached. Badly. And Alex hated invalids. Anne was surprised

herself at her constant physical complaints in Sydney. She had
never been sick at home, except for an occasional cold. It had
to be nerves. Apparently only a spiritual athlete could stand
being married to Rigby. Anne wanted to be loved in her way,
not in Alexander's domineering and unpredictable way. There
were weeks when he paid no attention to her whatsoever, and
then, suddenly, as last night, without any preparation, he had
wanted to be tender. As if he were throwing alms to a beggar.
But he hadn't counted on Anne's response. She was certainly
not as talented, nor as popular, nor as charming as Alex, but
you couldn't treat her like that! Drag her out of her corner
because it happened to suit him, only to put her back in the
corner again afterwards. For Anne, sympathy, to say nothing
of love, was a thing of consistency.

She combed her beautiful long hair agitatedly as she thought
of Alexander's mood yesterday. Perhaps she shouldn't have
rejected him so brusquely. Perhaps marriage demanded constant forgiving and never-failing tolerance. But all her honest
efforts had aroused no love in Alex. It wasn't surprising that
this condition of disappointment and isolation was making her
ill. She was only thirty-five. And of course the fact that they
had no children was the worst failure. Although Alex spent
almost all his evenings away from home, he had wanted children. That was why he had married again. Naturally he couldn't
have known that a healthy twenty-eight-year-old girl would let
him down in this respect too. Besides that he accused her of
being cold, indifferent, shy, and a spoilsport. What she held
against Alex she preferred to keep to herself.

She appeared on the breakfast veranda, her present in her
hand, just as Alexander's big white car was racing out of the
garden gate. Anne's heart beat fast. The heat made her dizzy.
Alex would never forgive her. Of course Mrs. Andrews had
wakened her too late on purpose. She hadn't looked like the
cat that swallowed the canary for nothing. Anne felt ill.

"Am I the one who is fifty today?" she asked her husband's
empty wicker chair. There were lines on her forehead, like
veins in marble. How could she give her life a new purpose?

If only she could still write poetry. That had always relieved her, but she was too hollowed-out, and she felt she couldn't say anything that others hadn't said better before her.

If only John Darling had been there last night! But her only friend in Sydney was with his family in Camden for the reading of a will, just on Alexander's big day. Alex had accepted the fact grudgingly. John was part of the inventory. But Alex would have his whole mob assembled around him tonight, and Miss Rigby would see to it that all ran smoothly. She took everything off Anne's hands in spite of her legendary workload. She would be astonished to hear that Anne resented it. Miss Rigby had never felt superfluous in her life. She couldn't imagine that Anne had grown so shy because there was nothing for her to do in Vaucluse. Because the household had been run forever by the competent Mrs. Andrews. And Anne was the last one to project herself or go in for power plays. She needed to be encouraged. Only her father had understood that.

Andrews brought Anne's breakfast on the silver tray that Elizabeth West had given her as a wedding present. Miss West would have been much better suited to Alex, Anne thought. She couldn't imagine why the two hadn't married. Both had been born and brought up in this country, and Miss West was resilient, even though she was of only medium height and not as slender or well-proportioned as Anne. But she was lively and self-assured, and Alex respected her for her achievements. Like the girl she had been in London, Anne saw perfectly clearly that everybody was right. What on earth was she doing here?

Mrs. Andrews put the breakfast platters and Anne's teapot down on the table and looked at the second Mrs. Rigby triumphantly before retiring. Anne drank the iced pineapple juice and sat there for a while, brooding. After a while she drank two cups of tea and with revulsion looked at the steak, which had grown cold, and the runny fried egg. Perhaps her great mistake had been to see a father figure in Alexander just because he was so much older, although she had always known that calendars lied. She felt a hundred and fifty years old, withered like a tree for which the centuries no longer counted. Dead eucalyptus trees were an ordinary sight in Australia.

And John Darling wasn't in Sydney. Anne was fully aware of the fact that it was ridiculous for her to need John so much, and how impossibly she was behaving when she occasionally told him so. He didn't want to hear it. He was Rigby's best friend. Anne often asked herself how Alex could deserve such a friend.

Mrs. Andrews appeared with a letter which she laid discreetly on the table. "Is there anything I can do for you, Mrs. Rigby?"

Anne thanked her. Andrews had done quite enough for her this morning.

Anne cut up the steak and fed it to her dog, then she opened the fat letter. It was from John Darling in Camden. He had never written her a letter before. Usually he addressed his letters to Mr. and Mrs. Rigby.

Anne had to read the letter three times before she had digested the contents. This was impossible! No, it *was* possible, and John had kept it to himself all these months.

Anne went back to bed as if in a trance. She was so tired that she fell asleep at once. The letter fell on the floor. Andrews came into the room on tiptoe to fetch Anne's blue evening gown that needed pressing. Rigby liked blue.

Mary Andrews saw the letter lying on the floor. Since hers was an orderly nature, she picked it up and laid it on the bedside table of the sleeping woman. Then she left the room on tiptoe again, the blue dress over her arm. Yes, of course, she had also read the letter. After all, she had to know what Professor Darling was writing to the wife of her Mr. Rigby. Six pages . . .

Anne slept for quite a few hours. The pills she had taken the night before finally worked. Whens he awoke, she read the letter again. Then she called her doctor. She felt feverish and wanted an injection. Alex would never forgive her if she was unable to attend his birthday party.

Mrs. Andrews knocked and brought fruit juice and the blue evening dress. On the hanger it looked like a blue corpse swinging on a gallows in the wind. "Thank you very much." Anne could hear her own voice as if from a great distance. Her bedroom was split up suddenly into white and blue-gray shapes that interlocked. The blue corpse was still swinging back and forth.

Mrs. Andrews put an ice compress on Anne's forehead. Alexander was there suddenly, asking, "What's the matter now?" Anne was coming to after a brief fainting spell, and seemed to be looking for something. Alexander, who was always one jump ahead of her, asked, "Are you looking for John Darling's letter?" Then he turned to Andrews, who was standing beside him, a half-full bowl of ice in her hands. He looked at her for a moment and knew at once by her expression that she had read the leter. "It's all right," he said calmly. "It's just the heat again. I'll help my wife to dress later."

He laid John Darling's letter back on Anne's bedside table and watched Andrews until she left the room. Then he opened the curtains, let the afternoon sun into the blue-white room through the corner window, and told his wife not to talk. "You must rest now, or you won't be fresh for this evening."

"Have you read John's letter?"

"Yes, of course. A big surprise, isn't it? Wouldn't have thought the old codger capable of it."

8

The Small Pleasures of Life

Rigby's birthday party outdid everything that had gone before. It was an open-air fête in the best of taste, arranged by a city elite with arcadian inclinations. After the reception in Vaucluse, in which official congratulators and members of the Architects Club participated, Rigby and his friends from the yacht club drove to his summer home in Manly. He had ordered a moonlit night. Except for Anne, everything was as it should be.

Rigby's white country house in Manly was surrounded by pines and looked down on the ocean from a wooded height. Whoever didn't want to enjoy the roof garden with its flowers, went swimming. Rigby's bathhouse in the garden offered everything conceivably necessary for improvised water games. Manly lay like a glittering jewel between harbor and ocean. Excursionists coming from Sydney could reach Manly by the ferry leaving Circular Quai every half-hour, and get off at the harbor bathing facility, or at the magnificent beach promenade, flanked by pines. If any of the swimmers found themselves in the neighborhood of sharks, in spite of all safety measures, they were invariably brought back to safety by the Volunteer Lifeguards, an Australian organization of men who practiced their dangerous, self-sacrificing duties year-in and year-out at the numerous bathing resorts and beaches. Rigby too had saved quite a few swimmers in the days of his youth.

Rigby was a radiant host. Whoever didn't know him well would never have guessed that on this day someone had thrown a monkey wrench into the proceedings. When he had read John Darling's letter to his wife, he had felt very simpleminded.

122

Also he had felt dimly that Anne's indefinable relationship to his best friend was somehow the result of his own neglect. Actually he couldn't explain to himself why, in spite of his frequent absences from Vaucluse, he had to think so often of his wife. Her shadow darkened his small pleasures. Sometimes, during a conference at the office, he would see her suddenly, powdering herself after a bath, her face hard, or in an empty room, doing some little household chore rigidly and absent-mindedly.

Rigby saw something almost funny in his marital problems. Hadn't he had to run away from women all his life? But there you were . . . the second Mrs. Rigby had fallen in love with his best friend. John Darling's letter left no doubt about that. Rigby couldn't think of anything more ridiculous.

While he was receiving his guests on the terrace at Vaucluse with Anne, he studied her unobtrusively. So she had more initiative than he had thought her capable of! And he had thought he knew women! Moreover, to his vexation, he found Anne looking especially pretty tonight. She was wearing the long pastel-blue dress he had picked out for her. So he was still good for *something*! And she was smiling her disinterested smile that always drove him crazy. Today she reminded him of the figurehead on a sinking ship, staring with indifference at the wild sea. During the reception he had to remind his figurehead from time to time that this was not a funeral. Once he grabbed her brutally by the arm and murmured, "Pull yourself together, for God's sake, or you'll be sorry! I've had just about enough!" Smiling at his wife as he said so, because of all the people around them.

At that moment Marchmont arrived. Rigby hurried to greet him. Anne was surprised to see with what warmth he greeted the old man with the eagle profile and his shock of white hair. No son could have been more loving. Alex helped his boss slowly and carefully up to the terrace. The senior partner of Marchmont, Rigby & French was not supposed to exert himself in any way right now, but of course Alexander's fiftieth birthday was a big exception. Stanley Marchmont sat on the terrace quietly and happily, in a comfortable chair, and all the important guests gathered around the founder of the famous architectural firm. But Marchmont had eyes only for Alex—God bless him! Since Rigby had constantly to greet new guests, Miss Rigby, Elizabeth West, and Robbie French looked after Marchmont. The old man shook his head impatiently: they were blocking his view. He wanted to enjoy his Alex.

The babel of voices was suddenly silent. The great moment had arrived. Speeches for Rigby. The first to speak was Robbie French, in the name of the firm and the generation to follow Rigby, to whom he had taught the tricks of their trade. Robbie French handed his senior partner a little statuette that he had sculpted himself, fortunately not a lady with two heads, but an emu in bronze. Rigby looked at the bird for a moment, silently and critically, until the pause became embarrassing for his audience. Then he slapped his junior partner on the shoulder so hard that it shook him. "Thank you, Robbie. The bird's not bad."

Coming from Rigby this was such high praise that French, confused, murmured that he had done his best, after which he took refuge behind old Marchmont, who nodded approvingly.

The "boys" from the government and city administration weren't going to be outdone. They expressed themselves with the customary brevity but with so much approbation that Marchmont had to cough twice. Rigby, according to them, lived for Sydney's architectural future, and the city wished to thank him today for past and future achievements. At that moment old Mr. Marchmont could see his cobber, Jonathan Rigby, and how he had shoved his beanpole of a son up to him like a piece of furniture and said, "Make something of him, Stan."

Parramatta was also represented. Their ambassador was much younger than Stanley Marchmont, but the green young man knew that Adam, Colin and Jonathan Rigby had planned and built Parramatta, and that Alexander's first architectural experience had been with the stone house the family had built. Marchmont looked sharply for a moment at his still youthful and now famous partner. His Alex was blushing like a school-boy as he accepted a plaque with a painting on it of the first Rigby home in Parramatta, as a token from his native city. Miss Rigby looked pale, Elizabeth West was red as a beet, and Anne look stupefied. Architect Rigby, cobber Rigby, and husband Rigby were very different people. The mob didn't move; they were so proud of the old devil!

Old Marchmont stayed exactly an hour and twenty minutes; that was all Dr. Dobson, the young doctor on Macquarie Street, had allowed. Plenty of time for such an old heart. Anyway, after the ovations, Marchmont was glad to go back to his quiet terrace in Mosman Bay and think everything over quietly again. Dr. Dobson and Alex took him to his car, then went back silently to the guests.

And now Rigby was standing beside his wife again, on the terrace, greeting the latecomers, in the course of which he crossed silently and smoothly over the hill of his anger. His self-control was perfect. He looked radiant and invincible, and not even his wife knew what it was costing him. Anne found him even more of a stranger than during their happy London days. His metallic smile was threatening, like a mask in a nightmare.

Rigby handed his wife a full glass of wine and looked deep into her eyes in front of everybody. Anne shivered. Was she already standing on the brink of an abyss like the first Mrs. Rigby?

"Your health, Anne!"

The mob cheered. Wasn't she to be envied? And Alex? Some people had all the luck. Rigby was not only professionally successful, on top of everything else he had managed to snap up this pretty little doll! She sat at home like a good girl and waited for him. Try to find that again! Long live the old bush bandit! The drinks were first-rate.

Miss Rigby raised her glass. "Cheers, little brother!"

Rigby and his tall sister clinked glasses; he was still taller than she. He asked the old girl if she was satisfied. Miss Rigby thought it was a good show. "Father should have lived to see this," she said, her eyes on the dark trees around them. Then she clinked glasses with Alexander's young wife and told her she could be proud of her husband.

Dainty Elizabeth West's eyes were shining, her hair curled wildly. She whispered, "I'm so happy, Alex! It's a big day for you." Rigby replied, "You could have had your hair done for this big day. Look at my wife, for example."

At last it was Mrs. Andrews's turn. Until now she had kept modestly in the background. "My best wishes, Mr. Rigby."

"Why the funereal expression? This isn't a funeral, Mrs. Andrews. I keep having to tell the members of my household that."

"Is that a joke?"

"Maybe."

Andrews mumbled something to the effect that she would stand by her benefactor, come what may. Alex accepted the threat with a sour expression. If only Andrews would shut up! If only she would fade away! In her gray dress she reminded him of a room that wasn't lived in, with dust covers on the furniture. Yes, he'd have to let Andrews go; she read his wife's letters. No married man could permit such a breach of conduct. He would have to make quite a few changes in Vaucluse. Quite a few? Everything! But when he thought of firing Andrews, he got a queasy feeling in the pit of his stomach. She would make a scene. The thought of the possibilities inherent in the Hungarian temperament made him shudder. Naturally he couldn't fire her overnight, after so many years of faithful snooping. He'd have to talk with Bertie Dobson. Perhaps he could take on his Hungarian jewel. But at once dropped the idea. Old lady Dobson, who sat around in Bertie's bachelor apartment all the time, wouldn't put up with Andrews for ten minutes. Bertie's mother cooked very well and wouldn't let any cook spoil her broth! Meals at the Dobsons were remarkable. Bertie was very attached to his mother's cuisine. That was why he hadn't married yet, at thirty-eight. He'd never find anything to equal the life he was leading: peace and quiet and fabulous meals, a lucrative practice in Macquarie Street, and a little girl friend. All the boys were smarter than Rigby . . .

Meanwhile Andrews had moved off in the direction of the cold buffet. "Such junk, and for all that money!" she thought. Just to torture herself, she tasted one dish after the other. She had made up her mind not to enjoy the party for a single moment, and it satisfied her to see how successful she could be. When she looked at the former Miss Karasz, who had managed to catch rich Patrick Trent, she'd had it. This vain hope of Hungarian literature had ignored her guardian angel from the immigration station with unabashed impudence. But Andrews could remember how seven-year-old Klari Karasz had wept on her shoulder because she was so homesick. At the time she had been scared to death of the Aussies; and the friendlier they were, the more they frightened Klari. Tonight she was laughing loudly for all Australian ears to hear, and was strutting around in a dress that consisted for the most part of decolleté. Andrews was ashamed of her. Certainly it was hot in November, but that was no excuse for a Christian to run around three-quarters naked! Besides, Klari was flirting outrageously with Rigby. Disgusting! Andrews was sickened. Even on this day of honor, her Rigby was studying Mrs. Trent's voluptuous bosom whenever he had a chance. And this on the day that had shattered his marriage! Of course Andrews felt sorry for him, but at last, he would experience for himself how it hurt to be betrayed.

Although still waters ran proverbially deep, she had never thought it possible for the second Mrs. Rigby to have an affair. In Australia, one never knew where one was at with people. Even one's former compatriots weren't the same. Miss Karasz, for instance, had changed almost unrecognizably. Before her brilliant marriage she had been modest, unworldly, and dreamy. As Mrs. Patrick Trent she had developed a pathological and insatiable urge to shop, dress luxuriously, and make eyes at every man in New South Wales. The spectacle revolted Mrs. Andrews. Now she was laughing over one of her husband's jokes which no immigrant would ever understand. Who in Budapest had ever heard of *diggers* (war veterans), *graziers* (sheep station owners), or *sheilas* (girls)? But Miss Karasz was laughing hypocritically right along with the rest. She couldn't possibly find any of it funny. Andrews knew her too well.

Miss Rigby looked upon her husband's housekeeper as a hopeless case. She had observed, with irritation, that Mrs. Andrews's anger was directed at all those who had accepted the Australian experience positively, and they were in the majority. Why did Mary Andrews stick to her provisional attitude toward Australia? She would never go back to communist Hungary. She knew very well on what side her bread was buttered. Moreover, shortly after Alexander's second marriage, Miss Rigby had offered to find a new position for his housekeeper. With Mrs. Andrews's capabilities and the many bachelors in Sydney, this would not have been difficult, but here Miss Rigby had hit granite. As soon as the source of his food was endangered, there was no reasoning with Alex.

Meanwhile Andrews had arrived at a torte iced with baroque magnificence. Her recipe was better. Of course in the case of such huge cakes, butter, eggs, and sugar were used sparingly, but Rigby apparently wanted to throw his money into the Pacific. The icing, though, *was* remarkable. The Aussies could be effective on state occasions, when they took the trouble. She must remember the icing for Rigby's seventy-fifth. Not that he deserved it, but she loved even her enemies ...

She saw Rigby whisper something to his wife. His smile couldn't deceive Andrews. Her boss was furious. She knew the wild look in his eyes by experience, whether it was aimed at a burnt omelet or adultery. Mrs. Rigby could consider herself fortunate if she met the dawn unharmed. There was something hunted in the expression of her eyes and the way she carried herself, because she couldn't put on nearly as good an act as Rigby. That was how the political prisoners in postwar Budapest had looked when the communists had interrogated them. Mrs. Andrews couldn't understand the second Mrs. Rigby. How could one run after a boring bookworm like John Darling when one had Rigby? Although he was a murderer of the spirit, Andrews still preferred Rigby to any of the rest of the mob. And how he still looked at fifty! Not easy to duplicate. Unfortunately Mrs. Rigby seemed to be in a state of panic. Andrews noticed how her long white hands moved restlessly over her hips. And for that she had pressed the blue dress? Andrews didn't envy Mrs. Rigby the discussion that would surely follow the party. Rigby would question her mercilessly: when, where, and how often? The tongue would stick to the mouth of this arrogant little fool. And in hell it was probably hotter than in Australia, and there were no iced drinks. The thought made Andrews smile for the first time that evening.

Anne looked from the roof garden across the illuminated scene below, and the dark blue ocean shore. Under the luminous moon the world looked calm and glowed in the pure colors of its spectrum. The miracle works of technology sank into the Pacific. Voices rose up to Anne. Daisy Andrews, the housekeeper's daughter, was laughing softly with Robbie French. A record was singing somewhere of love and the pain of separation. The ocean moved gently in an eternal rhythm. The sand shimmered like eggshell porcelain. Couples, their arms entwined, wandered along the beach, under the pines. Every now and then shining spots moved across the water along shore: ruby red, silver and green bathing caps. The world was unbearably still. Only the ocean waves rolled powerfully across the sand and were lost in it. Like love and hate, hope and disappointment. Everything was incomplete and fleeting. Why did she seek escape in cold symbolism? The others were enjoying the festive scene. Alexander too stepped out of the illuminated sphere into the dark of night. She was the only one stranded on the roof of the house.

Miss Rigby brought cold drinks and two plates of cold cuts. She couldn't possibly be enthusiastic about vegetating up here on the roof with Anne, because she had just been chatting animatedly in the garden about *Insight* and other lesser stars in the media heaven. But years ago Miss Rigby had also visited poor, giggly Flora Pratt in Vaucluse once a week. Really unfortunate that Alex kept getting married!

"Why don't you come down in the garden?" Miss Rigby asked. "Paddy Trent is telling jokes."

"I felt funny enough this afternoon," said Anne.

"I know, I know," Miss Rigby said impatiently. She pulled up a chair and put the food and drinks on a table. Anne was correct in her impression that Miss Rigby was making a big sacrifice on her behalf.

"Aren't you tired, Grace?" Miss Rigby had at last suggested to Anne earlier today that she call her sister-in-law by her first name.

"I am never tired."

Anne sighed. The tireless ones had no idea how tiring they could be. "Wouldn't you say it's a real Italian night?" she asked, just for something to say.

Miss Rigby answered promptly, "What do you have against an Australian night?" Her moon, here in Australia, was every bit as good as the one in Florence, if not better. Water was water wherever you were. And swinging lanterns were not a specialty only of Italy, even if the immigrants thought so. A stupid lot!

Grace Rigby hungrily ate her way through all sorts of different delicacies with no sense of order. She never had an upset stomach and nobody knew where she put all the food she ate. "Did John write?" She was eating fruit cake with whipped cream and looked at Anne sideways.

"He sent Alex a telegram."

"That was to be expected," Miss Rigby said drily. "I mean, he must have told you about the big event. After all, one doesn't get married every day. I would never have thought it of the old codger."

"Of course he wrote to us about it." Anne's voice sounded flat. "In all the excitement I forgot it."

Miss Rigby swallowed her next remark. The whole thing was too stupid. Anne and old John Darling had been insepa-rable. Was that why Anne was so crushed? Had there been any real intimacy between her and John? Anything was possible in this lousy world, but she didn't think so. Old John was a man of principles, and had now married a woman with prin-ciples. Besides, Professor Darling hated complications which might rob him of the concentration he needed for his work. She knew the old codger like her own pocket.

"Do you know John's wife?" Anne asked. She hadn't intended to ask it, not at any price—it had just slipped out. John's letter had exhausted her. Delicately and anxiously, as was his nature, John had made clear to her that she was a young romantic. He had noticed, and it had worried him, that she had slipped into a certain dependency on him, quite unintentionally on his part. He was not as important as she thought. She shouldn't see anything special in him. He was a perfectly ordinary old codger; Miss Rigby had always said so. In short, Anne had to try to understand Alexander better, and knock all this nonsense about John out of her pretty little head. He remained her devoted friend and hoped sincerely that she and his wife would be good friends. That was the essence of his long and cautious letter. She had thrown herself at him, and John Darling had probably experienced moments of great embarrassment. He had none of Alexander's brutal nonchalance. John could feel his way effortlessly into a lonely young person's heart. She hadn't needed his company more and more for nothing. She had even toyed with the idea of marriage since Alexander seemed to be going his own way. But of course had never mentioned it. She had only envisioned this happy ending in her wishful dreams.

"Of course I know Ruth Eastman," said Miss Rigby. "A very efficient woman. Around forty. Ruth has worked for years for our natives, in missions and reservations. *Insight* once published an article on Eastman and her black sheep."

"Then she shares John's interests."

"Naturally," said Miss Rigby. "That's the basis of every sensible marriage." She wasn't looking anywhere in particular. She went on to say that the Eastmans were landowners in the Camden area, not as important as the Darlings, but good enough. Good fruit and excellent cattle. Miss Rigby found the marriage suitable. Yes, Ruth Eastman had worked for a year now on the Aboriginal Mission Board in Sydney, and over the weekends John had dictated his anthropological textbook for students to

her. That was why John had never been able to come and see
them on weekends, thought Anne. She had never visited him
where he worked. For that she was too shy. She hadn't even
read the paper, *Dawn*, that explained about the demands and
integration of the aborigines. At first John had brought her
several copies, but then he had stopped.

"I never visited John in his office," said Anne. "I was afraid
of disturbing him."

"And you certainly would have. Anyway, during the last
years the only way to John was over Ruth Eastman's dead
body." Miss Rigby added that Miss Eastman—for a week now
Mrs. John Darling—wouldn't put up with any nonsense from
anybody.

"Have you known them both for a long time?"

"Since the creation of New South Wales," said Miss Rigby.
"I haven't the faintest idea why it took John fifty years to
propose to her. But there was something that prevented it.
That's right—Ruth first had to nurse her mother and grandmother until they died, not both at the same time, of course."

Miss Rigby lit a cigarette, then offered her sister-in-law one.
Anne thanked her—she already had enough smoke and fog in
her head. Miss Rigby explained that on birthdays all the Rigbys
turned up in a body at the Eastmans. "I have never seen such
sob sisters as Mother and Grandmother Eastman," Miss Rigby
went on. "Those two would have liked to tie Ruth to their
bedposts until Judgment Day. Stupid people!"

"My mother wasn't so keen about my presence, either."

"Your mother has managed to make a marvelous career for
herself, my dear Anne. You must ask her to visit us. We'd
give her a dinkum reception at the club, get the press in on it,
and all the rest. You see, my child, a career makes all the
difference in the world. The ideas of the Eastman ladies on
family life go back to the time of William the Conqueror. But
you can't get away with anything with Ruth. She always knows
what the score is."

Anne said nothing.

"Grandmother Eastman's funeral was really exceptionally

nice," Miss Rigby went on. "Much more enjoyable than Ruth's mother's. The mimosa was in bloom, a beautiful sight—the bushes blooming. You sit around in Vaucluse much too much, Anne . . . What else did I want to tell you? Oh yes—in the case of Ruth's mother, they couldn't get her under the ground fast enough. The Eastmans, of course, had all the time in the world. But the guests wanted to get it behind them. Here everybody's always tearing back to their animals. And they're right. All the chatter and the masses of food aren't going to bring the dead back."

"That's right," said Anne. Miss Rigby was always right. Somehow Anne couldn't imagine herself spending many evenings in the future with the Darlings. In order to contribute something to the conversation she asked what Miss Eastman's father had been like.

"Tom Eastman was great, absolutely great." Miss Rigby lit her fourth cigarette. She smoked as quickly and methodically as she did everything else. "Ruth's father was a loner. And when the weeping and wailing and shivering at home became too much for him, he went walkabout."

"What's that?"

"He wandered off. That's a word you should know by now, Anne. We took it over from the aborigines. Sometimes Tom Eastman turned up in Queensland, or in South Australia, where Betty comes from. And he spent a year in the Northern Territory. We've got plenty of room in this country if anybody finds his four walls too much for him. Every now and then he'd come home and attend to business. Ruth's brothers looked after things pretty well. When Mother Eastman died, the old man came back for good. Then he was alone with his two sons, and everything ran smoothly, the way he wanted it. Ruth went to the mission. We published Tom's report from Alice Springs in *Insight*. People like Tom die out slowly. The industry in New South Wales overpowers the old bush myths. I don't object. I'm always for the day after tomorrow."

Anne saw Miss Rigby as if through a veil. Where were they anyway? Still on the roof garden? She was exhausted, and fell suddenly into that light-headed condition in which, in the old ivy-overgrown house behind Avenue Road, she had once written poetry. She saw, heard, and understood with greater clarity than usual. Persons, things, landscapes, and dream pictures stepped forward, painfully lit, out of the dark zone of the consciousness into the light of conscience.

Perhaps this vast and mysterious continent bestowed a glowing vision on those very immigrants from more pallid regions. The first, second, and third periods of assimilation were hard because the land and people were no different from what they had been at home, in the old, tired, more skeptical lands. Not until the blazing sun on the country roads, the crippling summer heat, the indifferent looks, or the coarse jokes of the native population no longer tortured the new Australian, did the stoical, taciturn loneliness and courage of this virile continent begin to speak with a thousand tongues. Then Australia sang. After years of painful adjustment and absurd misunderstandings, the cities spoke with a new, buoyant voice, and this corner of the earth expressed itself through its last original inhabitants, who had strayed from the Stone Age into the twentieth century. Then the prehistoric mammals, the nightmare birds in the bush, the deep-sea wonders of the tropical north, came to life for the stranger. And the shower of blossoms on the monotonous garden houses gave the sprawling Australian suburbs a touch of poesy.

Anne had not yet reached the stage in which Australia would enrich her. Until now this sunny land had only robbed her of strength. But on Alexander's birthday, on the roof garden in Manly, she had an Australian vision for the first time. She saw the dance of the men and the sharks.

Young Australians, in the colorful uniforms of the Volunteer Lifeguards, passed across the beach like living bronze statues. Their light hair fluttered in the breeze. And at the head of the procession of the joy of life and the danger of death, marched Alexander. Anne recognized him. He walked like a boy and glowed without exertion. Anne had never known young Alexander . . .

The young demigods danced along the shores of the Pacific, rulers of Oceania, unfettered by the shackles of civilian existence. They dived into the sea, surfaced jubilantly, and celebrated their rebirth. Business and sheep stations, bank accounts, social status, electric toys, newspapers, tea kettles, blankets, razors, responsibilities—all were left behind on the shore somewhere, in stone palaces or bush huts, in hotels, boarding-houses and narrow marriage-barracks, where wives and tax officials waited.

They sang without words. Primeval, lusty sounds issued forth from their throats, an elementary shout for the nymph with no address, with no demands, and with no vocabulary. These swimmers were Neptune's bastard sons in Australia, and at last they knew it again. Never again would they crawl back into the homes or high-rise houses of the twentieth century! Never again would they lie to their loving women about where, how, and with whom they were spending the evening. From now on they would ride into infinity on the backs of the sharks. They would become one with the water, with the moonlight, and with the silence of the night.

The sharks heard their song and swam greedily toward the shore. They reared up high, as if they were greeting the audience in a theatre, and opened their predatory jaws as the intoxicated mob came dancing up and threw themselves, arms entwined, into the ocean. "Alex!" Anne screamed from the roof garden, but she screamed only deep inside her. Helplessly she watched how young Rigby moved fearlessly closer to the jaws of the tiger shark, while warning searchlights cut across the sky, and an invisible chorus of kookaburras, with their horrible humanlike voices, began a concert of laughter. Anne's outcry died away in the cosmic storm. Alexander hadn't shied away from danger at any age. It fascinated her, because he was forever in flight from familiar shores. Anne's voice hadn't even reached him when she had still loved and admired him.

She closed her eyes.

"What's the matter with you?" Miss Rigby tapped Anne gently on the arm.

Anne stared at the disappearing vision. Then she asked where Alexander was. On the beach, where else? said Miss Rigby. He was either running around with Paddy Trent or Betty. Alex and Elizabeth West were old beachcombers.

"I suppose they are," murmured Anne. Alexander could evidently not be separated from his dear Betty on land or in the water.

Miss Rigby rose. "Come, child. Off to bed with you. The whole thing's been too much for you."

"I hoped I'd make it."

"You made it," said Miss Rigby, but she didn't say what Anne had "made" on Alexander's birthday. She took the young woman to her bedroom, shaking her head. Anne swayed as if she had drunk several glasses of gin instead of fruit juice. Was she pregnant? That would make Alex very happy. But she said she was just exhausted.

Miss Rigby plumped up the cushions and exuded the horrible liveliness of a trained nurse. But she meant well, and Anne was grateful. She would have liked to please Miss Rigby with a nephew, but unfortunately there could be no thought of that.

Miss Rigby went back to the beach and looked around her. Where was Alex? It was high time that he paid some attention to his wife. Miss Rigby couldn't understand Anne, and her lifelessness made her impatient. But the young woman was actually quite brave. She had unfortunately remained an outsider in Sydney, but the pommies had a hard time acclimatizing, and besides, being married to Alex wasn't much fun. Granted, he knew a thing or two about buildings—the honors bestowed on him today had surprised her—but for all that he remained a lousy husband. He pursued his small pleasures and had no comprehension whatsoever for a sensitive creature like Anne. And she was too young for him. Grace Rigby had said so right away. She was thankful that dear Betty West hadn't fallen for Alex. For a while she had thought the two were seeing too much of each other. But she had kept her mouth shut, and so had Betty. Which had suited Grace Rigby fine. She found outpourings of the heart between women horrible. Anyway,

Betty had had enough gumption in her little red head not to move from Bellevue Hill to Vaucluse. Anne, on the other hand, had walked from a nice, monotonous life straight into the jaws of the shark. Poor young creature! She had liked Anne at once. A decent girl with substance to her. She could sense anything like that from miles away. Much too refined for Alex, who took his marital duties too lightly. After a while he went his own way. Flora Pratt had also eaten alone until she had finally turned the house in Vaucluse into a men's bar. Miss Rigby hadn't like it, but Flora had asserted herself in her own way. Anne never asserted herself. She treated Alex with cool rejection. Anne had just told her something that, even if one was used to taking a lot from Alex, was more than the traffic could or should bear.

Miss Rigby frowned as she looked across at the neighing mob. Alexander was not with Paddy Trent. So he was probably "on his way" with Betty West. Of course you could depend on Betty, but Miss Rigby felt it was high time that Alex gave up these amusing digressions. His little pleasures made him smaller than he was.

Miss Rigby had reached the promenade, and looked around for Dr. Dobson.

Although he was only in his early thirties, Bertram Dobson was automatically a member of Rigby's mob. His father had been their doctor. Then Bertie had taken over his practice on Macquarie Street. The elder Dobson meanwhile preferred to fish or listen to music or carry on friendly arguments with his wife. The mob was used to the Dobsons, and to the festive palm trees on Macquarie Street. And if Bertie sometimes couldn't get things straight, he could always consult his old man. Since Rigby's mob had known Dobson as a young rascal, and had frequently beaten him up, none of them had really noticed that Bertram had meanwhile become quite a famous internist. In short, whenever one of the cobbers had a bellyache, or his heart was acting up, or his gall bladder was behaving strangely, he'd toddle off to see Bertie, and that was that. While visiting him they could also run over to the wool exchange, or sit on Macquarie Plaza around the obelisk. This was where Australia's first orchard had stood. The plaza was still a peaceful patch of green in the centre of the metropolis. Or one walked over to the public library of New South Wales and did something for one's mind. A call on Dr. Dobson therefore included all sorts of other possibilities.

The young doctor was of medium height, reliable, and just as quick-witted as his father, and one could see that he was a hearty eater. Bertram was professionally successful because he evaluated his capabilities correctly. When in doubt, he called in a specialist. He was very modest, although he knew a lot more than the mob realized. His father was sure that Bertram was headed for a splendid career, but this was never mentioned. All the Dobsons were brilliant doctors. They were situated in Sydney, London, New Zealand, and some nephew or other was practicing in Brisbane. Besides medicine, they loved music and the classical philosophers. In his leisure time, Bertie read Virgil, and was terrified that the mob might find out. The mob liked sports, betting, and beer sessions. People with inclinations like the Dobsons had to watch their step. Except for the Virgil bit, they were of course dinkum through and through. On this continent everybody was equally good or equally mediocre. Bertie had learned this credo in his infancy, but newspaper reports about political catastrophes or the Australian labor unions, about cricket and gossip-column scandals, didn't satisfy him. As a student he had foraged around in old John Darling's books, and in Horace, Virgil and Seneca had discovered comrades of the spirit. On the day he had discovered the classics outside the schoolroom, his mother had been cooking some fowl or other in wine. Bertie could recall it exactly. When she was young, Mrs. Dobson had visited a friend in Queensland. The girl's family had owned French sugar plantations. Bertie's mother, an intelligent and enthusiastic woman, had learned to cook so well that even the toughest steak melted in your mouth.

In spite of being so much younger, Bertram was a close

friend of the Rigbys, even though he never looked at *Insight* and didn't appreciate Alexander's way of life. Bertie had a residue of the puritanism of his English ancestors in his blood. He had fought with his conscience before he had finally acquired a girl friend. The thought of a lasting marital dialogue, such as his parents indulged in with obvious pleasure, frightened him. He started an affair with a nice, decent young girl who worked in an office on the next street, Bridge Street. Mavis had brought her mother to him as a patient. Her mother had heart trouble, and after that Bertie discovered that he was having trouble with his own heart . . . Now he and the young lady had been together for three years. That her office was nearby made things easier. Although a visit to a patient could never be too late or too far away, in the little free time he had, he liked his comforts. Once Rigby, with a wink, had asked him if he wouldn't like a change. After all, said wise Alexander Rigby, a man's wishes and needs changed every couple of years or so. Young Dr. Dobson had replied that one girl was pretty much the same as the other, since one always wanted the same thing from the sheilas. Why spend time looking and courting all the anxiety involved until one finally got to the point? He knew all the advantages and disadvantages of his Mavis, and the advantages were greater. He could still marry his girl friend from Bridge Street if worse came to worst, but there was plenty of time for that. Right now he preferred to watch soccer or listen to a concert—you could admit to hearing a concert to Rigby—than to waste time looking for a new girl. He didn't mention Virgil. Those were his strictly private friends. *Res severa est verum gaudium*—yes, serious things were a joy. Cobber Horace had already known that.

"It's sheer unbelievable, boy," Rigby had said. "You don't have a spark of erotic fantasy."

"Thank God!" young Dr. Dobson replied, very pleased with himself.

Rigby's fiftieth was dinkum. Bertie had swum for a long time, and was now strolling along the Pacific, alone. He was pleased with himself and the world because he knew all its tricks. One was never disappointed when one wished only for what was attainable. Perhaps, behind the wall of good sense, there were irrational pleasures, the kind Rigby was looking for, but Bertie stuck to the small, inconspicuous ones. What was wrong with his friend Mavis? She was no dazzling beauty, but she was pleasant to look at, played a good game of tennis, and kept her mouth shut when Bertie preferred to fish over the weekend. At first Mavis had of course tried to remodel Bertie and make a romantic lover of him, like the ones in Elizabeth West's novels. Naturally Mavis subscribed to *Insight*. But Bertie had come through this period unscathed. He had explained to the young lady that he was not a film star. Anyway, in private life film stars were either boring or alcoholics or neurotic sob sisters, or all three together. Mavis hadn't wanted to believe this, but Bertie had explained it all in detail until she'd got the picture. He was her first man. That worried him sometimes. He would look for a nice young man for Mavis in case she suddenly began to talk marriage. Until now the subject hadn't come up.

Miss Rigby walked up to him. "Too bad that you don't have office hours on the beach, Bertie."

"What's the matter, Grace?"

"I wish you'd take a look at Anne."

"She was perfectly all right this afternoon after that little fainting spell, or I wouldn't have let her come tonight. I think it's nerves. Since when are you a mother hen, anyway?"

"Perhaps she needs a stronger sedative," Miss Rigby said hesitantly. "I was with her just now on the roof garden and got the impression that she wasn't exactly herself."

"Is she in a rage?" asked Dobson.

"Don't be silly!" Miss Rigby said indignantly. "Anne is never in a rage. She's not Alex."

"All right. I'll have a look at her again."

As they walked back to the house, Miss Rigby asked about Stanley Marchmont's heart. "He's got to be careful," said young Dobson. "An old heart like his needs rest."

"Nonsense!" said Miss Rigby. "My grandfather Colin ran around Parramatta like a weasel when he was eighty-five."

"Why do you ask if you know better?"

"I'm sorry, Bertie. I only meant that Stan Marchmont . . ." She stopped, then finally mumbled, "He'll have to answer to me if he signs off."

"Fortunately he won't be alive to oblige."

Miss Rigby was silent for a moment, baffled. Then she said good-humoredly, "Bertie Dobson, you always were fresh!"

They had reached the house. "Anne's upstairs in the bedroom," said Miss Rigby. "Go on up, Bertie. Do something for your money."

Miss Rigby waited. Why did Bertie stay so long upstairs? When he finally appeared, she looked at him questioningly. "Nothing wrong," said Dobson, his eyes on a platter of ham that looked tasty. Miss Rigby shrugged, and fixed him several open-faced sandwiches. She knew Bertie!

"Thanks, dear. After swimming I'm always terribly hungry."

"You can always eat, Bertie. One can see where it goes."

At last Dr. Dobson had had enough. "I don't like the way Anne looks," he said slowly. "Everything's all right physically. As I said—it's nerves. I think I'll make an appointment for her with Morty." Dr. Gerald Mortimer was a nerve specialist on Macquarie Street and an old friend of Bertie's father.

"But she's not a mental case!"

"If she were, I'd send her to Frank Norfolk," Dr. Dobson said patiently. "But she is extremely nervous." He scratched his head, embarrassed. He couldn't possibly tell Miss Rigby that Anne was in a panic of fear of Rigby and believed that he intended to kill her. Such nonsense!

"Well anyway," he said calmly, "I want Morty to take a look at her. Perhaps she's unhappy."

"You're joking," said Miss Rigby. "Alexander is destroying her."

"It's not entirely impossible that she is also destroying him."

"You'd better go to a nerve specialist yourself, Bertie."

Dr. Dobson finished his beer. Beer was a great invention. Then he said amiably, "I don't know how you feel about it, but when there's something wrong between two people, every arrow comes back to the one who's shot it."

Miss Rigby said nothing. "Alex still has a lot to do," said Dobson. "He needs every ounce of strength he has."

"I've been worried for a long time," said Miss Rigby, "but about Anne. She's the weaker one."

"She has the resistance of the weak. I know that sounds funny," he said apologetically. "Perhaps all Anne needs after these seven years is a change of scenery. Couldn't you go somewhere with her?"

"Don't be foolish, Bertie. I'm in the office all day and every day."

"Couldn't Betty West take your place for a while?"

"Betty writes novels. And wherever she goes there's chaos within three minutes. Or she has another one of her imaginary illnesses. You know how fond I am of Betty, but at my desk? Over my dead body."

Bertie didn't want to hear another word about *Insight*. Mavis was always rebellious after she'd read the rag. "Maybe Morty will send your sister-in-law off to London for a while," he said.

"What an idea! She'd never come back!"

"Exactly," Dr. Dobson said quietly.

They walked back to the beach together. The sea glittered darkly. In the distance Rigby and Elizabeth West were walking arm-in-arm under the pines. "They were talking so animatedly a little while go," said Dobson, "they didn't even notice me."

Miss Rigby was asking herself what could possibly be wrong with Alexander's marriage. She had the feeling that in spite of his misdemeanors, her brother was fond of Anne, and every now and then tried to do something to please her. But this evening he was different. "You're smart, Bertie," she said. "You have peace and quiet."

"One should never praise the day before the evening," he

said. "But I'm going to do my best to preserve my peace and quiet." He looked at her from the side and thought she looked exceptionally pale. "Would you like me to prescribe something to pep you up, Grace? No extra charge."

Miss Rigby laughed. "Prescribe something for youself!" She mustn't let Bertie see how worried she was. He was too smart. "Go back to your friends, Bertie. I'm no company for you."

"You can't order me around any more, Grace, however much you'd like to." He grinned. He had always had a soft spot in his heart for Grace, God only knew why. He had no intention of leaving her to her dismal thoughts.

"Should I speak to Alex about it?" she asked.

"For heaven's sake, no! Your talks always make everything worse. You know you're my only true love, Grace, but you don't know how to handle Alex!"

Miss Rigby looked at the ocean. "You know everything, Bertie. Can you tell me why Alex can't stick to one woman; why he changes them all the time?"

Miss Rigby could sense change in the air around Vaucluse. Before the tragedy of Flora Pratt she had felt it too. But this time there must not be a scandal. Stan Marchmont's heart couldn't stand it. Why was Alex so restless? Miss Rigby looked at the paradisical shore silently. Manly was being slowly hidden by the cloak of night. The houses, with their lights, lay in the mist of the moon, the living quarters of the well-to-do. Miss Rigby thought some times that only lucky people lived in these country houses, with washing machines and television sets and electric blenders. But actually she knew better. The bitter honey was locked away in the pantry.

"I don't really know Alexander very well, in spite of the fact that I'm his sister."

"Just because of that, Grace. And by the way, in the times that lie ahead, if you ever feel like talking, you know where to find me."

"If I'm not mistaken, you're in my address book. Listen, Bertie, I have a great idea."

"And that is . . ."

"Why don't you marry our Betty West?"

"Why should I marry your Betty West?"

"You'd be a very suitable couple. And your dear mother cooks so well. You can't expect that from Betty, of course."

"As far as I know, I've never asked her to cook for me."

Miss Rigby had been considering for some time how she should settle Betty favorably, just in case something should happen to her. Grace Rigby was only fifty-seven, and hoped to become just as old as her grandfather Colin, but you never knew. Betty had pots of money, but had no idea as to how to manage it. And when she wasn't writing, she needed somebody to look after her. She was a great big, precocious child.

"Don't be so stubborn, Bertie. You're in your mid-thirties now. It's high time, my son. Worse food would only do you good. Anyway, you should start eating less, considerably less."

"Why?" Dr. Dobson asked indignantly. "I hate meals thrown together, and Mother is happy when I enjoy my food."

Miss Rigby gave up. Old lady Dobson was happy above all that. Bertie was still attached to her apron strings. Both her daughters had gone off with absolute strangers.

"Come to your senses, boy!" said Miss Rigby. "Think of your big, empty house. What do you do in it all alone?"

"Enjoy my peace and quiet, just like you. Sorry, darling, but I never marry authors."

"You prefer illiterates?"

"There's a golden mean," Bertie said gently. His friend Mavis was solidly entrenched between the two.

"I'd like to know what you have against authors."

"They have too much imagination for everyday use. Let it be, Grace. Everybody is happy in his own way."

Young Dobson gve Miss Rigby a friendly dig in the ribs, since he couldn't pat her on the shoulder. He didn't reach that high.

Boys and girls paraded along the beach with torches. They belonged to some sports club or other, and were celebrating something. The red glow of their torches lit up Rigby and Betty West. For a moment it looked as if the two were walking through a provisional purgatory. Dr. Dobson reflected that Betty West was part of the inventory at the Rigbys'. On the other hand, a husband should be walking with his wife. Or what sense was there in marriage?

9

On the One Hand, On the Other Hand . . .

On the one hand Rigby enjoyed walking arm-in-arm with Betty West along the shore; on the other hand, right now she was nowhere near him. On the one hand Rigby was hungry to possess; on the other hand he found possession a burden. Was that why Elizabeth had turned him down seven years ago? All in all Rigby was astonished, and in a way insulted, that his relationship to the weaker sex didn't give anyone, not even himself, much joy.

His relationship to Elizabeth West, which had endured through so many storms, was basically too complicated. If she had married him, everything would have been all right. Would he have fled from little Betty four times a week? No. There would have been a togetherness between them. Probably children too. That would have made a hell of a lot of difference to him. Besides, Betty had a profession of her own which took up most of her time. In short, it would have been a dinkum marriage. The mob would have been astounded. Naturally Betty always had a heap of nonsensical ideas in her little red head, but he would have driven them out lovingly. Nothing had hurt him as much as Anne's reproach that he was brutal.

Elizabeth West had enjoyed Rigby's fiftieth birthday hugely.

She was still thinking of all the honors he had received. "The mob was really surprised at all the speeches, Alex. Such praise!"

"That's the trouble. The boys always believe everything said about me."

"Too bad that John Darling couldn't be here."

"A terrible shame."

"You must be very happy today."

"I'm always happy."

When Rigby was in this kind of a mildly aggressive mood, Betty kept her mouth shut. He had seemed nervous all afternoon, but that could have been joyous excitement. One could talk to Rigby only about the weather, sports results, and occasionally about his work. Betty understood this because she too evaded questions about her private life. In interviews she gave information only about her professional life.

Rigby felt almost content as he walked beside the sea with Betty. The Pacific helped him to forget space and time, and the solemn pines moved in the evening wind. Rigby liked to wander with Betty because then the way was clear. They left all vagaries and concealments, and the tyrannies of convention, behind them. If he had paid more attention to the conventions now, he would have gone to his wife. At the thought of Anne his lips compressed into a thin line. Now, at last, he wanted to celebrate his birthday in peace.

On the one hand he would have liked to talk his marital difficulties off his chest; on the other hand one never spoke about one's wife. It was strange, but in Betty's silent sympathy he felt confirmed and secure. In spite of past misunderstandings—all Betty's fault—today they were good friends. Naturally one couldn't compare dainty, elegant Elizabeth West with a pair of old slippers, but she gave him that old-slipper feeling. No other sheila had ever been able to make him feel like that. Was it because he and Betty had known each other for so many years, and loved their country just the way it was? He didn't want to think any more about it. God bless the old slippers!

"You haven't grown all these years either. I was always able to spit on your head easily. Not that I ever did!"

Funny . . . the successful Elizabeth West still had an air of innocence about her, in spite of her Sydney polish, her style, and her wonderful sense of humor. "Withers from Adelaide" peered occasionally out of a corner of her consciousness and looked at the great Rigby with awe, as she had done years ago in the little office in George Street. And Rigby was usually tactful enough to ignore "Withers." As a matter of fact she surfaced rarely; usually West was in full charge.

Rigby wondered if Betty would have liked a closer relationship with him. On Sundays and holidays he sometimes thought along these lines, but he was never sure. Betty still had her puritan upbringing in Adelaide in her bones. Married men were taboo. And he was never able to rid himself of guilt feelings where Betty was concerned. He had really behaved badly, damn badly, during their springtime. But all that was over. There was much to be said for love cooled off. The soul took a lukewarm bath and passion was as unthinkable as black snow. The fire in the hearth of memory burned softly and pleasantly, no ecstasy, no neuroses, and no roses!

Betty too wanted things as they were now. When, after Rigby's disappearance, steak had tasted good to her for the first time, she had felt saved. It was a wonderful feeling and a healthier experience than Walpurgis nights in neon lighting.

"Don't regret anything, girl," said Rigby. He must have lived Betty's journey into the past with her. "I know you've had horrible experiences with me, but they're better than none, aren't they? Wear them like black pearls." Then Rigby asked how the big novel was going. Betty had started it before his marriage to Anne. Rigby had read the first chapters before he had flown to London. There had been something about it, even if it hadn't been right for the magazine.

"I couldn't do anything with it for a long time," said Betty. "It was as if the novels for *Insight* had taken the substance out of me. But a year ago I started all over again. It's going to be a quite different book. I've changed too."

"May I read some of it?" In the moonlight he could see Betty flush. How young she was! And how ambitious!

"You don't have any time, Alex. And it's probably no good."

"Probably. When do I get to see it?"

They walked on arm in arm. Betty was happy that Alex was so calm and content. Perhaps she had influence over him because for years now she had preserved the aloofness necessary for creative people. Sometimes she felt a vague pity for this brilliant and successful man, and this pity quite possibly neutralized the senses.

"How are you living nowadays, Betty? Do you have a new friend again?"

"I'm not a hundred years old yet," Betty West answered crisply. "When I have writer's cramp I occasionally need a man, but that has nothing to do with love."

"I have no idea what you're talking about."

Miss West cleared her throat. "Probably I've written about love so much, I can't participate in it any more. A professional disease, my dear."

"You're too young for that kind of withdrawal, pet. Does public acclaim at least pay you damages?" Rigby pulled her hair and Betty yelped. "Just don't drop dead," said Rigby. "Any new ailments in sight?"

"With your disgusting health you don't want to hear about anything like that."

"Correct!" Rigby heard about nothing but backaches, headaches, and exhaustion at home.

Betty sensed his sudden coldness and bitterness. "What's the matter at home?" she asked, quite against her principles.

"Nothing," Rigby said harshly. He tickled her neck. "So laugh, for God's sake, you little twerp!"

Rigby had taken his arm off Betty's shoulder. With every step she could feel him wandering away from her, but she pressed his hand impulsively. Was she the only one who knew about his virtues, which he liked to keep hidden? Actually she was showering Rigby with illusionary laurels. He had done her too much harm, but she knew his value. The fact alone that Rigby existed made her happy. The old love had grown away from the status of enchantment and torturous dependency long ago. Now she could present Alexander Rigby with a liberated heart. He probably had no idea of the value of such a gift.

Betty had to think of his son, to whom she had given birth alone and buried alone. Alexander had no children. Although Betty had sometimes been tempted, she had never told him the truth. In lonely hours, when her typewriter seemed to provide only destructive material, she thought sometimes of this decisive experience and felt that her life was proceeding without love and was bearing no fruit. She was in her mid-thirties now. Why had Rigby sent her away seven years ago? At the time she had told herself that she couldn't bear his faithlessness, and would lose him because of her reproaches. Today she was more mature, and Rigby was older. But his sister had told her that he still played around. Who really knew or understood Rigby?

He had embraced her, hurt her, and left her. On the other hand, he had driven the small town out of her soul and pushed her onto a different path. And now they were strolling peacefully, hand-in-hand, along the seashore. Rigby had put his arm around her again.

"What would you have wanted to write about if I hadn't made you so angry?"

"About nothing," she said. "I would have been happy, just like other women."

"That's the simplest thing in the world!"

"We'd better go back, Alex. It's getting cool. I still have five installments to write for *Insight*, and can't afford pneumonia right now."

Rigby put his sweater on her and laughed because she was swallowed up by it. Betty said, "No, no! You'll catch cold."

"I'm not you!" Rigby buttoned up the sweater and kissed her on the nose. In spite of her protests, he took her to friends of his in Manly to spend the night.

A striking pair walked past them: a very beautiful young girl and a slim, dark-haired man who looked Italian. Rigby's sharp eyes recognized the model, Candy, and the necklace he had given her. His small pleasures cost money . . .

"Wasn't that Candy? The one who models for *Insight*?" Betty asked.

"No idea," said Rigby.

On the one hand Rigby had given his wife a lecture, and she had stared at him wide-eyed, as if he were about to wring her neck. On the other hand, he had by now got over his vexation and was ready to compromise. He was no model husband, and Anne was much too lacking in temperament to actually deceive him. He had been an idiot to even think so! If Anne would just make the least bit of a fuss of him, he'd stay home more. After all, he'd married her because he'd found her attractive. And one could really converse pleasantly with Anne, when she wanted to, whereas Candy had nothing but sawdust in her head. And Anne wasn't interested in his bank account. He'd always found that charming. In short, he was ready and willing to forgive her for this idiotic adoration of John Darling. He felt quite stimulated at the thought of a pleasant truce, which might eventually develop into a lasting marital peace. Anyway, there were a lot uglier girls around than Anne. She had looked absolutely adorable this evening.

He ran into her bedroom. It was empty. For a moment Rigby stood absolutely motionless. Was she still on the roof? It was much too cool up there. The night on the sea had its treacherous aspects. But Anne was nowhere to be found—not on the roof, not in the cellar, nor on any of the verandas or in any of the rooms, nor in the garden.

She had moved out. She had chosen to do so on the one day when he had been happy. A red hot rage welled up in him, to the roots of his hair. This was unforgivable. He had always considered Anne a decent human being in spite of her frigidity and chronic somnolence. After dinner Miss Rigby had given him John Darling's letter to Anne to read. It was quite evident that the old cobber had denied himself certain pleasures with Anne. And now she had deserted Rigby. But no divorce, please!

He couldn't afford another scandal. She could go or stay wherever she damn pleased, but nothing was going to be made public this time!

Rigby was standing in Anne's bedroom. The curtains waved in the night wind like gigantic butterflies. He began to laugh loudly. He found his role as the abandoned husband funny. But he found the fact that he was a human being especially funny. Funny, and somehow eerie. Too many different Adams were alive in him. And something else . . . his bourgeois existence was beginning to fall apart, slowly and imperceptibly. Good fortune, or whatever one thought came under that heading, was dissolving like a chemical substance. On the one hand, private citizen Rigby was wandering on a jagged path, on the other hand he was looking for a code of law that brought order into the life process. Yet he was standing today, on his fiftieth birthday, in the impenetrable bush, and the seconds stretched to hours and eternities, and ran out between his fingers.

Rigby picked up the large Sèvres vase he had given Anne in Paris. His hair tumbled across his forehead and a murderous rage flamed in his narrowed eyes. One day he would wring that treacherous woman's neck! She didn't deserve anything better. He flung the priceless vase against the built-in cupboard of Queensland wood. He had designed the room with walls that had a transparent effect. Here he had wanted to sing the duets of a pleasant life with Anne, goddammit!

Miss Rigby appeared in her dressing gown, buttoned up to her neck. From her room next door she had heard Rigby laugh and the noise of the vase breaking. Her long housecoat made her appear even taller than she was. Her clear-cut face with its narrow, scornful lips looked stern.

"What's the meaning of all this noise so late at night, Alex?"

Rigby stared at his sister. He had forgotten that she didn't drive back to Sydney when it got late. They had bought this house and the land it stood on together, with Patrick Trent's help. Alexander had renovated it and Grace looked after the garden when they spent weekends in Manly. Miss Rigby didn't seem to notice that Anne's bed was empty.

"What *are* you doing, Alex?"

"I'm smashing porcelain," Rigby said in a soft voice.

"Why don't you take the kitchen cups?" Miss Rigby asked. "But I suppose it's *your* porcelain. Don't you think you've smashed enough?"

"Stop talking," said Rigby.

"I've only just begun. Can't you speak a little louder? I'm not a lip reader."

Perhaps he couldn't speak louder. He was white now, as if the red anger had flowed out of him and drained him. He wiped the chest with his handkerchief. He hated scratches. Scratches spoiled the picture. Suddenly Miss Rigby had to think of their father who, on his deathbed, had asked her to look after Alex. But Alex had been a green boy then; now he was gray at the temples and was staring into dead-end streets.

"Sit down, Alex."

He fell into Anne's big, flowered chintz chair and stretched his long legs. Suddenly he was dead tired. "I'll make her pay for this," he mumbled. "These pommies with their goddamned refinement!"

"Don't be foolish. Anne is as she is."

Rigby jumped to his feet and kicked a blue brocade slipper under the bed. Anne had written him off, out of her life and he, Godforsaken ass, still wanted her in spite of her coldness. Her narrow little waist had enchanted him right from the start. And how grateful she had been to come to this wonderful country!

He might perhaps have learned to love her if she had let herself be loved. But she hadn't even played the game right on their honeymoon. For years now she had been putting him off like a beggar, with a smile or an excuse. For years she had neglected the simplest marital duties. Long before he had smiled at the little piece of Irish candy in Darlinghurst!

What else could he have done? At his wedding he had been forty-three and robust as a bull. When the hunger attacked him, he couldn't work. To this day he'd grow so restless, his pencil would go its own way. Damn it all, he hadn't married to receive

charity! He hated martyrs in bed. And today he was only fifty
and could tear up trees, clear a whole bush acre, roots and all
if necessary . . . did Miss Rigby know anything?

"Why did she leave me?" he asked, his voice choked. "I
didn't bother her much."

Miss Rigby said nothing. For the first time it dawned on her
that perhaps Alex had also been denied a lot of what he had
coming to him, but he had behaved abominably to his wife,
and not only today.

"For a while now Anne has been receiving anonymous letters." Miss Rigby didn't look at her brother. She would have
preferred it if Anne hadn't told her.

"What do you mean?"

"Can't you speak English?" Miss Rigby said sullenly. "The
sort of thing you usually find written on toilet paper with no
return address. That you spend your evenings with whores.
And Anne should follow you some Wednesday to a certain
boardinghouse in Darlinghurst . . ."

Rigby's face was red. Had Andrews followed him? Wednesday was her day off. Miss Rigby was thinking the same thing.

"I advised you after your marriage to get rid of that hysterical
woman. She clings to you like a leech."

"At least there's one woman who clings to me."

"Anne is at Shirley Cox's in Lane Cove. Bertie Dobson took
her with him because she insisted."

"She has a thing or two on her conscience as well," said
Rigby. "But that's no longer interesting."

"Maybe she'll go to Queensland with Shirley."

"She has my blessing," said Rigby. "Desertion is grounds
for divorce, but I'm not doing her the favor. If she sues me
for adultery, then we're quits. I'll ask my lawyer. James Battleship is an old friend of mine and one of the best lawyers in
Sydney."

"I know," said Miss Rigby. "You and your lawyer."

"It's all her fault!"

"That's what you think."

"Yes! That's what I think!" Rigby pounded his fist on the

rosewood table he had found for Anne in Chelsea on his last trip to England. "I didn't have a marriage," he said, "whether you can grasp that or not." He wiped the sweat from his forehead and murmured, more to himself, "I couldn't stand it any more."

"You have no idea how much one can stand," said Miss Rigby, with a fleeting sense of compassion. "And just put all that nonsense about a lawyer right out of your head. Jimmy Battleship had quite enough of you last time round."

"You think so?" Rigby asked, menacingly, softly. "I was just going to propose a trip to the Blue Mountains to Anne."

"Don't, Alexander! So... what are you going to do?"

"I'll have to think it over," Rigby said harshly. "To a certain extent I'm grateful to have my peace and quiet. I wanted to change a few things in Vaucluse anyway." He frowned. If Andrews had written those anonymous notes, she'd have something coming to her. It could only have been his jewel. She hated Anne. She had been plotting these last seven years to get rid of the second Mrs. Rigby. She'd hear the angels in heaven singing tomorrow...

Miss Rigby was watching his face. "Please Alex—don't do anything stupid now."

"Goodnight." Rigby opened the door for his sister. "Terribly sorry, Miss Rigby, but I'm an old cobber now. My party has tired me a little."

"So—until tomorrow."

"Yes," said Rigby. "Until tomorrow."

10

Mama Doody's Boardinghouse

On the morning after Rigby's fiftieth birthday the papers featured illustrated accounts of the event, in which Miss Rigby played no small part. She was somehow connected with all the newspaper people in Sydney, and would return the favor when the opportunity arose. Everybody read about Rigby's reception in Vaucluse and the party in Manly. From top-ranking business executives to harbor workers, from salesgirls to models, everybody knew who had been invited and how graciously the enchanting young Mrs. Rigby had treated her guests. From Balmoral to Darlinghurst, from Rose Bay to King's Cross, the subscribers found out at breakfast that the famous author, Elizabeth West, had been present too. Miss West was an old friend of the young Mrs. Rigby. The pressmen stuck to the official reception at which Marchmont, almost a legendary figure now, and the boys from Parramatta, had played a big part. The lady reporters described the women's clothes, the cold buffet, and the radiant mood of the ridiculously young-looking and charming fifty-year-old who had received his guests at the side of his beautiful English wife. Architect Rigby was a great man, no doubt about it, who practiced the Australian bush virtue of hospitality as a matter of course in the big city of Sydney. The pictures showed Rigby and his wife, arm-in-arm—it was touching.

In a boardinghouse in Darlinghurst, where the tired plaster dribbled from the walls, Molly Fleet and Mama Doody were enjoying the Rigby report over their morning tea. There you could see again how the rich amused themselves. Mrs. Doody scolded in a fine rage, that is to say in high spirits, about the bloodsuckers who could afford summer houses, perfumed women and expensive food. Mama Doody herself liked to celebrate and eat. She would have had nothing to say against Rigby's house if it had belonged to her. She considered all rich people lazy and herself a busy bee, because she had the enviable Irish gift of dressing up the naked facts in fantasy until they became wish fulfillments of pure silk. Now she sat in her sloppy housecoat, her hair in curlers, drinking her tea and talking without cease.

Candy yawned. She had been on the beach in Manly yesterday evening with Carlo Pressolini from the Restaurant Rosso. She had had eyes only for the handsome Italian and not even noticed Rigby's mob. Molly Fleet was not to know anything about this outing because Carlo was Molly's boy friend. But after all, Molly didn't own him, and he couldn't seriously be considering Molly as a girl friend. In her indolent way Candy had fallen in love for the first time. She had never met such a darling man, not in her West Australian home nor in Sydney.

"How was it yesterday with the new one?" asked Molly Fleet.

Candy started and looked sharply at Fleet's expression. She didn't seem aware of anything. It was simply the curious question of a girl who had never experienced anything.

"Quite nice," said Candy. "He says he's crazy about me." This was followed by a recital of what he said, what Candy had replied, what both of them had said, and what the new fellow had said on parting. Molly listened greedily, Mrs. Doody yawned. Men were dumb. "Does he have money?" she asked sharply. Candy said she didn't know yet.

Carlo of course didn't have a red cent. Candy had already loaned him money three times. He put every loan down in his notebook, although Candy would gladly have given him the money. She earned that much half-asleep! But Carlo was very strict with Candy. The thought of accepting money from a woman was unbearable. He didn't come from a background where men thought things like that were all right. After all, he had attended the university in Genoa. He came from a fine, wealthy family and had come to Australia straight from his father's villa with the marble columns. Candy wondered why he had given all this up. But then she found out: his father had disowned him because he had wanted to be an opera singer instead of going into his father's business. Candy had never heard of La Scala in Milan. Apparently they sang there. She had listened to Carlo, mouth agape. Even if he was only a waiter now in the Restaurant Rosso, his background was impressive. He looked like a film star, and in her eyes life was an exciting film.

Both of them laughed secretly over Molly Fleet. Candy had advised Carlo to go on taking Molly out on Monday evenings. That was the evening Candy always received her rich sugar daddy. Molly's suspicions must on no account be aroused. Candy didn't rightly know what it was about Molly that she didn't like. She was diligent and devoted and even wrote Candy's love letters. Of course Candy paid her for that. But Candy had an undefinable fear of the girl, and was therefore exceptionally friendly. It was ridiculous, but the thought that Molly might find out about her love affair with Carlo Pressolini made Candy tremble.

Molly Fleet read the account of the Rigby festivities with an expressionless face, and looked at the picture of the happy couple. But the Sydney *Morning Herald* had a surprising final notice: Mrs. Anne Rigby had flown to London the following morning to visit her mother after an absence of seven years. She had only wanted to be there to celebrate her husband's birthday. Lady Carrington, Anne's mother, wrote popular thrillers which Molly Fleet devoured evenings in bed. She let the newspaper fall . . . Mrs. Rigby had not cancelled her massage, and she was always considerate about things like that. She must have decided to leave overnight . . .

Mrs. Doody went on expostulating about the rich men she and Candy lived on. Molly shrugged. As if money grew on trees! In a city like Sydney everybody ran hectically for a place in the sun. Molly sensed that yachts and dream villas cost money.

"You are perfectly right, Mrs. Doody," she said.

Nobody replied. Molly Fleet lit a cigarette and went on looking at Rigby's picture. Funny, but in Parramatta she had envisioned quite a different man. She hoped his wife would come back soon. Molly didn't feel right about the letters she was writing regularly for Candy. But Rigby would go his own way anyway, whether he got the letters or not. Since one could talk oneself into anything in the world, Molly had gradually convinced herself that with these letters she was doing Rigby's wife no harm. She also told herself that she wrote these letters because Candy paid her well for it, and she needed money for the farm. She hadn't yet admitted to herself that she felt more alive and happier when she was writing to this man, to whom she had never spoken and who never answered. But whether Molly Fleet admitted it to herself or not, she needed this one-sided correspondence. Her interest in Rigby had been theoretical for a long time. Now she *had* to find out what he told Candy, how he kissed, how he behaved when he came to see her ... everything. Everything. Animosity toward this beautiful, carefree creature who couldn't tell the difference between a man like Rigby and her other lovers, welled up wildly in Molly Fleet with every letter she wrote. When Candy was amused by Rigby's changeable moods or spoke disparagingly of his portrait sketches, Molly Fleet shivered and felt a strange pain. She was furious with this golden goose. She was furious with Father O'Brien, who sometimes admonished her. She was furious with God! But above all she was furious with Rigby because he had fallen for a shop-window mannequin who unscrewed her head at night. Mrs. Doody was right: men were fools!

Molly was still staring at the photo of Rigby in the paper. In spite of her reserve, Mrs. Rigby had always been nice to her, and had mercifully chosen to overlook her birthmark. But a few weeks ago she had sent Molly at her own expense to a skin specialist on Macquarie Street. Although she had never mentioned the disfigurement, she must have sensed how unhappy Molly was about it. It wasn't Mrs. Rigby's fault that the specialist had advised against an operation. Miss Fleet's fiery birthmark—*naevus flammeus*—was too deep and too large for deep X-ray treatment or other radiological methods. The scars could result in an even worse disfigurement. The doctor had also advised against plastic surgery. In the case of such a large mark, there was the danger that with time, the scars could sink in and distort the features. Only small, port-wine spots could be operated.

Mrs. Rigby had told Molly the results. She had ordered tea and spoken quietly, yet so compassionately that Molly had drunk her tea together with the bitter tears of disappointment. Anne Rigby had murmured that there were worse things in life, and that Molly was so efficient and energetic, she would make a go of life in spite of the birthmark. After that Mrs. Rigby had closed her eyes for a moment. Molly had sat very still. Was Mrs. Rigby experiencing difficulties? Anyway, the girl from Parramatta had found out that afternoon that luxury and money were no guarantee of contentment. She'd wanted so much to do something for Mrs. Rigby. She wasn't used to having other people worry about her. But what could she do for Anne Rigby?

People had to fight and pray alone for the peace of their souls. As a child in the Parramatta church, Molly hadn't found this difficult because she had seen how Grandmother Fleet, with her wooden rosary attached to her belt, got through life very well. If Molly only knew why she stayed in Sydney! In this vast, soul-consuming city, life was dangerous, disappointing, and frightfully confusing. The people in their luxurious show places in Vaucluse weren't more content than Molly Fleet in Mama Doody's boardinghouse. The only truly satisfied person was Candy, but she was imperilled by her beauty. When she looked at Candy's enchanting, empty face, Molly Fleet sometimes pictured what Candy would look like with a birthmark on her face, or with horrible, badly healed scars. That was something Candy wouldn't be able to live with. The goose pimples ran down Molly's back. How could she think such dreadful things? Candy was always so nice to her. And Candy couldn't get along without her any more. No wonder—Molly had gradually learned the art of making herself indispensable.

What was it like in the arms of a man, she wondered. Molly Fleet was twenty-two, and her wild, innocent dreams swung like storm lanterns in the dark. Was the love of a man a feast or a fire or a sin? Candy had given her the impression that sex was important to men only now and then. Sometimes Rigby only sketched her, Candy told Molly indignantly. But he paid just the same. Again Molly felt that strange pressure in the region of her heart. She even longed for a big disaster; if only she could experience something. She felt like the dry rocks and brushwood in the mountains.

Mama Doody snatched the paper from her and studied Rigby through the glasses that were slipping off her nose. "Candy!" she exclaimed. "This architect looks like our traveling sales-man, Ritter!"

"You always find look-alikes, Auntie. To me all the men in Sydney are the same."

"And they are all the same," said Mrs. Doody. "Pigs, all of them! Is your sugar daddy coming today?"

"It's his Monday." Candy closed her eyes. She was bored with the whole thing. Molly Fleet was to be envied. Nobody bothered her.

"Come, Molly." Mrs. Doody pulled enviable Molly Fleet to the door.

"Molly!" cried Candy. "Do you see any resemblance be-tween Ritter and Rigby?"

"Sure. They're both men." Molly grinned. "Have a nap, Candy. For your sugar daddy."

"He doesn't give a damn. He's crazy about me."

"Crazier than Mr. Ritter?" Molly asked hesitantly.

"Ritter is never crazy. That man doesn't have a spark of feeling. He gives me the creeps. But he pays."

"And that's all we want from him," murmured Molly. It was time for a love letter to Ritter. Molly blushed as she asked what he was most interested in. "In me, of course," said Candy. "What else?"

* * *

Mrs. Doody's boardinghouse in Darlinghurst was different from the houses next door only because of its inhabitants. These narrow, two-story tenements were waiting stoically to be demolished. The neglected, airless houses knew nothing about "Gracious Living"—a popular series in *Insight*—nothing about hygiene, nothing about the new status symbols. The houses had come to terms with their inhabitants and vice versa. Junk was hallowed by force of habit. The houses had high old-fashioned doors of dark wood, and narrow balconies with railings of rusty wrought-iron. This formerly attractive decoration in Colonial style couldn't banish the general air of neglect. The walls were tired and dirty; the sediment of earlier tenants stuck to them. Identical chimneys gave the crowded buildings a dreary uniformity. There were of course houses in Sydney's old section that were not dreary and ready to collapse. With their fenced-in front lawns and balconies, their attractiveness wasted here, these row houses bore witness to an earlier building period, like the old monuments in an ugly, crowded industrial city in England. And then there were the gloomy stone barracks down by the harbor which were built by the sweat of their brows and with their memories of a cozy, smoky pub in the fog at home, by the convicts imported from England under Governor Phillip. Whoever was freighted from the old country to the colony of New South Wales after 1788, found life in the settlement bitter as gall and unbearably sunny. The dusty confines of Mrs. Doody's boardinghouse still exuded the old nostalgia for a small, jolly, slovenly, pleasantly alchoholized world as the natives of Dublin or Manchester had known it.

At the time many residents of the old houses in Surry Hills and Darlinghurst had already moved out. These people moved with outspoken resentment into the clean, light apartments the city had built for its citizens. Mama Doody would pour a pail of dishwater on the head of any member of the building commission who dared to touch her house. In it she had things the way she wanted them: the heap of trash in front, the dirty wash in the kitchen, the dark, worn stairs, her neighbors, and the "living room" with its ancient, moth-eaten plush furniture, yellowed photographs of Dublin, and hideous plaster of paris figurines. The plaster Virgin Mary stood on the buffet and was astonished. The wallpaper with its faded flower pattern was peeling. A chronic faint odor of gas from the kitchen penetrated all the rooms. The living room was used only on holidays. Mrs. Doody lived in her chaotic kitchen, or she sat in Candy's room, scolding the girl whom she secretly loved. Candy's room lay to one side on the first floor, and Molly Fleet kept it clean. Candy's visitors got to her room through a narrow passageway. Nobody could understand why a model who earned such a lot of money didn't get herself a better apartment. But then nobody understood the strong family feeling of the Irish. Anyway, Candy had lived in even poorer surroundings in Kalgoorlie, as the great-granddaughter of an unsuccessful gold prospector.

On the attic floor lived the Umbrella Man, an old vagabond with the weathered face of an eagle, who had suspended a collection of umbrellas from his ceiling. Occasionally he sold one. He himself never used an umbrella. He had a gas hotplate in a corner under the sloping roof. He was either alone with his umbrellas or chatting with the old Viennese actor who lived on the first floor. Mama Doody took the Umbrella Man's meals up to him. He had appeared one day straight out of the limitless Australian loneliness, and looked as if he had years of wandering through deserts without an oasis behind him. His name was Doody too. Perhaps he was a relative. Anyway, he was Irish. He could do cabinet work when he felt like it. For the most part he drank gin and listened to Irish songs on the radio. He didn't know what he wanted, not in Sydney. Nobody knew. People just happened to come to the big city. Everybody in the house called him "Uncle," although he was pretty grumpy. Mrs. Doody loved him, and he seemed to be fond of her. When he was in a good mood he went to the tavern around the corner with the Viennese actor who had emigrated to Sydney shortly before the Second World War. The man from Vienna worked in a factory in Sydney, and came back to the boardinghouse in the evening. Then he sat in his narrow, hot room and conversed with his dead wife about performances at the Burg-theater or at the Josefstadt, performing-arts centers which none of Mrs. Doody's guests had ever heard of.

On the attic floor, beside a small room filled with junk, lived an abo, short for aborigine, a black, wiry-haired Australian who had somehow drunk his way to Sydney from somewhere in New South Wales. When he felt like it, he worked in the harbor. His demands were so modest that he could afford to work part-time. He swept the house, carried heavy things up and down the stairs, repaired the gas stove, and sang when the clouds weren't depressing him. The clouds were mysterious moods that whirled around him like giant bush birds.

When Candy went out to eat or dance with her friends, the abo watched her go with glowing eyes in which the darkness of the Stone Age burned, and sang softly, "Lemon tree . . . very pretty." In his thoughts he called Candy "Lemon Blossom," and did what he could for her. Once he brought her some crushed mimosa. Candy smiled and said, "Thank you, Charlie Rainbow." He had received the first name, Charlie, and the family name, Rainbow, at a mission in New South Wales where his mother had abandoned him. He had been five when his mother's tribe had broken up camp and wandered farther into the bush. They hadn't been too pleased at the mission when they had found Charlie Rainbow. They had a lot of much nicer and diligent black children, and half-breeds who were cleaner and more grateful. Charlie didn't love anything or anybody except for flowers and Candy. He had enjoyed gardening at the mission, but when the other children had washed their hands after work, he had run away. His hands stayed black, it didn't make any difference whether he washed them or not. He had tried once in vain to soap away the black color of his skin. Since then he looked upon soap as his personal enemy. He had made no friends among the other children. He lived for himself and couldn't think of any other way to live. Nothing attached him to his white teachers, although they did their best to win him. In the end he ran away. As a child he had been afraid of the whites; they reminded him of the dead white trunks of the eucalyptus trees, and the hair of one of his old teachers was gray bush grass.

Now Charlie Rainbow lived in the great wilderness of Sydney, but Candy reminded him of his beloved flowers that stood in boxes on Mama Doody's little balcony. Sometimes he looked in at a milk bar or, later, at beer halls, but he didn't dare to enter. He was not one of the abos to whom the government had issued a card for alcoholic beverages. In his case the powers that be were right, even if Charlie couldn't see it that way. The gin he got at Mama Doody's went straight to his head. Then he danced wildly all over the place and sang too loudly, or more accurately, howled like an Irish banshee. Mrs. Doody laughed. She had no nerves. Why shouldn't the blackfellow be merry too? Molly Fleet warned Mrs. Doody. Charlie Rainbow with gin inside him didn't know what he was doing. On the farm they had once had a good, nice abo and one day . . . Mama Doody laughed loudly and said nobody knew what they were doing when they had too much alcohol in them. She only had to think of her old man . . .

Charlie Rainbow had wandered a long way before finally arriving in Sydney. He had worked on a sheep station for a while, then he had moved on. When he finally arrived at Mama Doody's, all he had was a teapot, a bundle of dirty laundry, and his "garden" on his back. But he was so obliging! He hammered or carpentered or was busy with his plants. His garden was a box of seedlings, and now there were three. He had picked up the boxes at the harbor and filled them with earth. They had the necessary holes and cracks through which superfluous rainwater could run off. Charlie had lined the bottoms with stones, and shoveled the earth and sand over them. He put the boxes out in the sun in the morning and in the shade in the afternoon, and kept them carefully watered, just as he had learned from the bad white people in the mission. And when winter came—that is, when it was summer in Ireland and everywhere else in Europe—then Charlie covered his little garden with glass panes. He'd learned that too. He belonged to a union, and he worked in the harbor, but he only got paid when he worked and wasn't "crook" from gin. He had even made friends with a white colleague who got him gin on the sly. But suddenly it was all over. The white man avoided him. Perhaps the police had found out about the gin. So now Charlie hated his former friend. The whites could do what they liked with him. Sometimes they were friendly to the black man; sometimes they pushed him into a corner and walked off to a pub, arm-in-arm. They teetered all over the place, just like him, when they came out of the pub. A white drunk had stepped on Charlie's foot once as he, sober as a judge, was standing in front of the tavern, watching the people come out. Charlie had howled like a dingo, a wild Australian dog, and drawn his knife, whereupon the police had locked him up. He was booked for attempted murder, and all Charlie had intended was a warning to the drunken white buffalo. Charlie cried in prison, because of his flowers, but when he got back to Mama Doody's, his flowers had been watered and were blooming. Molly Fleet had looked after them. Charlie carved her a little arrow for thanks. It didn't have a poisoned head like some arrows in the bush; Charlie had painted it painstakingly with mysterious geometric lines and symbols. Miss Fleet had been very pleased. At first Charlie had been afraid of Miss Fleet. People were either black, which was the natural color, or they were pale as corpses. He had never seen a spotted face. Only tigers had spots...

A while ago Miss Candy had given him a mouth organ, and now he wasn't lonely any more. He blew the melodies of the forest, like the wind blew, or like the kookaburra laughed. It was great fun. Now Charlie Rainbow worshiped the beautiful white girl with the light hair.

Miss Candy should take care not to reject him when he asked what he could do for her. That was something Charlie Rainbow couldn't put up with. But Candy was a friendly creature and she felt a little sorry for the blackfellow. Not that it really hurt; just a whiff of compassion. She couldn't understand why he sometimes laughed aloud crazily, and danced up the narrow stairs. His flower boxes and the cheap harmonica were his entire delight. Sometimes he was as violent as a sandstorm.

In spite of his beautiful black eyes, Candy found him horribly ugly, but she instinctively hid her revulsion. As an additional slave, he was welcome. Sometimes he hid for weeks from Mrs. Doody's lodgers; sometimes he ran away. But when he came back and rushed to his flower boxes, fury raging inside him should his flowers be dead, he always found everything green and blooming. Once he stole a red watermelon from the market and laid it in front of Miss Fleet's door. She was a benevolent tiger. He played something on his harmonica for her and she listened. Her hair was like the yellow poplars, and the right side of her face glowed like a red half-moon.

For some reason or other, Charlie Rainbow couldn't stand being in Sydney too long a time. Most of the people knew nothing about the forests. In Sydney the whites were innumerable and as much of a nuisance as sand flies. They were immodest in their hearts. Charlie Rainbow was as modest as the salt bush at the desert's edge.

On the day after Rigby's fiftieth birthday, the abo disappeared. Nobody seemed to notice it, but Molly Fleet went around with the watering can again. A whole world lay between her and Charlie, but both of them loved the Australian earth and everything that blossomed, bore fruit, or tried to. Just the same, neither of them could find their way anymore out of the city back to the country. Sydney held them with a thousand entrapping arms. However, they visited New South Wales. Molly Fleet went to the farm. She rarely went to see her father or her bitter sister in Parramatta. Charlie went walkabout, or he visited a blackfellow friend, who lived with his wife and children in a shack with a corrugated tin roof on the outskirts of the big city. The hovel stank of the sweat of many people; it was baking hot or dripping with rain, but it was cozy. Empty beer bottles, rusty pieces of iron, kitchen garbage, and trash lay in the narrow backyard. The dirtiest WC in New South Wales stood in one corner. It didn't bother anybody. Charlie's cobber was a good fellow. He liked his home.

The torn venetian blinds at the window let in the green, flickering light. One sat inside as in a pond. That was fun.

They spent the evenings on the little wooden veranda that Charlie had built onto the shack. The big tropical stars and the cooler air calmed their confused and restless souls. The dark was comforting, a wide cloak from a dream world. All of them felt less helpless in the world of the whites after night had fallen. The stars belonged to everyone; they also looked down at the blackfellow amiably. But this magical union, which healed a torn ligament of nature, came and went with the night. Morning in the big city brought with it new misunderstandings, monotonous work, the unstilled thirst for *corroborees*—the native festivals—and for alcohol. The black and white world became a nightmare of sunshine and fear. Yes, all of them were afraid of their white brothers, even when they were friendly and helpful. They sent them, surely for their own good, to missions and reservations, but Charlie and his cobber were not packages. Wandering was in their blood. The whites also went walkabout. They even had a magazine with that name, which they had picked up from the native population. And why did the whites call themselves "old Australians"? All of them had come here recently. Charlie and his cobber were the *real* old Australians because their roots and soul pictures reached back into the time of dreams. In Sydney there was nothing but houses, humans, events, doubtful and incomprehensible projects of an alien spirit, which depressed the blackfellows. They experienced a quite different fulfillment and void, and stumbled—mute and crippled by not knowing—between the functional buildings and symbols of the whites.

Not far from the shack there were desolate little stores that sold cigarettes, soap, coffee, and sugar. The service was friendly, in the ice-cream parlor too, which the whites also frequented. Charlie's cobber worked in a little factory nearby.

Charlie Rainbow repaired the tin roof. There was enough bent metal and other junk lying around. His hands were quick and clever, as if they were additional live creatures attached to his thin arms, and independent of them. Charlie Rainbow knew that his know-how wasn't in his head; clever hands were more important. Charlie constructed a fence around the tiny plot for his friend, so that the neighbor's children couldn't trample over his "garden." The sweat poured down Charlie's body as he laid out a garden for his only cobber, which the latter didn't even want. But Charlie planted a few simple shrubs on the bare spot, with its tired, dried-up earth, and giggling all the time, even stuck some flower seeds into the loosened earth. They were to be a surprise for his friend and his *gin*, his native wife. The shrubs grew in this climate without any help, and a little fruit tree, which Charlie had stolen from a garden, already looked pretty and out of place in this miniature plot at the edge of the city. Charlie's friend was delighted with the fence. In the dark he passed his hands surreptitiously across the rough wood. The fence was a friend. It gave him a sense of security. It protected him from visitors and wild dogs.

Charlie Rainbow could have stayed with his cobber, and that would have been very good for him, but he didn't have an eye for what was good and useful. He saw the beautiful blond girl in Mama Doody's roominghouse. When the vision of Candy hurt very much, he crept back to Darlinghurst.

He often brought a present for Candy. Once he stood a cleverly carpentered and painted shelf in front of her door. He had never dared enter her room. Candy forgot to thank him, but Charlie didn't expect any thanks. After quite a time of brooding, he asked Miss Fleet if the shelf was a "bad shelf"? But Molly said it was a very fine shelf, and beautifully painted. Candy had all sorts of things standing on it, and had told Molly to thank him. Charlie let out a shrill cry of joy, then he ran up to his attic room. All he had wanted to know was if Miss Candy had thrown the shelf away.

Next morning, when Charlie was creeping past Candy's room, she came out of it. There she stood in her flowered dress and her shining hair. She murmured, "Thank you, Charlie Rainbow," and smiled at him. For a moment he was standing on the sunny side of life. Molly had reminded Candy to thank him.

Otherwise Candy never spoke to Charlie Rainbow. What could they have talked about? Charlie couldn't lay out a garden of words. In the daylight his mind was silent and fled to the dimly conscious memories of his tribe. Only his hands belonged in the twentieth century. They did good and bad things. They were immensely strong or immensely gentle, all according to whether he was furious or happy. Sometimes Charlie's hands were a bridge for Candy. She was night-blind. One night she was feeling her way home alone, and Charlie had been waiting for her, as usual. She couldn't see him. He was a twin of the dark. But he held out his hand to her, and his heart beating fast, helped her up the dark, wobbly stairs. That night he had sung for joy in his room and had danced until the Umbrella Man had knocked furiously on the wall.

Charlie Rainbow could have told the beautiful blond girl a lot of what he had seen with his eyes and smelled with his nose, but Candy never stayed long enough in one place for his heavy tongue to loosen up. Probably this girl didn't want to hear anything about sheep herds and hillsides, nothing about the luminous red-green rosella birds in the bush, nothing about horses bursting with strength and sunshine as they rushed to a waterhole. Charlie could also have told her about the mysterious twilight that tinted the blue sky of New South Wales, and hunted the cloud horses, and enfolded the rainbow snake, and summoned the spirits. The fractured light between day and night did all those things. Like all the members of his tribe, Charlie could smell the spirits of nature. He knew when they were approaching or remembered what his tribe knew. And then it didn't make any difference whether or not one had learned in a mission to sit still and how to dress, or whether one was naked and restless and destined to die out in the bush.

Miss Candy would never have listened to Charlie. He knew it in his heart, which was more agile and clever than his head. And he didn't have to tell the girl from Parramatta anything. Molly knew from childhood all about the desolate eucalyptus, the wide-fleeing horizon, the country road and burning dust, and the honey-sweet mimosa tree. She knew everything in New South Wales that greened, and its struggle against the wildness of nature; everything that bore fruit or withered stoically. Perhaps the girl also knew about some of the dark corners in Charlie Rainbow's soul. Molly had never forgotten her childhood friend, Goonur, who had stroked her golden-red hair and plaited wreaths of wild flowers for her. She had never told Charlie Rainbow about Goonur. The girl was hers alone, although she had not really known the child from the bush.

Until now Charlie Rainbow had always come back to Mama Doody's. It surprised Molly Fleet. Goonur had had a much better life with them on the farm. She had been allowed to help Grandmother Fleet to preserve fruit; still she had disappeared without saying goodbye. Who knew anybody anyway?

On the Monday after Rigby's fiftieth birthday, Molly Fleet was sitting alone in her room. Carlo was so busy at the restaurant that his day off had been changed. He was sorry, but he couldn't tell Molly when he would be free.

She sat in her narrow, hot room with nothing to do, and the emptiness and disappointment stuck like a knot in her throat. Why wasn't Carlo going out with her this Monday? Had he told her the truth? She had caught him telling all sorts of lies, and first-rate lying was requisite for anyone trying to test a memory like Molly Fleet's.

It never did her any good to sit alone and think. Although she didn't trust a living soul, it had never occurred to her that Candy, who had such rich friends, had taken her young man away from her. It was quiet in the house. The November heat had made Mrs. Doody drowsy. Now she was in her room, snoring. The abo was away, and Candy was waiting for her sugar daddy, who had no idea that right now he was paying Carlo Pressolini's debts.

The bell rang. Molly started. Candy's Monday visitor never came before seven. But it was he. She recognized him at once. A big, corpulent man with a full red face and dark Irish eyes. He was dressed impeccably and had curly black hair that was combed over the beginnings of a bald spot. A loose curl fell across his round forehead. His nose was fine and straight, his full lips drooped a little, as if with slight revulsion, or so it seemed to Miss Fleet. A hidden melancholy lay in his deep-set eyes with the dark rims around them. It didn't go with the laughter wrinkles in the corners. This gentleman was known in his circles as a prankster. He was a fleshy colossus, with a lot of thinking power behind his wrinkled brow.

Patrick Trent smiled at Miss Fleet, a little unsure. He saw her for the first time. "Excuse me, please," he said formally. "Could I speak to Miss Blyth?"

Molly said Candy was in her room. Perhaps she was still asleep. It had been such a hot day.

"Yes," said the stranger. "Very hot."

He could feel the girl's strange, flickering eyes examining him. Dammit! Candy had told him to come an hour too early. The girl had a memory like a sieve. Perhaps it wasn't a weak memory but only a lack of attention. To pay attention was important, and a rare thing between a man and a woman.

In spite of his smile, the visitor seemed to be apologizing for his presence in Mama Doody's boardinghouse. He seemed to feel even more uncomfortable than Albert Ritter. He looked around nervously, as if someone . . . his wife perhaps . . . was on his heels. At the same time he was surreptitiously looking at the girl with the birthmark. One of nature's bad jokes. He hated bad jokes. His were always funny . . .

He held his head a little to one side. Either it was too heavy for him or he wanted to excuse himself for his size. Nobody in this house knew that Candy's sugar daddy was an old member of Rigby's mob.

"Pardon me." The stranger laughed, suddenly and very naturally, and pushed his way past Molly Fleet with the odd agility of fat people. He had talked about the weather, as was proper, and that was enough. Molly Fleet would have liked to converse some more. There was something comforting about the visitor.

The old stairs creaked under his weight. Then Mr. Patrick Trent finally disappeared from Molly Fleet's hungry eyes.

11

A City Like Sydney

After Anne's departure, Rigby was as free as the kookaburra in the bush, but he didn't laugh as much. Never had a husband, who paid bills uncomplainingly and now and then even did a thing or two to please his wife, been deserted in such fashion! And on top of that, in a city like Sydney where life was so colorful and exciting. But in Vaucluse things were momentarily at a standstill. The big house was empty. Rigby's relief at the beginning not to hear any more complaints about backache, and to leave his cigarette case where it suited him, was gone. From the start, it hadn't been the relief he had felt after Flora's death. Perhaps he had only talked himself into thinking he would prefer to live alone. Anne must have become a treacherous habit. And he clung to his habits. That was why he still had Elizabeth West on his list. He hadn't heard from Withers in a long time, and he wasn't about to call her, not in his present situation! He thought friends looked after friends. Miss West had evidently never heard of such a thing. All Rigby would really have to do was ask his sister if Betty was dead or alive, in Sydney or away. He wondered if she was working on a new book or just loafing. Or swimming. Sydney was the right place for swimmers. Anne would never again find beaches like the ones here, five minutes from the heart of the city.

Rigby put out his cigarette furiously. He didn't know why, but right now he couldn't stand his house. Uncertainty and doubt had crept in at the gate. But perhaps security and permanence in private life were illusions for which every husband paid, sooner or later. Rigby didn't consider the fact that his frequent absences from home might have contributed decisively to the crisis in his marriage. He hadn't left his wife, and he had to have a little fun in the evenings. His visits to Candy Blyth didn't count. Besides, he had been on the verge of giving them up, whether Anne believed him or not. After all, marriage was the only satisfactory union: you had everything at home and didn't have to prowl around in strange, sleazy bedrooms. But Anne hadn't cooperated. It was all her fault.

Mrs. Andrews was no help either. She fluttered around like a tired swallow. She stuck her nose up in the air the same way too. Andrews got terribly on Rigby's nerves, but what could he do? He had to eat. Besides, Andrews was the only one who was fond of him. He'd always said so. And even his sister had to admit he was right. He hadn't seen her since his fiftieth birthday because right now he wasn't going to Manly on weekends. Miss Rigby was decent to the core, but he just couldn't stand women who had "always said so." Naturally he could never fire Andrews now. He wasn't totally crazy! Nobody could make Szegediner goulash like her.

As far as he could recall, he had finally decided to fire Andrews on his fiftieth birthday, and it was entirely Anne's fault that he now had to listen to her pearls of wisdom, just when his steak was tasting right again for the first time. Andrews always tried to ruin his steak for him; she considered steak unimaginative. But when he pounded on the table with his fist, Andrews and the proper steak appeared. Until now, what the master of the house wanted was still being carried out in Vaucluse. In seven years, Anne hadn't been able to grasp that.

When he thought of his many good resolutions which now couldn't be realized, Rigby felt lousy. Of course he now visited Candy in her old roominghouse. Since Miss West remained invisible and his wife had fled back to the pommies, he had to have something attractive to look at now and then. Candy at least didn't talk about metaphysics, and she never had a headache. She wasn't the worst girl around, if you overlooked her vocabulary. A ten-year-old was more articulate. But Candy was always in good spirits, not a nag like his wife. When he looked at it from every angle, Anne's absence was a blessing in disguise.

Rigby was absolutely furious when he thought how he had decided to make a fresh start on his fiftieth. He had wanted to sit on the terrace with Anne at least four evenings a week, in spite of her sour expression, and instead of his visits to Darlinghurst, he intended to visit Stan Marchmont more often. To be sure his boss needed a lot of rest now, but whenever Rigby went to see him, he was so pleased and didn't want to let him go. Marchmont couldn't sit with him on the terrace in Vaucluse as he had done after the disappearance of the first Mrs. Rigby. Why didn't he visit his old friend now? Marchmont said too little rather than too much, but to Marchmont, ridiculous as it might seem, Alexander Rigby was still "the young man." And he didn't want to see the disapproval in his boss's sharp blue eyes. He could sense it in every bone in his body: Marchmont was beside himself over the breakup of Rigby's second marriage. He worried about him. *That* wasn't necessary. He had always managed himself splendidly in the past. But tomorrow evening he would go to see Marchmont. No knowing how long he would still be able to do that.

A few evenings ago Rigby, in a feebleminded moment, had walked into Anne's room and in silent fury had tidied her drawers. She had left nearly all her dresses behind, but Rigby wasn't deceived by that. The full closet didn't necessarily mean that she was coming back soon. It might just as well mean that she didn't want to wear the dresses because he had bought them. As he tidied, Rigby came across an expensive, crushed chiffon dress. Anne's silver shoes with the high heels had torn a hole in it. It was scandalous, the way his wife had treated the things he had bought for her, *his* things! In that dress Anne had looked like an airy white egret about to fly away. Well, she had flown away.

Rigby was so disturbed that he pressed the dress to him. It was wrinkled anyway. And who should come into the room at that moment but Andrews! Rigby might have known it. With her mania for cleanliness, the woman could drive you crazy! Why the hell did she have to dust Anne's room? The second Mrs. Rigby would never see the dust. And even if she had stayed home, she wouldn't have noticed it. Rigby threw the white dress at Andrews to be mended. Andrews, accustomed to having things thrown at her, picked it up with dignity. She asked pointedly if the dress should be cleaned and sent to London.

Rigby's answer was unprintable, whereupon Andrews gave notice yet again, and Rigby had to talk her out of it. Again. How would she manage with strangers? In a city like Sydney, where nobody cared about anybody else? Andrews said she would get more appreciation anywhere than in this house. Rigby said he'd never heard anything so funny. Of course Andrews stayed. What would her Rigby do without her? One had to grant him some consideration. His wife was heartless. Andrews had always known it, but for once she kept her mouth shut. She didn't want to be strangled by Rigby just before going to the movies.

Rigby spent the evening alone on his big terrace, staring out to sea. Incredible how ill at ease he felt in his beautiful home! In spite of her nagging and constant ailments, Anne must have created an atmosphere that Rigby now missed. Anyway, Andrews had *not* written the anonymous letters to his wife. He knew when his jewel was lying. Andrews had been indignant that he had thought her capable of such a thing. Never would she have fallen so low! She loved her enemies and included them, grudgingly in her prayers. And of course she had given notice again, dumb creature!

So *who* had written those letters? It had to be someone who watched his little side steps. A damned uncomfortable feeling. As if someone were creeping up behind him and leaping out of a doorway when he turned around. Then he forgot about it. Whichever way you looked at it, Anne had flown away.

Rigby fell back on his work, because right now his fun was no fun. So why in heaven's name did he go to see Candy? Damn it all! He wasn't a hundred yet. Like every man, he needed distraction and a pretty female to look at. In a city like Sydney, you could find one on every street corner in King's Cross, on every beach, in every third villa . . . but Candy happened to be an exceptionally nice girl to look at.

Once he drove to the Blue Mountains, but it was not a success. Memories were too obtrusive. Either he had suddenly turned into an old woman or he was crazy: he could hear Flora Pratt giggling! He had jumped into his car and taken the Great Western Highway nonstop to Sydney. This was the road taken by settlers, soldiers, convicts and gold prospectors in the early colonial days. From the year 1793 people had tried to find a route across the stern, wild mountains. Rigby had spoken once at the Architects Club about the connection between Sydney and Bathurst, and had explained how in New South Wales nothing had been impossible, nor was it today. In 1850 Governor Macquarie, with his wife and an official commission, had driven across the new highway. Mrs. Macquarie had always taken part in anything her husband undertook, as was to be expected from a wife. That was why to this day the famous lookout spot was called "Mrs. Macquarie's Chair." Rigby had often stood there on his way back from the botanical gardens. Mr. Macquarie had never realized what a good thing he had had in his wife. He had probably taken for granted that Mrs. Macquarie lived and sweated with him. There were marriages like that too.

That evening Rigby got drunk with his mob.

As in his bachelor days, he now made frequent forays through the city. Sydney never disappointed nor tired him. Here he found unparalleled riches: beauty, new ideas, and old English traditions. The panorama of the sea and the uniform ugliness of many buildings and streets bore as many contrasts as Rigby's soul. The fragmentary and episodic character of this sprawling former settlement excited Rigby's fantasy, and his desire to shape things. A city like Sydney was rich, versatile, intoxicating. Sydney not only *was*, it *became* with every new year, with every new building. Every architectural dream was given form and life in the sober air under this blue sky. It was a delight to build here.

In the second half of the twentieth century, Sydney couldn't expect to be a showplace. 'Thank God!' thought Rigby. The city didn't shine with perfection. It had its memories and came up with honorable, anachronistic jokes. Because the Victorian houses and the fates of the wild convicts, the early settlers, and the English adventurers with sideburns, had put their stamp on the panorama of Sydney, just as much as the high-rise houses of glass and metal, and the sensual beauty of the luxury villas on the water. The Victorian houses with their columns and high, narrow windows and their ostentatious portals were legends in stone that made Sydney a gigantic bridge between the English past and the Australian future. The town hall or the post office or Martin Place were, for Rigby, touching, monumental monstrosities. You wandered around Sydney as in an architectural family album. He stood on York Street, in front of the ornamented cement facade of a palatial department store of the nineteenth century, or he let the hideous portal of the customs house on Circular Quai astonish him. He shook his head over the Witches House in Annandale, a naive Victorian freak that didn't fit into a climate where palms and tropical flowers grew amid spired towers and "romantic" narrow windows ... all of it built for eternity. But in a city like Sydney, eternity only lasted decades. What place did a revival of Gothic architecture have in Australia? What room was there for Greek Classicism in this tropically tainted and hypermodern world? Time would tear more and more pages out of the old family album, and that was sad. It aroused in modern spectators a presentiment of loss, however ridiculous such Gothic jests may have been. Time raced on, nothing could stop it, and one day the buildings of Marchmont, Rigby & French would be just as anachronistic in an unknown Sydney as today's ornamental Huddart Parker House on Bridge Street. Or like Cochrane's Hotel, 1850, the consoling Colonial tavern that didn't try to be more modern than it was, and that, as the greatest concession to the present day, had only exchanged its wrought-iron fixtures

for ones that used electricity. Rigby looked at the stylistic
efforts of the past with affectionate eyes because he knew that
never again would a wave of English civilization, with the
historic pomposity and ornamentation intended for a foggy
climate, flow over this city of the future. These high, solid,
mercantile houses and public buildings would disappear with
time, like the frock coats, the sideburns, and the piety of the
English settlers.

Rigby stood on the quai of Darling Harbour where wool and
other wares were being loaded for export. He looked across at
the high-rise houses, but today he didn't feel his usual joy over
the present Sydney. Who fitted into these high houses of glass
and metal? Was architecture more progressive and less com-
promising than its creators? In the stern new palaces—Vaucluse
had been built with the same idea—there were no shabby, cozy
corners and alcoves as there had been in Anne's parental home
behind Avenue Road, which had combined old-fashioned ornamentation with a certain naive dignity. No clean-cut lines,
no feeling for material, no economy of design! But Anne, even
after seven years of brooding and instruction on esthetics by
Rigby, seemed to prefer this house to his model residence in
Vaucluse. And of course she would prefer any pommy to old
Rigby!

When finally, deep in thought, Rigby found himself standing
in front of his former office on George Street, Elizabeth West
suddenly appeared. He had just been wondering how many
tears Withers must have shed for him in her little anteroom
. . . oh yes, for him! Today Withers probably only wept within
her own four walls in Bellevue Hill. Miss Rigby must have
taught her to stop crying in public. Actually Withers had looked
quite cute and rather touching with the tears running down her
apple-fresh face. Rigby had often had to lend her a handkerchief. Withers had been born without a handkerchief.

Rigby turned his back determinedly on Miss West. She was
with a man, and Rigby didn't want to intrude. She seemed to
be enjoying an animated conversation with him. The man
laughed like a neighing horse. Rigby was surprised. Betty had

never been particularly witty. And he felt no desire to talk to her. She had behaved miserably. Or did she think Anne had withdrawn because of her? On his birthday, of course, it was she and not Anne who had spent hours with him.

"Alex!"

Rigby turned around. Miss West murmured introductions. The man with her was a journalist from Queensland. His name was Frank Grierson. He had taken a trip from Brisbane to New South Wales, and had naturally ended up in Sydney, like everybody else.

Rigby surveyed Betty's new man with shameless interest. The ash-blond gentleman could be forty. He wore glasses. Naturally. Glasses made one appear intelligent. He looked at Rigby amiably out of his light-blue eyes. To do this he had to raise his head. With his arrogantly hooked nose and wrinkled forehead, Rigby looked pretty formidable, but the gentleman from Brisbane seemed incurably friendly. He had a neutral, bookish face, but his movements were lithe and free. He was probably a good swimmer when he took off his owlish glasses, but then, every Queenslander swam like a fish. Rigby could find nothing exceptional about the fellow.

"Shall we have tea together?" asked Miss West. She sounded embarrassed. Rigby noticed it and wondered why. She could go out with whomever she pleased; fortunately, she was not married to him. Her question hovered in the air like a ball that didn't want to drop back on the pavement. When he found it fun, Rigby was a master of the embarrassed pause.

"Frank is thirsty," Miss West said, sharply now.

Rigby looked down his arrogant nose at his watch. "Sorry, my dear," he said amiably. "I have a pressing appointment."

Miss West reddened with vexation. Rigby had quite obviously been strolling along George Street. He had all the time in the world.

Mr. Grierson shifted from one foot to the other. Miss West had funny acquaintances. At this very moment Mr. Grierson took an instant dislike to this very tall, elegant man with the restless eyes and the cruel mouth. The man looked dangerous.

Didn't Miss West notice it? To sum up people correctly was his business. Mr. Grierson would have liked to protect little Miss West from this man, but he didn't know how.

"Have you been in Sydney long?" Rigby asked the younger man.

Frank Grierson had been in this turbulent city for fourteen days. Rigby hadn't heard from Betty in fourteen days, nor had he seen anything of her. Not that he had missed her. Paddy Trent had been very good about seeing to it that he wasn't alone too much. John Darling was too intensively married now, and the former Miss Eastman got on Rigby's nerves. Trent always had time for a beer or fun of some kind, but right now Rigby didn't want to hear any of Trent's jokes, and had told him so. Paddy never took offense. He had only mumbled guiltily that all he'd wanted to do was cheer Rigby up a little. "Are you crazy?" Rigby exclaimed. "I'm in a terrific mood. Any camel could see that!"

Perhaps any camel would have seen it but it had escaped Paddy Trent.

"How do you like Sydney, Mr. Grierson?"

"Rather chaotic. Such disconcerting contrasts. And too much painterly dirt in the older sections for my taste."

"That's possible," Rigby sounded more aloof than ever. "For us it's good enough."

"Oh, Sydney is wonderful, of course!" the gentleman from Brisbane hastened to say. The people here were ridiculously sensitive. They couldn't take the slightest criticism of their imposing but disorderly city. "The new buildings are fantastic."

Rigby raised his eyebrows. Miss West would have liked to slap his face, but for that she'd have needed a footstool.

"The high-rise houses have nothing whatsoever to do with fantasy," Rigby said gently. "Every measurement is exact. Only people are fantastic, don't you think?"

"Hm," said Mr. Grierson. He sounded and looked uncomfortable.

"We must go," snapped Miss West. "We have a pressing appointment."

"Don't bite my head off!" Rigby gave Miss West an enig-matic look. "We're all friends here. So have a good time, Mr. Grierson. Are you going to write a book about Sydney?"

"I'm reporting for the radio."

"Then you're lucky," said Rigby. "A talk is not a piece of writing. I'll hope you'll do honorably by us on the air."

"I'll do my best."

"Very good, Mr. Grierson. I'd like to talk on the radio too. Small mistakes are never noticed."

"I collect my material as conscientiously as possible," Mr. Grierson said stiffly.

"That's rather difficult in a chaotic city like Sydney," Rigby said gently. He looked at his watch again, a present from Elizabeth West. "When do we meet again, little one?"

"Not right now. I'm going to Brisbane with Frank."

"How come I don't know anything about it?"

"Is this a police interrogation?" asked Betty West. Frank Grierson listened to the dialogue, his face expressionless.

"Miss West is part of our inventory," Rigby explained. "We look after her because she's still so little."

"Don't be foolish, Alexander!" Miss West was furious. What would her colleague think?

"What are you going to do in Brisbane?" asked Rigby.

"I'm going on the air."

"Reading your own works?"

"Naturally," said Miss West. "Just imagine, there are still people around who haven't read my books."

"I envy them," said Rigby. "I mean, I envy them the pleasure of getting to know your work. Bon voyage! Don't get stuck there."

Rigby nodded to both of them and walked off into the traffic. "Who on earth was *that*?" asked Grierson. He hadn't caught the name when Betty had introduced him. "Tell me, Betty, when do I finally meet the famous architect, Rigby? They told me at home that an interview with him was an absolute must in Sydney."

"He just interviewed you," said Betty West.

* * *

Rigby drove straight to the Hungarian restaurant. He'd had enough of women for today and decided to leave his jewel in Vaucluse to her own resources. Somehow they had settled down to their own mode of conversation again since the second Mrs. Rigby had left the arena—that is, Andrews talked and Rigby pretended not to listen. When enjoyed at cautious intervals, Andrews's conversation wasn't as dumb as might have been expected. Just the same, Rigby was cautious.

Restaurant Szabo in King's Cross was pretty empty. It was early evening. Szabo's place was one of those small cellar restaurants which gave King's Cross an international ambience in the eyes of European immigrants. Besides the food, such places also offered the conversation and sometimes the music of the homeland. Rigby enjoyed the informal atmosphere. He liked to talk to Mr. and Mrs. Szabo, who with their harsh English and melting sentimentality, lived on the periphery of an alien Australian world. They had never penetrated outside this international zone of King's Cross. They served their own countrymen and the old Australians with the same zeal, and with the same interest in the personal affairs of their guests. They were burning to fathom the private lives of the Australians even more than those of their compatriots, but in this they were not successful. The Aussies were stubbornly silent when it came to their private sphere. They didn't even seem interested in their own business. If Andrews hadn't occasionally come out with some of the details of the Rigbys' married life, Mr. and Mrs. Szabo might just as well have been waiting on the Sphinx. Naturally they never mentioned the untimely demise of his wife in front of Rigby—for that they were too tactful, also too businesslike. In the many years they had spent in Sydney, they had had ample opportunity to study the reactions of the Aussies, who hated personal questions, whereas their Hungarian guests would have left the restaurant deeply hurt if Mr. Szabo hadn't questioned them about their ailments, business, mothers-in-law, vexations, amusements, and grandchildren.

There was usually little to tell about the grandchildren. The older generation rarely saw these young people. They had become Aussies. They were startled when their parents spoke Hungarian. They changed their names, frequently married Australians, and never came to the Restaurant Szabo. They weren't sure enough of themselves yet. They chatted among each other about racing, politics, newspaper articles, farming, films, about everything that contributed to their upbringing on this continent. Mr. Szabo nodded wisely when his old steady guests complained. Nothing to be done about it! After all, old Mrs. Varady could try to get accustomed to her Australian daughter-in-law. But Mrs. Varady shrugged in her inimitable way. She had nothing against dear Helen, but the paprika was missing. Mr. Szabo nodded again. The daughter of his friend, Ferenc Kuncz—Frances Connor for years now—had married the owner of a sheep station in Queensland. She had given up the violin, and visited her father in Sydney once in a blue moon. With the son-in-law the paprika was missing too. Nothing to be done about it! Curious people. The son-in-law didn't think much of his wife's father either. He told his best cobber confidentially that old Connor was a cranky old bastard, whereupon the two gentlemen drank a few more beers to which they treated each other with gales of laughter; then they spoke about more important things: sheep, and the price of wool. Mr. Connor had visited his disloyal daughter in Queensland once, but never again! Mr. Szabo had had to cook chicken in tokay sauce for him when he got back, he had returned so indignant. His son-in-law had treated him with a total lack of respect for his age, nor had he listened to Mr. Kuncz's opinion of Australia. Mr. Kuncz had tried in vain to start a really loud quarrel with his son-in-law, hoping for a touching reconciliation, but the Aussies would rather die than quarrel with him. Even his daughter had said, "Do be quiet, Father. I'm happy here. It's the best country in the world."

Mr. Szabo cooked, and calmed down old and new immigrants. It wasn't a bad country. Fair enough. Whoever wanted to work made headway here. That the Aussies didn't inquire

about the health and the children of Mr. and Mrs. Szabo was
something the couple had become accustomed to long ago. In
a city like Sydney, you couldn't expect personal interest. And
one should not try to be different from the rest. At home
everybody wanted to be a genius, or at least for the children
to have a better life than any other children, but that was
frowned upon in Australia. Other countries, other customs.
There was only one thing Mr. Szabo had never been able to
grasp: the way the old Aussies insulted each other amicably,
how they swore, and how rarely they turned around to look at
a pretty girl. Was the paprika missing in their love life too?
Mr. Szabo had bigger worries.

Rigby, however, liked to look at a pretty girl occasionally,
despite the fact that he was a true-blue Australian. And his
married life seemed almost as turbulent as in the best families
in Mr. Szabo's homeland before the Communists had come.
Rigby's jewel was not exactly discreet. And if she could make
her stories a little more spicy, she dramatized shamelessly. The
Szabos got the impression that Rigby beat his second wife
regularly. No wonder the poor woman had fled back to England. Mr. Szabo found Mr. Rigby very nice, just a trifle brutal,
and unapproachable like all the Aussies.

Rigby had his table in a far corner of the restaurant from
which he could observe everything without being seen. Mr.
Szabo always waited on him himself with special care. He had
read in the paper what a famous regular he had in Rigby. And
Rigby was generous. He gave terrific tips when something
tasted especially good. A Magyar nobleman in old Hungary
couldn't have been more generous. But Rigby didn't hurl his
plate against the wall when he wasn't pleased with the food.
Other countries, other customs!

Rigby was just discussing the menu with Mr. Szabo when
he caught sight of Candy. It was his lucky day, apparently: all
the women he knew were off with other men. Candy was
accompanied by the man with whom she had been walking on
the beach in Manly. He reminded Rigby of a greedy shark.
Rigby missed the gold necklace he had given Candy. She al-

ways wore it. In all probability the shark had managed to get the necklace from Candy.

What Rigby was eating almost stuck in his throat when another well-known lady walked into the restaurant, accompanied by a Hungarian. This was the bloody end! Klari Trent, the Hungarian wife of his good cobber, was talking now in a dimly lit corner in her incomprehensible mother tongue! She couldn't see Rigby, so she didn't exercise any self-control. Her decolleté was just as low as it had been at Rigby's party. The sight of Klari Trent was nothing to complain about, but the devil take her! Naturally Rigby wouldn't tell his friend Trent anything about this meeting. The poor fellow was often away on business in the evenings, and here his wife was two-timing him right under Rigby's very nose. Paddy deserved better. That was the trouble with these foreigners; as if there weren't plenty of girls that were good to look at in a city like Sydney!

Rigby paid and left. Candy had eyes for no one but the young Italian. Klari Trent's eyes were closed. Probably all for the best.

Rigby drove back to Vaucluse in a foul mood. His house was deathly still. Life was being played out elsewhere, in the many small suburban villas Rigby had always felt were so boring. Where man and wife stuck to each other and brought up their children together and worked at their marriage. Where everyday life passed uneventfully, and the husband worked in the garden on weekends and washed the car. The wife had her midmorning coffee break with her friends, she cooked plain food, she loved her husband docilely, and before you knew it you were old and sat contentedly on your little veranda, while in the city the high-rise houses grew into the sky. But here, Rigby enjoyed the harbor panorama of Vaucluse in lonely glory, and Patrick Trent looked for his new wife in his new house. Anyway, that was how Rigby saw it. Why had Paddy married again? To sit alone in his big new glass palace?

Although he was no longer in the prime of life, Patrick Trent had married a second time for a very specific reason. But only he knew the reason...

12

A Man in His Second Prime

The first Trent had emigrated to Queensland from his starvation district in Ireland in 1867, eight years after the political separation from the mother state of New South Wales. In the new colony, Shawn Benedict Trent became a gold prospector, and experienced the whole adventurous gamut from the gold rush to the bitter awakening in the bush. He had two invaluable characteristics for a pioneer: he accepted conditions on the fifth continent as they were, and he could stand aside and see himself as he was and laugh at his misfortune. His disappointments in the new colony were bitter, but not important. Only one thing meant anything to him: the welfare of his soul. He had to live in harmony with God. Not that Shawn ever said so, or thought consciously along these lines, but he felt he would be insulting his Creator if, like most of the prospectors with no gold, he felt sorry for himself or cursed the new land. The first Trent had brought one treasure with him from his homeland: the energy of faith. In Queensland in those days, he needed every ounce of it. The country was not yet the "sunshine land of tourists" nor the "tropical wonderland" of today's travel brochures. All Trent experienced was the merciless miracle of the sun, and the perilous bush. The thousand miles of elegant beaches on the Pacific, the exploratory trips to the Great Barrier Reef arranged by the government, and the El Dorado of the rich were events that took place a hundred years after the first Trent's appearance in Queensland.

In 1867 they found gold in Gympie, on the shores of the Mary River, a hundred and twenty-three miles north of Brisbane. Shawn Trent became one of the thousands who looked for the mythical treasure in Queensland, New South Wales, and South Australia. Whenever Shawn thought he had reached his goal, a stubborn, unpretentious Chinese beat him to it. The Chinese took the search for gold more seriously than anything else life had to offer. They had identified happiness with riches for thousands of years. In this respect too they came from another part of the universe. Shawn had choked a Chinese man because the latter had tried to jump him when he had seen a gleam of the metal. Shawn was incredibly strong. The dainty little Chinese had looked like a pesky fly to him. But Mr. Li had not joined his ancestors. He had quickly played dead in order to remain alive. Next morning, when Mr. Li walked out of one of the Chinese tents, very much alive and smiling, Trent was so happy that he gave the little man the only lump of gold he ever found in Gympie. Of course Mr. Li despised the Irish giant for his naiveté, but he hastily pocketed the gold. Soon after that he opened a shop in Gympie, where he sold produce, tools for prospectors, and a Chinese miracle medicine at steep prices. In his own eyes, Mr. Li was the most successful gold prospector on the Mary River.

In the first year, Gympie produced eighty-five thousand ounces of gold, which saved the economy of the land after the big depression. Shawn's offspring in Queensland saw nothing more of the gold rush. When Patrick Trent was born in Brisbane, shortly before the First World War, there was already a modern dairy industry in Gympie, and the finest fruit in Queensland. Patrick Trent never visited the place where his ancestor had prospected in vain for gold. He had developed a distaste for the city that had made a fool of old Shawn. All the Trents were allergic to defeat, just as all of them loved music, and hid their love of God and humanity behind jokes. They had big hearts in which there was room for many things; for example, private disappointments which they tried to overcome silently and without anger. They felt compassion for every living creature, but hid this irritating Christian weakness behind ribaldry and anecdotes, roaring laughter, and the vain effort to be overlooked by everybody in general. The latter they might have spared themselves because they were a very striking family. To begin with, nobody could overlook their size and corpulence, and they betrayed their compassion with sidelong glances of their dark, Celtic eyes, a sudden lowering of the voice, and by a ceaseless running back and forth, which made whomever they were talking to nervous. The wives especially couldn't stand it. Moreover, the Trents had to be damned careful in the new land, because if there was one thing beside status differences and arrogance that the Aussies detested, it was the feeling that they were being pitied.

The first Trent had come to Australia in a sailing vessel, because in those early days the government of Queensland had offered each passenger two and a half pounds of bread or crackers, one pound of white flour, five pounds of oatmeal, two pounds of rice, and two ounces of tea, eight ounces of sugar, and eight ounces of syrup weekly. Shawn had never seen that much food on his isolated Irish farm. The food alone was worth a voyage to Queensland. It would have been worth a trip to the southern Australian desert! Every Trent could manage on what he found on the edge of an oasis, and what he didn't find, he invented.

The first Trent had been cook on the sailing ship for a short while because the hired cook had been unable to withstand the rigors of the trip. Trent's cooking was indifferent, but he spiced his improvised menus with jokes and words of encouragement. He had never cooked for so many people before. This pioneer in the ship's galley was a huge, childlike fellow who silently pitied the seasick boasters, who on their way over to the fifth continent were already planning to transform the new land into settlements of small Irish towns with churches and taverns. On the ship the Irish were more or less on their own, as they were to remain in their first decade in Australia. During the many months they spent at sea, they were homesick, with choral singing and a prodigious thirst.

The first gold had already been found in Queensland in 1851. The Chinese had also been faster as immigrants than Shawn

Benedict Trent. During the years to come, they peopled the continent so diligently that thirty years later the Australian government had to limit immigration. But even without the Chinese rivalry, Shawn wouldn't have found any more gold. It wasn't to be. At twenty-two he was too young to accept the judgment of fate without protest. He left the hovels of Gympie only to seek his fortune elsewhere. He had heard rumors of gold on the Walsh River, in the slimy sand of the Palmer Tributary.

Trent had only been in Gympie a few years, and left the place in good spirits, with a little money and his worn rosary in his pocket. He had taken on occasional jobs in Gympie, and now tried to get rid of his money as quickly as possible. Later he couldn't remember how long he had been on the road. Full of hope, he went the historical way of slow disillusionment in the northeastern section of the continent. But in these pioneer days, if a man wasn't stopped dead right away or didn't get lost in the deadly bush, he could be considered a success story. Australia had not yet fulfilled the wishful dreams of the middle class.

At last Shawn reached the Palmer Valley, in a blue shirt and torn pants, a cone-shaped straw hat on his head. He had taken almost as much time in his wanderings as Odysseus, but unlike the hero of that epic, he had not spent his time with giants, sirens, and king's daughters. He had done every kind of work, as one had to do on a new continent. He didn't want to starve before he found his gold in Palmer. Nobody sang the adventures of this Irish farmer in Australia; yet Trent, like thousands of immigrants, was an Odysseus who practically and heroically fought the monsters of thirst and hunger in the Australian wilderness.

The Palmer Valley brought thousands of Chinese and white prospectors their desired gold. In time it put the economy of Queensland on its feet. For a short while Cooktown was the paradise of adventurers, but for Shawn Benedict Trent it was a witches' cauldron. Everybody was suffering from incurable gold fever and fought with pickaxe, shovel, knives, and elbow grease for minute traces of gold in the sand of the damp, hot shore.

Two Irish friends had accompanied Trent from Gympie to the Palmer Valley. Like innumerable others, one of them was killed by an arrow of the wild blackfellows in the region. The other strayed too far away from the camp because he thought the big treasure would be in a lonelier spot. He got lost in the bush, and died of hunger and thirst. Shawn survived Palmer. Like all the others he shook his primitive sieve until the little gold kernels were washed clean, but his washed-out gold ran between his fingers in the dives and gambling dens of Cooktown. At first he swore all the Irish curses he could remember, then he prayed. He had sinned. He had sought earthly gold, although he knew that the true gold mines were not of this world. He had to shake his obdurate soul, not his sieve.

When, during sleepless nights, Shawn had finally recognized the truth, he was his old, jolly self again. He avoided the dives and gambling dens, and spent the rest of his money on a pair of cotton pants, food, and a horse. One morning, with his cobber, he left his Sodom of the fifth continent. His friend swore and cursed the murderous land; Shawn was silent. His friend from Dublin didn't know better. He had driven the saints out of his alcohol-besotted system. James Rowan was only forty-two, but he was as emaciated as a skeleton. The cruel sun had withered him. He reminded Shawn of a dying fig tree. Yes, Rowan had come to the end of the line. In Dublin he had been a prosperous businessman, but he had wanted to get rich quick and had forged checks. Queensland had promised him a new life and a new freedom, but the promises weren't worth any more than his forged checks. Palmer and rum had made a fool of him and sucked the marrow from his bones.

Sad and frightened, Shawn listened to the wild curses of his dying compatriot. He tried to conjure up the refreshing spring breezes of belief for his friend, but he was after all neither a preacher nor a prophet, and it was too hot to talk anyway. Even the shadows of evening glowed like a smoldering fire. The words of comfort remained stuck in Trent's dry throat. All he could do was start to sing an Irish hymn for the dying, but with his last strength, cobber Rowan shouted for him to shut his dirty mouth. He died as night fell over their provisional tent. Trent gave him a bush burial. He himself was at the beginning of his long Australian wanderings, and the beginning was in the bush.

Shawn Benedict Trent now rode on with two horses and his provisions in his knapsack. Then he sold the horses and worked on a cattle ranch which had sprung up on bush land. At night he slept happily on a cowhide spread across four flat, wooden blocks. His room on the ranch was wretched. The door hung loose on its hinges and the mosquitoes pursued him in his sleep. But there were wooden huts in the bush with bark roofs that were even less comfortable and hadn't even a chair or table. Shawn hadn't brought any pretentious demands with him from Queensland.

Later he worked as a woodchopper in the endless forest, and hummed cheerfully to himself when the overseer handed out flour and tea. One might have thought he had been given a sack of gold. The overseer decided that Trent was a naive fellow because he was content, but Shawn was completely indifferent to what people thought of him. He had the gift of being able to read their thoughts from their expressions, and his feelings were never hurt. He felt sorry for mean people.

For a short while Shawn disappeared in the eucalyptus forests. He had preferred the rain forests. He hated the bare eucalyptus trunks with the raggedly hanging-down bark. He was no longer the same man who had sailed to Queensland with a fresh face and sensibilities. Sometimes he felt very tired. The sun had burnt his white skin brown long ago, and in spite of his gentle behavior, he looked like a real bush man with his wild dark hair and beard. But he wasn't one, at least not the kind of bush man later generations imagined. Life in the bush was not romantic; it was hard. In periods of drought even a hardy and religious man like Trent lost courage and hope. Then he felt he was living in a landscape of dust, and longed for lakes surrounded by mountains and the still green meadows of his homeland. The gray-green scrub and the thickets of the bush depressed him. What a country! He couldn't seem to get accustomed to the screeching of the bush birds and the noise of the cockatoos, and the shrill laughter of the kookaburras startled him. Later, Patrick Trent would inherit his ancestor's sensitive ears. In the younger man's lonely, lean years, as well as in his salad days with Rigby's mob, he suffered from the shrill voices of women and birds.

On the other hand, all the Trents loved the kangaroos and the wallabies in the bush, and were highly amused by their leaps and the fur-lined pouches for their young. And when the Trents were very depressed their moods could hop back and forth, up and down, like a wallaby. Then they looked at the flowers and shrubs, and their beauty almost made them happy. The first Trent in Queensland had already found pleasure in the flowers. Whenever the rain forests in the north became a dreary, damp hell, somewhere the spring mimosa would shine, or the bluish-pink Cooktown orchid, the purple sarsaparilla blossom, and the vanilla lily would quench their thirst for beauty. Shawn Benedict Trent was probably the only gold prospector in Queensland for whom the golden miracle of the mimosa bush made up for a lost dream.

When Shawn had had enough of his nomadic existence, he worked on a small farm near Brisbane. There he met Rosaleen O'Grady, the sweet, robust farmer's daughter. The good-natured young giant from her homeland took to her at once, and with that Trent's wanderings came to an end at "the end of the world," as their Irish immigrants called the fifth continent.

Shawn Benedict Trent, who had become a roaming tree among trees, built fences to protect the sheep from the dingoes. Now he had a young wife in his bed and she gave birth to children. The farm was poor. From the start it had been nothing more than a piece of semi-dry grassland that had to be watered doggedly and laboriously. Trees had had to be burnt to make room for a house and grass. O'Grady and his son-in-law, Trent, had none of the machines or chemicals that help today in the fight with the tough, dry earth. They fought incessantly against drought and sickness of man and beast. When drought made life unbearable, O'Grady and the Trents, with their few sheep and household goods, wandered on, and in another area again built a primitive home and fenced it in against the wild dogs. Shawn Benedict had stopped singing songs long ago; his throat was as dry as the grass around him. But he never lost his good humor nor his appetite, and he never cursed the dry land or his hard life. Sometimes he thought of his search for gold in the days of his youth, and smiled indulgently. He had had six children. Four had died on their wanderings. Shawn grieved for them deeply, for a short while. God had taken the children to the eternal meadowlands, where they now sang and danced around evergreen fir trees. He lived contentedly and died contentedly. He left his progeny his wanderlust, his fine voice, his enormous appetite, and the vision of treasures in the Australian earth.

In spite of his poverty, he had possessed a lot because nothing had ever possessed him. Shawn Benedict Trent would have been astonished if he could have seen how Patrick lived in Sydney. He would have been deeply troubled about him because in his own gold-prospecting days he had seen the dangers and bitterness riches could bring. Shawn would have pitied Patrick. But the veil of time fell between the first Trent in his desolate grassland, watered only by the sources of mercy, and the last Trent. Patrick was a successful real-estate agent. He owned a luxurious villa in Barmoral, and he was a thirsty beggar in the aridity of a materialistic world.

Tyrone B. Trent, Patrick's father, was the first member of the family to move into the city. He worked for a short time in a rum factory in Brisbane. Before that, at the age of twenty, he had moved herds of cattle from Queensland to New South Wales. Then he suddenly gave up the life of a stockman. Like all the Trents, Tyrone liked change.

In Brisbane, the city of many hills, Tyrone married young

Mary Gallagher, a redheaded bar girl. She was half a laughing Eve, half a young mother. In the rum factory, Tyrone had acquired a taste for the liquor that set him on fire. He went to the cheap bar every evening and sang Irish songs for Mary Gallagher until she married him.

Both thought the marriage would be the beginning of a mutual hominess. Mary did stay at home in Brisbane with the children, but after the birth of the seventh, Tyrone went walk-about. Perhaps the tropical city made him restless, but in all probability he'd brought the restlessness to Brisbane with him. From then on he was seldom home. Patrick's mother worked in a jam factory to clothe and feed her children. Tyrone some-times worked as a seasonal laborer in the bush land, and sent a pittance home. For two years he disappeared into the sugar cane fields of Queensland, and came back to Brisbane with a little money because he couldn't get along with the Italian workers. But the money was spent in beer halls and taverns.

The rich plantations on the Queensland coast fired Tyrone Trent's restless fantasies. Tropical Queensland was a state with exceptionally brilliant coloring. Trent thought in color and be-queathed this ability to his son, Patrick. Neither of them could paint on board or canvas; their pictures remained unfulfilled and unpainted in their souls.

Tyrone Trent returned again and again to his narrow, fetid home in Brisbane, only to flee eventually to the plantations without a worry in the world. One day he would bring Mary and the children to such a plantation. He loved his wife in his way, but his wild Irish soul recognized all or nothing. And in the factories of Brisbane, nothing was waiting for him.

When Tyrone was at home he described to his silent wife how happily they would all live one day on a plantation, in a great airy house on the coast, surrounded by palms and fig trees. Who would ever have had anything like it in Ireland? Bananas, pineapples and earthnuts needed no particular care in this climate, Tyrone explained to his weary, worried wife, because that was what had become of the merry bar girl. Mary was an anxious mother now, working in a factory where the fruits of the plantation were canned. Tyrone fantasized with shining eyes about his future plantation. Somewhere far away the ocean would greet them day and night, and the mountains would nod to them like old friends.

"Aren't you happy?" he asked his silent wife. But Mary's dreams were modest. They grew on the hard ground of reality; a piece of land of her own would have meant bliss to her. Tyrone and the boys would build a wooden house, and she would plant vegetables and a few fruit trees. And herbs too, of course—watercress, and if the little piece of land was cool enough, she would grow cabbage, lettuce, and onions. She knew how to protect them from mildew with ash. Before she had served drinks and jokes in Sydney, she had grown up on a farm in Ireland. Her greatest wish was never to see a can of produce again. That was *her* idea of happiness.

Mary Trent made the mistake of indicating her idea of happiness. Tyrone reddened with fury and ran out of the house, wild with rage. Mary, deafened by his shouts, remained behind with her children in the stuffy room she had rented from some Irish people. In return Mary helped in the kitchen, and after her work in the factory, did her landlady's laundry. Patrick Trent saw how his mother lived, and swore that one day, should he ever marry, his wife would have a better life.

One evening his father got into a devilish fight in his favorite tavern in Brisbane. They brought him to his wife and children with a heart wound. Patrick Trent would never forget that his mother didn't shed a tear. He was still too young to recognize the dry pain that mercilessly tears the soul to pieces like the bush-saw rips the skin.

"I'll always stay with you!" Patrick promised wildly, and his mother nodded submissively. She'd heard that once before. Patrick was fifteen when his father died. Sometimes he was afraid of his own strength. It was a good thing for the family that in the end his father had managed to provide for his own Christian burial, because the man who wounded him in the tavern had fallen in the broken glass and pools of beer, and hadn't got up again.

Patrick's only amusement in the days of his youth were the droll koala bears in the Lone Pine Koala Sanctuary on the Brisbane River. He earned his money for such pleasures by helping out in a bakery and delivering orders by bicycle to the villas and bungalows of the elegant suburbs. The owner hired the fatherless boy out of friendliness, because actually his delivery truck brought his goods quicker and more reliably to the suburbs that rose, like an amphitheater, on the hills above the blue river. But Jimmy Hamilton had been one of Tyrone Trent's cobbers. After Tyrone's death, he employed Patrick's mother too, with light work in the bakery. Factory work had become too hard for her. The climate bothered her, and her husband's death had taken a great deal out of her. But like many of the Irish, she had indestructible vitality.

On his trips to the paradise of the successful, Patrick acquired his first knowledge of the value of real estate. In his thoughts he promptly chose a villa for his mother. It was like the castle-in-the-air his father had built for merry Mary Gallagher. The future Sydney financier explained excitedly to his mother that he intended to make enough money to set her up one day in a fine villa, where from the wooded heights, she could spit down into the Brisbane River.

Mary Trent said, "Don't shout! I'm not deaf!" But she passed her hand across the dark, tousled hair of her oldest son. His old man had fantasized just like that.

One morning Patrick was gone. He had left to seek the treasures of the land. Mary Trent's lips tightened. Then she went to work. The men went walkabout.

When, as an old woman, Mary lived in her white villa and looked down on the Brisbane River, she sometimes pinched herself to make sure she wasn't dreaming. With the help of God, Paddy had succeeded. The crazy little fellow!

Trent never forgot how he led his speechless mother into her house and asked fearfully: "What's the matter, Mother? Don't you like it?"

Mary Trent received her portion of luck in her old age. The Brisbane River washed away the tears of her youth. Now *she* could go walkabout. She traveled in Queensland, tirelessly and wide-eyed as a child, and at last got to know the tourist "Land of the Sun." With Patrick she sailed in a white launch from Cairns to the Great Barrier Reef, and through the glass bottom of a boat was astonished by the coral gardens, the tropical fish, and the iridescent shells that Paddy had described to her as a young man. She had thought it was all nonsense, but she found the silent, undulating deep-sea life eerie, and longed to be back in her garden.

Shortly after this trip to the tropical north of Queensland, Patrick married a young girl from Sydney. His mother came once for a visit to get to know her daughter-in-law. When, years later, Patrick married his young Hungarian, his mother had gone to her eternal rest in the Blue Mountains. And that was all for the best . . .

Patrick Trent had given his mother the only joy in her life. This knowledge comforted him in his dreariness. In his search for the treasures of the earth, he had found opals, but he had never been able to unearth the treasures of married life. And that didn't change. Everything he was able to give his wives in the best years of his life, they could have done without, and what he was looking for in women at the age of fifty, he failed to find, just as Shawn Benedict Trent had failed to find gold in Queensland.

Like all the Trents, Patrick succeeded in the Australian way: he took the bull by the horns. After his disappearance from Brisbane, he became a cattle drover. An enterprising young man could find work like this everywhere. Patrick at twenty was still slim and lithe. He had the strength of an ox, and wasn't suffering yet from compassion for the frail human creature. He breathed free in the wide landscape. Naturally things were much easier for him than for Shawn. He wasn't a pioneer any more in cattle country. In his day there were already chemically fertilized fields, canalization against drought, and all sorts of remedies and preventatives for disease. The cattle provided the best export. There was still a struggle going on against the eucalyptus bushes beyond the canalized land, but the clearing of the forests proceeded more quickly and easily with the help of machines. The governments of the states also helped by permitting the cross-country migration of the cattle that were still endangered by poisonous plants and the lack of water. The cattle had changed too. The Australian cattle were first-rate now, and provided excellent meat for export.

Patrick and a second drover wore enormous felt hats, patched riding trousers, and worn, elastic-side boots. They drove the herds to market miles from the interior, and had to watch them day and night. They wandered off for months, all the way to the coast or to a railway station. They sang and whistled the herd ahead of them, because the human voice calmed the cattle.

After that Patrick Trent tried his luck for a while as a kangaroo hunter, but all the time he had the feeling that these were temporary jobs. Most of what he earned he sent to his mother and brothers and sisters in Brisbane. He felt guilty because he, the oldest, had abandoned them, but he had had to do so. He hunted kangaroos doggedly and boldly, because every stockman hated the characteristic Australian animal that ate everything away from the cattle and sheep in the interior. But Patrick remained restless, and felt that he had not yet achieved what he had set out to achieve—a life of ease for his mother.

Gold prospecting was a thing of the past, but there were opals. Patrick said farewell to the kangaroos. He asked his friend, an elderly hunter, if he wanted to come along on his search for opals. The cobber laughed at him. Only a fool dug for gems! That was just as dumb as digging for gold! He knew all the Australian stories about gold prospecting, and served them up to Patrick. But Patrick had heard that the earth in South Australia and New South Wales was rich in exceptionally pure opals. He registered officially as an opal miner, and trembling with excitement read the *Guide to Mining Laws* in New South Wales. He found out that he had to report his findings to the mine overseer within fourteen days.

He had never been in a mine before, and had imagined it would be cool. But he experienced the hardest apprenticeship of his life. He wrote to his mother that he couldn't send any money for a while because at this point he had nothing but debts, but the opals would eventually make him rich. Mary Trent wept dry tears as she read the letter, then she tore it into little pieces and went off wearily to the bakery.

One day Trent found black opals. He knew the find might be a fluke, but he stayed in Lightning Ridge. He found more opals, light and blue-green, but the black gems formed the basis of his fortune. He bought his mother the white villa on the Brisbane River, financed his brother's career, married off his oldest sister, and paid for the younger one's medical studies. Then he became a real-estate agent and learned all the tricks of his trade in an old, reputable firm in Sydney. Later he bought a partnership in the firm. The new sign read: Coleman, Trent & Company. Daniel Coleman, his senior partner, was a tough businessman and a soft father.

At the inaugural banquet in the house of his partner, Patrick Trent met two people who were to smile on his life: Celia Coleman, the beautiful red-haired daughter of his senior partner, and Alexander Rigby from Parramatta, who had learned the architect's profession under Stanley Marchmont in George Street. On this occasion he also met Flora Rigby, at first taking her to be the architect's mother. Then he happened to hear Alexander Rigby call the lady "Auntie." To his astonishment it turned out that the heavily rouged woman with the stiff little curls, wearing glasses and a flower-printed dress, and laughing all the time, was the wife of the young man. Trent didn't know whom to pity more—the witty, adroit and extremely pleasant Alexander Rigby, or "Auntie," who was making such desperate efforts to appear young. Flora's broad, barmaid humor was not particularly noticeable that evening.

Daniel Coleman was a puritan with thin, compressed lips and sharp eyes. He drank milk; stomach trouble prevented him from drinking anything stronger. He ate oatmeal while his guests fared considerably better, and he ignored Flora Rigby as much as was politely possible. His daughter Celia was obviously in love with Rigby. Coleman would have welcomed

Rigby as a son-in-law in every respect, because he knew who the Rigbys were. He also knew who Flora Pratt was. He hadn't drunk milk all his life! He liked Patrick Trent, but would have preferred Rigby for his son-in-law.

Rigby and Trent quickly became friends, and Rigby showed Trent the consideration he evidently could express only to his cobbers. Trent suffered from his lack of general education and all his life felt a childish respect for those who had gone to a university. That was why he looked at Rigby's big library with awe. Rigby not only loaned his friend the right books, but recommended evening courses, and with astonishing patience discussed things with Trent. He could sense the spiritual strength in this highly talented, modest, and merry Irishman. You could steal horses with Trent! He soon became a member of Rigby's mob.

Shortly before Flora's tragic end, Trent asked his friend Rigby how he liked Celia Coleman. He wanted to marry her; her red hair reminded him of his mother. That was the only respect in which Celia Coleman was like Mary Trent. Rigby hesitated. Finally he said, "She looks like an angel."

But Trent wanted to know more. "Would you marry her, Alex?"

"No idea. I *am* married."

Trent was silent. After a while he said, "I think she's moody."

"All women are moody," said Rigby. "You should be married to my Flora!"

A few months after this conversation, Rigby suddenly began to sing Celia Coleman's praises. "She's really a nice prawn. You could do worse, Paddy."

"I don't think she cares a fig about me."

"Leave that to her. She likes you, you idiot! And what's more . . ." Rigby stopped abruptly. "Watch it! Here comes Auntie!"

After the wedding, Trent's father-in-law retired, and Patrick became top man in the firm. He had the real-estate business at his fingertips in no time. His friendship with Rigby helped too. But above all, Sydney was the right place for a man in the prime of life. There was still so much room for houses. There were thousands wanting to exchange a small house for a larger one, or one suburb for another. New department stores, supermarkets, movie houses, schools, hospitals, were being built constantly, pushing the bush of New South Wales farther back. Trent speculated cleverly and was lucky, because luck was just as much a part of success as was the manure in the earth of a flower garden. Every plan for a new center brought contracts for Trent's and Rigby's firms. Mr. Coleman congratulated himself on his son-in-law. He was a much more reliable fellow than Rigby, a solid fellow, as solid as the public library on Macquarie Street where Trent spent so much of his time. Coleman, ever the thoughtful father, was furious because his daughter, Celia, was evidently not as happy as Trent and Mr. Coleman.

When Celia had a miscarriage, Patrick Trent was in despair. It was one of those occasions when he had to test his faith and pray to God for mercy. It would have been a son, and, as was later ascertained, Celia could have no more children. She never shed a tear throughout the entire tragedy, but it left her moodier than ever. Trent couldn't do anything right anymore. If she ever *had* loved him, then her love was certainly not the kind that united two people. It only exposed their incompatibility. Trent didn't blame his wife for the wreckage of their marriage. Their estrangement was not a cause for guilt, and anyway, he always blamed himself for everything first. He felt sorry for this hectic, coquettish little woman who had married him so thoughtlessly.

Celia only became lively when Rigby appeared on the scene. Trent could understand this. Rigby was so attractive, while Trent was putting on weight and finding his marital duties a burden. He simply didn't want intercourse with a woman who had remained a stranger. He slept in a room of his own, and this seemed to suit his wife. Trent felt liberated . . . he was healthy and still in his best years, but he needed a deep, spiritual union in order to give or receive satisfaction. After the tragedy he became taciturn, and three years later, when he withdrew into a room of his own, he was a stranger in the beautiful new house that Rigby had designed.

The new house kept Celia busy, and she had all sort of plans which she often had to discuss with Rigby. It was just around this time that Flora Rigby died. Trent had never seen such a composed widower. One could almost have said he was cheerful, if the scandal hadn't fallen hard on the heels of Flora's death. Trent found the suspicion that Alex had murdered his wife outrageous and ridiculous. Why should he have done anything like that? True, Flora had transformed Rigby's house into a quasi-tavern, but Rigby had evidently had nothing to say against it. One had only seen him laughing and joking with Auntie. He wasn't even embarrassed when Flora was high and became tactless. She came from a world where one word led to the next, and nobody thought before they spoke, as she sometimes told her husband. She swam in her money like a fat, asthmatic fish. Trent didn't trust Flora Pratt; he didn't know why. And she hated him. Patrick was the only member of Rigby's mob whom she never invited to their festivities. The dislike was mutual, and was evident at their first meeting at old Mr. Coleman's. She sensed Trent's distrust, and it made her unsure. Shortly before her death, Patrick Trent paid the first Mrs. Rigby an unexpected visit. The visit ended in a hysterical fit of rage on Flora's part. She stood on the terrace and screamed unqualified obscenities after him as he left. He was speechless. How could Alex have married such a fury?

Rigby seemed never to have found out about Trent's visit. He was as friendly as ever when they met again, only perhaps a little too jovial. Now Trent forgave him for his nightly escapades. Who could stand being with such a woman? Still, in spite of everything, Trent was convinced even after Flora's death that Rigby had had nothing to do with it. After all, a man couldn't be cheerful, alert, and capable for years if his wife was slowly driving him crazy. Or could he?

After Flora's death, Rigby was suddenly isolated. When John Darling and Stanley Marchmont weren't sitting on his terrace with him, Rigby sat with Celia and Paddy on theirs. The new house was finished and Celia and Rigby were as inseparable now as they had been when Trent, with his opals and the lonely aura of the bush, had turned up in Sydney.

Once Trent came home early from the office and found Celia in tears, her arms flung around Rigby's neck. "She got the house number mixed up, Paddy," he murmured, pushing Celia away gently. "She's weeping her eyes out because of me. Quite unnecessarily. I like being alone."

Celia ran out of the room. Trent watched her go, shaking his head. "Are you grieving at all for your wife?" he asked abruptly. Normally he would never have asked such a question, but the sight of his wife in tears had upset him. She never showed *him* any compassion.

Rigby was evidently thinking the question over carefully. Was he mourning his wife sufficiently? Then he said gently, "Any more questions?"

Trent stared at him. Rigby had always been a good friend, even if he had talked him into the marriage with Celia Coleman. Trent recognized the fact that Rigby had wanted to get rid of Celia because Flora was constantly making jealous scenes. Every married man wants peace and quiet. Trent realized this. But Rigby seemed to be composed of so many different personalities, Trent couldn't make him out. Then again, wasn't every person a prisoner of his past, his dreams, his impulses, and his spiritual unrest? Sometimes Trent got the impression that Alex was in a torturous state of uncertainty or stubborn despair.

"Of course I miss the old lady," Rigby murmured. "Do you think I'm a monster, Paddy? I mean . . . after all, I was used to her. I never thought that we were really suited to each other, but not because of her age. That's nonsense!"

"Cigarette, Alex?"

Rigby smoked hastily. "What do you think of the land in Kempsey? Were you there again?"

So they talked about the land in Kempsey. The fine view across the Macleay River. Trent wanted to have another look at it. It was pleasant to talk about houses and property. Then one had firm ground under one's feet.

At the time both of them had been in the prime of life. Afterwards, when he thought about it, Trent decided that those had been the most difficult years. They had taught him to endure a spiritual loneliness, and make it bear fruit. After Celia's death he wasn't lonelier, only more forlorn. His empty house filled up with books, pictures, visitors, music—with everything a man can cram into a big house. But it remained empty. For years...

When he began to suffer because of the emptiness, he married Klari Karasz. He was about fifty then. He felt sorry for Klari because she was homeless, but she filled the house with such unrest that he recalled the former emptiness with nostalgia. By now he had become very heavy, and there was fat around his heart. A deep crease had dug its way between his dark brows. He was an authority in his field, and his cobbers loved him. He laughed and joked with them as he had always done, only his eyes seemed to have grown darker and sunken, as if they were trying to look inward. Sometimes he was as absent-minded as an old man. Had his youthful wanderings made him so tired?

The opals had lost their sheen long ago, but he apparently still had a share in a prestigious jewelry shop on Castlereagh Street, and occasionally financed the search for opals in New South Wales. Personally he was not in the least interested in mining opals himself. And it would have been senseless, because he had more than he needed. Even more than a young wife needed, and that was saying something! But sometimes, for memory's sake, Trent visited a narrow little house in Darlinghurst, where an old opal expert cut the stones and prepared them for the jeweler. In his youth Jerry Stevens had also mined opals, but then he had learned the difficult art of cutting a fine opal without destroying it. Lately mass production operations had penetrated the processing of opals, but there were still a few opal cutters who had learned their trade from father or grandfather, and they loved the noble gem just as they received it. The high polish and the cold sheen of the ready-to-sell stone meant nothing to them. They clung to the lump that had come to them straight from the mine, and gave it shape. The opals brought their legend with them:

> October's child is born for woe,
> And life's vicissitudes must know.
> But lay an opal on her breast,
> And hope will lull those fears to rest.

Trent's first wife had been born in October. On their wedding night he had laid a black opal on her breast and murmured the verse like a spell. Celia Coleman had found this funny. There was nothing wrong with her. She had just won two prizes in water-skiing.

One day Trent found the black opal on the floor under Celia's vanity table. He picked it up and looked at it. A red sheen gave the valuable stone a gloomy fire. Trent locked the opal away. His wife hadn't even noticed that she had lost it. That had been years ago...

Once, when Trent was visiting the old opal cutter in Darlinghurst and was admiring an especially clear, transparent opal, a beautiful girl appeared in the workshop. "Hi, Gramp!" Candy said, in her coarse Western Australian voice. Trent looked up. Where had he seen this girl before?

"Sit down and don't bother us," old Stevens said pleasantly. "If you want tea, you know where it is."

When Candy Blyth brought in the tea, Trent knew where he had seen her before—pictured in *Insight*. His second wife cut out the fashion photos, and had dyed her hair blond to look like Candy. Klari Trent didn't want to look like Klari Trent and certainly not like the former Miss Karasz. It was a sickness of the times. Film stars and models created the ideal images of the sixties...

Candy Blyth was a neighbor of the opal cutter's. Like Candy and Trent, he was a compatriot of Mama Doody's. All their ancestors had emigrated to Australia from Ireland. And now here they were in Sydney.

That was how Trent got to know the idol of the magazines. By now he was an ascetic in a solid flesh shell, and had drawn the curtain on such fun long ago. So he didn't write to Candy Blyth in order to enjoy bed for appropriate payment. He asked to visit her on Mondays for quite different reasons. In his prophetic compassion he could see the day coming when Candy's flesh could grow sere and her beauty fade. And what would she be then? A straw-haired old fool, boring the whole world with her withered blossoming. Then he would have to love her. It would be fatal and ridiculous and the end of him. Because Trent believed that even the emptiest marriage was a covenant binding a man and a woman irrevocably. He had never deceived Celia or Klari in the conventional sense. It was not their fault that they had remained strangers. He rarely performed his marital duties, but he had chosen to marry this young Hungarian, and that was that!

But Trent's vision of salvation left him no peace. He tried to arm the beautiful model against the ravages of time. Perhaps he wouldn't live much longer . . . then who would look after this sweet little fool? He sat with her patiently in the small eateries in King's Cross and tried to prepare her for the second-best years of her life. But Candy was so young and so satisfied with her way of life that Trent might as well have been praying in the Australian desert. Anyway, he opened a bank account for her. In ten or fifteen years she'd need every penny of it, the poor thing. It was sad to know beauty only as a triumph of youth and cosmetics. And did all pretty girls talk such nonsense?

Rigby had no idea that Trent was giving Miss Blyth instruction every Monday. He would have laughed himself silly if he had. And it really was silly. Candy had no idea what her sugar daddy was talking about, but she was grateful to him. She knew the meaning of poverty from her childhood in Kalgoorlie. In her ignorance she was surprised that such an eccentric fellow could make so much money. Candy would have liked to do him the only favor she knew how to bestow on men. But Trent insisted on talking about incomprehensible things, was ever so nice and sometimes even jolly. But when Candy laughed loudly over one of his jokes, he put his big, workworn hand over her mouth. He couldn't stand loud laughter.

"Did he? Finally?" Mama Doody asked from time to time. But Candy always shook her head.

Mama Doody gave this some thought. "Maybe he's too fat." In her time she had once had a fat one, but he had been first-rate. Nobody could expect Mrs. Doody to have any ideas on the psychology of the sexes. Either it worked, or the fellow was impotent. That a client *could* but didn't want to was un-imaginable. "What is he paying all that money for?" she asked, baffled.

"No idea!" Candy frowned. "I find him rather funny too. Actually I feel sorry for him."

"What's this country coming to when men in the prime of life . . . My steak!" she screamed. "Is he coming today?" she asked, as she ran into the kitchen.

Of course he was coming today. It was Monday. Candy found her aunt funny. Her benefactor was *not* in the prime of life. Besides, she respected him like a father.

When Mr. Trent turned up at Mama Doody's boardinghouse, Miss Blyth had gone out. That had never happened before. Silently he read the note Molly Fleet had handed to him without saying a word. She studied his face with consuming curiosity. Trent pretended not to notice. Silly young creature! She should be happy that men left her in peace.

Candy's handwriting hopped all over the paper like a wallaby. *What* had happened? Molly couldn't enlighten him. Her beautiful red-blond hair fell artfully across her face. Why didn't this friendly gentlemen go out with *her*? It was, after all, his Monday? She would sit quietly beside him and let him talk. But Candy's friend left hastily. Molly always stayed behind, alone. She had no one to amuse her in the evenings but herself, and that wasn't enough. Or she watched the colorful lights in King's Cross, which never burned for her. They shone only for the big sharks and their dollars. Of course Molly Fleet knew why Candy had run away. She knew all about Candy, and hated her more every day.

13

Sharks and Dolls

Candy had always used her beauty as a tool: hammer, arrow, sword or hypodermic needle. Only with Charles Preston, whom in tender moments she called "Carlo," which annoyed him, did these weapons fail her. She was crazy about him. Despite her many affairs, her senses had slumbered until now. Perhaps that was why her effect on most men had been that of a picture. She was no more than a fabricated idol, cleverly manipulated, romantically photographed, and framed in artificial taboos. Yet only Charles remained unimpressed. He knew that this dream girl of the magazines brushed her teeth like everybody else, had to use deodorant, and had corns from wearing narrow shoes with too-high heels. For him the idol was a sheila like any other. His feelings for Candy were not deep. She had realized this long ago. What he really found wonderful was her money. But she didn't earn it quite as easily as he thought. It only looked that way.

She was not as naive as she pretended to be. She had no book wisdom, but life had taught her a thing or two: how one could get as much as possible out of a man with the least exertion. Or that a steak on one's plate was more important than a castle in the air. With Trent, Candy played the helpless child because she had noticed right away that this was the way to hold him. But one thing was clear to Trent: all Candy's thoughts were concentrated on her beauty. This was to be expected from a model, but in his wanderings in the bush, Trent had never come across such a specimen. She loved the life of ease. Her greatest fear was not God's anger, but any gain of weight. Candy made heroic efforts not to eat sweets. Trent's soliloquies were agony for her because for the life of her she couldn't grasp what he was talking about, and lately his voice sounded like the muted, dismal cry of the dugong. Candy had tasted and enjoyed this unique aquatic mammal with the pearl fishers in Broome. Prepared as they did it, dugong tasted like steak with bacon. In those days she hadn't been worrying about her weight. But when Candy told her benefactor about roast dugong, he had explained that the creature had nothing to do with food but was a singing mermaid, half-fish, half-girl. Odysseus had met her on his travels. Candy, irritated, asked, "And who is Odysseus?"

Lately she had rarely been able to make her corpulent guardian angel laugh. What was wrong with him? Candy looked surreptitiously at the deep groove between his brows. He wanted to send her, grown-up as she was, back to school. He declared that there were teachers in Sydney who could make her rough western Australian voice sound more pleasing. Apparently, like the dugong, she was expected to sing for her sugar daddy. She stared at Trent, her mouth open wide. What was wrong with her voice? Anyway, it didn't get photographed. Candy smoked sullenly. She felt insulted. Trent took the cigarette away from her. Smoking would make her voice even rougher. Candy shrugged. Why didn't he go to bed with her? Her voice wouldn't bother him then.

She asked the traveling salesman, Albert Ritter, if her voice bothered him. Rigby laughed uproariously. He didn't visit this beautiful call girl to hear her sing arias. But when he sensed Candy's feelings of insecurity, he said there were louder and rougher voices—the cockatoos in the bush, for instance. Ritter-Rigby was no consoler at a sickbed. Sometimes Candy envied the girl from Parramatta. Molly didn't have to be annoyed or bored by men. What was more, she was raising her price for writing Candy's love letters to Ritter. Which brought Candy's thoughts back to Molly Fleet again.

She was annoyed about having to leave Trent in the lurch today. Even more annoying was the fact that Molly knew why, because she had had to give her the note for Trent. Mama Doody was always visiting a neighbor when she was needed.

"Where are you going?" Molly Fleet had stared at Candy scornfully.

"To meet somebody."

"Don't be an idiot!" Molly Fleet said, her voice sharp. She had given up speaking to Candy in honeyed tones, and was no longer humble, nor was she so eager to be of service. "As if I didn't know whom you're meeting!" Molly's laugh was disagreeable. She had found out about Candy and Carlo Pressolini long ago. What did they think she was? A hollow nut? That Molly Fleet now didn't have a man to go out with anymore didn't improve her spirits. Carlo hadn't called again. Candy Blyth, who had a man for every finger on her hand, had taken the only man who had occasionally rescued Molly from the loneliness of her four walls. "Be careful!" she called out as her best friend walked off. It was said calmly, almost gently, but, although it was ridiculous, it caused a shiver to run down Candy's spine. She even looked around to see if Molly was following her; then she hurried off to the Taronga Zoo.

Charles Preston had sent her a hurried message; she was to meet him at the shark tank. Candy found this horrible; she hated the sight of the predatory fish. When she had visited the aquarium with Aunt Doody, shortly after her arrival in Sydney, she had looked a tiger shark straight in the jaw and had been scared stiff. She hadn't recovered until she rode the carousel and was squealing along with the rest of the children. And the penguins in the Taronga Zoo had delighted her. Mrs. Doody had shaken her head. This niece from western Australia, with her tall elegant figure, sometimes behaved like a schoolgirl. Candy loved animals, but when it came to beasts of prey, she drew the line. "We'll be safe, in the aquarium," Charles had written. Safe with the sharks?

Candy caught herself thinking that today she would rather have been with Trent. He was soothing. And he was good to her. Charles wasn't good to her. He didn't have to be. She loved him.

He had made a strong impression on her at once, the first time she had seen him at the Restaurant Rosso. It must have been love or she wouldn't have lost her appetite at the beginning. She had also lost a lot of her naive good humor. She wanted to marry Charles, even though he was a dog and a pimp. She didn't believe anymore that he had never accepted money from women. She didn't believe in his palatial home with the columns, nor in his opera career. He didn't write down what he owed her in his little notebook anymore, either. Why should he? He was sure of this doll. But just the same, he was cautious. Every now and then he acted out a little love scene for her benefit. Charles Preston really understood women; otherwise how could he have exploited them so thoroughly? He told himself that if he went too far, he might lose Candy. She was not Ginetta. You couldn't insult Candy. So, in spite of his violent temperament, he controlled himself. Instead of rage, he displayed irony. Fortunately, Candy didn't understand irony. When Charles smiled, he couldn't be angry, could he? Every time he was in trouble, he fed her sugar. He knew that he had to admire her constantly: it was what nourished her. Candy didn't know yet how miserable Charles would make her, but she was beginning to sense it.

Ever since Charles Preston had walked into her life, Candy was troubled. But she was trained to be a sex symbol, so she continued to show her public a radiant smile. She hadn't chosen this lover. Like a shark, Charles had circled around her and finally swallowed her. She couldn't bear life with or without him. He remained a cool stranger, with alien memories from his Italian homeland. Without ever having seen it, Candy hated Genoa. Everything was better there: sympathetic neighbors, serious conversations over a bottle of wine, passionate and obedient girls . . . "Why did you come to Sydney?" Candy wanted to know. Her patience was giving out. She hated complications. To avoid unpleasant or painful experiences cleverly was an Australian article of faith. Therefore, in more sober moments, Candy would have left this unpredictable and money-hungry lover. You lived with Charles about as cozily as in a railway junction!

There were also quite a few things about Candy Blyth that bothered Charles Preston. First and foremost was the error of birth—she was Australian. These inheritors of a young continent, born in freedom, were either companions of everyday life on equal terms, or they were the untouchable idols of the newspapers, films, concert halls, and television. Charles Preston not only came from a foreign country; he himself was a foreign country to Candy: impenetrable as the forests, more violent than a bush fire, and more changeable than the wind over Sydney. His erotic tradition—twilight experiences, vaguely mysterious dialogues—lay disagreeably between him and his Australian Eve. Or was she Lilith, Adam's rebellious wife? Candy was as stubborn as a water buffalo. In his homeland Charles Preston had experienced either the gentle beloved or the stern matriarch. But Candy lacked the strength, the warmth, and the fertility to be a matriarch. This you could find only in the Australian Outback, in the lonely settlements beyond the cities. The civilization of the big city had changed Candace Blyth, a healthy Australian girl, into a baby doll with slightly neurotic tendencies. Sydney had robbed her of her naive sense of security.

Preston waited impatiently at the aquarium. Where was the girl? His Ginetta had always been a few minutes early. That had pleased him. In a foul mood, Charles stared at a tiger shark. The gigantic fish had been caught and brought to the tank in Taronga recently. Charles had read about it in the *Morning Herald*. The sharks didn't survive long in captivity. Perhaps the crowds watching them annoyed them. That was understandable. Charles Preston wouldn't have liked an audience to his captivity. After being robbed of their freedom, the sharks refused to eat for at least a week. They were really valuable only after they were dead. Their fins provided the Chinese restaurants in Sydney with their fine soup; their fat was used for margarine and soap, and their skin to make elegant handbags and shoes for the sheilas. Where was Candy with her sharkskin bag? In any case, dying captive sharks were worth more than a dying man in prison. Charles frowned. He had no intention of dying in an Australian prison. But there was a chance that he might . . .

Candy was twenty minutes late. She had rested a while in a Taronga rock garden. She wasn't used to hurrying, especially in December, when it was much too hot. She hoped that Charles was planning a nice, tropical Christmas party with her, and would spare her the description of all the Christmas festivities and midnight masses in Genoa. Then Candy had visited her beloved black swans, an Australian specialty. Candy had seen them sometimes in coastal areas and rivers. In Taronga they were proud and serene, and their silver-gray young swam peacefully around them. The sight of them had calmed Candy. Charles didn't care for the animals in this unique natural park. He hated the Tasmanian devil, and had dreamt about this weird, coal-black, greedy mammal, living behind strong bars. It ate wallabies, birds, lizards, rats, and would certainly eat Charles Preston too. Nothing good had ever come to him from Tasmania. But his Uncle Fabio was getting wealthier there all the time, and right now Charles was flat broke.

Candy would have preferred to meet Charles on the upper floor of the aquarium, where the glittering tropical fish lived in illuminated tanks. But what could she do about it? Something must have happened. She sauntered with her studied, swaying walk down to the lower floor, and out of habit registered every admiring glance. She was troubled by a mute fear. Suddenly she felt unsure, as if she were stumbling at night, hand-in-hand with Charlie Rainbow. Only the abo and Mrs. Doody knew about Candy's night blindness. Molly Fleet had often wondered why Candy let her light burn all night.

Candy looked around the aquarium. There was Charles, in his new white linen suit, talking to the sharks. And what was that? There were two suitcases standing beside him. Was he going to run away?

Candy screamed, "Charles!" Some of the visitors turned to stare at her. One didn't scream in Sydney. A few stuck their heads together. Wasn't that beautiful girl in the white dress the model . . . Charles Preston looked around for a moment, furiously. Then he smiled and said, "Why not a little louder, baby doll?" Everybody smiled. The young man was apparently very much in love. What a pity that the beautiful girl had such an ugly voice!

"Where are you going, Charles?" Candy asked, her voice hoarse.

"Closer to the sharks," Preston whispered, and playfully drew Candy nearer to the edge of the tank. Candy drew back, afraid. Why didn't they sit down on one of the chairs or benches? Charles drew her right up to the edge to see the man-eaters better. But Candy was only imagining this. Preston just didn't want the people on the benches to hear him. Facing the sharks, nobody listened to the chatter of lovers. In the light, the steel-gray captive sea-robbers didn't look demonic. They aroused fear only because the Australians knew what they were capable of. Charles pointed out one of the slowly circling giants. "That tiger shark spat out a man's arm the other day. It was in the paper."

Candy ran out of the aquarium in a panic. Was that all Preston had wanted to tell her? He ran after her and grabbed her arm. "Not so fast! It was a joke!" His smile was distorted.

"Are you going away?" Candy caught her breath, looking around her. "Your suitcases. You've left them in the aquarium."

Preston went and got them. They were new, and real alligator leather. He despised synthetics. "Why so excited?" he asked irritably.

"They could have been stolen." Candy had been poor once; she knew what it was to feel the loss of an object as a personal anguish.

"Then they'd have been gone, and I'd have traveled without luggage."

Candy stared at him, wide-eyed. "No," she whispered.

"Yes. In an hour I'm leaving for Tasmania."

"Why?"

"I need a change of climate. Can you lend me some money?"

* * *

Next morning there was a quarrel at the Restaurant Rosso between Raffaele Rosso and his wife. "I'll report him," said Muriel Rosso from Darwin. "The bastard took my gold bracelet with him. My wedding present!"

"I'll give you another. Please, Muriel, don't bring the police in on this! Carlo is young and rash. He'll send us the money some day."

Muriel looked at her husband, her expression worried. "The little one," as she called the much younger Raffaele, had tears in his beautiful dark eyes and had turned yellow-gray.

"Don't get excited, Raff," she said sharply. "The doctor's forbidden it. A thief is a thief. Maybe a stay in jail will bring him to his senses."

"I won't let it happen! I'd rather go to jail myself!"

"Are you crook?" asked Mrs. Rosso. Her husband must have gone out of his mind! With her own sober little brain she always stood helpless in the face of such emotional explosions. "Why shouldn't I report him?" she asked gently.

"He comes from Genoa." Rosso's voice was choked. "His father is a civil servant. Fabio Pressolini in Tasmania is a respected businessman. His daughter married a wealthy man a month ago in Hobart!"

He was gasping. Mrs. Rosso, resigned, wondered how many more details of the family chronicle she would have to listen to. But Rosso had finished. Right now he wasn't in King's Cross. "I can't bear it when a Genoese is slandered," he murmured. He was trembling.

"All right, Raff. Take it easy. We'll drink a nice little beer now, all right? No, no, I won't tell a soul!"

"You do understand?"

"Of course not," Mrs. Rosso said energetically. "But that doesn't matter. What can I do about it?"

"I'll never forget what you've done for me." Rosso was as grateful as a child. He laid an arm around his colorless, overworked wife. "Muriel!"

"What now?"

"You are an angel!" His kissed her and whispered, "I'll buy you a much prettier bracelet, *carissima*."

"As soon as we've paid for the new refrigerator," Mrs. Rosso said quietly.

"When is Mr. Preston coming back?" Candy asked at the Restaurant Rosso. How should the new waiter know? Mrs. Rosso was not to be disturbed. She was keeping an eye on both waitresses. Raff was nowhere to be seen. A burning angle-light cast a dreamy reflection. Candy wasn't hungry, but she had to order something. Perhaps she'd catch a glimpse of Rosso later. She had the feeling she'd get nothing out of Mrs. Rosso. She ordered pizza and a shandy, a drink the Aussies often ordered—an ice-cooled mixture of beer and lemonade. The Italian guests, or the new Australians from Italy, of course drank wine with their meals.

Candy downed the shandy and asked for a second one. What had she done wrong? Why had Charles left her? She didn't believe for a moment that he had just gone to Hobart on a visit. He couldn't suddenly have felt a longing for Uncle, Aunt, or one of the Cousins Pressolini. Candy had never been able to make him out. He was full of contradictions. He was young, just the same, he was age-old. Sometimes his bed was a heaven, sometimes hell. And of course he drank wine. His disappearance had the advantage that Candy could at least drink her shandy in peace.

She had made a scene. In spite of her indolence, she had plenty of the explosive Irish temperament. After the outburst, she had begged him to forgive her. She had tried all evening not to interrupt him. In the end she had implored him to take her to Tasmania with him. She would work . . . He had laughed. Then he had made it clear to her how lazy and spoiled she was. Did she want to take her financial benefactors to Tasmania with her? Did she want to stand in a hot kitchen at Aunt Pressolini's instead of earning a lot of money as a model? Would she please come to the little senses she had! Charles had promised to write to her. Now five weeks had passed and not a word. She realized that she had miscalculated—she, who was so good at calculating. She had begged Preston to be kind. This she should not have done. In love one should never be modest. One should ask for all or nothing. Because nothing was more than a little . . .

Candy wouldn't have grasped the meaning of love with a clear head, but even the dull realization that she had made a mistake gave her a headache. In her misery she ordered a piece of cake with candied fruit, something she wasn't allowed to eat for professional reasons. Who had ever spread the idiotic idea that worry wasted you away?

Candy had just arrived at her fourth shandy, and wasn't seeing the world and King's Cross all too clearly anymore. How small and narrow and ridiculous this little bit of Italy in Sydney was! Actually, it was rather touching. The menus were printed in Italian, but the Aussies were offered the food in the Queen's English. Chianti bottles—that in every trattoria in the old country were filled with wine—hung from the ceiling. Of course there was chianti in the Restaurant Rosso too, for homesick immigrants. A well-intentioned oil painting of Genoa hung on the right wall; a faded picture of Rosso's parents, surrounded by a radiant group of children, hung over the bar; the grandparents kept a sharp watch over the cold buffet. Everybody was drinking red wine. Groggy with shandy, Candy could see an old wooden house in Western Australia through the walls of the restaurant. That was where she had seen the light of *her* world. Kalgoorlie, the city of the gold prospectors, had brought the Blyth family neither happiness nor wealth. Just the same, Candy had been content. She had felt firm ground under her feet until she had run away from Kalgoorlie. Every adventure of her life had begun with a drink: Kalgoorlie—Darwin—Broome—last stop, Sydney. Everywhere an absolute stranger had drunk a shandy with her.

14

Shandy with Candy

Candace Blyth had grown up in an Irish-Western Australian immigrant family whose only blessing had been children. At age twelve she had exhibited three traits that were later to bring her to Sydney: first, she couldn't listen; second, as a result of her exceptional beauty she developed a ruinous thirst for admiration at a very early age; and third, she couldn't see well in the dark. She never admitted to anyone that she was night-blind. She just couldn't see too well in the dark. She couldn't bear to have anything wrong with her, and never learned how.

Her need for admiration was energetically suppressed at home. Her mother removed the hazy mirror from her daughter's bedroom, and Candy's brothers beat her up just as if she were any other girl. But Candy knew better. Secretly she looked down on plain women like her mother and sisters, hiding her scorn behind an enchanting smile. That was easy because she mirrored herself in unattractive women as in a murky pond. Later, in Sydney, she was secretly delighted with Molly Fleet's birthmark. She enchanted strange men and women with her charm and brightness: it was her mother who discovered, early in Candy's life, her daughter's stony indifference to the sufferings of others. She fought this lack in her daughter with sharp words and secret prayers.

Candy's mother was faded before her time. She worked in a chocolate factory. Occasionally, when the girls fetched her, Candy waited eagerly for the admiration of her mother's co-workers. "Such a beautiful child, Mrs. Blyth!"

Caroline Blyth always answered, "Beauty isn't everything."

She would have like to see the big, strong girl help more at home. But Candy left that to her brothers and sisters. "Lazy as sin," said Mrs. Blyth. She had very little to entertain her in Kalgoorlie. Finding fault with her husband and children was her main form of amusement.

Candy loved sweets, but there was chocolate in the house only at Christmas. Mrs. Blyth brought it home with a sour face, a present from the factory administration. She wouldn't have brought the children sweets even if she had had the money. She was of the opinion that sweets ruined teeth and character. She had firm principles: enjoyment came from the devil.

Candy's father worked on the Western Australian Railroad. He was a sociable but naive man who lived either in the past or in the future, depending on how he happened to feel. With amiable indifference he overlooked the problems of the present—clothes for his seven children, the rent, the burden of work his wife carried. As a young man James Blyth had had the Irish charm which his wife, after years of marriage, saw as a disaster. After work he went off to a tavern where he could impress his cobbers. The pubs of Kalgoorlie, even in their early, primitive condition, had been an agreeable diversion for his gold prospecting ancestors. As time went by, Jimmy Blyth preferred his pub to his home, where his wife reproached him mercilessly for his failings. Her harsh voice didn't make her judgments easier to bear. Yet Caroline Blyth managed to keep the family together. Unfortunately Jimmy heard so often that she was the backbone of the family, that after Candy's birth he put in only the briefest appearances at home.

At twelve, Candy worshipped her father. Whenever she was able to get hold of him, he was so much more fun than her mother, and besides, he admired her. On Sunday, after mass, he would show off his youngest child to his colleagues from the railroad. His wife stood there with a sour face. "Come on, let's go home," she'd say irritably.

Later, when Candy left Kalgoorlie, her father envied her. As the years went by he turned more and more to the past. What else could he do? His future lay in the beer pools of the taverns. There everybody liked old Jimmy, but his health no longer permitted him to drink as much as he used to. Now he spent more time at home, but still didn't participate in the family's life. He studied the sketches of his ancestors who had worked the gold mines of Kalgoorlie in vain. Ignatius Blyth from Dublin had been the first member of the family to dig for the treasures of Australia. When Mrs. Blyth saw her husband poring over the yellowed pictures and chronicles he brought home from the library, she was furious. "There's no money in reading and lazing around," she yelled. "You're a failure, a drunkard, a fool!" (Later she used some of Ignatius Blyth's foolish sketches to start a fire.)

James Blyth went on reading as if he hadn't heard. He envied his ancestor because at the end of the nineteenth century, life in Perth had still been an adventure, however treacherous and godforsaken the gold fields may have lain in the blazing sun. In the year 1887, a young man had lifted a stone to throw at a crow. The stone had glittered strangely. Gold! For more than forty years, huge amounts of gold had been taken out of Kalgoorlie, but Ignatius Blyth had only been whipped by the desert wind and fooled by his illusions. Still he didn't leave. He cursed "the miserable hole" and "the death trap," but gold dust was in his brain. He stayed in the alien country of desert sands, oceans, mountains, swarms of insects, and heat waves, and was happy with his wife and children. When he watched the golden hills in the evening sun, he was content. Tomorrow was another day. They weren't starving. They were working for the conquerors of the gold fields. They had a few hens, their own hand-hewn hut, and the children laughed when a kangaroo hopped by.

Candy's father envied Ignatius Blyth because he had had a sweet, gentle wife. He mentioned her constantly in his diaries. Jimmy's wife, on the other hand, was like the spinifex, the inflammable Western Australian bush from which the abos made fish nets and baskets. Candy's mother was just as useful and thorny. James Blyth ignored his scolding, exhausted wife and read on. She was probably right a thousand times over, but he hated repetitions. His life in Kalgoorlie was not a tragedy; it was just sad, boring, and ugly, and that could have been termed a tragedy for a son of Ireland, but he had no intention of making one of it. His wife felt at home in Western Australia. Everyday life there suited her. The tragedy for her was that her husband didn't want to share it.

James Blyth knew without his wife's remarks that he was a failure and a beer drinker. But he was not a drunkard. He did see himself as a fool. Otherwise why would he have chosen this decent and self-righteous wife? Actually she had chosen him, but that had been so long ago, James had forgotten it. Who could succeed in anything if his wife thought nothing of him? Jimmy needed admiration just like his daughter Candy, and poor Caroline couldn't possibly admire him. She was too disappointed and too tired from hard work and noisy children to put on a show of what might have made a different man of him. In thirty years of marriage she had served him vinegar instead of honey.

In Candy's childhood, Kalgoorlie, situated on the "Golden Mile" of Western Australia, was already a sober, modern city which still figured as the center for the eastern gold fields. Still, the region had become a part of Australia's past. Candy couldn't understand why they were poor. After all, the gold mines were so near. More than thirty million ounces of gold had already been taken out of the mines, but Candy couldn't buy herself a candy bar or a silk ribbon. As a teenager she was already thinking of how she could adorn herself as cheaply as possible. A good-natured friend sometimes invited her to the movies, where she learned how one got a man who could shower his girl with gold. Her mother didn't give her any money for the movies. Hollywood films came straight from the devil, too. Candy was such a good liar that even her mother didn't know what was going on. When there was no other way, Candy used her clever little head.

She was not unhappy at home. She laughed and chattered with her sisters, and interrupted them constantly. That was something else she didn't shake off later. But this rudeness wasn't a result of her vivacity; she simply wasn't interested in what other people had to say. She was also not interested in what happened to them. When her sister Brigid broke her arm, Candy wept buckets. But after that she never asked how her sister was getting along in the hospital. She visited Brigid not of her own volition, but because her mother ordered her to. She had watered the mishap with her tears for a few hours, then forgot it.

But Candy was always friendly, and became more beautiful every day. Although she was by now a big, well-developed girl, her father still called her "Sugar Baby." When she drank her first shandy with a young man from Darwin, she confessed her nickname to him. Mr. Kearney found it a little infantile, but Sugar Baby stuck to her like syrup to a dessert dish. She didn't really want to grow up.

She found her first experience with a young man romantic because she had seen something like it in the movies. Her soul was as dry as the earth of her home, although by now, with the help of artificial irrigation, there were flowering gardens in Kalgoorlie, and attractive parks where before there had been only hard, red earth, salt deserts, and thickets. But the aridity must have crept in and taken possession of the souls of some people. Candy was not the only one who was as hard and merciless under her beauty as the earth the first diggers had worked. Until Candy fell in love with Carlo Pressolini, she had never felt anything for her lovers. They gave her the cool poise and porcelain attraction that delighted her first man in Kalgoorlie, the journalist Rick Kearney, who mistook a lack of impulsiveness in this girl for strength of character.

At the age of sixteen, Candy was working as a packer in a small factory in Kalgoorlie, and turning the red head of the young foreman. She didn't stay long in the factory; her mother found a job for her as a domestic. She told Candy to work harder and be more modest. Beauty was a chance thing, nothing earned. But even Mrs. Blyth couldn't talk her daughter out of the belief that beauty wasn't the luckiest thing in the world. In the villa of her employer, Candy saw silk underwear, real jewelry and well-dressed men for the first time. When there were visitors, she served drinks and smiled radiantly at the men. For the ladies she had a different set of smiles. The only one who ever saw her with a sullen face was her mother. Candy couldn't stand criticism.

The master of the house followed Candy with his eyes, and when he secretly tried to kiss her, she laughed at him. Mr. Cook was very good looking and an important figure in the railroad hierarchy, but Candy didn't start anything with married men. Not because it was a mortal sin, but because with a married man you always ended up with the short end of the stick. Candy knew this from her conversations with factory women. Mrs. Cook fired her because Candy had smiled at her husband. She didn't know that Candy smiled at most men. It didn't mean a thing.

But now Candy was on the street. She didn't want to go home. She had her salary for the week in her pocket as she stumbled across the twilit garden. She wasn't afraid because she had no imagination as to what might be awaiting her in the dark. Three days later her father got her a job in a cafeteria.

Again she had to sleep in her family's dismal wooden house, and hated it. Her mother yelled at her not to interrupt her all the time. "Spinifex!" thought Candy, and smiled to herself. How could she get away? A few of her sisters were already married, or working hard and contentedly in shops or offices. Brigid was already fading. Candy looked scornfully at the tall, thin girl with the loving heart. A girl who refused to brush her hair for hours had to get by without men. But Brigid loved a man whom, to her sorrow, she couldn't marry. Candy despised her sister for her sentimentality. Brigid's eyes often betrayed the fact that she had been crying, whereas Candy looked bliss- ful. Not a shadow of passion or renunciation darkened her enchanting face.

If she hadn't met Rick Kearney in the cafeteria, she would have run away with any other young man. All she wanted was to get away from the narrowness and the nonsense of her "Irish street."

Rick Kearney wrote articles about the "Golden Mile" of Kalgoorlie, those few miles of "the richest earth in the world." James Blyth could have told him a lot about it. There was the legendary Patrick Hannan, for instance, the redheaded Irishman who had found gold in the vicinity of Kalgoorlie, and the mine with the funny name, Hannan's Reward, which still reminds people today of the founder of Western Australian wealth. James Blyth would probably have shown the journalist the list of his ancestors, but Kearney only got to know his daughter.

He fired questions at Candy like pistol shots. Did she have a boy friend? How old was she? What did she do? Where was she living? Alone or with her family? Where could one find some harmless amusement in Kalgoorlie? Until how late could you drink in the bars? Every Australian asked this all-important question on arrival in any strange city. In this best of all worlds one couldn't drink whiskey at all hours.

Candy knew as much as a newborn koala bear. Funny creature! Where had she learned her affectations? From the magazines? The movies? Instinct? In spite of her young, blond charm, Candy gave the impression of being strangely tough. Mr. Kearney really preferred to devour his girls like soft-boiled eggs, but he was bored to death in this city with its faded gold brilliance. He was known in his circles for being able to enliven any party. He managed this with his hearty laugh, his anecdotes which were often cleverly concerned with himself, with his thirst and his vitality. Unfortunately, except for this half-frozen Sugar Baby, there weren't any people around to amuse.

Kearney's tactics weren't exactly subtle, but good enough for shandy with Candy. After giving it a little thought, the young man with the jolly eyes behind his glasses decided to take the girl with him to Darwin. She kept begging him to do so. Why shouldn't he invite her for a visit to this strange city on the edge of the desert? He was cautious enough to buy only one return ticket to Kalgoorlie.

Candy told her family that she had a job in Darwin, thanks to one of the guests at the cafeteria, as maid in a Darwin hotel, with good pay. She had to leave Kalgoorlie in a few days. Her father was beside himself, but Mrs. Blyth thought it was for the best since they weren't satisfied with Candy at the cafeteria anyway, and her days there were numbered. She was a dud, like her father, and she would soon find out when she got away how easy she'd had it at home, Mrs. Blyth said reproachfully. One lazy person less in the house! The girl would rather run around with holes in her stockings than darn them, she added after a pause. She stood there in her spotlessly clean kitchen, tall, gaunt, and gray-haired, like a vengeful goddess.

Understandably, Candy was dreaming of marriage. She expected Kearney's family in Darwin to receive her with open arms. You couldn't find such a pretty, pleasant daughter-in-law in ten golden miles. Candy let Rick kiss her, but wouldn't put up with any nonsense. There was time enough for that on the honeymoon.

Kearney was thirty years old, alert, intelligent. Marriage could wait. A long time. Besides, he would never marry a girl who constantly interrupted him. Kearney liked to hear himself talk, and he really did have a lot to say. He said it concisely, clearly, and with authority. Journalists are on the whole allergic to interruptions in the middle of their best sentences, but Kearney was positively rabid in this respect. He didn't show it, though, because this little Sugar Baby was absolutely delectable.

This experience taught Candy that one can't believe what a man says over shandy. In Darwin Rick declared that he wouldn't dream of marrying at this point. Candy couldn't possibly have taken him that seriously. Mr. Kearney had no family in Darwin, nor did he live there. He lived in Sydney, and at the moment was writing articles about Western Australia for the *Morning Herald*.

A week after their arrival in the Darwin Hotel, where they had separate rooms, Rick Kearney flew back to Sydney without any embarrassing farewells. He had wanted to seduce Candy, but after mature consideration had decided against it. When it came to virgins, he drew the line. Besides, the doll didn't care a damn about him. He'd found that out quite a while ago. A frigid young thing with a hideous voice! Why, for God's sake, did she always interrupt when he was telling his best stories, *and* with nothing to say? The only thing she was first-rate at was arithmetic. Mr. Kearney had found that out damned quickly too!

He left her a jolly farewell letter with a generous check. He left her unharmed and as gorgeous and dumb as the day he'd met her. He regretted having spent so much money on her but he could write some of it off as business expenses.

A few days later Candy had forgotten him.

Of course Candy didn't go back to Kalgoorlie. She had never seen so much money at one time, but she knew how quickly it disappeared. She had to find work. She remembered the alleged job at the Darwin Hotel where until now she had been a guest. A Greek maid had just left, and Candy was hired, with a good salary.

In Kalgoorlie, Candy had had a support of sorts in her family life, even though so much hadn't suited her. When she left her home town, she walked out into a void on an empty continent. She didn't know how lonely one could be in her country. In the end she moved on to Sydney, where her Aunt Doody lived, not because she loved her but because she needed someone who admired her. And she was charming to Molly Fleet until the young man from Genoa turned up. She could never get enough of seeing herself mirrored in men's eyes. She even beamed on abo Charlie Rainbow because his humble worship gave her a feeling of power.

But for the time being she was in Darwin, and Darwin was the capital and administration center for the vast Northern Territory and the revolving door to the Outback, the "dead heart" of Australia. Darwin was the civilized oasis for the transients and farmers of the Outback, and the focal point for various races. With its modern airport, the city crouched like a gigantic black and white bird on the northern edge of the huge continent. About two thousand white Australians lived in the territory, and six thousand blacks, and during her stay in Darwin, Candy got to know a lot of them. She was there for the wet season, and the rain and the many strange faces confused her. She bought chocolate for herself so as not to weep for homesickness, and for the first time in her life tried to hang onto a job. After all, she was only eighteen and a stray child. But she didn't want to go home. Did she sense that never again would she have the courage to go walkabout?

But the strange world of Darwin was empty and indifferent after Rick Kearney had left. The tropical flowers and colo:ful mix of people were no consolation. Nobody was admiring Candy, and she swallowed her tears as she made beds. The government officers in their snow-white uniforms, the abos in their shiny bush shirts, the Chinese women with their bright umbrellas, and the beautiful, aloof Greek girls all walked past her without paying any attention to her, as if she weren't the most beautiful girl in Kalgoorlie. The heavy scent of the frangipani blossoms gave her a headache. She had come from the Irish quarter of her home town to a city in Australia, that exotic continent tainted with practicality, where what was left over from the Stone Age and the numerous lonely white men from the no-man's-land of the bush, came together. An airport, a football field, and an air-force base stood like gigantic toys of the present, facing a vast emptiness.

Candy would have liked to run away, but where to? She sauntered all by herself through the Chinese quarter, and when it grew dark, crept back to her room which smelt of rain. She swam, lay on the beach under coconut palms, and gradually lost her roots. And after Rick Kearney had left her, she didn't trust any strangers. Moreover, all the young men seemed to have girls of their own. The color of their skin made no difference. Candy wafted in midair like the planes that landed in Darwin on their way from London and Malaya to Australia.

Candy spent the first bitter weeks of her life in Darwin. She found out that she couldn't stand her own company, and that was odd because until now she had been so very pleased with herself! She envied her sister Brigid who, safe in her mundane existence, was listening to their mother's harsh tongue. Candy would really have liked just once more to hear that beauty was a gift from the devil! If only to hear one familiar voice!

On Saturdays, Candy went to the movies. One day, in the lobby with its garish film advertisements, she ate some french fries which the Chinese cooks prepared on their little carts, and walked too late into the dark auditorium where government officers in their snow-white uniforms, graziers with their big felt hats, and half-breeds were buying themselves illusions. The usher, with her flashlight, was gone. Candy, in an ocean of darkness, panicked. Suddenly she saw a flickering white column and clung to it. But the white column was a man. In the semidarkness he clutched the girl. You never knew who was going to run into you in Darwin! Mr. Muir smiled. It might be worth while to take a look at this bit of clinging ivy in a decent light. Without any further ado he dragged Candy back into the lobby. Jeee-sus!

"Why are you afraid?" The sheila stammered that it was dark inside. "Of course it's dark inside," said Mr. Muir, "or you wouldn't see the picture. Why are you shivering, miss? Have you got rain fever?"

Candy shook her head.

Mr. Muir, a dealer in pearls from Broome, didn't ask any more questions about her health. It didn't interest him any more. Either this pretty sheila was drunk or she wasn't all there. But he was ready to buy her a drink. And he was looking for a young lady who did *not* come from Broome. What was this girl doing in Darwin? He had never seen her before. She looked lost. Mr. Muir recognized things like that. A single sharp lookout of his dark, shining eyes had sufficed. Had the little thing done something wrong? It wouldn't surprise him. In the bright light of the sun everybody had done something wrong, even if it never made the papers. "How about a drink, miss?"

Candy hesitated. She wasn't trembling any more, but she was bathed in the perspiration of fear. The stranger's eyes were dark and startling as the night, and the way they glowed gave them a lightning sharpness. Mr. Muir's lips were pressed tightly together as he looked Candy over mercilessly. His brutal lower lip dominated his bitter mouth. His big, prominent nose was very Australian. His powerful bald head looked naked, like a mask with glittering black eyes. They were not western eyes. They were almond-shaped, ancient, and could look into far-off worlds . . .

"Well?" the stranger asked, not very amiably. He wasn't accustomed to waiting for answers. Besides, Mr. Muir, who was a very rich man, didn't indulge in the complicated ceremony of politeness if he was going to pay. Finally Candy said she would like to drink a shandy.

Mr. Muir questioned Candy thoroughly over their shandy, but revealed nothing of his private life. At last she could chatter to her heart's content, but Mr. Muir only allowed her this pleasure over the first shandy. He had no intention of listening to any reprise of all this nonsense. He sat at the bar like a statue with glowing eyes, was silent, and didn't seem to hear the roaring, raucous laughter of the men who were celebrating their weekend in Darwin. When he spoke to Candy, he looked across her shoulder and saw Broome, city of the pearl fishers, a part of Candy's homeland, but a wall of mother-of-pearl separated this legendary place from the Irish quarters of Kalgoorlie. He hoped that his household staff weren't stealing any of his deep-sea treasures in his absence. Robert Muir knew how to treat thieves quickly and efficiently. They didn't steal his pearls or mother-of-pearl twice. Naturally every child in Broome knew that mother-of-pearl was much more valuable than pearls. That was why Mr. Muir's rage over its theft was feared more than the whirlwind or death by drowning.

Would Miss Blyth like to work at his house in Broome? Mr. Muir said, "We could do with a young girl." We? So he was married.

Candy hesitated, whereupon Mr. Muir quoted a fabulous salary. Candy grew increasingly suspicious. She hadn't learned anything. What would she be expected to do in his house? Mr. Muir said the first thing she would have to do was make up her mind. She would find out later what he expected of her. Then he was stonily silent. If Candy hadn't been so young and so forlorn, she would have let Mr. Muir fly back to Broome alone. While she was thinking it over, he took a costly mother-of-pearl brooch out of his pocket and laid it in her hand. At the same time he watched her eyes. A greedy doll. He had known right away that she could be bought. She reacted in a lively but superficial fashion to excitement, and wasted her emotions, like most women. Even those you couldn't buy with toys from Broome. Miss Blyth gave the impression of being soft and malleable. How could Mr. Muir have known that she was also stubborn and loved her freedom. At eighteen she was naiver than most girls and knew little about herself. At this point she had not yet grasped that she was white, of age, and sitting high and dry! She told Mr. Muir that the man she was engaged to had gone to Sydney, and she hadn't yet heard anything from him. Her parents didn't like him very much, and that was why they had thrown her out.

"Too bad," murmured Mr. Muir, with an expressionless face.

Candy didn't know that such transparent lies lowered her value. Muir took a quick look at her well-groomed hands—she didn't do a thing at the hotel without rubber gloves—and eyed her beautiful body and the way she moved. This girl was made for love and indolence. Robert Muir wouldn't have kept a girl like this in his office for a moment. Whites, Malayans and Chinese worked there, outstanding for their diligence and speed. In the warehouses they also packed the priceless mother-of-pearl shells, as big as eggs, for export to Singapore, London, New York. A Chinese-Australian foreman, who could be trusted implicitly, never moved from his stand. But the abos in Broome didn't steal the big "eggs" anyway. When they found pearls on the beach, they gave them away for rum or cigarettes. There were still plenty of pearls in the city with its penetrating smell of oysters and its mother-of-pearl ornamentation on cars and cutlery. Besides, after the Second World War strict immigration laws had been enforced for the Japanese. After 1945, with patriotic zeal, European divers had been tried out, but no European had the strong heart, and skill, and the patience of the Japanese expert in deep-sea fishing. The fiasco of the dives from the West had elicited one of Mr. Muir's rare smiles. He could have told the government people ahead of time, if they had asked him.

Candy's voice reminded him of a creaky door. Muir was extremely musical, but he wasn't hiring the young girl as a lyre bird. Beside his hunger for power, his record collection was his only form of amusement in Broome. Not that he didn't have enough distraction. Jewel dealers from London, New York, Paris, Amsterdam, Singapore, and Sydney visited him regularly in the Muir villa. Framed by palms and illuminated poinciana trees, it looked down from a rocky promontory on Dampiers Bay, just as Mr. Muir looked down at the rest of the population. For a man born in Broome, this was not exactly a typical Australian attitude, but it was not Mr. Muir's ambition to be classified as a top-ranking dinkum Aussie.

His mother had been Japanese. From her he had inherited the inclination to treat all women despotically. That was all right with the lubras (the black natives), and the Chinese washerwomen in Broome. A Japanese cook came three times a week and reverently prepared the delicacies for the pearl fishers. On the other days there was steak, as there was everywhere. His gardeners were abos; his chauffeur was a Malayan.

The villa had several guest rooms which united the best of Eastern and Western decor. The beds were soft and comfortable, and there were chairs and desks for guests from the West. Japanese guests naturally slept on mats and used the traditional hard headrest. All the mirrors had costly mother-of-pearl frames. The toilet articles were of tortoise-shell and gold. The rooms were never locked, and no guest nor staff member had ever stolen anything. The walls, except for a few Japanese wall hangings, were bare. For Robert Muir the woodcuts by Japanese masters were a penetration of pure poetry into the Australian living space.

Only his Japanese servants had access to his private quarters. In these light, almost empty rooms, the pictures were changed constantly in order to freshen and renew the spirit during the hot season. The pictures in the Western guest rooms were never changed. Why? Because the Western visitor found beer more refreshing than cherry blossoms on a white piece of paper.

This was the house to which Candace Blyth of Kalgoorlie came.

Robert Muir had grown up in the family of his Japanese mother until his father, who had gone back to Scotland before the birth of the boy, had sent money to a bank in Broome for Robert's education. Young Muir had an Australian guardian with whom he spent his childhood in Dampiers Creek. He hated the friendly, cheerful lawyer, but there he was, like the sand hills, the abos, the red eucalyptus trees, the ruined hulls of old fishing boats on the beach, and the blazing tropical sun. Robert Muir's guardian gained the impression that this alert boy, with his father's build and his Far Eastern eyes, was very fond of him. As long as he was dependent on adults, Muir smiled and was exquisitely polite. His real life—a separate existence full of subterranean tensions and protests—was played out on the weekends, and sometimes, at the end of school vacations, in the Asiatic quarter of Broome. It was during these years that he learned all there was to learn about Japanese pearl fishers, Chinese dealers, Malayan travelers, and Indonesian boatsmen. Robert's Japanese uncles and his grandfather had hacked the shimmering shells out of the oyster beds at the bottom of the sea as long as the heart, lungs, and tenacity of the diver's life permitted. Robert hated his guardian's car that always brought him back to the Australian world. It was during this time that he developed the strong urge for spiritual and financial independence.

Robert Muir never forgave his country for deporting the Japanese to other parts of Australia, which took place because the government was afraid of spies. Muir forgot that during the Second World War the city of Darwin had been bombed by Japanese fliers, and there had been fear of a Japanese landing. He himself came back to Broome after the war as an officer of distinction.

During his school years in Perth, Robert Muir had been lonely. But he didn't want friends. He was a good student, even if his mind got results which could have been reached in much simpler ways, via very subtle deviations. But he was the unrivalled champion swimmer in the school. He hid his burning ambition behind his impassive face. Nobody really liked him, and he really didn't like anybody. You couldn't quarrel and laugh and joke with him. He was quiet, like a tiger stalking his prey. In Australia people step forward so that you can see somebody is coming; people help each other even when there's no advantage to it; people are younger, more naive, and heartier. In many respects Robert Muir had the advantage over his comrades, but advantage doesn't make friends on this young, self-conscious, democratic continent. Robert Muir had never been to Japan in his youth, and his family in Broome was not in a position to develop prejudices in him, nor to point out differences in status. He must have been born with both.

In postwar Broome, Muir built up an international pearl trade with Australian partners and his own fleet of divers. His Aussies were first-rate, quicker to grasp what was going on than he was, but not as smart. The firm flourished just because of this collaboration of diverse mentalities. At first his partners had offered Muir friendship and warmth but had been politely rejected. Mr. Muir found the arrangement pleasing as it was, and the lack of social contact didn't break his partners' hearts. They had their own friends and families.

After the war Muir traveled to the United States and Europe, alone or with his partners, also occasionally to Darwin where there was pearl fishing and gold too. Between business conferences and formal banquets, Muir had always found an opportunity to go to the art exhibits and museums of the West, and to the temples in Japan. His house could have stood just as well in New York, London, Paris or Tokyo, but the garden was luxuriously tropical. Muir loved Australia's flowers and Western music. He was a bachelor, and at forty-seven felt that he was too old for experiments. He lived exactly as it suited him. He had offered Candy a high salary for specific reasons, although he was just as frugal as his Scottish father. And what did he want from Candy? She was to entertain his friends from all over the world like a geisha. Of course she had no idea of his intentions. She lived in the Western-Eastern house in a state of stupefaction, and asked herself sometimes if she really was Candy Blyth from Kalgoorlie. She also asked herself sometimes if Mr. Muir had forgotten her.

No doubt about it: he was a master at the art of forgetting. The social climate of the fifth continent was foreign to the Japanese spirit in him. The idea of being "matey" horrified him. He did not share the Australian belief in equality. There were masters and convicts, wise men and fools, and there was Robert Muir and the cobbers. He had guilt feelings when he came upon a careless waste of food, feelings, or speech. He did not feel the strong, generous need for human contacts that created oases in the arid soul of this continent.

Candy looked at him with helpless astonishment, but she admired his wealth. Besides, she was afraid of him. If her congenital inertia and her thirst for a luxurious, indolent life hadn't paralyzed her, she would have run away again. She still had her money from Darwin.

Mr. Muir gave her priceless jewelry whenever he happened to remember her existence. Occasionally she was dusted off like an object to be exhibited, and displayed, namely when Mr. Muir was expecting guests, business friends from all over the world. Not that he cared in the least for their friendship. He had bought Candy beautiful dresses, and it was he who decided what she should wear and say on such occasions. But Candy was not a trained geisha; she was a naive but free Australian. When an American guest at a party in the Villa Muir found Candy bewitching, Mr. Muir politely offered him the girl for the night. This was why he had engaged her, and in spite of her meager talents as a conversationalist, was paying her very well. Candy screamed and tore out into the garden while the American tried to apologize. Since it was dark in the garden, she fell. The American picked her up and brought her back into the house. He apologized to Mr. Muir. He regretted infinitely not being able to spend the night in his house. He had forgotten that a friend from home was waiting for him at his hotel.

Next morning Mr. Muir dismissed the ignorant schoolgirl. He had never been so surprised in his life. It had never occurred to him that a girl, who after one shandy had been willing to fly to Broome with him, would suddenly put on the airs of a virgin! How could he know that Candy had never slept with a man?

"Where shall I go?" Candy's lower lip was trembling like a child's.

"I don't know, Miss Blyth." How could Mr. Muir know? Dreadful, the things girls asked! "Don't cry, Miss Blyth. It is undignified."

"Thank you very much for the jewelry and the dresses," Candy stammered. Crying was unbecoming and bad for one's complexion, but what on earth did tears have to do with dignity? Candy swallowed her tears and asked if Mr. Muir wanted his presents back.

Mr. Muir, who in his life had met a lot of women who could be bought, stared at Candy, speechless. Had he become so old and stupid that he couldn't tell a decent girl from a whore any more?

"Why on earth don't you want to go back to your parents?" he asked brusquely. "You're still a child. You need a mother's care."

Candy was silent.

"I guess you weren't punished enough as a child, Miss Blyth." For the first time Mr. Muir smiled and looked almost human. "Of course you keep the presents. It is impolite to denigrate something beautiful so much that one prefers to offend the donor rather than keep them. Do you understand?"

"No," said Candy, with Australian candor.

Mr. Muir hadn't really expected her to because he didn't even get angry. He shrugged, resigned, and gave her a generous check which was in no way commensurate with her services. She had forgotten that Mr. Muir didn't want a whole flowering meadow on his table, only one beautiful branch. What *did* the whites learn in their schools? "Don't you have any other relatives?" he asked irritably.

"There's my Aunt Doody in Sydney."

"Who?"

"Aunt Doody. But she doesn't know me."

"Then she has that pleasure in store for her," Mr. Muir said drily. "Now listen to me and don't interrupt. *That's* something you've got to learn. I'm flying——"

"I never interrupt," Candy said, offended.

"I am flying to Sydney next week. I shall send your aunt a wire. If you don't like it in Sydney——"

"I'll love it in Sydney! Why shouldn't Sydney——"

"Shut up! If you don't like it at your aunt's, you have enough money to get back to Kalgoorlie." Mr. Muir cleared his throat. "If you like you may be my guest until you leave."

"You're terribly good to me!"

"Nonsense!"

Mr. Muir wanted to be rid of this little girl as quickly as possible. Her beauty and her affectations had deceived him. Hadn't she thrown her arms around his neck that night at the movies in Darwin? At the time he had thought she had mistaken him for a young man. Naturally he could still hold his own with any young man, and knew a lot better how to please a woman. But of what concern was Miss Blyth to him? His house wasn't a mission school, much less a home for infants. Very well, then—he'd made an ass of himself. He had hired a very beautiful girl as an entertainer and ended up with a stupid little fool. He would get hold of the real thing as soon as possible. There were plenty of pretty, adroit young girls in Broome, who didn't interrupt you and who knew how to behave with guests.

"Isn't your fiancé in Sydney?" Mr. Muir asked absentmindedly.

Candy grew fiery red.

"All right, all right." In his thoughts Mr. Muir was already with a jeweler on Martin Place. He would put Miss Blyth in

a taxi at the airport in Sydney, and that was the last he wanted
to see of her.

Candy had left the room. Mr. Muir watched her move slowly
and attractively across the garden. She stopped at the oleander
bushes to pick off a few twigs for good Mr. Muir. The sun
shone on her gold-blond hair and gave her sweet little face a
mother-of-pearl shimmer. If she had been born mute, Mr. Muir
would have managed to resign himself to her inadequacies. He
had never seen such a perfect white beauty. There had been a
certain evening when he had felt the desire to see this young,
perfectly formed body with nothing covering it. He would of
course have paid for the pleasure. But the child would probably
have screamed her head off as she had done last night. Fortunately he had fought this impulse stoically with well-organized
artistic distractions. He had looked at several exquisite pictures
and then listened to Mozart recordings. Since his youth he had
suppressed desires which, as a bitter core, might conceal vexation or rejection.

In the garden Candy was wondering why Mr. Muir hadn't
admired and loved her. He hadn't even gone swimming with
her on the beach. And in her bikini she looked adorable. But
Mr. Muir always swam alone before the sun rose and the moon
had disappeared. It would have amused Candy to excite this
cold man. That was really all she wanted. In Kalgoorlie, Rick
Kearney had mussed up her hairdo, groaned ridiculously, and
in the end had torn his own sparse hair. Candy wanted men to
admire her, dream about her, and give her presents. But men
were rough . . . Candy frowned. The best thing would be if,
after a few years in Sydney, she married a man who was too
old for love and too rich for a pretty girl. These frigid dreamers
were fun. Sydney was a big city. There had to be a lot of men
there.

Candy brought her flowers into the house. Mr. Muir permitted only one spray, or nondescript-looking grasses to be
displayed. They didn't look in the least elegant on the table,
with its cutlery with mother-of-pearl handles, and the hand-

painted china. It was painted in such faint colors that at first Candy had thought the dishes were old and faded, and had thrown a few away. Mr. Muir had *not* been pleased.

At home Candy had seen a film about Sydney, but she had chattered with her friends and couldn't remember any of it and that's how Candy came to Sydney.

Her first lover was a taxicab driver. Michael Browne was an acquaintance of Mrs. Doody's, and was doing pretty well financially. He treated Candy to quite a lot of shandy until he lost patience with her. Since she sensed that he would soon leave her, like the journalist in Kalgoorlie, she did Mike Browne the small favor. After all, it would have to happen sometime! Her first night made little impression on her. *That* was all? That was what the movies and novels made such a fuss about? Mr. Browne, on the other hand, was not satisfied, although strangely sobered. Seen by the light of day, this gorgeous sheila had given him her all, yet nothing. But she was very young and inexperienced. Surely it would be possible to get her going. But not too stormily. Mr. Browne wanted to marry Candy. He was a jealous fellow and hoped she wouldn't start anything with his cobbers. Sex didn't seem to mean anything to her. Mike Browne couldn't have wished for anything better in marriage.

Candy would probably have married the nice but hotheaded young man if she hadn't experienced a form of luxury in the Villa Muir that had estranged her from reality. Mike Browne passed out of her life just as suddenly as he had turned up. With delight Candy had imagined his despair when she suddenly turned him down, but Mike had laughed at her. She wasn't the only pretty girl in Sydney, even if she thought she was. He tapped his forehead with his finger and laughed again. Candy screamed at him: get out! And he did, whistling as he walked to his car. Now would have been the time for repentance. This love was her great sorrow . . . on the other hand she no longer had to listen to Mr. Browne babbling about football and racing. He had never taken her to the movies. He had never paid her a compliment nor given her any jewelry. She didn't shed a tear over him. It was a young press photographer who discovered Candy in the Restaurant Rosso. After a shandy, he brought her to the *Insight* office.

Until she became a model for *Insight*, and Alexander Rigby turned up, Candy drank shandy with several passersby who were much more attentive than Mike Browne, and who didn't want to marry her either. On the contrary. Then she met Ritter, alias Alexander Rigby, and finally Patrick Trent turned up. And then, one evening, when she was dining with Trent in the Restaurant Rosso, Carlo waited on them. He avenged her for all her disappointing men because he aroused real feelings in her.

While Candy was smiling at all Australia in *Insight*, she had sent a few copies of the magazine to Mr. Muir with a dark wish for self-justification. Now at last he would realize that he had thrown out the most desirable model in Sydney. She wasn't childish enough to wait for weeks for a sign of recognition from him, which never came. Had she really been in Broome? The Asian quarter, Sheba Lane, the pearl fishers, the abo camp, and the Villa Muir, high up on the ocean? Had it all been as real once as Mama Doody's boardinghouse was now? Anyway, now she no longer felt any need for new horizons. In that part of the world where walkabout is a natural philosophy, Candy was satisfied with her explorations in King's Cross. She couldn't understand the restlessness that sometimes drove Rigby or Trent or even Charles Preston away from Sydney.

Candy was all alone in the Restaurant Rosso, and the memories of Kalgoorlie, Darwin, and Broome did nothing to cheer her up. She was overcome by the old insecurity. Why had Charles left for Tasmania? To be alone was dreadful. One sat in the open air, whipped by heat waves and wind, and on the whole brown plain there wasn't an inn, not a man, not a sound. Loneliness was the wing-beat of the dully shining owl—soundless, soundless—and then, suddenly, a screech!

But Candy wasn't alone in the Restaurant Rosso. A young

man had been watching her for some time. "Is that she?" he asked Mrs. Rosso. "She's even more beautiful than in the magazines. Do you suppose I could go over and sit with her, Muriel? I mean..."

"Since when are you so shy, Curl?"

The young man, who was called Curl because of his shock of curly hair, grinned. He tapped the evening paper he'd been reading lightly on Mrs. Rosso's shoulder, and whispered, "Does she know yet?"

"No idea," said Mrs. Rosso. "I don't think Miss Blyth is an avid newspaper reader."

"Good for her! Do you think she remembers the fellow? He doesn't give me the impression of a murderer, but mostly they don't. Or how would they wriggle out of it? See you later, Muriel."

"Excuse me, please. Is this chair free?"

Candy looked up at the lean, suntanned face with sharp, light blue eyes. The young man's blond hair tumbled over his forehead like a boy's. But he wasn't a boy. He was thirty-seven years old, and when you took a closer look at him you could see the lines of experience in his long, hard face. "May I order something for you?" he asked.

"I'd like a shandy," said Candy.

The stranger was a traveling salesman in sportswear and related items, but he didn't bore Candy with talk about football or tennis records. He let her talk. She brightened right away. No screeching owls were fluttering around in the restaurant now. Once, as a child, they had frightened Candy; the night was bad enough without the threat of birds. At the end of their amusing conversation, the traveling salesman in sportswear showed Candy the newspaper. He evidently found her so beautiful that he didn't take his eyes off her as she looked at the headline: CRIME OF PASSION. And the pictures that went with it. "The things that happen," said the stranger. "Did you know about it?"

"No. I haven't seen him in ages."

"So you knew him?"

"Of course. He wanted to marry me. But then one day he was gone."

"Then you were lucky, young lady. How about another shandy? Don't be angry, but you *are* the most beautiful girl I have come across in a long time."

"I'm a model," said Candy, with modest pride.

"You are?!" Boundless admiration. Candy gained confidence. The stranger found out that she had often gone dancing and swimming in Bondi with a traveling salesman. He wasn't all that young, but smart. Albert Ritter. Candy hadn't intended to mention the name; it had just slipped out. But she didn't mention Trent. Gratitude and respect stopped her. And anyway, Albert Ritter didn't live in Sydney but somewhere in New South Wales. Candy hadn't been listening attentively, but when the stranger had shown her the paper, she had felt dreadful. Murder! How horrible! But she didn't feel sorry for the accused. He had deserted her. Blood was disgusting . . .

Curl was called to the phone and got up, grinning. "My girl friend. Just a minute."

Candy waited, but the stranger didn't come back. He was probably a good dancer: tall and slim, with quick, lithe movements, like the panthers in the zoo. Perhaps his girl was mad at him over the phone. Candy thought sometimes how pleasant it would be if there weren't any other women in the world.

"I can't get anything sensible out of the girl," Curl told Muriel Rosso. He had hung up the phone. "After all, Miss Blyth must have known the fellow pretty intimately if they were planning to marry. If she had, she'd be lying in the coffin today, under flowers."

"One can be with a man for quite a while without really knowing him," said Mrs. Rosso. The Aussies were silent even when they were in love. Her Raffaele was different. He expressed his fury, his joy, and his suffering to Muriel. Raff gave his all, body and soul; he didn't dish out alms to his Muriel.

"You're a smart woman, Muriel," said Curl. "If there's another call for me, tell them I'm on my way. Okay?"

"Okay. If you see Raff, don't tell him, please. He gets so excited about everything, even if it's none of his business."

"Okay," said Inspector Douglas Cox, and walked out of the back entrance of the restaurant into the hot Sydney night.

15

Love Letters

Elizabeth West, Brisbane to Alexander Rigby, Sydney

Mental draft:

Why haven't you answered my letters? Beast! This is my last private communication to you. We won't see much of each other in the future. I've had enough of borderline cases and the wretched years with you! You never knew the meaning of love, and you won't learn it now. How could you, since you avoid any true intimacy like the plague? Your wishes are satisfied shamelessly fast. For you an embrace is the beginning of the end. Shortly before I left Sydney I saw you with the model, Candy, on Bondi Beach. Are you teaching her how to write too? In case you think I'm jealous of the little idiot, go right on thinking. I was only surprised how modest a man *I* once loved could become with the passage of time. You'll end up with a seventeen-year-old illiterate! It always boils down to the same thing: you can't stand being with any woman for any length of time because you love only yourself and your work. Nobody admires your work more than I do, but you have made a habit of shutting out all emotion. That remains a deadly sin, however funny you may find it. You will gradually become a stone among stones, Alexander! That's why I didn't marry you. It wasn't easy to give you up. I had to carry my decision as high as a flag during the many empty years, and I'm not much good as a flag bearer. The damn things are too big and heavy. I was happy only when I could feel calm friendship for you, as on your fiftieth birthday, when we walked along the ocean, side by side.

But after all, I'm only in my mid-thirties, and friendship alone doesn't suffice. Meanwhile life is tearing along, happily passing me by. If your son had lived, everything would have been different. Yes, Alexander, we had a child. I was often on the verge of telling you, but since your marriage with Anne produced no children, I didn't want to see your face. Anyway, your son only lived for a few hours. He wouldn't have wanted to wander around the world, fatherless. For me he would of course have meant a certain fulfillment. Forget it! Naturally I would have seen to it that our son didn't develop into a caveman. He might have learned to show a little consideration for the girl who happened to be sharing his bed. I guess even you will calm down eventually, with bedroom slippers instead of your seven-league boots, and with the melancholy comforts of your second-best years. It's none of my business. My present is moving with giant steps away from the past we shared.

During these last months you have become a piece of the past for me. You won't like that. I imagine you are still recalling the time when I was a mute songbird in your female zoo. To be sure you managed to squeeze a few songs out of me, and I'll always be grateful to you for that. But under what conditions did you teach me to sing? For days, weeks, months I saw and heard nothing from you after you fired me. I can understand that you found Betty Withers very funny. And what do you know about me today, Alex? For years now you've been seeing "Elizabeth West," the polished personality I've become. But I am still a woman just the same. The cage of ambivalence has become too narrow for me. Hate-love and love-hate can be quite amusing, and certainly better than nothing at all, but in the long run they're not enough. At last I realize that lions should never enter into a personal union with lambs. Naturally, at thirty-seven, I am not a lamb any more but a full grown sheep. Who knows that better than you?

I have often asked myself: why didn't I stay in Adelaide? Life in my home town is not as hectic as it is in Sydney. Compared with the traffic on Pitt Street, Rundle Street is idyllic. Shops and places of amusement are separate entities. The weekends are peaceful, with a glass of wine and soft-spoken conversation, and the golden autumn on Mount Lofry! Why did I come to Sydney? Why did you have to cross my path?

Now I am going to throw you out of my life, Alex! From now on I shall wear my glasses without embarrassment and eat whatever I feel like eating. You can't stand girls who wear glasses, and in the last ten years you never saw me with them on. At last I intend to live without waiting for you to call me. It is marvelous when one straightens up the household of one's feelings. I never want to be teased, kissed, punished, or rewarded by you again, you phony father-figure! I don't want to believe any more that there isn't another man in the world for me except you. There are a lot of nice men around, and I would like to belong to one of them before it is too late.

I am going to get married.

You met Frank Grierson briefly in Sydney, and treated him with embarrassing arrogance. You will understand when I tell you that he isn't exactly eager to see you again. We are going to be married very soon. I shall do my best to make Frank happy. He is a wonderful person—friendly, considerate, patient, faithful, and sensitive. To put it in a nutshell—the exact opposite of you. He has already managed to make me feel happy and content for the first time in years. I shall at last be leading a normal life, something you have successfully managed to prevent for fifteen years. And if in the future I don't have as much time to write as I used to, what does it matter? Too many novels are being written anyway.

I wish I were less bitter, considering the fact that you gave me so much. But you never gave yourself! Not even in the years you were free. That's why I'm grateful to you for everything and nothing. I can't help it, but actually I feel liberated. And only the free like to live, and live long . . .

The letter:

Dear Alex,

I haven't heard from you in weeks, and hope you and Anne are well. If your sister didn't write to me regularly, I could believe my life in Sydney had been nothing but a long dream!

You will be glad to know that I am about to settle down too. I am going to marry Frank Grierson. You met him once with me on George Street. He wishes to be remembered to you, and both of us hope that Anne and you will visit us one day. Through Frank I have already made some very nice friends in Queensland. Dr. Catherine Trent, for instance, a sister of your friend Patrick. She has a children's practice in Bundaberg, on the Burnett River. I've visited that attractive, peaceful city three times with Frank. Bundaberg is surrounded by sugar-cane fields, its streets are wide and shady, and I was especially attracted to the Burnett River. We celebrated our engagement at Catherine's summer place. She had already written to Patrick Trent about it. Right now I'm writing short stories because I don't want to let Grace down so suddenly. Would you please let me have my novel fragment back when you have a chance? I sent it to you after your fiftieth birthday. No hurry—I'm terribly busy.

I hope our friendship of so many years will endure even if we are not living in the same city any more. And I'd like to hear some time what the two of you are up to. We are going to live in the beautiful house Patrick Trent bought years ago for his mother. It's been standing empty for a long time, since right now Trent is living in Brisbane. The house has enough guest rooms for my many friends in Sydney.

Very best greetings and all good wishes for Anne and you,

Yours,

Betty

Alexander Rigby, Sydney to Elizabeth West, Brisbane

Mental draft:

You are an idiot! That boring ass in Brisbane will drive you up the wall with his sensitivity. You need excitement, my dear. You thrive on disappointments. You are prettiest when you are desperate. I'm laughing myself sick, Betty. But go ahead and marry this doormat. Frame the wedding certificate and hang it over your bed! That's all you seem capable of at the moment. But don't come weeping on my shoulder. You never did know what was good for you, or you would have taken *me* seven years ago. It was sheer stubbornness on your part.

Be bored to death with your Mr. Grierson as far as I'm concerned, you little dope! On George Street it looked to me as if, after an hour's animated conversation with him, a jump from Harbour Bridge would be imperative! But there's one good thing about this marriage—you won't have to take sleeping pills any more, and I won't have to worry about you. Why do you want to get married anyway? You had a lot of fun in Sydney. But above all, you're talented, girl. You have better things to do. Afraid old age is creeping up on you? That's nonsense! All you've got to do is look at yourself. You're terribly young and crisp, and truly sweet when you're het up. Of course, and much to your disgust, I know, you were never able to let your repulsive moods and your *idées fixes* about illness out on me. I imagine that this is why you are marrying Mr. Grierson. But you have absolutely no talent for marriage. If a good idea occurs to you, you let the steak burn. I hope this happens so often that Mr. Grierson, who understandably is amiable and sensitive, smacks your little behind for you! Even marital patience has its limitations, my dear, especially at the kitchen range.

You write sometimes as if you'd swallowed the wisdom of Solomon, in spite of which you seem to believe seriously that marriage can solve emotional problems. My experiences should have warned you! Your imagination is running away with you again. You want to have a home, Betty, because that's a toy you've missed until now. Yet for years you managed to develop an exemplary routine without it. You have grown accustomed to the voluntary and bitter discipline of intellectual creativity. You're horrid on the phone if anyone so much as dares to call you while you're working. Mr. Grierson will call all the time. He'll call you from the office, he'll interrupt you in the middle of a sentence, he'll distract you and drive you crazy! You don't know yet that husbands are a disturbing element who don't want to be disturbed themselves. And what does this admirable Grierson know about you? How often has he seen you? He has no idea of the ghastly disorder you can create in five minutes wherever you go. And your thirty-five ailments per month are something else he doesn't know about, I am sure. The poor fellow will of course demand that from now on every one of your thoughts be directed toward him. I am sure he has no idea what it means to marry an author. You would have done better with me in this respect too. Because I can't stand it when a woman thinks of me all the time. That makes me as nervous as if ants were crawling all over me!

Naturally you will marry Mr. Grierson because that's what you've made up your mind to do in that pretty little red head of yours. You were always a hopeless case, Withers. By chance you know how to express yourself, but nasty old Rigby had to teach you that too.

I shall keep the fragment of your novel as a souvenir of Elizabeth West. *That* would have been a book! But you prefer to marry, so there's nothing we can do about it.

As a fatherly friend, may I give you a last piece of advice? Never look back at your life in Sydney. Remember that Lot's wife was turned into a pillar of salt. Go on having a good time. You always understood as much about men as my foot! But if . . . oh, forget it!

The letter:

Dear Betty,
    Patrick Trent has already told me that you are going to get

married. That was good news! My best wishes to you and Mr. Grierson. I had the pleasure of meeting your future husband on George Street.

I am very well. My wife is still with her ailing mother in London, but Lady Carrington's condition seems to be improving, and I imagine Anne will be able to come home soon. My house is pleasantly quiet since Daisy Andrews, my housekeeper's daughter, married a sports teacher last week. Lately everybody's marrying!

I swim a lot, and plan and build, and seem to be all over the place. Your marriage will make Sydney the poorer of one nice young woman. Fortunately there is no dearth in a charming new generation.

Of course we remain friends! Why not? By the way, I know your future home. Trent showed me the house when we were in Brisbane a year ago. It's gloriously situated, and the house itself isn't bad either, when you consider the time it was built. Of course you'll have to remove all that gingerbread in front, and if I were you I'd build a big glass veranda at the back. You'll need it. I take it you're buying the house from the Trents? Not a bad investment. I'd tear it down and build something new. The view of the Brisbane River seems to demand that. Of course I never told Trent what I thought of his big barn of a place. For him it was never a home, but a symbol. In such cases the professional keeps his mouth shut . . .

My very best to Cathy in Bundaberg. A great girl! When is she going to get married?

"Miss Rigby" is a brave woman, but I can tell how much she misses you. Of course Grace would rather die than admit to anything like that. We're worried about Marchmont. Bertie Dobson is silent about it.

Grace will buy a suitable present from both of us. You're to write and tell her what you would like.

All the very best, and much fun at the wedding! Warmest regards from Mrs. Andrews.

Yours,
Rigby

Alexander Rigby, Bowral, N.S.W. to Anne Rigby, London

Mental Draft:

What's the big idea of not writing for such a long time? I love

Happy New Year wishes in March. Pull yourself together and come home. I have to lie to everybody that your mother's ill because not a soul here can imagine you'd rather be in London than in Sydney! I don't want another scandal—do you understand? I have no intention of giving you a divorce. It would be absolutely sense-less because we could live very nicely together if you'd just throw your immature ideas into the Thames. I can't help it that you dreamed up a father-image that time in London, nor is it my fault that you're an icy virgin. Evidently you can't disassociate your image of what a man should be from the real thing! And that's foolish. After all, at thirty-five you're not exactly a teenager any more, and you're living in the same world and under the same natural laws as the rest of us.

I would be grateful if you would take a moment to think the matter over soberly, and I continue to wish your mother a speedy recovery. I shall try to drive the fear of love out of you. Do you need money? Anyway, here's another check.

Come home. I need you, you idiot!

The letter:

Dear Anne,

Thank you for your letter. I was glad to hear that you and your mother are well. I am spending a long weekend here in Browal with Trent, who is temporarily a grass widower, because things at the office are hectic. Did you get my Christmas package? If not I must put in a claim at the post office.

Betty is getting married next month. Do write to her. You set such store by good manners.

It's pleasant and refreshing here between the mountains and the golf links. I make Paddy play golf every day. It's good for his stomach. The Hobart races were terrific. We celebrated for a long time afterwards with the mob.

I hope to hear from you soon. It must be near springtime in London. I'd like to walk in Regent's Park with you again, when everything starts to bloom so very gradually. Unfortunately I'm swamped with work and can't talk anything over with Stan March-mont, because Bertie Dobson stands watch. Grace and I are only allowed to visit him for half an hour, once a week. We're hoping he'll make it after the last heart attack. He was always a man of iron.

An architect from California is coming to see us. That will keep us busy. That's why I'm spending a quiet weekend here

with Trent. Bowral would do you good too, if you found it too
hot in Sydney. There's always a fresh breeze from the mountains,
and the air up here is crystal clear. I could visit you every
weekend. Trent and I enjoy the farms all around. Maybe I'll
build a country house here for us. It's quieter than Manly, and
you'd be undisturbed. It's autumn here now, as I guess you
recall. It's going to get cooler gradually, and if you came, let's
say end of May, it would already be winter in Sydney. Of course
there's no law against your coming sooner. You'd soon be rid
of your headaches up here.

Very best greetings to your mother and Miss Jennings.

Alexander

Candy Blyth, Sydney to Charles Preston, Hobart, Tasmania

The letter:

Darling!
Why don't you write to me? I'm downright foolish with longing
for you. Just a minute, my aunt wants me . . . The bulb in the hall
burnt out and she can't reach it, and our Umbrella Uncle up in
the attic is drunk . . . There. All set. It's a little cooler in Sydney
already. I've bought myself two new dresses, marked-down because I'm such a famous model. They show off my figure beautifully. One is white, the other is green, with a pleated skirt. I've
dyed my hair red. The photo boys say I should be piquant for a
change. I'm sending you three prints with my new hair. There are
an awful lot of flies today. Do you have flies in Hobart? I'm doing
without almost any sweets because of my career. Our neighbor, I
mean her cat, had six kittens. They're adorable! I use silver nail
polish now. Very sophisticated! I'm sending you money with the
same mail, darling. I eat cake twice a week to cheer me up.
Yesterday I drank quite a lot of sherry because I felt so blue. I
won't be able to stick it out much longer without you. The other
day they were selling black nylon lingerie in one of the department
stores. I bought some for you! Do you remember our abo, Charlie
Rainbow? He came back yesterday. Aunt Doody has a cold. That's
because she runs around with just a towel over her head when
she's washed her hair. The owner of the laundromat was operated
on for appendicitis at St. Vincent's Hospital. I cried. Molly Fleet
is terribly unfriendly to me. I don't know why. I'm so nice to her
and gave her one of my cast-off dresses the other day. It was still
fairly new and only had a little tear at the back. The zipper was

broken, and there were two coffee stains. She threw it on the floor at my feet! What do you think of that? As if she could afford to buy herself such a good dress! Her figure is quite nice, but can't be compared with mine. I would even have paid her to have it cleaned. I mean the dress. Why did you send her a postcard from Hobart? Now I'm sure she thinks you'll want to go out with her again when you get back to Sydney. Which would be ridiculous! Fleet is very busy and makes a lot of money with her massaging. She wants to go back to the farm later. Then you can't go out with her any more anyway. She never gets any presents. Who would give Fleet anything anyway? I don't mean because of her birthmark. You don't see that in the night. I mean because of her character. She snoops and spies—things like that. I don't know why Aunt Doody doesn't throw her out. But she doesn't. She's too good-natured, that's why she has no money. I always cry when somebody's unlucky, but just the same, I know how to look after myself. That's my duty as a model.

The other day I was in Luna Park with my sugar daddy. It's great fun. We must go there right away when you get back. When are you coming back anyway? I don't know Hobart, but I'm sure it can't compare with Sydney. And I've been around in Australia. Our neighbor who cuts the opals is in the hospital too. He's very old. Fifty-eight. Aunt Doody visits him and says "hi" for me. I don't go to the hospital until things get really serious. I'm modeling fashions on television too. The other day I saw a neat movie about love and adultery in Rome. Cried my eyes out and had to borrow three tissues from my neighbor. The lover looked like you. The poor wife had to suffer a lot. In the end her husband threatened her with a carving knife. He wasn't particularly good-looking, but then he was the husband. Yesterday, in Martin Place, I saw three girls, laughing. They were wearing chic dresses. One of them was bowlegged. I wondered how she could be so cheerful with legs like that! Charlie Rainbow made me a frame for my mirror, and painted it. The poor fellow's black as the night, but so nice and helpful. And loyal! Of course he worships me. Just a minute, Aunt Doody's calling me. The food smells burnt. I love you so much, Charles! When are you going to write to your baby doll? I cry every night because of you, I mean every night I'm home. Sometimes I go dancing. What else can I do? Dancing distracts me. After all, I'm still young. The other day they arrested a fellow because he's suspected of murder. He wanted to marry me once. His name is Michael Browne, and he drives a taxi. I found him too vulgar, especially the way he spoke, and he didn't like to treat very much. That was when I'd just arrived in Sydney from Broome, and wasn't a famous model yet. When it was all over between Mike and me, I had to take the bus. Lucky me, or I might have been the one konked off! On the same evening that there was a picture of Mike Brown in the evening paper, because of the murder he'd committed. I met a nice, jolly young man at Rosso's. He treated me to a shandy. He showed me the paper all about the murder in it, and I knew Mike intimately! It made me feel sick! He was a traveling salesman in sports gear, I mean the nice stranger at Rosso's. He had thick, curly blond hair. Mike Browne had a head of hair like that. I hope the strange young man isn't a murderer too! Haven't seen him again. He travels around too much with his sports stuff. Aunt Doody bought biscuits in the bakery around the corner. They were hard as nails, and she was furious. Nothing seems to turn out right for her these days. I laughed. The strange young man at Rosso's said I was the most beautiful girl he had seen in New South Wales in a long time. No, that he'd come across, that's what he said. That comforted me, since I'm so absolutely miserable because of you. The faucet in the kitchen is dripping again, and the plumber . . . oh, never mind. The other day I had ice cream for breakfast, from the Italian ice-cream parlor across the street. I had to cry because you're from Italy too. The ice cream was first-rate. You see, I like everything Italian! I hardly look at anybody else. Molly Fleet is moody and won't play along any more. She must have thought that you were going to go on going out with her. Such an idiot! Aunt Doody gave Charlie Rainbow gin the other day and he looked wild. She shouldn't give him any hard liquor. I don't know why she coddles him the way she does. After all, he's an abo and isn't used to it. The other day he was mad at her and put soap in the jam jar! But all she said was he could have jam for tea, and both of them laughed. The fence next door is broken. That's all the news from Sydney. I hope they build the opera house soon so that you can sing there.

How are you? How do you like living with the Pressolinis? Why don't they call themselves Preston too? Nobody can remember a long name like that. Yesterday we had cabbage and fruit jelly out of a package. Do you still love me? Is it really cool in Hobart? King's Cross gets more and more crowded at night. Two new restaurants and a German coffee shop. The owner is a German woman. Her husband died in Adelaide. Car accident. Now she runs the coffee shop. Her name is Gretchen. I mean the widow. We sweated terribly here at Christmas time. The only place you could breathe in was in church. Molly Fleet helped Gretchen at Christmas. The shop's doing very well because the pastry is divine! Aunt Doody is going to visit her friend with the wooden leg in

Surry Hills tomorrow. Aunt Doody helps her to take a bath. Afterwards they play cards. I have new bedroom slippers with feathers on top. Last night I sat on the balcony. Charlie Rainbow went out. Aunt Doody says he has a friend just outside the city. Her varicose veins are bothering her, but she won't go to a doctor. All her friends who went to a doctor died one after the other. But the population in Sydney is enormous just the same. You don't notice it when there's one or two less.

I can't think of anything more to write. Please come back soon, Carlo. I'll never interrupt you again. Word of honor! Lots and lots of kisses.

Candy

Molly Fleet, Sydney to Alexander Rigby, Sydney

Mental draft:

Dear Mr. Rigby,

I must tell you the truth at last. It is not right that a man like you should be exploited and deceived by Candy Blyth. She is a selfish, heartless little fool who gets money out of older men and gives it to her pimp. He is in Tasmania right now.

Quite by chance I found out from the newspaper that you are not the traveling salesman, Albert Ritter. You are Alexander Rigby, the architect. But I am keeping this strictly to myself. This is not a blackmail letter.

You are wasting your attentions on Miss Blyth. Please forgive me for interfering in your affairs, but Miss Blyth goes too far. She even lets me write her love letters! That surprises you, doesn't it? You don't know me and I don't want you to know me, but what I wrote in those letters is true. I think you are wonderful, Mr. Rigby. I would do anything for you. I hope you believe me.

Candy's friend is a foreigner, a wop. Why didn't he stay in Italy? It's a famous country, isn't it? I wouldn't mind seeing Rome myself, but who would invite me?

This is the first and last letter I shall ever write to you personally. My heart beats fast when I see your name in the paper. Your buildings are marvelous. I think Sydney is marvelous too. I come from Parramatta.

I am already twenty-two and I don't have a man. People think that doesn't matter, but I know better. I could tell them a lot of things that a decent girl doesn't tell. If only I could go out with you just once—nothing more, you understand—I would be the happiest girl in the world. I have a good figure, but that doesn't help. If you didn't have any money, I'd work for you. Unfortunately I am not the right girl for you. If you saw me, you'd know why. But you will never see me, Mr. Rigby.

Miss Blyth tore off to her fellow in Hobart a few days ago. That's what she's like! He didn't invite her to visit him. He's probably got another, richer pigeon. That's what he's like!

I massaged your wife. She is the best and sweetest person— Miss Conroy in Parramatta excepted. Unfortunately Miss Conroy is dead. I hope your wife comes back soon. I think sometimes it must be lonely for you in that big house with only that funny housekeeper. I think a lot about you, Mr. Rigby. Sometimes I have to laugh out loud because you don't know anything about it. I have already kissed you twice in my dreams, but not on the mouth. Just so . . . And I pray for you every night. I don't know how to kiss a man so that he forgets everything. Miss Conroy, my teacher in Parramatta, always said it was inner beauty that counted, but that doesn't hold in Sydney, or Miss Blyth wouldn't have such rich friends.

Charles Preston went out with me first, then Miss Blyth took him away from me. I don't care. He's a stinker and a bastard. Miss Blyth made him believe she was only eighteen. She is twenty years, five months and three days old. She has a mole on her left hip. But you know that.

Her aunt is in a fine rage. I mean Miss Blyth's aunt. I asked Mrs. Doody what had she expected from Candy, who is after all a treacherous bitch. So now Mrs. Doody is angry with me! Nobody can say a word against Candy. What do you think of that?

When I see a really gorgeous built man in a film, I always think of you. You don't mind, do you? How do you like my love letters, Mr. Rigby? Parts of them I find in novels I borrow from the library, but most of what I write is out of my own poor head. Honestly! Sometimes I'm at the Taronga Zoo when you're sketching birds or just walking around. But I *never* follow you. I love to watch the birds in Taronga too. I love all animals, especially cows. And the emus with their soft feathers and helpless wings. But I imagine the emus are perfectly happy because none of them can fly. If every girl had my bad luck, I think I'd be content too.

The other day somebody from the police came to Darlinghurst. I recognized him from the newspaper. He was working on the Mike Browne murder case, Mike Browne the taxi driver. The man from the police was Inspector Cox. He is very friendly, and has a shock of curly hair, but his eyes are like knives. When he came to our boarding house, Mrs. Doody had just gone out to see a friend. I'd just got home from work and ran straight into the entry of the house opposite. Curlyhead had wanted to ask our other roomers about Miss Blyth, but only Uncle Doody was there, and he was drunk. Good for him! We don't want anything to do with the police. The fellows snoop around until they find something. I think if one snoops around long enough anywhere, one finds something. The papers call Inspector Cox the toughest scoundrel between hell and New South Wales. Of course they don't write scoundrel, but that's what they mean. Perhaps Candy's fine friend has been up to something in Hobart. Or she has. She never has any money now because it all goes to her wop. Mrs. Doody is furious, and says Candy will come to a bad end. But Mrs. Doody always sees a bad end to everything. It's all the fun she has.

I followed Inspector Cox when he finally left. He went to the Restaurant Rosso. I asked Mrs. Rosso if she knew him. She said she didn't.

Please, Mr. Rigby, don't come here anymore.

This letter was never sent.

16

It Is Cold in Tasmania

Because of its cool climate and fruit plantations, Tasmania is a popular holiday paradise, but Candy Blyth was aware of none of this. Perhaps she shouldn't have followed Charles. But she was too young and too much in love to do anything else. In pretty, sunny Tasmania, which is known as "the Apple Island" or "the Diamond of the South Pacific," Candy was sitting on a milestone in a dark street. It was the street of sorrow, and you can find it anywhere—in Sydney, in Broome, in Darwin, and of course in Hobart. On this whole vast continent there isn't a single hiding place from sorrow. It finds its victims everywhere, and lurks especially in those vacation resorts that inspire travel bureaus to poetry. Like the octopus, sorrow has innumerable tentacles, and they are ice-cold. In Tasmania, Candy felt their frigid breath. This was especially unfortunate because it was cold anyway in Van Diemen's land, and it is just for this that visitors pay high prices, especially the people from Sydney, who this year, had had enough of the blazing-hot Christmas festivities. Although the height of the season was over by the time Candy arrived, it was still as cool as in Europe. If the invisible Preston had been as faithful as the gold he had managed to squeeze out of her in the form of bank notes, everything would have been all right.

Some people have a sixth sense for invisible threats from behind. Like the funny little wombats in the bush, who sense danger even when the lyre is still trilling, and the old trees stand silently and unmoved by storms. The wombats burrow quickly into the earth, or hop away when the dangerous man approaches, while the giant trees don't notice that the sly lianas are choking them to death as they entwine around their trunks and tighten their grip gradually, until the eucalyptus or that legendary tree that still looked upon the black man in freedom, fall to the ground. The fat, nearsighted wombats save their lives, and the majestic tree giant is felled with a crash. In Australia nature is the great teacher.

The old bush runners can sense danger in time too, just like the wombats. They run away with their billies and waltzing Mathildas to where it is safe. But Candy Blyth came from Sydney. She was a city flower and a roaming fashion plate. Her face came to life thanks to the artistry of the photographers. She could smile and look dreamy only with their help, and assure readers that the new soap powder washed whiter than white, and would brighten their lives fundamentally. Although Charles Preston had lived in cities too, he instinctively recognized the trickery of the bush and the creepers' tactics. But Candy knew nothing of all this when she flew to Charles Preston in Hobart. She had got the address of his relatives at the Restaurant Rosso, and that's where she went. Where else could Carlo possibly be? Fabio Pressolini had meanwhile become a wealthy man. He had developed his one garage into a whole chain of garages, and had put Charles in charge of one of these little gold mines. The Italians are incurably family minded, and the Pressolinis in Hobart were no different from those in Genoa. They didn't think very much of Charles—he'd always been a showoff—but Uncle Fabio felt that blood was thicker than water, and that was that.

When Candy drove out to the Pressolinis' pretty house in one of the suburbs, Charles Preston was conspicuous in his absence. "Where is he?" Candy asked, horrified. All the Pressolinis—father, mother, married daughter and Mr. Millington, the Australian son-in-law, nodded their heads. They looked like Chinese mandarins, sitting there and nodding. Uncle Fabio, intelligent and sympathetic, asked the pretty young girl from Sydney a lot of questions, then he nodded again. Why hadn't she written to them? Candy got the feeling that the family knew very well where Charles was, but they wouldn't tell, and talked about all sorts of other things, mostly about the neighbors—what they did, what they said, and where they traveled; who was going to get married, who had died, and who had bought a new car. Italian and Australian names whizzed past Candy's ears. She was stupefied. Of what concern were all these strange people to her? The Australian son-in-law was silent too. He looked Candy up and down, not in a friendly fashion: a flighty little chit! Suddenly father, mother and daughter were speaking Italian. Mr. Millington raised his sandy-colored brows, smiled pleasantly, and said, "Hey!" After which the Hobart saga was continued in the language of the land. Candy was stunned. Where was Charles? Why wasn't he living with his relatives any more?

"Angela has twins," Mrs. Pressolini was saying. "Sweet, God bless them. Angela's grandparents—they live in Spezia, no, in Filanesi—they had a fruit store and . . ."

"Nonsense, Mama!" said Mr. Pressolini. "They came from Ventimiglia, and they didn't have a fruit store. Shoes! They sold shoes! And Emilio drove a tourist bus to Genoa, and Angela's grandmother..." Mr. Pressolini continued in Italian. Mr. Millington cried, "Hey!"

"Where is Charles?" Candy said harshly.

At last they told her. They were familiar with Australian doggedness. Mr. Millington looked at his compatriot from Kalgoorlie even more critically than the rest. What did this sheila want from his in-laws? She was only wasting their time. Millington still wanted to mow the lawn in his father-in-law's garden, and Claudia had to feed the baby. This city pigeon from Sydney in her low-cut dress, spoke in a voice that could rival a creaking door. He liked her less and less the more he heard and saw of her. He stood leaning against the door as if half asleep, his hands in his trouser pockets, his shirt open, a cigarette between his narrow, scornful lips. But he wasn't half asleep. He noticed everything. It was he who had thrown Charles Preston, formerly Pressolini, out of his in-laws' house. The elder Pressolini was the best cobber Millington could have wished for, but he was too guileless. A belief in "mateship" and all the rest was properly included in Mr. Millington's comprehensive system, but he looked people over carefully before he came closer. For "Presso," as he called his father-in-law in affectionate moments, it sufficed if a goddamned ne'er-do-well came from Genoa! Yet where business was concerned, Presso was a bloodhound, sly but absolutely honest. He was dinkum. Mr. Millington gave his father-in-law a sign, while Candy went on besieging the family with questions. Mr. Pressolini was helpless in the face of this flood of words until he caught his son-in-law's eye. The wink and surreptitious nod meant: Get her out of here!

Like every Aussie, Mr. Millington was a perfect mime. He offered Miss Blyth a cigarette. "Smoke-o?" And Mr. Pressolini wouldn't let the confused young thing go without a glass of beer. In his boundless benevolence he drove her back to her hotel. In spite of the wonderful big car, the trip was not pleasant because Mr. Millington sat like a watchdog beside Presso, and Claudia Millington, with the baby, sat in the back with Candy.

The baby, with its apple-red cheeks finally upchucked its milk on Candy's suit. Candy shrank back with a cry of horror. Mr. Millington turned around and laughed for the first time "Give me the baby, love," he said, took his son and heir on his lap, and hummed some Aussie songs, while Candy and Claudia conversed across an abyss. "It's cold in Tasmania," Candy muttered. "I think it's wonderful," said Claudia. For the life of her Candy couldn't understand how anyone could find it wonderful here if one had to share one's life with Mr. Millington.

When Mr. Pressolini deposited her at her hotel, and looked at her sympathetically out of his lively dark eyes, Candy thanked him for his kindness more warmly than was usual for her. There was a slight pause. Mr. Pressolini opened his mouth twice, but then seemed to think better of it. Like every good Aussie he simply said, "Orright," and drove off with his family to the Millington's fruit plantation.

After her introductory visit to the Pressolinis, Candy Blyth had to put up with her own company for a while. She wandered around the city with the European climate and the Dutch and English names in the telephone book, without a plan, and tried to think how she could tear Charles Preston out of the clutches of a certain Mrs. Pugh. It never occurred to her that he might not want to be torn out of Mrs. Pugh's clutches. She didn't know what to do with herself in this strange city. Slowly the old feeling of insecurity came back, and she had to force herself to think of her success in Sydney in order to still believe in it. In the evening she crept into her bed, dead-tired, and wept. She couldn't help it, even if tears made your skin blotchy. But she was only twenty, and her skin was smooth. The cooler air in Tasmania even painted a delicate natural rosiness on her face, as if by magic, but nobody admired it. She was too indolent to go back to Sydney, and surely *something* had to happen soon! Some day a nice man would put in an appearance, and inflate her self-confidence like a balloon, and take her *somewhere*!

But nobody came. The days passed. She was condemned to a monologue in her hotel room.

* * *

. . . Why did I fly to Hobart? I'm all through with the bastard! This hotel isn't worth the money. This morning my breakfast was cold. Everything's cold in Tasmania!

Nobody notices me. And I'm supposed to be known in the whole country as a model. A couple sits at the table next to mine in my hotel. The man has eyes only for his wife, in spite of the fact that she's wearing a dress you could have bought a year ago at a sale for a song. No sense of style! Has no idea what to wear! Her permanent is second-rate and her hair is cut too short at the back. I suppose she's never lived in Sydney, only in this dump of a city with its frumpy people. I wouldn't like to see her in a bathing suit! What on earth does the man see in this dud of a woman? She has no taste, and I'm sure no idea how to handle a man. She doesn't even use nail polish. Hasn't the man got eyes? She reminds me of my sister Brigid. I haven't written home for a long time. The last time when my father died. He was the only one who was fond of me. I should have visited him sometimes. He kept writing: when was I coming at last? Or I should have sent him the money for the trip. I had such a lot of money in Sydney until Charles ran through my account. Funny how one always thinks of what one should have done when it's too late. I cried terribly when Father died. Why do I have to think of Kalgoorlie now? I really must send Mother something once I start making money again. I wanted to. Twice. Something always prevented me. But first I've got to get some new clothes and costume jewelry, things like that. Business expenses don't stop, even if right now . . . Anyway, Mother's got along without my help so far. She'll just have to wait a little longer. But I'm really going to do it this time.

Father called me Sugar Baby.

I've been sitting two weeks in this expensive hotel and had to sell a ring. I can't go on like this. Charles, the bastard, isn't doing a thing for me. It's very cold in Tasmania, but the apples are first-rate. I must speak to Mrs. Pressolini. I'm still so young and don't know what to do. Mrs. Presso is a very good, sweet person, but she interrupts all the time when I'm talking. I've got to tell her about it sometime, just between us. One doesn't interrupt in our country . . .

Spent the whole day at the Pressos. They're very glad when I come. I'm moving into their house this evening. Of course as a paying guest. But I don't think they'll take any money from me. They're stinking rich. Still, Mrs. Presso wears dresses I wouldn't touch with a ten-yard pole! Not because they're dirty. Mrs. Presso washes herself and her clothes like crazy! But they're so old-fashioned. Well, with her figure it would be a lost cause anyway. Flat and spread out like a pancake. But I like her a lot. Like a daughter likes her mama. She is gentle and has such beautiful eyes. I think she'd really be unhappy if I went away. Her daughter, Claudia, is busy with her husband and the baby, and Papa Presso has his garages to look after. She wouldn't have said I should come if she hadn't wanted me. I asked her twice if it was all right with her. And I said she was alone such a lot. She said she didn't mind, but I'm sure she only said that so as not to complain about her boring life. You can tell when somebody likes you. Tact tells you that. And when you're unwanted, people let you know soon enough. Mr. Millington certainly let me know! But perhaps he was so grouchy because he didn't want to make his wife jealous. I had on my white dress with the blue jacket, real sharp. My best outfit. Molly Fleet altered it for me before she went bonkers. I have lots of time to think but I still can't understand why Fleet got so nasty to me. Aunt Doody says she has a hard time, and so on. But that's ridiculous! Fleet is quite used to her birthmark. I'm looking forward to Mrs. Pressolini. At last I can talk sense with somebody! Aunt Doody is sweet and all that, but I can't talk to her. She always starts talking about something else. She jumps from one subject to the other. No connection whatsover. That's crook! But when I told her, she said people in glass houses . . . That's gratitude for you! When you think of all the things I did for her as long as I could. They're all good at taking from you. I learned that from dear Charles. A pimp and a liar. Mrs. Pugh should be ashamed to take on a low type like that!

If I babbled like Aunt Doody, I wouldn't have benefactors like Albert Ritter and Trent. They're spoiled. They hang on my every word, especially Ritter.

I've been with Carlo's relatives for two weeks now. I'm a little disappointed in Mrs. Presso. Either she was putting on an act, or she didn't want me here as much as she pretended to. Now that she has a nice jolly girl to talk to, she hardly says a word. Of course she's very busy in her big house, and always cooks everything herself for her husband, in spite of the fact that they have money to burn. They could eat in the finest restaurants, which I'd enjoy a lot more than eating at home. Or Mrs. Presso could buy canned and frozen foods instead of spending all her time cooking. "We don't like to eat out," she told me. I'm speechless! Italian men are the biggest tyrants in the home. Our men are satisfied with anything. They know very well that we're not going to spend all our time on their food. We live in a free country. I told Mrs. Pressolini so with the best intentions; one has to explain our customs to the new Australians. But she said, "Wait until you get married, Candy. If you want to keep your man, learn to cook from me. I'll be glad to show you." I thanked her politely. If one's got a figure like Mrs. Presso, I suppose one has to cook and bake for one's man. He's not bad-looking, actually quite interesting, and much younger than she is.

I help Mrs. Presso in the kitchen when I'm not too tired. She finds my rubber gloves funny. I find a lot of things funny in this house too, but I'm a guest. They won't take a penny from me. "It's only for the time being," said Mr. Presso. "Hang onto your money, Candy." Very decent of him! Of course I'm only a temporary guest. What did he think? I rather like him. Not as fat as Trent and not as arrogant as Albert Ritter. I wonder what Ritter's doing without me? I'd love to see his long face when he comes to the house!

This evening Mr. Pressolini said, "Go back to Sydney, child. My nephew isn't going to do a thing for you. You see, we threw him out, and that's something we don't do easily with a rel-

ative." When I didn't say anything, he went on. "*I'm saying this for your own good.*" I asked him if he wanted to be rid of me. "*Heavens, no!*" he said, quite startled. "*But you're still too young to be sitting around here. You have possibilities in Sydney.*"

I didn't want to tell him that I dreaded Molly Fleet's malicious satisfaction, and that Aunt Doody is used to seeing me at the top of the ladder. I can't bear to be pitied. Not by women! Mr. Presso and I went for a walk in the garden. He got one of his wife's woolen shawls for me because it's cold in Tasmania. "*I'm so alone,*" I murmured. He didn't reply. And he talks a blue streak to his wife. I laid my head on his shoulder. "*Fabio, help me,*" I whispered.

"*What on earth are you talking about, Miss Blyth?*" he said, and marched into the house without looking back at me once. Perhaps he's so much in love with me that he's playing it cool. His wife can't possibly satisfy a man like him. That same evening I heard voices in the bedroom. I was getting some coffee for myself in the kitchen. I don't listen at doors like Molly Fleet, but perhaps he was saying something about me to his wife. He said a lot, unfortunately in Italian. His wife seemed to be trying to calm him down. Suddenly he opened the door, but I turned my back on him and took my coffee to my room. He seems to think I'm running after him! Men are ridiculously conceited. If Fabio wants something, let him come to me.

Mrs. Presso makes marvelous coffee. She puts more in than Aunt Doody. I don't know why she's so silent. I was really quite mistaken about her. I discover new unpleasant sides to her every day. Fabio is still friendly, but at a distance of ten miles! I wonder if he dreams about me. Italians have so much imagination.

A week later:

At last I told Mrs. Presso that I've lost my work in Sydney. *Insight* and the other magazines and television stations have dropped me. I couldn't fulfill my contracts because I had to *fly to Hobart with my broken heart. After all, people should understand that. But nobody did. Not even the photo boys who made such a lot of money from me. Beasts! The only thing the whole beauty mob can do is make money with you. And I thought Australia was a free country! Only on paper.*

I must write to Aunt Doody that she must put more coffee in her coffee. And the food here is never burnt. If the Pressos were nicer I wouldn't mind staying here longer. Why aren't they nicer to me? Don't I bring life into their house?

I have advised Carlo once more to remember his true love. I wrote to him against my will, that I'm ready to forget and forgive. He must have a lot of money now from his old lady, but I didn't mention that I'd like to borrow some or I'll never see him again! The bastard only knows how to take. I am beside myself. Not that anyone would notice it. That would be the bloody end!

Miss Rigby's secretary wrote that they've found somebody to take my place. To take my place? I had to laugh. Bought a copy of Insight *to see what my replacement looked like. The dog comes from Mittagong. What can possibly come out of Mittagong? She is seventeen and has enormous ears. I am very relieved. The people at* Insight *will soon find out who made their subscription list shoot up sky-high! Especially in the Outback. Charlie Rainbow used to look at my photos, even though he's ill . . . illi . . . even though he doesn't like to read or write. I mean illiterate. I learned the word from Trent. He didn't mean me, of course. He compared me once to a mimosa blossom! I mean, I'm not a mimosa! Just because he won't touch me . . .*

Heard a story over the radio of a pickaninny brat that got lost in the bush. Very sad. Pressos were not impressed. She cried, "Cooh-eh!" I mean the mother of the pickaninny did. She followed the traces like a bloodhound. These lubras see in the dark just as well as in the light. Can't compete with them in that! It's thundering in on the radio, and a dingo is howling. He isn't in Tasmania. There are no more dingoes here. Except Charles Preston. I cried for the pickaninny child.

Mrs. Presso asked her husband if he liked the fish with the new sauce. These people are heartless. And I always thought the wops were so emotional. Just an act. If I only knew where to go! At last Carlo is back from his trip. I read about it in the social column, where I always used to be featured, but this was only about Hobart: Mrs. Kenneth Pugh and her secretary, Mr. Charles Preston, have returned . . . so they call that a "secretary" now! I laughed myself sick!

Mrs. Pugh is the widow of a rich director of the electric works. Apples and electricity make up the wealth of this state. Now Charles Preston is spending his money. If I were the dear departed Mr. Pugh—according to Fabio he was decorated in the Second World War, and made great contributions to charity—I would be turning in my grave three times a day! The Pugh woman is gaunt and has a sour expression and red veins in her face. I could see that even on the photo, but she carries on like a young girl. I thought widows were supposed to grieve.

Saw Mrs. Pugh and her secretary drive off to the golf club today. I was waiting outside the villa. Charles had to come out some time! He drove. She looked a hundred and thirty-two years old! Charles was enthroned beside her. And to think that in Genoa he was a chauffeur, according to his uncle. In Genoa he was milking some old woman too. His parents were poor. All the things he told me in Sydney were stinking lies! That's him! I lie only when my self-respect demands it. I've written to Molly Fleet that I love it in Hobart, and that I'm a guest at the home of Charles's fine relatives. She'll bust! And I really am a guest. Mrs. Pugh and her secretary play golf at the Royal Hobart, I followed them in a taxi. When they stopped at the club house, I ran out and cried, "Hello, Charles!" I was wearing my pink dress, a dreamy creation. And a white coat and long gloves! "Hello, Charles!" I cried, louder. I was freezing, although the sun was shining.

Mrs. Helen Pugh, the famous hostess and widow of . . . anyway, Pugh's widow looked at me with piercing eyes and asked, "Who's that?" Charles was silent for a moment. He didn't

*look at me, although I was wearing my pink dress for him.
"Somebody I knew in Sydney," he mumbled. "Come on, Helen." He wanted to get Mrs. Pugh into the club house fast. "I think I went dancing with her once," he added hurriedly.*

I ran after them. They had to move slowly because of Mrs. Pugh's age. At least forty-three! I had to laugh and couldn't stop! Everything was going around and around in front of me. "He thinks..." I screamed finally. "I want you to know, Mrs. Pugh! The dog lived for months...months...on my money! I want you to know..." I stopped. There was nothing but air around me. The two had disappeared into the club long ago. I wouldn't have thought the old bitch could run that fast! I stood in the sun and froze. A policeman came up to me. "Are you all right, miss?" It was then that I noticed I was still laughing and crying, "I want you to know..." Luckily a taxi stopped right in front of us. The policeman must have hailed it. "Go home, miss," he said, real friendly. "You're a little crook."

"There's nothing wrong with me!" I screamed. "I want you to know..."

My teeth were chattering. Mrs. Presso put me to bed and gave me aspirin with hot milk and honey. Oh yes, there was an egg yolk in it too. Aunt Doody would never have done that, I mean, beside everything else, add a whole egg! "Why are you shivering, Candy?" Mrs. Presso asked.

"It's cold in Tasmania," I replied hoarsely.

Next morning things went my way. Fabio had gone to the office, I had slept late because I'd had chills, Mrs. Presso was making fresh coffee. "I can do that," I said. She's quick as a race horse in spite of being so fat. Practice, I decided. I wouldn't like to be running back and forth all the time.

"You gave me a good scare, Candy." Mrs. Presso was pouring my coffee. Now she put an omelet down in front of me. It had not stuck to the pan. "What are you going to do now, girl?"

"How is it that your omelets never stick to the pan?" I asked. At last I wanted to learn something about cooking and she wouldn't explain it to me. She's not easy to live with. I don't know why I suddenly felt flat in my stomach in spite of the good breakfast: two pieces of toast with butter and orange marmalade, besides the omelet. Mrs. Presso was staring at me, her eyes wide. A strange look. As if she were sorry for me. With my figure? And as if she'd had enough of me. Who wants guests whose teeth chatter? It dawned on me at last— she wanted to be rid of me. Nicely. She is gentle and always friendly, but I don't know . . . It was weird. I left the room. I hadn't quite finished my toast, but there was a lump in my throat. Not that Mrs. Presso had said anything nasty, but there was no warmth in her eyes any more. They were hard as gravel. I hadn't done anything. I asked her twice if my visit wouldn't disturb her, and I've only been here five weeks. Baked beans for lunch. I hate them.

In the evening Fabio, in a very friendly tone, told me that his daughter, Claudia, and the baby were coming to stay with them, and he was sorry but they were going to need my room. Mr. Millington was coming a week later. I asked when Claudia was coming, and could I stay three more days? Of course, both of them said. They would phone Claudia and tell her not to come until then. I felt so cold that Fabio had to turn on the electric fireplace. I'll sell the mother-of-pearl brooch and the gold necklace Mr. Muir gave me. Charles sold the necklace Ritter gave me in Sydney, but he forgot to give me the money. I can't write to Trent for money. I don't know his address, and if his wife opened the letter! I'd open every letter my husband got, if I had a husband, I mean, a man. I know the sheilas . . .

In this morning's paper I read that there was a burglary at the Villa Pugh. Charles Preston was arrested. A pearl necklace had been missing. She had found it in her secretary's room, skillfully hidden. He was having a bit of fun with the gardener's daughter while Mrs. Pugh was searching his room. So in her case love didn't seem to be blind. I wonder if Charles will go to jail now. You can't be too careful about the company you *keep. The Pressos are very upset about it. I would be too if Carlo was my nephew.*

The pearl necklace he had stashed away fortunately reminded me of the pearls in Broome. I had never thought of Robert Muir, but now I remembered how good-natured he had been. Money, presents, and a free airplane ticket to Sydney. Anyway, the Pressolinis paid for my ticket to Broome. Not because they wanted to be sure to get rid of me, but because I'm still young and can't look after myself. Anyway, not right now, with Insight behaving so shabbily.

It was an absolutely crackpot idea of mind to come to Hobart. Nobody in Sydney told me how cold it was in Tasmania. I wonder if that is why the Pressolinis were so frosty during the last weeks of my stay there. I'm glad I'm leaving. I tried very hard with them, but it's not like being with our old Aussies.

Mr. Muir may be a little surprised, but I'm sure he'll pay for my flight back to Sydney later. Perhaps the new prodigy at Insight will get sick, or the girl from Mittagong will pick up a lousy lover. I wish her all the best, but in case anything should happen to her and Insight needed a new model, I could go back.

If Muir lets me go!

I hope he's in Broome! But I don't like to ask. There's no time anyway. Mrs. Pressolini is making up the bed fresh for her daughter.

Candy landed at the airport in Broome toward evening. She was afraid of what the dark was hiding and what the morning would reveal. But the Villa Muir was brilliantly lit. Guests were walking up and down in the garden, which was festively illuminated by lanterns. Candy told the driver to wait a minute. Then she drove to a hotel in the Chinese quarter. She had just remembered that Mr. Muir didn't receive uninvited guests.

She phoned from the hotel and was told that Mr. Muir was busy. "It's an emergency!" Candy sounded desperate.

"Who's speaking?" the secretary wanted to know. Candy recognized his voice.

"Candy," she said. "Candy Blyth."

"And what do you want?"

"I want to speak to Mr. Muir personally. Please ask him to come to the phone."

There was a click on the line. The secretary had hung up. He couldn't remember any lady called Candy Blyth, and Mr. Muir was busy.

Candy sat straight upright in her little hotel room. What would she do if Mr. Muir didn't remember her?

17

Cultured Pearls and Butterflies

Robert Muir took his Japanese guests to the airport next morning, and on his way home picked up Miss Blyth at her hotel. Despite his secretary, who watched over him jealously, Mr. Muir had not forgotten Candy. So the stupid girl was on the skids again. Mr. Muir had no illusions that she had flown to Broome because of his beautiful eyes, but why shouldn't he have a bit of fun with her? His Japanese guests had been with him for two weeks; he could do with a little relaxation. Candy was in luck, but she didn't know it.

When she had called Robert Muir, he had been discussing the price of pearls with his friends from Tatoku Island. He had only just returned to Broome after visiting the famous pearl culture station in Japan, on dreamlike Ago Bay. These pearls offered considerable competition to the pearl-fisher stations in Broome, but in Broome mother-of-pearl had always seemed more important than the pearls. And after the Second World War, even the high point had been surpassed.

Muir had never felt so content as on this visit to Japan, and he was thinking seriously of spending his remaining years in the land of his mother's ancestors. He wanted a town house in Tokyo and a country house on one of the many islands. In any case he had no intention of keeping up the villa in Broome for Miss Blyth's occasional visits. Candy hadn't grasped yet that everything in life changed faster than one realized, and that men could change too. Mr. Muir was so friendly this time that she wasn't the least bit afraid of him. He gave her some presents, but no cash. Candy was so speechless that she began to look more attractive to Mr. Muir.

She had now been living for fourteen days in his magnificent house and couldn't understand why Mr. Muir had turned into such a lamb! He wasn't *that* old! In his middle forties, at most. Candy believed that aging men were calmer and more generous because they no longer had the strength to be angry or passionate. Mr. Muir, age forty-seven, did not feel old, but it was the time of life when a man starts to meditate, leaves the business of the day to his partners, and thinks of a home in solitude. His metamorphosis from Australian businessman to a student of wisdom had begun in Japan. Since people and things gain in value in an aura of impending farewell, Robert Muir saw in Candy this time an Australian Venus, who would hardly cross his path in Japan.

On the evening after the farewell dinner for his Japanese guests, Robert Muir lay naked under his mosquito netting and did breathing exercises. Candy was in the garden, chattering with his secretary, a student from Perth, who was as faceless as required by Mr. Muir. He was nice to Miss Blyth now because Mr. Muir had taken her in. Mr. Muir yawned, and thought with satisfaction of the dinner. He had supervised his cook as the man had filled the beautifully lacquered platters and trays with exquisitely garnished delicacies: grilled lobster and crab, artfully fringed tentacles of roast octopus, consommé with seaweed (which was supposed to increase a man's potency), and naturally the Western Australian type of sashimi, a raw red fish served swimming in soy sauce between little heaps of horseradish. During the meal Robert Muir had been pleased to think that his steak days were nearly at an end.

He had also examined a collection of cultured pearls, and his Japanese guests had presented him with a few spectacular examples as a farewell gift. Mr. Mikimoto, the son of a poor pearl fisher, had produced the cultured pearl. Nothing had been able to hold this clever, fanatic Japanese back from his experiments—not the infinitely fine work of opening the shell and introducing the alien body; not the destruction of his shells by the *akashio*, the red tide, the microbes of which destroyed fish and shells; not the atomic war nor the American occupation troops—nothing had deterred Mr. Mikimoto from the development of his craft. "Patience," thought Robert Muir, lying on his bed in Broome. "Who has patience in Australia or America?"

With eyes half closed he watched his white tissue-paper butterflies that hung suspended from the ceiling by thin threads. It was unbreathably hot tonight, but whenever the faintest breath of air wafted through the open windows and door, these weightless Japanese toys danced up and down and gave the motionless man an illusion of coolness. The butterflies fulfilled their only function in the mechanized present with perfection, and Mr. Muir didn't expect anything more from them. He didn't expect these dainty paper dancers to make classical music or converse with him about the French theatre of the absurd. He had seen a few performances of Ionesco's short dramas during his last visit to Paris, and had been entranced by their existential nonsense. What was happening on the stage had been going on in Japan for thousands of years. But the mundane common sense of the West, all practically oriented, couldn't be expected to grasp the drama of existence.

Mr. Muir watched his dancing butterflies and in a roundabout way his thoughts reverted to Candy Blyth. As long as she fulfilled her function to his satisfaction, like these butterflies, she could go right on being charmingly inane as far as he was concerned. She provided the illusion of perfect beauty as long as she remained silent. On this pragmatic continent, Robert Muir needed certain illusions, and was prepared to pay for them.

* * *

Muir had noticed at once that the butterfly dust had fallen from the wings of his young Venus from Kalgoorlie. The girl lived in a consumer society and was the victim of frivolous and merciless male lust. She had told him that she had missed him. He had laughed aloud. Whom did she think he was?

Mr. Muir spent most of his evenings with his butterflies. Another week passed and he hadn't called Candy into his private rooms, which one entered only in stocking feet. She entertained his guests as best she could, and he didn't seem to notice her, although he was watching her all the time. After her arrival he had sent her to the hairdresser. Her red hair was impossible. The girl had all the guile of a butterfly; not even her alliance with the shark from Genoa had robbed her of her lighthearted optimism. This Mr. Preston had of course helped himself to her money and jewelry. Mr. Muir missed his presents too. He had his Scottish memory for things he had bought.

He put on his black silk robe and rang for Candy. He wanted to talk business with her. Candy smiled at him coyly. She could never tell whether Mr. Muir was in a private or official mood.

"I have bought an oyster bar, Miss Blyth," he said. "You will work there from five to seven. I take it you don't want to sit here forever doing nothing."

"Of course not," said Candy, against her convictions.

"The manager will show you what to do. I'll take you there tomorrow morning, and I hope you'll like the work."

Mr. Muir hoped nothing of the sort—he was giving orders. Candy nodded. She knew that tone. "I hope it won't be too much for me," she said hesitantly.

"I hope not too, Miss Blyth. So what's new? Why so silent?"

Candy opened her eyes wide. Wasn't Mr. Muir always telling her to keep her mouth shut? "Something terrible has happened, Mr. Muir."

"Here in my house?"

"Nothing ever happens in your house. I mean in South Australia."

"I am not a mind reader, Miss Blyth. So . . . what happened?"

"I'll get the paper."

"Don't flutter around all the time. Try to think for a change."

His bright, dark eyes were fixed on her with a strange expression. They were boring holes into her. Suddenly she felt hot and cold. Was he trying to hypnotize her? After all, he was half a Jap, and the old people in Australia still told horror stories about the dirty deeds of the yellow man. Candy couldn't move. The butterflies on the ceiling weren't moving either.

Mr. Muir looked down again and asked if Candy had lost her tongue. She pulled herself together. She must have been mistaken because Mr. Muir was a hundred percent Scottish again. Candy reported that an immigrant family consisting of five people had lost their way in the northwest desert, miles from Birdsville. The poor creatures, tortured by unbearable thirst and hunger, had perished in the so-called "sand hills of the dead."

"Why do the fools come to Australia?" Mr. Muir lit a cigarette. "That wouldn't have happened to them in England."

"Don't you think it's terribly sad, Mr. Muir?"

Muir went on smoking, unmoved, and looked up at his lifeless butterflies. He asked languidly how the bodies had been found.

"By the blackfellows. Funny, but the blacks can follow any trail better than the dogs."

Mr. Muir said nothing; his face was a mask.

"The blacks led the boys from the police to the bodies."

"Did you think the police would have found them alone?" Mr. Muir asked gently.

"It must be terribly hot in the desert."

"It's colder in Siberia," said Mr. Muir.

"I know an abo in Sydney. His name is Charlie Rainbow, and he lives with us. He came one day with his box of flowers . . ."

"No biographies, please, Miss Blyth. I'm allergic to them. Besides it's too hot for them in the desert of Broome. Why are you crying again? Are you longing for the abo?"

"I'm sorry for those people." Candy's voice was trembling.

"The blackfellows or the English?" Mr. Muir asked in a

strange voice. He closed his eyes. Lately he found talking to Miss Blyth enervating. For a moment he had to let his mind carry him away. This happened to him quite often when he dealt with certain types of Australians. Then, with the utmost concentration, he would manage to see waterfalls, rock formations, and clouds—the primeval stuff of the universe. They were an insurance against sensual attraction, because this foolish girl was becoming more and more threateningly attractive daily.

Candy's strident voice tore into his thoughts. He looked at her in silence. It was ridiculous, but for him this young creature had become a visual object of esthetic desire. Was it possible that he could conjure up a magnificent landscape of the spirit and in spite of it pine for this little fool? He knew that the struggle was lost. He had to touch those breasts and the narrow, swaying hips of this marble idiot! He had to shatter this sugar doll. After that he was willing to be poor, banished from the paradise of the senses, and would walk upright across the threshold of old age. Miss Blyth was not a child any more. She was sated with cheap and humiliating experiences. She couldn't express herself, but her body spoke. Her body was a hymn of immaculate beauty, the kind the white race produces only occasionally among thousands of misprints. Her body was a gift of God which this young creature was selling at marked-down prices between Kalgoorlie, Sydney, and Broome.

"Isn't it gruesome, to die so young?" Candy asked. "The youngest of that immigrant family was only ten."

"What's gruesome about it? Those people were spared a lot in Australia."

"It's the best country in the world!" Candy cried indignantly.

"And that's why. Too much preoccupation with body welfare leading to the typical sickness of spiritual deficiency."

"We're very progressive, Mr. Muir. We have a lot of universities and movies and television."

"Ah yes. Television." Mr. Muir was interested to see Candy's eyes fill with tears again. "And what's wrong now, Miss Blyth?"

"I can't stop thinking of those corpses in the desert. They can't ever go to the movies again. Or eat ice cream."

"Horrible!" said Mr. Muir. "You are enchanting when you cry, Miss Blyth. Unfortunately you were born without a sense of compassion. In five minutes you will have forgotten those unfortunate people in the desert."

"That isn't true!"

"Oh, but it is, Miss Blyth."

Unlike the casual Australians, Mr. Muir used the formal address. Candy had once called him "Bob" and he had given her a look that had nipped any further attempts at informality in the bud. Mr. Muir decided who could be intimate with him, and when.

He moved closer to Candy. "Why do you feel so sorry for absolute strangers?" he said harshly. "If you want to weep, then weep for me!"

He had lit another cigarette and was smoking calmly. Candy was baffled. This man had everything—money, a luxurious villa, he traveled, gave parties, he had women! In Broome, gossip didn't stop at the Villa Muir. A while ago a French woman from Queensland had been a steady guest there.

"I should weep for *you*?" Candy asked. The bottom had fallen out of her world with a crash.

Muir was silent. He couldn't talk to this girl about the nature and the problems of this lonely continent. He couldn't possibly bare his soul to her. Should he tear open his wounds in front of this beautiful ignoramus? This country had given him nothing voluntarily. He had fought grimly and with very private difficulties for every success and all the respect he enjoyed today in Australian society. Not even in love had he been accepted without having to pay. Although he was in command of a whole repertoire of delights, no woman had ever left his house without a check. He was not simple or vain enough to give the appearances of love to the tyrannical demands of the flesh, but even the most unvarnished pleasure lost vitality and charm with the checkbook. That was why Mr. Muir had been living for months without the consolation of Venus.

"I think you are to be envied," said Candy.

"Let's stop this nonsense, Miss Blyth." Perhaps this blind

chicken had found a kernel of corn? After all, he knew how to make his loneliness bear fruit, and was thus perhaps to be envied, even if the child had not meant it.

"Would you like tea?" asked Candy. Mr. Muir's silence was making her feel more and more unsure of herself.

"I don't want tea," he said brusquely. This girl, who was staring straight at him without a spark of understanding, was, perhaps for that reason, becoming increasingly irresistible with every passing second.

He had to embrace her, wound her. Through Candy he would humiliate the white Australians. Then he would squash the butterfly in his fist and throw it away. The old dangerous hate-love, the basic motif of his divided existence on this continent, was concentrated at this moment on this unsuspecting girl. Robert Muir stood like a statue in his own twilight. He felt dizzy, with an avidity he was still trying to suppress. But it was too late. He had undressed Candy so many times in his mind. Why had she come back?

He closed his eyes again, but he was cruelly awake. This destructive lust, which in sober moments Mr. Muir found absurd and monotonous, had to be expiated! Sex was monotonous, but it brought deliverance from treacherous tensions and left him liberated, and with the reawakened desire for solitude and abstract thought . . .

Seconds had passed, but time seemed to be standing still. Candy tried to avoid Mr. Muir's eyes. They were black, hypnotic pools that grew increasingly eerie, a thunderstorm with lightning. Candy was trembling, but she couldn't move. She had never seen this man naked. This wasn't Mr. Muir who advised her kindly to shut up, and gave her dresses and jewelry. A strange, powerful figure, inexorable and terrifying, was moving toward her slowly, resolutely and mercilessly. The powerful shoulders, the bald head, the narrow hips and the long, sinewy legs were like marble, gleaming golden and barbarically in the dark. This was the night itself, which had always made Candy shiver. She stood naked and helpless under the spell of those eyes, their animal glow blinding her. With a childish motion she put her arms up in front of her face and screamed, "No!" But not a sound came out of her throat. The light and the everyday things as she knew them had fled.

"No! No!" In vain. Too late. The night was deaf and mute.

After that night Robert Muir found Candy's presence hard to bear. He was overwhelmed by a dark feeling of guilt right in his office, and it grew in his leisure hours. He had lured an ignorant young creature onto forbidden ground, and he didn't want to repeat the experiment. Candace Blyth lived in a different climate, on another emotional level—besides, she always remained the same. The rhythm of the seasons and feelings were foreign to her. The chain of absurdity that ran through her existence now weighed also upon him, and in a roundabout way conjured up guilt feelings. True, he had given her a valuable piece of jewelry, but he had the feeling that this time it had not roused the same enthusiasm. He had thoroughly confused the girl and now he was sorry. She crept around like a sick young animal. She worked at the oyster bar at the time assigned to her, dully and automatically. Dead inventory. He might have known. Politely and silently he began to hate her. He didn't desire her any more. She had given him all and nothing. An oyster without a pearl.

Mr. Muir lay all alone again in his immaculate room after work and the many business meetings. He looked at his butterflies. They were less impersonal than Candy Blyth. Why couldn't he get rid of this feeling of guilt? Finally he shrugged and told himself that the struggle between the sexes was waged with boomerangs that came back in deceptively playful detours to the ones who had thrown them.

Miss Blyth had to leave.

One morning Mr. Muir was gone. His secretary, who wasn't experiencing the end of an affair for the first time, brought Candy a letter. Mr. Muir suggested that she work in his oyster bar all day, because one waitress was out sick. But if she preferred to leave, his secretary would buy her a ticket to Sydney. Neither cash nor a check were enclosed this time.

On his return Mr. Muir found the young lady still at his house. His secretary, a young man with no attributes, experienced an uncomfortable half hour. Naturally he defended himself. He had tried his best but Miss Blyth was hard of hearing. Moreover, her listless behavior at the oyster bar had reduced the number of clients. Mr. Muir chose to overlook this observation. The oyster bar was none of his secretary's damn business!

That evening Mr. Muir spoke to Candy about her future. They were sitting on the big balcony facing the ocean. The moon shone dreamily in the tropical sky, but Mr. Muir was not feeling dreamy.

"I am going to write to my aunt in Sydney," Candy told him finally.

"Do that, child." This was followed by an uncomfortable silence. "Forgive me," Muir mumbled, "but everything has to end some time, doesn't it?"

Candy didn't notice the trace of impatience in his voice. "What did I do?" she asked stubbornly.

"Nothing," Mr. Muir replied truthfully. "What are you waiting for?" he asked irritably. Then he sank back into his basic and merciless introspection. He had talent for creating a vacuum around himself.

He watched Candy as he had done at the end of her first visit, wondering that such an attractive body did not include an attractive spirit. He had tried at least to produce an artificial pearl—in vain. The girl's spirit was weighted down in a mundane life. Her soul was asleep. She was wandering along the edge of an abyss and didn't know it.

Muir frowned. At twenty Candy had seen and experienced more on this sprawling colorful continent than most young women in Europe or Japan, but no one and nothing made a lasting impression on her. And that was the true tragedy of any human being.

At last Candy wrote to Lydia Doody. They hadn't heard from her in months because she only remembered her relatives

Dear Candy,

I'm glad you thought of your aunt at last. We've been racking our brains where you could possibly be. Your mother didn't know either. But I wrote her that you couldn't expect chicken meat from an ox.

That you want to come back to Sydney is the dumbest thing I've ever heard of. What do you expect to do here? You won't like it after Broome. You can't just throw over your elegant job in the oyster bar. You're twenty years old now, and still don't have any more gumption than a little brat. How do you think you can earn money here? I'm sending you—printed matter or it costs too much—a few issues of *Insight* with your successor in it. I cry often because you gave up your elegant job as a model where you earned so much money. Molly Fleet makes tea for me when I'm mad. She's a good egg.

Sydney has changed a lot. I'm broke because I miss the money you used to pay me. But I manage. I've had to raise the rents, though, so everybody's mad at you. But I always say—you can't count on anybody in this lousy world. Not even one's own flesh and blood. Charlie Rainbow laughs at me. I let him. A blackfellow doesn't often have anything to laugh about.

Our Albert Ritter, you know—the traveling salesman from New South Wales with the snotty face—never came back. Do you suppose he's dead? If only you didn't always forget to get his address, I'd have sent a wreath. Two of our neighbors died. I don't know what's come over Sydney. Everybody's dying! I hope I don't catch it.

Our dear Mr. Trent has been in Queensland now for quite some time. He came to see me a few times after you left, and helped me out with money and tried to comfort me because you were so disloyal. He said, Youth has little virtue, but that's nonsense. Even a young dog sticks to his master, doesn't he?

How can you ask if Molly Fleet is still with me? Of course she is! She's like a daughter to me. Don't know what I'd do without her. She comes home tired from work and scrubs the kitchen floor! I always say: it's heart that counts!

Mr. Trent is going to have a baby, I mean, his young wife is. Isn't that dinkum? I cried like anything when I heard the good news. Dear old Mr. Trent kept beating about the bush until he finally told me before he left. He gave me such a big check. I guess he was so happy, he didn't know what he was doing! I can do with it, I mean the check. Molly

Fleet says Mr. Trent can't have been so unhappy with his wife as you always tried to tell us. A baby speaks its own language, says Molly. Mr. Trent sent you best greetings and all good wishes. He said, "I am truly happy that my young protegée is doing so well in Broome." By the way, I know Mr. Muir. I met him at a friend's house right here in Sydney! What do you say to that? Australia is a village. Trent and Muir never mentioned you. I made a point of asking because I wanted to know where you were. In the end Mr. Trent said he *thought* in Broome.

I would love to visit you at the Villa Muir. After all, you are my favorite niece and lived with me for a long time, didn't you? The fence is broken again. Charlie Rainbow has planted new flowers. But I guess all that doesn't interest you. You're an elegant young lady now in a luxurious house in Broome. Molly Fleet says there must be something fishy about it if you want to come back to us. But Molly sees something fishy in everything. Everybody has a little something wrong with them, like that. She also says she hopes you don't come to a bad end. I said if anybody has money to burn, like you do now, the bad end must be pretty far away. I know life and what I'm talking about. As soon as you send me the plane ticket, I'll come. I think it'll do you good to see an old piece of furniture out of your own family. I pray for you every day, and my friend with the wooden leg sends best greetings. Molly Fleet does too. We've all grown used to her birthmark. We don't see it any more. Charlie Rainbow and Uncle Doody send greetings too. Uncle wants to know if Mr. Muir would like to buy an umbrella. When shall I come?

But if you'd rather come back to us, you'll have to work. You can't count on your men any more, nor on the photoboys. Write right away what you decide. Molly Fleet is altering my best black dress. She says there are so many pearls in Broome. We'd love to have some! Molly says the pearls lie on the street in Broome. I hope I get to see them.

Your loving Aunt Doody

Candy tore up the letter. Did the friend with the wooden leg, Miss Fleet, Uncle Doody, and Charlie Rainbow perhaps want to settle down in the Villa Muir too? Why had she boasted so much? If she had written her aunt the truth, it would have been better. Mrs. Doody melted with pity for anyone unlucky, but she reacted sourly to lucky people. Candy felt panicky. She could only stay at the Villa Muir a few days longer, and the secretary wasn't the least bit helpful. Candy suspected him of being homosexual, but that wasn't the case at all. He was engaged, and spent all his free time with his fiancée.

Mr. Muir had given Candy her farewell present the night before. His meaning couldn't have been clearer. He was flying to Paris and bringing guests with him on his return. He gave Candy a butterfly of mother-of-pearl, set with pearls. The pearls were tears that wouldn't dry up, and the whole thing had to be worth a lot of money. Candy stared at the brooch, her lower lip trembling. Where was she to go? Nobody wanted to do anything for her. Nobody seemed eager for her company. But she was Candy! What was the matter with people?

She put the butterfly in her suitcase. She had to go walkabout again, and that was a nuisance and frightening. What had she done wrong in the Villa Muir? She didn't know and would never find out, even if she spent years thinking about it. She had only discovered one thing in Broome—there were tears behind everything . . .

"She's gone!" said Mrs. Doody. "Now I can't fly to Broome."

"It's all for the best," said Molly Fleet.

"But you said the pearls lie on the street there! And where is Candy? Maybe something's happened to her. I wrote her such a nice letter. I said she'd be welcome any time. After all, she's my own flesh and blood!"

"That's right," said Molly Fleet. "So where is she?"

"How should I know? You know, Molly, she goes walkabout, and that's that. She'll come to a bad end."

"She always lands on her feet," said Molly Fleet, unmoved.

"But you said yourself she'd come to a bad end."

"Possibly. I must have picked it up from you. Here's a tissue, Mrs. Doody. Don't cry. You won't get Candy's address that way."

Miss Fleet gave Mrs. Doody a sharp look. Except for the red veins in her fat face, she thought Mrs. Doody looked alarmingly pale. What on earth had the old woman written to Candy?

"If you wrote to her so nicely, and she still wants to run around all over the place, there's nothing you can do about it. I'll make you a quick cup of tea, Mrs. Doody. If you don't mind waiting a moment, I'll run over to Gretchen's and get us some pastry."

Mrs. Doody began to look in her bag for change. "My treat," said Molly. "We'll make it a little farewell celebration."

"Why? Are you going to take off too? I love you like my own daughter! And who'll scrub the kitchen floor?"

"Don't get upset, Mrs. Doody. I'm only going to Parramatta for a few days. My grandmother on the farm is ill."

"What's the matter with her?" Mrs. Doody asked animatedly.

"I don't know. My brother just wrote that she wanted to see me."

"And you'll surely come back?" Mrs. Doody sounded worried.

"I'm not your niece," Molly Fleet said with dignity.

18

How Big Is Parramatta?

After Grandmother Fleet's funeral, Molly sat with her brother, Stephen, on the big wooden veranda. The farm seemed empty. Molly didn't know what to say to her brother. She was like a bird dropped out of its nest. Stephen was silent. Molly looked at him shyly, sidelong. The protector of her childhood was now a strong, capable man who seemed to have forgotten how to speak. Molly looked around her. Everything was as she had always known and loved it—the house, Grandmother's kitchen and pantry, the living room with its worn furniture and an aroma of childhood, the stalls, the meadow, the evening stillness. Had it only been Grandmother Fleet, who with her sharptongued kindness and her faithfulness, made this place a home? That had to be it! Molly felt that with her grandmother's death, her youth had ended. But she was only twenty-two, and as people were always saying, her whole life still lay ahead of her. She pulled her grandmother's white shawl, that she'd been wearing for years now, tighter around her shoulders. Her grandmother had knitted it. Heaven only knew how she had found time with the work on the farm, to sew and knit for "the young one."

Molly had considered life on the farm as something indestructible. Every shilling she had set aside in Sydney she had thought of as something toward broadening and modernizing the place. And suddenly everything was different. Molly couldn't say what was separating her and Stephen. Evening had always been their most peaceful time. Stephen had taken his ledger—the little dog had sat beside him next to the wooden table—and had teased Molly every now and then. Grandmother had darned or rested after the strenuous work of preserving fruit and vegetables and all the business of the farm. Molly and the abo girl, Goonur, had sat around with her grandmother or played "farm" on the wooden veranda. Stephen had carved little animals and houses and a tiny fence for them. He had always been clever with his hands. And then there had been Lily, the good, clever cow. Molly hardly knew any of the cows now. She had only come to the farm for Easter and Christmas. Funny, there'd always been the three of them, as if her father and sister lived in another country. Yet the city of Parramatta wasn't far away. But the farm was the only place that had given Molly a feeling of belonging, and surely something like that had to remain, Molly thought, even when her grandmother wasn't sitting there any more. Milk and bread and the fields were . . . eternal! The big word startled Molly, but that was the way things were when you looked at it all in the light.

Molly had come too late to see Grandmother Fleet alive. None of them had known how serious her illness really was. Two days before her death she had made breakfast for Stephen and the farm hands, and declared, heroically and stubbornly, that she was feeling dinkum and the doctor was an idiot! He had threatened Grandmother Fleet with the hospital when Stephen told him she was still getting breakfast and shooing the girls out of the kitchen. And when nothing came of the threat with the hospital, and Grandmother finally realized that old Dr. Hodge was not an idiot but knew what he was talking about, she had capitulated.

She had decided all by herself and all alone that she would die on the farm. That was where she had lived with and labored for her grandchildren, and prayed for "the young one." Then she had told Dr. Hodge he should tell his old friend, Reverend Campbell. Not until the Reverend drove up in his rattletrap wagon and brought everything requisite to saying farewell to the farm, did Stephen see the light. That was when he had written express to Molly, and his father and April. Nobody reproached Stephen. They had all thought Grandmother Fleet would never die, in spite of the fact that she had been rehearsing that ritual for quite a few months. Nobody was allowed to watch her because it was an act of love, totally private and only God knew about it. Yes, Grandmother Fleet had made her peace with the Lord in profound silence. She had been angry with Him for years because of "the young one." Such a little lamb shouldn't have had to bear a fiery mark on her face. It wasn't fair! Of course all people were subjected to trials, and they had to be borne, and they had to say to themselves over and over again that the Lord knew how much one could bear. But Grandmother Fleet had found this too heavy a burden for Molly. Grandmother Fleet had broad shoulders and would have liked to take this burden upon herself. The child wasn't a vain little brat, like April. Grandmother had never ceased bringing the matter to God's attention, as if He didn't know his creatures! And in the end she had spoken about it to Reverend Campbell, and after confession had felt much calmer. For the first time she believed that Molly would know how to cope with it. With God's help. And so, after a laying down of arms, had come the great peace.

Half a year ago, Grandmother Fleet had begun, beside her housework, to pack up her earthly existence. You had to start some time. Stephen, grumbling, had driven her to the notary in Parramatta. What did Grandmother want with the notary? There was plenty of time for a will. And she didn't have to make one anyway, Stephen said. Molly would always have a place on the farm, all of them knew that. What was there for the old pen-pusher to scribble? But Grandmother was not to be shaken. She had signed various "scribbles," and the papers had remained with the notary. Then she had driven home with Stephen, content. Yes, they had drunk a beer at Father Fleet's house, and Grandmother had even asked why April came to the farm so rarely. In spite of the fact that she couldn't stand April, that was how peaceful Grandmother Fleet had been after the visit to the notary.

After that she had sat on the veranda again every evening with Stephen and still enjoyed many healthy, contented days. She had sewn quite a few things for "the young one," and embroidered some dresses. She didn't trust the job they did at the factory in Sydney. Molly had such a beautiful, straight figure. Everything fitted her as if poured on her. Yes, Grandmother had still had time to embroider a white dress with mimosa blossoms for Sundays. That was during the last weeks, when sewing and embroidering were already torturous, and Stephen was right to make a scene about it. That was Stephen. When he wasn't silent, words poured from him like a raging waterfall. She would have to leave her sewing machine behind, Grandmother thought sadly, but then had called herself to order sharply. She had to start behaving like a proper candidate for death. And that was how she had stubbornly practiced for enternity.

In the end Grandmother had asked constantly, "Has the little one come?" By that time all of them were gathered around the bed: Father Fleet, the Reverend Campbell, and April, and the boys and girls who worked on the farm. But then there was nobody but the family and the Reverend. Suddenly Grandmother cried out, "Molly! Come closer, child!" She couldn't recognize the people standing around the bed properly any more. Stephen pushed his sister April forward. She stood there as usual, stiff as a ramrod, but finally she did kneel down, and Grandmother laid her old, work-worn hand on April's head. Then the prayers for the dead began. Grandmother Fleet looked damn peaceful, Stephen thought. Younger, too, and smoother. He couldn't understand it.

Father Fleet and April went straight back to Parramatta after the funeral. The brewery had to go on functioning. Father Fleet had even asked Molly to stop and visit them for a while before she went back to Sydney. Molly wanted to pack up slowly in Sydney. Now was the time. She couldn't leave Stephen alone for good. She had saved quite a lot, and somebody had to do Grandmother's work. Mrs. Doody would understand. She would have to find one or two nice, decent girls to rent from her because there was no relying on Candace Blyth. She just bummed around.

Molly wanted to stay with her father for a week. He was lonely. He couldn't bark at his wife any more or scare Grandmother Cocker half to death. In the end, the two had escaped him. And April? His favorite daughter was as bitter as blackthorn. Molly knew that it was partly her fault. Why had she, stupid brat that she then was, got herself mixed up in April's affairs? But there was nothing to be done now about the broken engagement. She didn't hate her sister any more as she had done when April had called her Mole. April had become a stranger. Molly would spend a week in her father's house as an act of contrition. She found her father had aged considerably. "Is Father all right?" she asked Stephen.

"Sure. But he isn't getting any younger."

Finally Stephen told her that their grandmother had left her all sorts of things in her will. She had told him so during her last days. "The sewing machine too. And her only ring."

"There's time enough for that, Stephen."

"We're going to town tomorrow. They'll open the will."

Molly looked up at the violet night sky. The clouds were crowding together like strayed sheep. Molly said hesitantly, "Grandmother was first-rate. *She* was always there."

"She lived here."

"Father ran away from us all the time, Mother hid from us. Have you forgotten it all, Stephen? And Grandmother Cocker scurried away like a scared rabbit when I wanted to go up to her. She was a dud."

"Let's not bring old Cocker into this, Molly. The poor woman didn't know any better. Father wasn't nice to her."

"Anyway, Grandmother Fleet never ran away when we wanted her." Molly swallowed hard. "That's a wonderful thing. I mean—to be always there for your family. Grandmother Fleet..."

Stephen pounded on the table with his fist. "Stop it!" he yelled. "You don't have to explain her to me." He turned away brusquely. His dog licked his shoe, and Stephen mumbled, "Scram, you bastard!" But the dog wagged his tail, and Stephen forgot him. He stroked Molly's hair clumsily, as he used to do when she came running to him, weeping. How could he have yelled at Molly? She had only told the truth. Grandmother Fleet had been unique, and it was a good thing that the young one knew it. "Let it be, Molly. I'm not myself."

"I'll make tea for us, Stephen. Two sugars for you, and a lot of milk. Or has it changed?"

Of course Stephen drank his tea as he always had. Molly never forgot later that it had calmed her.

Shortly before she left for Parramatta, Stephen asked his sister what her plans for the future were. She had grown accustomed to being at home again. In these two weeks, Sydney had begun to fade. Mrs. Doody's roominghouse, Molly's clients in their fine villas, her lonely wanderings through King's Cross, her love letters to Rigby and her own last letter, which she had torn up—everything lay far behind her. She thought often these days that it might have been better if she had stayed on the farm. This was the place for her. Grandmother had left her her share. The farm now belonged to Stephen and her. But even without the will, it would have been the only home for her. Stephen and she had always held together. When he yelled at her it was only because he had to let off steam. He was the salt of the earth.

Molly had soon made friends with the new cows and helped wherever she could. She hoped this would please Stephen, but he didn't say anything. When one tried not to find one's home empty and worked as hard as the boys and girls on the farm, life was good and made sense. The only thing she and Stephen didn't touch were the preserves in the pantry. One day the wooden shelves were empty. Stephen had given Grandmother's preserves, in their glasses and stone jars, away. He had always experienced a slight shock when he had seen her clear script on the labels: content, date, how prepared, and how long the contents could be kept. Stephen had brooded. It wasn't right that things should outlive the person. Molly saw the empty shelves, but she said nothing. She had some of Granny's preserve jars in Sydney. She would remove the labels and keep them.

"What are you planning to do, Moll?"

Molly looked at her brother, surprised. If Stephen didn't know what she wanted to do, then who would? But she said quietly that she'd like to go on making money a while longer and then...

"Of course I'll come back to you, here on the farm. I may stay only a few more weeks in Sydney. I can't let Mrs. Doody down at a moment's notice."

Still Stephen said nothing.

"I've read a lot about dairy farming while I was in Sydney, and I've been to quite a few lectures. I think we should go right on modernizing. But I think I wrote you all that."

Stephen puffed on his pipe. The silence gradually grew oppressive. Why didn't he say anything? Molly sat up stiffly in her wicker chair with the faded cushions. Her hands were ice-cold. Didn't Stephen want her? When he still didn't say anything, she asked him, taking care that her voice shouldn't tremble.

"Don't ask such stupid questions," Stephen said gruffly. "This is and remains your home. Only . . . I want to . . . I intend to . . ."

"Do you want to sell the farm?"

"Don't shout! Granny hated it when you shouted."

"What's the matter, Stephen?"

"You don't have to whisper, either. Well, Moll . . . I'm going to get married at last."

He drew a deep breath. Praise be the Lord, he had spat it out! The young one sat there stiff as a statue. As if lightning had struck. Stephen began to feel uneasy.

"That doesn't mean you won't be welcome here, Molly. I've explained everything to Jennifer. Her folks have a farm near here. Not as many cattle and machines, but nice enough. Jenny grew up on the farm." Stephen couldn't remember ever having said so much in one go. He wiped the sweat off his brow.

"When do you intend to get married?" It cost Molly effort to ask.

"Pretty soon. Look, ducky, I can't run this place alone. I mean, there should be a woman here. And children."

"Of course." Molly Fleet got up. "I'm tired."

"Are you going to bed? Shall I bring you milk and honey?" He'd done that when the school children had called her Mole. Or when things had gone wrong with her.

"No thanks, Stephen. Goodnight."

"Goodnight."

Stephen Fleet sighed. What could he do? The girls in and around Parramatta were marrying all the time, only his sisters didn't. And April was twenty-seven, Molly twenty-two, and Stephen had finally reached thirty. And he hadn't told Molly the most important thing, although he had promised Jennifer he would. Perhaps Molly would want it herself. "Moll!" he cried upstairs.

She came back slowly. She had on a flowered nylon robe, made in Sydney. You could see that ten miles away. Her golden hair fell over the side of her face. She looked thirteen, not a day older.

"What do you want, Steve?"

"Nothing. Go to bed, little one."

"But you wanted to say something."

The way she looked at him! Did she know anything? Stephen Fleet felt damned uncomfortable, but he had promised his fiancée ... Jennifer was a decent girl, but she was an outsider. She didn't know Moll and she didn't know ... Dammit! He couldn't let Jenny think he was a softy!

"There was something I wanted to discuss with you, Moll. Because you're going to Father's place from here."

Molly said nothing. Why the hell didn't she ask what he wanted to discuss with her?

"Grandmother left you a share of the farm."

"Yes."

"Now listen carefully, Moll. I thought ... we thought, if you want to sell your share to me ... you only have to say so." Stephen spoke fast. "It won't be to your disadvantage, chick. And ... and your room will always be here for you. What do you think?"

When her silence became too pronounced, he looked at her. She was white as a sheet. He could see it even in the dim light. But she was standing up very straight, and somehow she reminded him of Grandmother Fleet. Godammit! Molly belonged here!

"I don't know what I'll do, Stephen. Not yet. I'll have to think it over." But she knew exactly—Stephen sensed it.

"As I just said, you ..."

"Goodnight."

She was gone. Stephen whistled for his dog. Nothing good had ever come of a threesome. Jenny was right. But why was she in such a hurry? Why had she pestered him until he had promised to discuss the matter of Molly's share now? Life went on, and sometimes it passed over little girls and their wishes. It wasn't Stephen's fault. His fiancée had an uncle, a wealthy sheep farmer in New South Wales, who was willing to spend

a large sum of money on their farm as soon as it belonged to
Stephen and Jenny in equal parts. All perfectly legal. But
Stephen knew that it was all wrong. He should have waited.
Moll was stupefied by sorrow. Only yesterday she had packed
Granny's things. Stephen had happened to see her with the old
sewing machine—outmoded, dented, but crazily durable. She
had been stroking it. When she had seen Stephen, she had run
out of the room.

On the other hand, Stephen hadn't wanted a lawyer to talk
to Molly about it. That would have been even more unsuitable.
Only right now he should have kept his mouth shut. He stared
at the river. "The young one" had always believed in him, like
the *Amen* in church. Molly was a good egg. He'd look her up
more often now in Sydney, when he spoke to the dairy co-
operatives, and she'd spend all her vacations on the farm, as
she always had done. And every damn weekend, if she wanted
to. And Jenny's uncle could keep his stinking money! They'd
gotten along very nicely until now without Jenny's goddamn
uncle; Granny, Molly and he. And if Jenny didn't like it, if
Moll decided to hang onto her share of the farm, then Jenny'd
see another side of Stephen Fleet! Yes sir!

Stephen whistled quite cheerfully for his dog. He really
believed he'd come to a decision, but the state of marriage had
its own battle plan, and Stephen had already lost the first
encounter. He didn't know it, but Molly did, although she was
so much younger and less experienced than her big brother.
Right then she was staring with burning eyes at the crucifix
over her bed. She was taking leave of her home. As a little
girl she had thought the Parramatta farm was vast. A whole
world! But tonight the farm had grown so small and narrow
that there was no room in it for Molly Fleet.

When Molly got back to the roominghouse, Mrs. Doody set
the tea table with the good china Candy had bought for her.
"What's the matter, Mrs. Doody? Is Candy back?"

"You know better than that!" A shadow crossed Mrs. Doody's full-moon face. "Damned little tramp! How was it in
Parramatta?"

"Except for Grandmother's funeral, just the same."

"Nice or horrid?"

"Nice, of course," said Molly Fleet, her voice flat. "My brother's getting married."

"Everybody's getting married these days! I'll be the next one!" Mrs. Doody roared laughter. "I'm glad you're back, Fleet. Did you meet your sister-in-law?"

"Not yet. Stephen says she's very smart."

"When should he find that out if not now?" Mrs. Doody said slyly. "You stayed such a long time, I thought you weren't coming back."

"Who's coming? I don't want to disturb anyone."

"Are you crook, girl? Gretchen's coming. She's bringing German crumb cake, and some news!"

"Is she getting married too?"

"Of course! She can't manage the bakery alone anymore."

"That figures," said Molly.

"I don't know what it is, but right now everybody's dying or getting married. What do they do in between?"

"Act dumb."

"Did you eat a lot of lemons in Parramatta?"

Gretchen Curtis, née Breitschneider, had changed a lot since she had gone to school with Elizabeth West in Adelaide. She didn't tell anyone Grimm's Fairy Tales any more, and she shared the opinions of her deceased husband about Australia in general and in particular. The only German thing left was the diminutive of her name, Gretchen, to which she stuck stubbornly.

Gretchen thought often of Elizabeth West, née Withers. Life was a carousel. When Betty had turned up in Adelaide, tired and indifferent after her first stay in Sydney, Gretchen had been a happy wife, well-off, with children, and Betty had been a bored secretary in Mr. Curtis's office. And Betty's mother had begged Gretchen constantly to find a husband for her difficult daughter. Then Betty had gone back to Sydney, and everybody in Adelaide, Betty's mother and Gretchen in the lead, had thought that this would be the end of Betty Withers. Funny the way things turned around. Today Betty was a famous writer and Gretchen had turned into a shadow of her former youth.

Gretchen opened the latest copy of *Insight* and showed it to Mrs. Doody and Molly Fleet. "Doesn't Betty look elegant? Except for her messy hairdo."

The three ladies looked at the pictures of Elizabeth West and her fiancé from Brisbane. *Insight* had devoted a whole issue to its famous writer, with pictures of her in Adelaide, Sydney, and Queensland, with interviews and quotes. It had apparently been a whirlwind romance. "Some people have all the luck," said Mrs. Doody. "What was Miss West like when she wasn't famous?"

Gretchen thought hard. "Betty? Nothing special." She cut off a piece of cake for herself. "I know it must sound funny, but in school I wrote much better compositions. I don't know what got into Betty. You can believe me, but not a soul at home could understand how little Withers could suddenly write best sellers. My husband always used to say that successes like that in Sydney were fabricated." Gretchen drew a deep breath, and began to eat her excellent cake.

Molly Fleet said nothing. Mrs. Doody gobbled her cake as usual. "I'd like the recipe for that cake, Gretchen. Who fabricated Miss West's success? I don't think she's pretty. Her nose is too big. Can't be compared to my Candy."

Gretchen barely knew Candy, and Molly Fleet had written her off completely.

"Betty and I were always good friends," said Gretchen. "I wrote to her, care of *Insight,* and she answered. Now what do you think of that?"

"Why not?" said Miss Fleet. "I massaged her for a while. I congratulated her, and she answered."

"Have you been invited to the wedding?" Mrs. Doody asked Gretchen.

"I'm much too busy at the bakery. Miss Rigby's giving a big reception for Betty. I got an invitation, of course. Engraved."

"I did too," said Molly Fleet. "Miss West and I are good friends."

"*We're* going to have a real wedding with good eats and coffee," Gretchen said dreamily. "I don't like cocktail parties with a crowd of strangers."

Gretchen was marrying a restaurant owner of German extraction in King's Cross. Perhaps they would add on a coffee shop. She gave Mrs. Doody and Molly Fleet printed invitations to the wedding.

"I always thought Miss West was sort of married to Miss Rigby," said Molly. "Whenever I went to Bellevue Hill, the two seemed to be like two peas in a pod. It's not going to be easy for Miss Rigby."

Molly grew thoughtful. Her first piece of cake lay untouched on her plate. It was funny . . . you'd have two or three people from the big herd living peacefully together for years, and then one of them got married, and the herd scattered. The one left behind sat high and dry. As if a billabong in the desert had suddenly disappeared. The thirst, of course, remained.

"Don't you get married now, Fleet!" Mrs. Doody warned her. "Or who's to scrub my kitchen floor?"

19

A Wedding in Sydney

It wasn't easy for Miss Rigby, but she had wanted Betty to marry. At Alexander's fiftieth birthday she had tried to hang her onto Bertie Dobson. Miss Rigby still didn't know why Bertie and Betty hadn't done her that small favor. It would have been a fine thing. Miss Rigby could reach Macquarie Street easily any time, and Alex would have built them a house, if Bertie had decided to move. In any case, Miss Rigby would have been able to keep her eye on them.

Why Bertie Dobson didn't want to marry Elizabeth West became evident to Miss Rigby at the big press and wedding reception for Betty. Bertie brought his bonny bride Mavis to Bellevue Hill. Miss Rigby couldn't find anything especially wrong with the girl. Betty was ten times as famous, ten times as witty, but of course ten years older than Mavis. But Bertie was beaming. It was simply ridiculous how Bertie, who had always clung to his mother's apron strings, showed his bride off. As if Mavis were a seven-day wonder! Men! thought Miss Rigby. She stood tall, distinguished, and charming beside Betty and Mr. Grierson, and greeted all who had come to congratulate. She also told her colleagues, the photo boys and reporters from Sydney, Adelaide, and Brisbane, how very suitable the marriage was. Frank Grierson was a well-known journalist and radio personality in Brisbane. When a young reporter suggested that perhaps Mr. Grierson could help his wife to write her novels, Miss Rigby thought it a brilliant idea.

She was being asked all the time: *Where* was Alexander? And she told everybody that her brother was going out to Manly, where there was to be a little extra celebration only for closest friends and relatives. It was absolutely disgraceful of Alex! But she was used to that sort of behavior from him. He thought it was funny! She didn't even know if he was in Sydney. The young couple would fly to Cairns right after the reception. They were honeymooning on the Great Barrier Reef. Everything as it should be. Miss Rigby looked across the battlefield: nothing was missing—i.e., her old friend Stanley Marchmont was not present. A reporter from Brisbane was sitting in his chair. Bertie Dobson had forbidden Marchmont to attend weddings and funerals.

Where was Alexander? thought Elizabeth West Grierson. She had been married for four hours and should really be thinking only of Frank, but four hours is a relatively short time. The years with Rigby would probably take time to erase. "I am happy," she told herself stubbornly. She pressed Frank's arm, feeling guilty, and he responded. "When can we get out of here, Betty?"

"Not yet. Grace would never forgive me."

"But that's ridiculous!" said Mr. Grierson, slightly irritated. He didn't know that Betty had already reserved one of the loveliest rooms in the big house in Brisbane for Miss Rigby. "Grace is sensible. Let's go, Betty," urged her very new husband.

At that moment Alexander walked into the flower-filled reception room. He was in great form, and greeted all his cobbers from far and wide, and the boys from the press. Marchmont, Rigby & French never turned down free publicity. Rigby didn't seem to see the young couple, but he chatted jovially and with flattering interest with some reporters from Adelaide. They were printing extra editions for the wedding of the famous novelist.

Patrick Trent, his young wife, and his sister, Catherine, followed Rigby around. For the first time in many years, Trent was the happiest man in this room. A heart-to-heart talk with his wife had cleared the stormy air, and now a baby was on the way. Grace Rigby watched Trent, more moved than she had ever been in his dismal days. At that time all those who knew him well were fully aware of the fact that his joviality was a mask. He had hidden behind it, resigned, for years. Now he looked years younger. It was almost ridiculous the way he danced attendance on his young wife. "Don't eat the fish salad!" he was just telling her, as he took the plate out of her hand.

Rigby and Catherine Trent watched the scene and smiled ironically. "Holy Moses!" cried Rigby. "Your wife isn't made of sugar!"

Trent told his wife to be sure to tell him when she felt tired. And she was pink as a peony! He was the one who felt weary. Did happiness make one tired, he wondered? Then he shook hands with Betty. "Do your best, little one," he said. "And God bless!"

Elizabeth didn't look at her old friend. Trent alway saw too much. He seemed to know that it would have been easier for Betty to break with the past by writing...

"I'm so happy for you both," Betty told the Trents. "You must visit us soon in Brisbane."

Just then Rigby walked up to her, smiling radiantly. He looked bigger than ever, and was dressed to the nines. Had she really, seriously thought that her marriage would unhinge him?

He congratulated Betty as conventionally as if he were seeing her for the first time in his life. He chose to overlook the groom, but that may have been because Grierson barely reached his shoulder. "All the best, Grierson," he said finally, casually, and turned to leave.

"You're not leaving yet?" Betty cried, and reddened. Which did not escape Rigby. She was trying hard to control herself. She hadn't seen Alexander for a long time. He looked very much alive and as enigmatic as ever, like a giant python in the bush. His eyes glowed just like one.

"I'm terribly sorry, but I have visitors from California," he said gently.

"I thought they visited you a few weeks ago!" said Betty. It just slipped out.

Rigby was almost touched by her naiveté. "They postponed their visit, if you don't mind. All the best, girl. I've got to go."

"Stay!" Betty cried impetuously. Something was tying her up in knots. Fortunately Frank was talking to some friends from Brisbane. He had turned his back on Rigby. Frank was no fool, and everybody who knew him well knew it.

"You can't leave right away, just like that, Alex!" said Betty in a choked voice.

"Were you planning to take me on your honeymoon with you?"

He turned brusquely and left the big reception room in which, seven years ago, he had introduced Anne to his sister.

Grierson grew more and more impatient. The papers had

everything they wanted, but he didn't have everything he wanted yet. He was happy to see that Betty was now ready to leave. She ran, eager as a little girl, over to Miss Rigby with whom she had worked and been friends for so long. Happy, rich years. Miss Rigby had protected her without mothering her. Suddenly Betty couldn't speak. Frank Grierson was standing beside her like a sentinel.

"Thanks so much for everything!" Betty finally managed to say.

"Don't forget Sydney, little one. And when you need your thirty-five medications, write to me."

"Believe it or not, Miss Rigby, we have pharmacists in Brisbane too," said Mr. Grierson.

Miss Rigby ignored the interruption. "When do I get the next manuscript, Betty?"

"As soon as I can, Grace. Promise!"

"First we're going on a honeymoon," said Mr. Grierson.

Miss Rigby also ignored this bit of information. "Be careful not to catch cold, little one. We'll send you anything you may have forgotten."

"Which will be just about everything," said Mr. Grierson. "But from now on I'll be looking after Betty's luggage."

"I've reserved the loveliest room in the house for you, Grace. You must visit me often."

"I have a small career on the side," Miss Rigby said drily. "But it's sweet of you."

She adjusted Betty's hopeless hairdo and held her protégée close for a moment. "Do your best, child. I don't want to hear any complaints, Frank."

"I never complain, Miss Rigby." Grierson's smile was ironical. He had had enough of the Rigbys, of Sydney, and of the circus on Bellevue Hill.

Miss Rigby had had enough of Betty's wedding too, but she still had to go through the traditional post-celebration in Manly. It would all look exactly like Alexander's fiftieth birthday, only she would feel the emptiness. Alex should have sacrificed this evening for his sister; it would have been

the thing to do. She had sacrificed more than one evening
for him when the scandal over Flora had hit him hard. Grace
Rigby smiled stoically at a few latecomers, a famous lyricist
from New South Wales, the gossip columnist from a rival
magazine, and Mr. F.B. Lawson, one of the most important
backers of *Insight*. "May we expect further contributions from
Miss West?" he asked Grace Rigby in the course of their
conversation.

"But of course! I'll see to that, if I have to go to Brisbane
personally to get them!"

"I wouldn't put it past you." Mr. Lawson laughed, and Miss
Rigby joined him. "You're unbearable, Grace! The pioneer
spirit! What would we do without you?"

"That's what I'd like to know too," Miss Rigby said. She
was satisfied.

Rigby drove straight to Vaucluse. The house was empty.
Mrs. Andrews was on vacation. She was visiting her married
daughter in Mittagong. The brand new son-in-law would be
delighted, Rigby thought, as he walked onto the terrace.
There was nothing as empty in the world as an empty terrace.

He got a beautifully bound book from his library, a mono-
graph on Edmund Blacket, who had designed the universities
of Sydney and Melbourne, and several cathedrals, schools,
hospitals, and department stores. Blacket was also one of those
architects who had begun gradually to transform Sydney into
a metropolis. Rigby studied his plans. You couldn't think of
Sydney without thinking of Blacket.

Edmund Blacket had landed in Australia on October 3, 1842.
He and his wife had come to the colony as free immigrants.
Blacket's first impression in the harbor of Sydney had been
the tower of the Church of Saint James, which Francis Greenway had built. A clear line ran between these early architects
to Marchmont, Rigby & French. But those immigrants of the
mid-nineteenth century had still been so closely tied to the
motherland that Edmund Blacket's first lodgings had been close
to the Methodist chapel in Sydney, because the landlady re-

minded him of someone he knew well in England. And for that reason alone, the man had settled down in Princes Street. Rigby frowned. Princes Street, and the chapel with the Doric-columned portal, had disappeared long ago. Anne was like Blacket. Since nothing in Sydney reminded her of Avenue Road, she had gone back to London. Pommies remained pommies!

Rigby looked at the plans for the country homes Blacket had designed for prominent members of the colony. Gothic arcades in the Australian landscape! Had Sir Thomas Mitchell, the Colonial official who had traveled around the world, wanted arcades for his Park Hall? Probably. These people had preserved their English outlook on the new continent. Marchmont, Rigby & French, on the other hand, aspired to an open-air synthesis in house and garden. Frank Lloyd Wright, the great American architect and city planner, had already tried to introduce this to the midwest bourgeoisie in his country. The Japanese had been doing it for centuries. And here, in Australia, there was a new feeling for the endless spaces. The creators of a freed architecture smiled at the megalomania expressed in styles that were foreign to the land. Informal arrangements with wide, sliding glass windows and sundecks, had replaced the old-fashioned, unimaginative symmetry. Strange, thought Rigby. Architecture seemed to be far more advanced than the people who brought their dusty conventionality into these new buildings.

Rigby sat motionless, watching the darkening harbor scene. His own marital conflict could have taken place just as well in Victorian England, in festive rooms dimly lit by crystal chandeliers, with heavy drapes, clumsy furniture, hideous little ornaments, and a few really beautiful pieces of porcelain that were in everybody's way, just waiting to be knocked down. Formal, straitlaced sentimentality. Not a piece of furniture built in; everything on display as in a high-class junk shop, creating a static, stuffy atmosphere in which no Aussie could breathe! Of course buildings and furnishings had changed with time also in Europe, but more slowly, and soul and spirit came limping behind. Anne, with her narrow waistline and her long, slim neck would have fitted charmingly into one of those Victorian dresses, stiffened with whalebone, that contained the human body like valuables in a safe. In Rigby's modest house in Vaucluse she had been as cold and reserved as her ancestors in their Victorian salons. For a moment Rigby had the impression that the technology of the twentieth century played rounders with its dull victims...

He closed the illustrated Blacket biography with a bang and began to smoke hastily as he crept out of the glassy light of ideas into the morass of emotions, and called himself to order. Did he want to end up in a labyrinth of unfulfilled wishes? Ridiculous! When you looked soberly at your losses, they could be transformed into winnings. Stanley Marchmont had always known how to do that. Grace managed it silently. Why couldn't he? Why, at his age, was he still unable to master the bookkeeping of his emotions? Why had Betty's wedding thrown him? She was neither his wife nor his lover. But for years she had been a source of joy and vitality for him, and he could not reconcile himself to the fact that this source had dried up.

He looked at his watch. He had spent nearly three hours studying Blacket's blueprints. Right now his house in Vaucluse resembled a ground plan; by chance a few pieces of furniture stood in it. Rigby stood stock-still on the terrace for a moment. Miss Rigby's guests would have left Manly by now so as to be back in Sydney before dark. How would it be if he kept Grace company tonight for a change?

So Rigby drove to Manly. He was in good spirits again and hummed his favorite song from the Outback:

> Get a bloody move on!
> Have some bloody sense!
> Learn the bloody art of
> Bloody self-defense!

"What do you want here?" asked Miss Rigby. "Everybody's gone."

"I want to eat. Did the mob leave anything?"

"Go and look. I've run around enough for one day."

"No more weddings?" Rigby grinned.

Later they grilled steaks, and fried potato sticks, just as they had done years ago after the death of their mother, when Grace had looked after her younger brother in Parramatta, before Rigby had burst into the lives of Anne Carrington, Flora Pratt, or Elizabeth West.

Grace ate heartily. She discovered to her astonishment that she had eaten practically nothing all day. Funny! She yawned, unabashed.

"Good night, old girl," said Rigby. "Get a bloody move on!"

Alex went walkabout for a while. Manly in the evening was refreshing. There were few people on the ocean promenade. Somebody called out, "Hello, Alexander!"

Rigby turned around, annoyed. *That* was all he needed: Shirley Cox, his wife's bosom friend! Anne probably wrote a letter to her every week. The devil take all women!

"Hello, Shirley!" He smiled brightly. "What are you doing in Manly?"

"We were visiting friends." At that moment a blond, tough-looking man with sharp eyes and curly hair walked up to them. Shirley introduced her brother. Inspector Cox of course knew who Rigby was. Who didn't know Rigby in Sydney? Friends of the Coxes had had a crazy house designed for them in Manly. Cox had read the rest about the great Rigby in the daily papers. His fiftieth had really been a good show. Cox looked at the architect with interest, and expressed his pleasure at meeting him. Rigby, stony-faced, also remembered from the newspapers that Cox had recently solved a sensational murder case. Mike Browne, a chauffeur from Sydney, had been the murderer.

"Are you working on another murder, Inspector?" Rigby asked casually.

Cox laughed. "Are you building another house, Mr. Rigby?"

They drank beer at Rigby's place and talked about all sorts

of things: the theatre, sports, and of course, new building. Anne wasn't mentioned. The Coxes left in fine spirits and Rigby accompanied them to the promenade. Then he walked off in the other direction. It was much too early to go to bed.

"How do you like the great Rigby?" Shirley asked her brother. Inspector Cox hesitated. Finally he said jerkily: "Not average. Hard to read. A little too amiable."

"Anne often complained about his unfriendliness. A lousy husband."

"That's often the case with impressive men," Inspector Cox said drily. "Nowadays most marriages are threatened. I'd like to know what Rigby has to complain about."

"Not a thing!" Shirley said angrily. "Anne is a saint. But in the end she lost patience."

"Just what is to be expected from a saint?" Inspector Cox lit his twelfth cigarette.

"Don't smoke so much," Shirley said irritably.

"Tell me, Shirley, some time in the Dark Ages, wasn't there a scandal about Rigby's first wife? I heard something to that effect."

"The first Mrs. Rigby met with an accident in the Blue Mountains."

"Was she drunk?"

Shirley laughed. "She's supposed to have been a bar girl. Much older than Rigby. Anne heard about it first from Miss Rigby. He hadn't told her a thing about it. What do you think of that?"

"Very sensible of him. There's much too much talk. What was the old girl's name?"

"Flora."

"And the rest?"

"I've forgotten. Why? Does it interest you?"

"Not especially. Rigby has a beautiful house here in Manly."

"He's a horror. But I'm sure he's not guilty in any way of his first wife's death," Shirley said quickly. She shouldn't have said anything. With her brother you never knew when it registered or when he'd choose to pick it up again. "I'm sure Anne will come back soon," she said. "How did you like her, Curl?"

The inspector had seen the second Mrs. Rigby frequently at Shirley's house. "I liked her. Why not? I'm not married to her!" He laughed, and Shirley laughed with him.

"Anne is sweet. When you think what a tough time she had with Rigby..."

"In what way?"

"He looks at every girl."

"He's got to look somewhere."

"I can't stand him," Shirley said angrily.

Her brother looked at her, astonished, and she blushed. "But don't think because of that, Rigby did away with his first wife!"

"I never think anything," Inspector Cox said calmly. "I believe only in facts. Besides, the Rigby scandal is water over the dam. I must have still been in school at the time."

A cool breeze wafted over the ocean. Shirley shivered slightly. Conversations with her brother sometimes had such curious endings. What had she said about Rigby? Why couldn't she stand him? He was very good-looking...

"Listen, Shirley... I've rarely enjoyed myself as much as tonight."

"Thanks for the compliment."

"Sorry, but for once, I mean Rigby. He makes one want to be an architect," Inspector Cox said dreamily. "He knows what he's talking about."

Perhaps Rigby also knew what he was silent about. "Come on, Shirley!" Inspector Cox said, suddenly lively. "Get a bloody move on!"

20

My Forefather's Name Was Adam

Dear Alex,

I should have answered your letter long ago, but it is so difficult, and I tend to put off difficult things, hoping that time will help. But it only hurts . . . The longer I carry this unwritten letter around with me, the more difficult it becomes to write. My reticence drove you crazy for seven years. I hope you get annoyed with me now for the last time.

I acknowledged your Christmas gifts and the checks long ago, by wire. It is truly scandalous to thank you for them with the right words at the end of May. They are all so wonderful—no wonder, with your exquisite taste—and much too valuable. I don't wear brocade dresses here, not even an evening dress. Why should I? And for whom? It's draughty here in summer and winter, so I've slipped back into my London uniform: jerseys and sweaters. I've packed away my beautiful robe from Sydney too. In the early morning the only people who see me are the milkman and Miss Jennings. Mother breakfasts in her room with her various corpses and the murderer of the chapter before the last. I mean, that's when he's revealed as the murderer for all to see. It doesn't interest me. Mother is unbelievably busy and writes so fast. Every thriller takes her about six months, and she works until late in the night. She still can't get over how I just sit around. But I don't just sit around. I go for walks in Primrose Hill Park, and brood. If you can recall, it's my only true talent.

I know how much you like to give me beautiful things, Alex, and I was very touched that you still remember my favorite color. I thought you'd forgotten everything. I really got that impression during the last years in Sydney. Forgive me for mentioning it. I know how you hate complaining women. You said once they were as attractive as vinegar in oatmeal.

Miss Jennings sends you her very best greetings. She goes crazy when I talk about Sydney. She would have fitted in better there.

How you do love that city! Of course nobody can resist its influence, but for me Sydney has too much fireworks and too little substance. Forgive me for boring you again with my opinions. I simply don't fit into such dynamic, ambitious, and extravagant surroundings. You didn't choose Sydney as your home for nothing. You are wonderfully suited to each other. Perhaps you and I would have had a better life together if you had stayed in Parramatta. I was in your native city with you twice, and felt the calm every country town radiates, even today. But perhaps I would have been able to cope better with Sydney's incomparable atmosphere if you hadn't left me alone so much. Why didn't you help me? You knew how slow I am. No, that's nonsense! I realize today that with your stormy vitality you couldn't have had any understanding for my tempo.

Dear Alex, I shall try to explain the necessity of our separation to you. Believe me, I am sad about the failure of our marriage. A lot of it is my fault. I was always an unsatisfactory person. Mother and Miss Jennings would corroborate that. I am so ashamed of my withdrawal because it solved nothing. But I don't want to go on ruining your life. I know that some time, somewhere, you will find a suitable partner. You are so much younger than I am.

Your suppositions are all wrong, Alex. I don't have another man in London. I have nobody at all and feel just as superfluous as before my Australian adventure. Perhaps I was away from London too long. Most people have forgotten me. I can understand it, and am not offended. I try to live with myself. This is difficult but—forgive me—not quite as difficult as living with you! Perhaps the relationship between every man and woman is difficult, but nothing is left of our marriage after seven years but a catalogue of guilt feelings on both sides. What has become of our hopes? Perhaps one shouldn't build such a realistic institution as marriage on hope. Our illusions are of course our private possessions. That's why I'd rather bury them alone.

Perhaps I really am an "old maid" by nature, as you reproach me. You write, "My forefather's name was Adam." I know that, dear, but there are many ways of being close. I couldn't bear your sporadic love making any more because you became increasingly alien. For me love and marriage mean the efforts toward intimacy.

It is very difficult for me to write you all this, but I had to explain to you why I can't come back. Neither of us are going to, nor can we change.

The spatial distance between us has helped me to understand you better. I hope that you too know me better now and realize that my little store of initiative is exhausted.

You know how very honestly I thank you for everything you have done and are still doing, for Mother and me during these years. May I beg you, please, not to send me anything more because I have taken a job as a secretary.

If you really want to talk things over, then come to London, please. But don't think you can change my mind. Poor Alex— you were badly served with me!

You are and remain my best friend, and I would be sorry to lose you entirely.

Farewell. I shall always feel indebted to you.

                                              Anne

Rigby sat in front of his cold breakfast. Anne's letter had robbed him of his appetite. That had happened to him only once before in his life: when the scandal over Flora Pratt broke out. He crushed Anne's letter in his fist and rammed it into his trouser pocket. Shouldn't he be congratulating himself that he was finally rid of this interminable brooder? But if Anne thought he would marry for a third time, she was on the wrong track. Way off! He was doubly annoyed because right now he could see her so clearly. What on God's earth did he see in this colorless, slow, discontented person? Anne was suffering from an inner life that had turned sour. She wanted a paradise without Adam. The devil take it!

Rigby decided not to give the nonsensical letter another thought. He had never understood Anne. A blessing that he was now free of a condition that was sapping his vitality. Rigby shook himself and was pleased.

He was still pleased when Mrs. Andrews appeared. She wanted to speak to him. He might have known it. She stood in front of him, motionless. What was wrong with her? Finally she came out with it. Rigby was stunned. She couldn't be serious! Mrs. Andrews wanted to leave! Impossible! She was as much a part of the inventory in Vaucluse as the harbor terrace, his workshop, and her goulash! But Rigby's jewel had made up her mind to move to her daughter in Mittagong. She had felt terribly forlorn lately in Vaucluse, and her daughter needed her. Daisy had married too young, and now she was expecting a baby. Her son-in-law too had begged Mrs. Andrews to come and live with them. The young man had taken a position in Blackheath, in the Blue Mountains. It was a well-known resort, seventy-five miles from Sydney, which could be reached easily by train. Mrs. Andrews wanted to spend the rest of her life there, recovering from Mr. Rigby. She could wander around in the Megalong Valley, and in the farming country all around, instead of being bawled out all the time ... Naturally she didn't say any of this. All she said was that blood was thicker than water. Rigby shuddered at the cliché.

"Naturally I shall wait until Mrs. Rigby has come back from London," said Mrs. Andrews.

"I have no idea when she'll be back," said Rigby. "Her mother is seriously ill. Blood is thicker than water."

Mrs. Andrews reddened with anger. "Then I'll stay until I've found somebody suitable to take my place," she said stiffly.

"You don't have to do that, my dear. Miss Rigby can send me one of her retired photo models. Good morning." And he tore off to his car.

Mrs. Andrews watched him go. Unbelievable! She had lived for this man for years—on an excellent salary, granted—and now he didn't seem to give a damn whether she stayed or left!

Of course she *was* leaving. She had only half made up her mind. She hadn't expected Mr. Rigby to fall on his knees and beg her to stay, but *now* he'd gone too far! Nothing seemed to mean anything to him. A true Aussie! And if she had to spend a hundred years in Australia—her great-grandfather had died at the age of ninety-two and a half—she would never grow accustomed to the insufferable rudeness of the Australians! If an Aussie happened to have feelings, he hid them like gold dust in the sand.

Mrs. Andrews wasn't getting any younger—lately she'd had to admit it—but she still had feelings, and showed them, as had been customary where she came from. Rigby became more incomprehensible daily. He was full of contradictions, and sometimes she was afraid of him. Before his second marriage he had dragged her off into the bush once, at night. It had been gruesome! Mrs. Andrews had never seen flying mammals

before. The gray-white animals with their fluttering eyes, gliding along the ground, had flown up suddenly between the
eucalyptus trees and wound their long tails around the branches.
She had screamed! Rigby of course had laughed. Then he had
explained that in Australia nature showed imagination. Europe
was a boring continent. The birds flew and the mammals stuck
on the ground forever. Whom did it interest?

She had stared at him. Suddenly Rigby himself seemed like
a gliding horror, who would crouch quietly on the ground and
then, suddenly, with a giant leap, disappear into the dark. That
was the time when Rigby wasn't sleeping with his pretty housekeeper anymore because unfortunately she served only what
was to be expected. But at the time she had still been desper-
ately in love with him. Of course the night in the bush died
away as if it had never happened. For months Rigby showed
her his everyday face and roared his disapproval when the food
wasn't to his liking. In the end Mrs. Andrews thought she had
dreamt it all.

She decided to look in the Hungarian restaurant in King's
Cross for somebody to take her place. Even if Rigby kicked
her around, she loved her enemies. She would find a cook for
him, not bad, but certainly not as good as herself. Rigby should
know whom he had thrown out! By now she was convinced
that *Rigby* had fired *her*. What a dirty thing to do! She took
away the breakfast dishes, trembling with rage. Rigby's big
teacup fell on the floor and broke. In Sydney, broken china
was unlucky. In Australia everything was different...

Mrs. Andrews understood for the first time why the second
Mrs. Rigby had moved out. Rigby would grow old and ill and
die forsaken by everyone. The idea cheered her up. Although
right now Rigby was enjoying the best of health and looked
it, misfortune moved fast! The new Australians knew this from
living in more thoughtful continents. Mrs. Andrews had often
imagined how she would be the only one standing at his deathbed. *That* dream he had shattered!

She walked into the bedroom and told the maid, in Rigby's
tone, to get a move on! Mrs. Andrews tore the bedding off

the bed and threw it on the floor, where it collected some dust, and watched Bessie Towner make the bed. Then she rode off on her bicycle to do the shopping. Bessie, who had only been working in the empty house for a few weeks, sat down on the terrace, lighted one of Rigby's cigarettes, and made fresh tea for the gardener and herself.

A wonderful job! Bessie worked only in houses where there was no wife. Mrs. Andrews could rant as much as she wanted to, Bessie Towner knew how to handle new Australians in her sleep! First, Andrews should learn to speak English. She spoke too harshly, and the abos had made mashed potatoes of the language. The gardener suggested a picnic for the weekend. Bessie would see what Rigby's refrigerator could contribute, not too noticeably. "Okay, mate?" asked Miss Towner.

"A-okay," the young gardener answered, grinning. For Bessie Towner of Surry Hills, life in this house was one continuous picnic.

Rigby couldn't agree. His jewel ruined his home for him as far as this weekend was concerned. By the time he had finished his business correspondence, it was eleven o'clock. Too late to arrange anything with his friends. They were all happily married now, and when things weren't going too well, they spent the weekend together anyway. Miss Rigby was entertaining guests in Manly, and Rigby was not in the mood to meet people from *Insight,* or even worse, poets! Grace always warned him ahead of time. When Rigby and his cobbers used the country house, she stayed in Sydney. It was an excellent arrangement, but this time it left Rigby at loose ends. Involuntarily he recalled several very nice weekends he and Anne had spent together. Then he had belonged somewhere and hadn't had to arrange anything. He shuddered when he thought of the empty terrace in Vaucluse. Foolish of him, but Miss Rigby's *Insight* party made him think of the model, Candy. He hadn't thought of the pretty little thing for ages. During the last months he had spent most of his free time with Paddy Trent, but Paddy had become a regular stay-at-home. When he wasn't getting along with Klari, you could go horse-stealing with him!

Why shouldn't Rigby treat himself to a fun weekend with Candy Blyth? Why was he avoiding the sweet little thing like the plague? Suddenly there was no reason any more to start a new life. The old life had had its charms too. The wise, self-possessed Rigby of the last months was suddenly in a state of revolt again, which could spell danger for his steady, middle-class existence. His wife had evoked this mood automatically. That had been her second great talent. When he found the conditions under which he was living insupportable, he reacted like this, had done so even in Flora's time. Now, ten years later, it was being alone that he couldn't stand. "It's just lasting too long," he had told himself aloud sometimes during the last weeks. The repugnance he felt for his present way of life had driven him to the bars of Sydney. He had never drunk so much as in these past months. Although he could tolerate astounding amounts of whiskey or beer, still Dr. Dobson had told him to take it easy with the drinking, and for once in his life he had accepted advice. He had big building plans and needed a clear head. Anne must have left him her headaches. He had never had a headache in his life, not even while he was being suspected of having murdered Flora. Perhaps they came on because he couldn't stand rejection. Then nothing helped—either alcohol, philosophy, nor hours in the surf. For his restoration he needed the uncritical admiration of a young woman. His forefather's name was Adam.

Rigby had arrived at William Street.

A neat young thing stood facing him at Mrs. Doody's boardinghouse. Nothing to be said against the sheila except for a birthmark on her left cheek, but her beautiful hair almost covered it.

"May I speak to Miss Blyth?"

"She's away."

Why did the young girl stare at him so? What was the matter with her. "When is she coming back?"

"Please, won't you come in and sit down?"

Rigby was led into what was probably the "parlor," a room filled with dank air, ghastly furniture, and a plaster statue of the Virgin Mary. It turned out that Miss Blyth, like every good Aussie, had gone walkabout.

Miss Fleet had no idea where Candy might be right now. She was looking at "Mr. Ritter" as if hypnotized. Almost pleadingly. Rigby was surprised. What was there to look at? Was the girl bonkers? Oh no! The young thing was sunk in admiration. Exactly what Rigby had missed for such a long time. This sheila had enough gumption to differentiate between a boring buffalo and an amusing man.

Rigby's mood improved at once. He even smiled at the young sheila. She seemed to be the victim of an empty weekend too. Rigby's disappointment that Candy was away had disappeared. From far away she was ineffective. She was Eve and Lilith in one small package, granted, but she wanted to be admired all the time. Actually a rather boring noode.

"What do you do on your weekends, miss?" he asked. Fatherly tone. "Are you going out with your boy friend tonight?"

Miss Fleet blushed. She was alone in the house. Mrs. Doody was visiting her friend with the wooden leg. Charlie Rainbow was holding forth with his cobber on the city limits about the old Australians who weren't really as old as the abos were. Gretchen had gone to Marouba with her fiancé. Every weekend the young couple forgot that Molly Fleet existed, but Molly didn't take offence because six days a week Gretchen was a nice, helpful person. Since her last experience in Parramatta, Molly knew that sooner or later a third person would always come and disrupt a beautiful friendship. She could of course have gone on an outing. Sydney was a wonderful starting point for outings. But foolish as it might be, Miss Fleet couldn't stand the sight of so many loving and married couples. She murmured something about having nothing planned, and that this was unusual. Rigby got the message.

Miss Fleet walked over to the window and with an abrupt motion tossed her hair forward over her cheek. She had an adorable profile. Rigby studied it as a connoisseur. Why shouldn't he give this lonely sheila a little pleasure? She didn't seem to have a soul who cared about her. And funnily enough, neither did Rigby!

"Who'd ever hang around Sydney on such a beautiful day?" he said. "Would you like to drive to the Blue Mountains with me?"

"I . . . with *you*?" Miss Fleet was blushing like a schoolgirl. She could barely breathe for joy. At first, because of her mature figure, Rigby had taken her for twenty, but she couldn't be more than eighteen, at the most. He wondered if she'd ever had a go with a man. He doubted it.

"Take a coat along, miss. It gets cool in the evenings in the mountains."

Miss Fleet tore upstairs and put on her best, light-blue dress. She couldn't grasp what was happening. Rigby—of course she would address him as Mr. Ritter—didn't seem to find anything wrong with her face. She poured half a bottle of perfume over herself, unfortunately also over the dress, and put on the opal ring Miss Conroy had given her. Then she powdered herself and arranged her mane of hair. Her big, floppy hat covered her left cheek almost completely. She presented herself to Rigby like a child thirsting for praise.

"You look very nice." Rigby ignored the radiant schoolgirl face.

During the drive to Katoomba, Rigby was enlightened about the character and habits of Miss Blyth. The explanation was longer than the Great Western Highway. He smiled indulgently. Women could not keep friendships. Miss Fleet didn't have to protect him from Candy Blyth. He had dealt successfully with more dangerous snakes. But he found out, to his astonishment, that his virtuous cobber, Patrick Trent, who prayed for him every Sunday, had visited Miss Blyth regularly for quite some time. That took the cake! "But Mr. Trent didn't have an affair with her. He's not her type," Miss Fleet went on hastily. Rigby couldn't imagine, however hard he tried, Paddy Trent visiting the young lady for her intellectual charms. Naturally he wouldn't say a word about Paddy's little indiscretion, especially since his wife, whom Rigby had witnessed two-timing Paddy a while ago in a Hungarian restaurant, was expecting a baby. It had saved Trent's marriage, and that was why Rigby was driving to the Blue Mountains now with this little girl. She must have been the one who had massaged his wife. There couldn't be two masseuses with a birthmark running around in Sydney!

Miss Fleet was a good hiker. She didn't take tiny steps like the first Mrs. Rigby on her high heels, nor did she complain, like the second Mrs. Rigby of headache and backache. Miss Fleet was a robust, solid creature. Rigby laughed aloud several times. The girl was really quite comical, and she worshiped him. She favored him with her exquisite profile as much as she could, the intelligent young thing! And then they were standing on a dizzifyingly high plateau, watching the sun set and looking across at the Three Sisters. These sandstone crags, swathed in gold by the setting sun, rose up high above the abyss of the Jamieson Valley. The plateau lay there in deepest silence. They were among the last visitors. Although Sydney was only thirty-five miles away, thousands of years separated the city from the primeval landscape. Here, in the old days, the blackfellows had wandered, designating the rocks, the streams, the valleys, and the sky as the homes of the spirits of nature. The vast forests, surrounded by stone, were already wrapping themselves in the veils of night.

"In the morning a blue mist covers it all," Rigby explained.

"Really?"

"Do you hang around Sydney all the time, Miss Fleet?"

"I used to hang around Parramatta. That's where I come from."

Rigby was silent. A twisted path had led him from Parramatta to the Three Sisters. They towered, monumental, over the abyss of time. Trees and fern grew around the crags, and some distance away, a few Australians had built their homes. They fought for bread and love, multiplied, had to adapt constantly to the shifting aspects of life, and innocently obeyed the laws of being born and dying. In his youth, Rigby had thought he stood like these craggy eminences: nothing could change or shake him.

From below came the gurgling sound of water cascading over precipitous rock. A call, a song, a cry . . . Rigby listened. "It must be like this in Switzerland," said Miss Fleet.

"It's like this in New South Wales. Good enough for me."

Molly looked at him shyly. Suddenly he was a total stranger, unfriendly, almost somber. She walked over to the edge of the plateau and looked down. Rigby yelled, "Careful!" and pulled her back brutally. "Are you crazy?"

Miss Fleet laughed. "I don't get dizzy."

She rubbed her arm, which hurt where he had grabbed her. Rigby apologized, but his mind wasn't on what he was saying. He was staring down at the abyss. This was where Flora had fallen into the depths below. Why in hell did he always come back to the Three Sisters? Only murderers with low IQ's did this sort of thing in the crime novels they sold in Katoomba.

"I'm hungry," he said brusquely.

Night was falling. Rigby led Molly back slowly to the City of the Blue Mountains. Suddenly she stopped dead.

"Are you tired, little girl?"

Rigby was standing close to her. The moonlight fell on his long, fine face, his nose with the arrogant hook, and his light, flickering eyes.

"I love you, Mr. Rigby!"

He was so astounded, he didn't even notice that she knew who he was. Before he could say anything, she had thrown her arms around his neck and was sobbing. Her hat had fallen off, and Rigby could smell the scent of her red-gold hair and her youth. He couldn't help it if youth sobbed and embraced him . . .

"I've loved you forever!"

"Nice of you."

"Not nice. Horrible!"

"Why?"

Miss Fleet said nothing. She covered her left cheek with her hand.

"There's nothing so bad about that, child." Rigby had understood. He looked at the young girl. He was ready to eat his hat if Miss Fleet had ever slept with a man. But no virgins for him. They clung like bees to acacia trees and one was never able to shake them off. He gave the girl a light kiss, and put his arms around her. Molly pressed close to him shyly. He had been right. The sheila didn't even know how to kiss.

"I'll bring you back to the lodge, Molly."

"And where are you going to sleep?"

"With friends." Friends, plural. That was a good idea. It should stop the lovesick little bird in her tracks.

"I . . . I want to stay with you."

"What would my friends say?"

The girl had intuition. She declared there weren't any "friends." Rigby laughed, but Molly Fleet didn't join him. With Candy he would have taken up quarters for the night in his friend's empty villa without giving it a thought. Miss Blyth was hard-boiled!

They drank a beer at the lodge. Rigby didn't entirely believe the young thing when she assured him that Mrs. Doody and Candy really thought he was Albert Ritter. He asked sharply if Molly was lying, but she assured him that she had seen a picture of him by chance when she came to massage his wife, and it sounded true. Then she said nothing more, just sat there innocently devouring him with her eyes.

Rigby thought it over. The girl was in love, beautifully built, and her disfigurement would dissolve in the dark. But he couldn't get Anne's letter out of his mind. If only the little thing wouldn't look at him so imploringly! He certainly had got himself into one hell of a mess!

"Molly," he said gently. "You're a sweet, clever little girl." No reply.

"You're terribly young. Or are you an old nag?"

"No!"

"You see? And I think that someday you'll want to marry and have children."

"Nobody'll marry me."

"Nonsense!" This child should have seen Flora Pratt! Still, Rigby had married *her*...

"I don't even have a boy friend!"

"That's just it," said Rigby. "But you may. Any day. If I were to start something with you now..."

"You'd *never* start anything with me!"

"May I finish?" Rigby asked with a trace of impatience. "I'm a rolling stone, little girl. You would cry your pretty blue eyes out. You need someone steady."

"Will I ever see you again?"

"You'll see me tomorrow morning," said Rigby, a little more impatient now. "I want to show you the stalactite caves of Jenolan."

"Oh, that's wonderful!"

"Then we'll have lunch and drive back to Sydney."

Miss Fleet digested this information.

"Whenever I have time, Molly, I'll drive you out somewhere."

"Word of honor, Mr. Rigby?"

"Word of honor. If you like you can call me Alex."

"You're dinkum, Mr. Rigby." She threw her arms around him again and he felt her breasts.

"That's something I like to hear from charming young ladies," in spite of which honeyed words, he pushed her away. She should go before he asked her to stay...

Molly walked into her room, partially consoled. A young heart is modest. *He* had said she was charming. *He* had said she had beautiful eyes. *He* had...

Molly Fleet slept.

When Rigby got back to Vaucluse, the terrace was already lit up with the white angle lamps. From far off his sharp eyes could detect two men with drinks on the table in front of them. So Mrs. Andrews was still there! He raced like a schoolboy across the garden to the terrace: his cobbers hadn't forgotten him! He recognized Paddy Trent at once by his silhouette, but who was the other man? Rigby had never seen him before.

21

Ovid in Vaucluse

"This is Mr. Muir from Broome." Trent introduced the man. "He's staying with us, and he wanted to meet you, Alex."

Rigby had heard a lot about Muir's visits to Sydney, and looked at the tall man with the bald head and deep-set eyes with interest. Were they Asiatic eyes? The man stood as motionless as a statue.

"What are you doing in Sydney, Mr. Muir?"

"At the moment I am studying Mr. Trent's collection of opals, Mr. Rigby."

"There's nothing very much to it." Patrick never found anything much to his collection nor to himself.

"A very rare collection, my dear friend, or I wouldn't have wanted to see it again."

Rigby mixed cocktails. He had decided that he liked Mr. Muir.

"Would you be my guest tomorrow evening at the Chevron Hilton, Mr. Rigby? With Mr. Trent? I would consider it an honor." Mr. Muir was more formal than any Aussie Rigby and Trent had ever enjoyed drinks with.

"Thank you very much. I'll be glad to come."

There was a pause. Mr. Muir seemed to have no intention of starting a conversation. Rigby stared at him with undisguised pleasure. Funny guy! The man looked forty, then again more like a hundred and forty.

"I would like to discuss a certain business matter with you tomorrow evening, Mr. Rigby."

Rigby hid his astonishment. Why didn't the man say what

317

he wanted right now? Had Trent sold him some real estate in New South Wales? Did he want to have a house built?

Mr. Muir was admiring the harbor scene. He liked the house in Vaucluse. Rigby, in his own way, built according to Japanese principles. Very impressive! Muir had seen residences, schools, and other public buildings in Sydney that all bore the stamp of this architectural firm.

"You've built yourself a very beautiful home here, Mr. Rigby."

"Your house in Broome isn't bad either," said Trent.

"More like a cake with icing than an organism, my friend." Mr. Muir understood the art of understatement of which, generally speaking, only the Japanese and the English were in command. "Have you been to Japan often, Mr. Rigby?" Muir asked abruptly.

"Unfortunately never."

"I thought that perhaps you had gathered some inspiration in my mother's country," Muir said casually. "I would like to express my admiration for your work. You practice architecture as a poetic act on a mathematical basis, and that's the way it should be."

Mr. Muir looked at the indigo-blue water. It was glittering greenly, then gray, then violet. It changed color constantly, thus inspiring waves of meditation. During a walk through the garden, Muir had been struck by how brilliantly the architect had placed solid stone and shimmering glass to face the water, and achieved the effect of the house's seeming suspension in a great sea, participating in the metamorphoses of the elements.

Meanwhile, during the pause in the conversation, Muir had settled down comfortably. He didn't look up until Rigby offered him a cigarette. "Have you read Ovid, Mr. Rigby?"

"The *Ars Amatoria*?" Rigby grinned.

Muir shook his head. Ovid's love poems did not appeal to him. In Mr. Muir's opinion the elegant poet had never experienced grand passion. "I meant the *Metamorphoses*."

"They're too highbrow for me," said Rigby. "I'm a little man."

Trent laughed loudly and Mr. Muir smiled. He liked Alexander Rigby.

"No, seriously, Mr. Rigby, I have the feeling that you would enjoy Ovid's *Metamorphoses*."

The stranger had hit the nail on the head. The *Metamorphoses* had delighted Rigby since his student days. The constant transformation of gods and humans into animals, plants, and stone; of nymphs into mute islands; the continuous interplay of conversion, change and renewal, of various viewpoints and moods—all of it was his element. Perhaps, in his poor efforts, he was just as much a virtuoso of the surface. Ovid was no mystic. And Rigby liked that. Mysticism came damn close to brooding.

Rigby asked Mr. Muir if he knew a lot of people in Sydney.

"Fortunately, no! Most people are two-legged streams of traffic."

"Or on wheels," said Trent. "Don't make yourselves out worse than you are, my friends!"

Only Trent knew how lonely Alex was. He had written to Anne about it but received no reply. He was very worried about Alex. Didn't the second Mrs. Rigby have eyes in her head? She'd never find a man like Alex again.

"A young lady from Sydney visited me in Broome," Mr. Muir said, communicative all of a sudden. "Trent knows her."

Rigby asked for her name. He was very interested in young ladies.

"Candace Blyth," said Trent. "Don't you know her, Alex?"

"I don't know *all* the young ladies in Sydney."

"She was a model. She used to work for *Insight*."

"Is she dead? Why the past tense?"

"She is more alive than is good for her," Mr. Muir interrupted. "I found her a short while ago in Perth. A few days ago I brought her back to her aunt in Sydney."

Mr. Muir had not yet recovered from Mrs. Doody's "parlor." Miss Blyth's pink room had been another nightmare. He wanted Rigby to build her a small house. The ignorant young thing could then perhaps learn a little something from her surroundings. If nothing else, her beauty would at least have a suitable frame. Of course Mr. Muir saw this house as an investment.

Miss Blyth could live in it, and the furnishings would be a gift. But if she scattered her junk and her pink spreads all over the place, he was sorry, but he would have to give her a good beating.

Mr. Muir had picked Candy up in pretty bad shape in a bar in Perth. Until then she had lived on chance encounters. He had bought her clothes, listened to the shabby stories of her adventures, and as a precautionary measure had sent her to a doctor. He had slept with her again only after that. She was more beautiful than ever but got terribly on his nerves. He was sorry for her, of course, but his compassion was tinged with contempt. Well . . . then he had brought her to Sydney. He didn't know why he felt responsible for her, but she always seemed to force her way into his life. As long as he lived in Australia, she was a burden he couldn't shake off. The house would be his last contribution to her welfare because it was his intention to move, in due course, to Japan. In his opinion Miss Blyth suffered from several failings which would prove fatal: she wanted the triumphs of Venus without working for them, and she filled her mind with trivia.

"She has no sense and no upbringing," said Muir, to no one in particular.

Rigby said nothing. He was still digesting the news of Candy's return.

"Could I ask you to do me a favor, Mr. Rigby?"

"Certainly."

"Miss Blyth was once quite successful as a model. She sent me several copies of the magazine *Insight*. Could you perhaps do something for her there? Is your sister still editor-in-chief?"

"In full regalia!"

"Perhaps she could be persuaded to make an exception in this case? The little fool has to find work. She seems to be afraid of Miss Rigby."

"So am I!" Rigby said drily.

Mr. Muir smiled for the second time that evening. He gave Rigby a card on which he had scribbled a few words. "Just in case Miss Rigby would like a report on Broome. My secretary does that sort of thing with his eyes closed."

"I'm sure Grace will be very interested, Mr. Muir."

"An excellent magazine. Astonishing, when you think it's a women's paper."

Rigby and Trent looked at each other. A Japanese viewpoint, undoubtedly. Rigby invited Muir for dinner on the following Thursday, and called his sister. She accepted the invitation. She liked to meet interesting people.

Mr. Muir was delighted. At last he'd be rid of Candy Blyth. He wanted to talk about the house in the country with Trent and Rigby in his hotel, but first he had wanted to meet Rigby. He didn't buy a pig—or an architect—in a poke.

After dinner, which Mrs. Andrews had cooked to perfection, Trent left the room to phone his wife. He wanted to know how she felt and to beg her to rest as much as possible. Yesterday she had had stomach pains. Could this possibly harm the child?

"Send Trent to a good doctor," said Mr. Muir.

Rigby was surprised. "Paddy is too fat, but he can uproot trees."

"I know," said Mr. Muir.

"Our Mr. Dobson is first rate. Internist in Macquarie Street. I mean . . . is anything wrong with Trent? Has he said anything to you?"

"Of course not. I'm afraid Mr. Trent eats and drinks too casually."

"I'll give him hell!"

"I wouldn't do that, Mr. Rigby. Please excuse me if I give you some advice. It would not be wise to alarm him."

"But what's wrong with him?" Rigby asked. "I'd like to know!"

Muir looked at Rigby for a moment silently. A splendid architect but a temperamental man. Impolite, like every dinkum Aussie.

"His breathing isn't right, Mr. Rigby. He is an unusually valuable human being. I want him to breathe for a long time to come."

"I suppose there's too much strain on his heart," said Rigby, feeling a sudden disquiet. He was very fond of his fat friend, very fond indeed. He'd better drag Paddy to Bertie Dobson. At once. Tomorrow. Whether he wanted it or not. Rigby coughed and said, "Excuse me, Mr. Muir. Ordinarily I'm no lamb, but I . . . I'm very fond of Trent." It all came out with great difficulty.

Muir was disarmed. "I understand," he said gently. "Mr. Trent may outlive all of us. There are so many people with dubious illnesses . . . isn't that so?"

"I don't know. Nothing's ever wrong with me."

"You are an exception, my friend. I heal my numerous ailments with regulated breathing and solitude. Trent is about fifty now. I think that is an age when one must face the fact that it is later than one thinks. A definite consolation in this miserable life, is it not?"

Just then Trent came back, beaming. "My wife feels wonderful!"

"And how do *you* feel, you old idiot?" Rigby asked angrily.

"Me?" Trent was surprised. "Don't have time to think about myself. I'm fine, as usual!"

Rigby drank several cups of strong black coffee. Trent sounded worried as he asked how could Rigby possibly sleep after that? "Look after yourself," Rigby said amiably. "I can always sleep."

"One can see that," said Mr. Muir. "I have a natural sleeping medicine for you, Trent." He didn't say what, and Trent didn't ask. It was so unimportant whether he slept or not.

Rigby was in a fine mood. He hadn't had such a nice evening in a long time. Contrary to all expectations, he'd even had a great weekend. He thought for a moment of Molly Fleet. So young and so much in love! Rigby thanked heaven that he had brought the little girl from Parramatta home untouched. He'd ask her out for dinner some time, or go for an outing with her again, since it seemed to mean so much to her. Really a nice, sweet girl. Much more serious, intelligent, and modest than Candy Blyth. According to Mr. Muir, Candy Blyth was considerably soiled around the edges but still looked like an orchid

But he had had enough of her. Odd! He was probably standing on the edge of a metamorphosis again. Did Anne's farewell letter have something to do with it? What could he do about it? Nothing. One should never detain people who were traveling. Rigby smoked hastily. The thought of Anne darkened his bright vision of the future, like an ink spot spreading over white blotting paper. How grateful Molly Fleet had been! For absolutely nothing!

Muir talked about Broome and Japan, and Rigby listened with great interest. Then Muir invited him and Trent to Broome, and said they shouldn't put off the visit for too long because he didn't know how much longer he would be living there himself. Like Rigby he seemed to be thirsting for change.

Rigby had never been to Broome, and promised to come soon. The evening became increasingly congenial. Rigby had forgotten the outing in the Blue Mountains. In a few hours the young thing from Parramatta had faded and become a memory. Tomorrow she would be swallowed up by the daylight. But Molly Fleet had not forgotten Rigby.

22

Miss Rigby's Cold Coffee

From time to time Miss Rigby invited her friends for a cold meal and hot coffee. When she gave her farewell party for Mr. Muir, it was winter in Sydney, but Miss Rigby didn't dream of serving a hot meal in July. Her recipes for convivial professional hyenas were inspired by the refrigerator. Not until late in the night did the survivors grill sausages, bacon and tomatoes for themselves in the huge kitchen on Bellevue Hill.

Miss Rigby and Robert Muir had become friends. They

appreciated the differences in their natures. Muir had found his stay in Sydney stimulating this time, thanks to Patrick Trent and the Rigbys. Now he would return to his chosen monotony interrupted only by his guests from abroad. Muir was in a meditative mood as he sat all alone in his room in the Chevron Hilton, furnished with all American comforts. Why had he been distrustful of his Australian compatriots for so many years? Had Sydney changed him? Or had Trent and the Rigbys done it? It seemed to him that the end of his long Australian day was to be enhanced by a glorious sunset. Muir had invited the Rigbys to visit him in Broome, and he hoped to be a host to them later in Japan.

Betty's marriage and Marchmont's illness may have made Miss Rigby more open to new friendships, but she had certainly taken to Robert Muir. Like Alexander, she recognized a free spirit and an individualist from miles away. Marchmont was a free spirit and Betty had imagination, but Muir had both in an elegantly unobtrusive balance which the Rigbys couldn't help but admire. Of course they treated him with perfectly natural friendliness, but that Miss Rigby, after their first meeting, spent some time every weekend with Muir in a restaurant in Sydney or in Manly, was most unusual. The Trents had also occasionally been present, but Mr. Muir could do very nicely without the presence of young Mrs. Trent. That was why he had moved into the Chevron Hilton. How Patrick could stand the young lady day after day was beyond his powers of comprehension. And Klari had once written poetry? Dear God in heaven! Poetry was an intimate dialogue, a delicate act of recognition between a soul and the primeval aspects of emotion. But Mrs. Trent spoke in her coarse and vulgar English solely about social events, the latest electronic gadgets, cars, the peptic ulcers of prominent people, and other status symbols. Sydney's *dolce vita*, the unsure, sleek, Americanized way of life of an urbane society, had not impressed Mrs. Trent. Patrick lived his own life, unperturbed. Muir asked himself if, perhaps before his departure from Australia, he hadn't met the true dinkum Aussies in Trent and in the Rigbys.

He spent most of his time with Patrick Trent. Actually he should have told Trent something he was going to find out sooner or later anyway, but he was silent. What one doesn't tell can hurt no one. He decided quite suddenly to ask Miss Rigby if he could come half an hour before the party, whereupon she had suggested that he breakfast with her on Bellevue Hill.

Miss Rigby, who was not easily surprised, could scarcely grasp what Robert Muir confided to her on this occasion. Her black coffee grew cold. Finally she promised that for the present she would say nothing. Muir asked if Alexander couldn't speak to Trent, and Miss Rigby said she knew her brother was very fond of Patrick, but he had as much tact as an elephant.

"What are you going to do?" asked Muir.

"Something will come to me. Trent left for Queensland yesterday, on business."

"Is he going to stay there long?"

"At least four weeks." Miss Rigby drank her coffee absentmindedly. She felt queasy. Patrick was looking forward so much to the child...

Muir looked at her fine, energetic face with its sharp eyes and the narrow, ironic lips. He felt that a human being was hidden behind the facade of this elegant, successful editor, a human being with whom perhaps very few people were familiar. Miss Rigby's persona was of exceptional perfection. Not a crack in the wall of her self-control. But behind this wall, Muir realized suddenly, there was a woman who knew that there were tears in things...

Grace Rigby took Muir's coffee cup from him. He drank his coffee black, sweet, and boiling-hot. "I'll make us fresh coffee, or you'll hate me."

"Not necessarily. *You* may even serve me cold coffee."

"Since when do you pay compliments?" Miss Rigby asked, laughing.

"I never pay compliments. May I call you Grace?"

Miss Rigby, who lived in an unconventional milieu, had no idea what this request cost a man like Muir, especially since

Miss Rigby's bluntness and dynamic energy would be incomprehensible, almost repulsive, to a Japanese. But Grace and he understood each other across the abyss. She had a profound and discreet understanding for Australian mixed races. In this sense she inspired and published a magazine that was read throughout Australia because of its varied points of view and reports. Muir had grasped that the fashion and cookery items were a necessary concession to the women on this male continent. Miss Rigby would have admitted it, smiling, and begged him to keep it to himself.

Muir had described his childhood and youth in Broome. After that they had become friends. Finally Grace had said, "You've had a hard time. But you have imagination, and that gives one power over circumstances. I am only a realist."

And then she spoke to this strange man who had become such a friend, about little Betty West, how she had brought color and joy into her sober working life. Muir sensed how much Grace Rigby was suffering because of the changed circumstances, and to his astonishment it touched him. Although he was considerably younger than she, he was emotionally just as secure and lacking in sentimentality. This wonderful woman needed a friend now to fill the gap Betty West had left. And here was Robert Muir, with his Scottish practicality, reliable and proud and humble as his Japanese ancestors. He was at her disposal. Of course they would only be able to see each other between long intervals, but his future island home in Japan was waiting for her.

His question still hung in the air. Why did Muir want to call her by her first name? Wasn't he a fanatic representative of aloofness, not spontaneous and warm like the Aussies? And of course he despised superficial contacts. In spite of which he was offering her, who did nothing but listen to him quietly, a pearl.

Miss Rigby's reaction was un-Australian. She said she was honored.

Robert Muir's farewell party was a huge success. Important people from the press and writers from New South Wales came, bringing healthy appetites with them. To say nothing of thirst. Robert Muir was introduced to a great many prestigious people and, ridiculous as it may seem, was treated as a guest of honor and interviewed constantly. Very few journalists had visited Broome, but Muir's name and his reputation as an international businessman, along with the stories of his regular visits to New York and Paris, had preceded him. His surroundings did the rest. Miss Rigby indicated that *Insight* was going to publish a series of articles on Broome. "Dammit!" thought her rivals. "She's beaten us to it again!" The Rigby nose was really long.

Miss Rigby's cobbers from the Sydney *Morning Herald* naturally turned up also, and everything proceeded according to plan, just as it had done at Betty's wedding. But today Miss Rigby was in high spirits. She actually looked beautiful, a Diana in a silk suit. She had obviously left her dragon's teeth at the office. She answered all questions about Elizabeth West with the patience of a saint, and what she didn't tell, Alexander Rigby made up for. The journalists were doubled over with laughter. For years there had been rumors in Sydney that Rigby had had an affair with young Elizabeth West. If so, the fellow had latched onto someone else long ago. Nobody asked about Rigby's wife, and it wouldn't have been good for anybody if he'd done so.

Bertie Dobson was present, naturally. He beamed at his young wife and introduced her to the intelligentsia of Sydney. Mavis behaved charmingly and modestly in this new world, and Bertie was bursting with pride. Miss Rigby winked at him. Both of them were thinking of Alexander's fiftieth, when she had tried to talk Bertie into taking on Betty. Miss Rigby was perfectly satisfied with Mavis: a nice, practical girl.

In the middle of all the fun, young Dr. Dobson was called to the phone, after which he told his wife and Miss Rigby unobtrusively that he was leaving, and made his way through the crowd. The conversations continued; Miss Rigby didn't seem to be quite as cheerful.

In a corner some journalists were talking about the daily papers in Sydney, Melbourne, Adelaide, and—in honor of

Robert Muir—the press in Broome. Mr. Muir said there was nothing to say about it, it spoke for itself. But nobody could get out of him *what* it said. The guest from Broome was almost as secretive as "our Rigby." After persistent questioning he finally told them that the Australian dailies were easy for teenagers to understand, and gave the impression that they were published mainly for that age group. That might be true for Broome, said a guest from the *Melbourne Herald*. Mr. Muir didn't contradict him. For that he was too polite and too indifferent. He hated any kind of sensationalism, and the Australian ranked the sensational item even above the sports news. How many people read the serious editorials and contributions in the papers and magazines? Pictures, crimes, society scandal, and again pictures. In the larger Australian cities a society bewitched by television and films was in the making which chose only the cheapest, most sensational items, some from the American press and certain London papers. But Muir said nothing of all this. The men from the press were far too intelligent not to know about it themselves. They wrote mainly for the subscriber—an old story in a young civilization.

Around Miss Rigby there was talk about the problem of power. The men were declaring that women were using their power professionally and privately, to gain ever more prestige. The men on the other hand used the ideas and technology of power for purely impersonal purposes...

"Robert," whispered Miss Rigby. "I've just had bad news. Please tell Alexander when our guests have gone. We can't both disappear at the same time."

Muir brought her a brandy. She looked pale but she went right on smiling at her guests who were gradually dispersing. The fun was over again for a while.

"Can I do anything for you?" asked Muir.

"Please stay with my brother. He should come as soon as he can get away." She gave Muir an address. Dr. Dobson had asked Miss Rigby to come first, alone.

Stanley Marchmont was waiting on the harbor bridge to eternity because before the big crossing he wanted to beg Grace

Rigby to look after Alex. Marchmont lay quietly and completely conscious in his sunny study on Mosman Bay, and was ready for the trip. It was very quiet all around him. The sounds of this world, to which he had listened tirelessly throughout his entire life, had turned into the drumming of raindrops on a corrugated tin roof in the Outback. It was strange, but even his beloved Sydney, with its high-rise houses and colossal Harbour Bridge, was barely different right now from the Outback. Even if Sydney were to grow farther up into heaven, the city would always remain of this world.

Marchmont had never had much talent for being ill, and he had had quite enough of being bedridden. All he still had to do was tell dear Grace to look after Alex. Who would bring the rascal to his senses when he wasn't there any more to give him hell? Why had Anne run away? He wanted to see Alex once more, but not to tell him off. Grace laid her ear against his blue lips. How weak his metallic voice had become! But she understood every word and nodded.

Alex stormed into the room. His features were distorted, but he forced himself to be calm when his boss gave him a sharp look. "Don't excite him," Miss Rigby whispered.

"Leave us alone." Rigby's voice was hoarse, but Grace had already left the room and was sitting in the breakfast room with Bertie Dobson.

"Alex mustn't stay too long," Bertie mumbled.

"Let him be, Bertie," said Miss Rigby. "It's the way Stan wants it."

Five minutes later Dobson left. Miss Rigby watched him go, but he looked strangely misty. She sat alone in the darkening room and bade Stanley Marchmont farewell. In her youth she had loved him and wanted to marry him, but he hadn't seemed to be aware of her deep attachment. Marchmont had had nothing on his mind but Alex. Like her own father . . . And no wonder. Alex had always been so much more brilliant and charming than she.

Just then Rigby appeared. He looked at his sister as if he had never seen her before and murmured, "He's gone and done it."

He drove straight back to Vaucluse. He wouldn't speak to anybody, he didn't want to see anybody. How fortunate that he was living in an empty house! Grace would understand. She had to understand! He felt torn inside. The spiritual umbilical cord that had bound him to Marchmont since his youth had been cut. How often had Marchmont thrown him out of the old office in George Street, and he had always come back! The silver teapot he had given his boss as a peace-offering . . . in the gray past . . . they had used it to the end. Rigby had seen it on a table in the room of the dying man. That was the moment when this wild, dark pain that was still tearing him apart had overpowered him like a Tasmanian tiger.

Rigby drove slowly up the hill to Vaucluse. The moon was up and was transforming the city that he had discovered as a greenhorn, with Marchmont's help, into a crater landscape— ashen, cold, desolate, a wasteland of stone and dead grass. And still this wasteland radiated merciless beauty, and was chastened by a lively wind. How much ecstasy, how many storms, how many dead had this city seen?

Marchmont had walked in these streets, and now they were empty and filled with dangers. Rigby would grow old, his senses dulled. He would succumb to illness and in the end have to retire. He would experience everything Marchmont had had to experience, but he didn't have Marchmont's dignity, his patience, and his resignation to God's will. He would be just as unable to resign himself to his exit from the stage of life as he had been unable to cope with the loss of Anne. He couldn't resign himself to anything! Marchmont had always said so. Why had everything run so treacherously smoothly for him for so many years? He couldn't shake the thought that at the firm, slowly, slowly, he was becoming "the old man." Just as Marchmont had. French sometimes jokingly called him just that: the old man. In time it would be meant seriously. Especially when an even younger partner would join them. Which of course would have to take place. Building, the shaping of the future—nothing else mattered. Marchmont had pounded it into him as a young man. And it still held good.

At home Rigby flung himself into a big easy chair and stretched his long legs. The telephone rang. He let it ring until it stopped, discouraged. Rigby had closed his eyes and was going walkabout once more, with his boss.

"Alex doesn't answer." Miss Rigby put down the receiver after her second try.

"Don't let it worry you." Muir had waited for her patiently in the empty reception room and ignored the astonished looks of the housekeeper Miss Rigby had had for years. In the end Mrs. Parker had brought coffee. Miss Rigby had told her what had happened and urged the good soul to go to bed. She could not stand tears. After her vain efforts to reach Alex, she sat in front of her coffee, speechless. Strange, but life kept getting emptier. She took a sip of the coffee and put down her cup. If there was one thing she couldn't stand, it was cold coffee. But life was gradually becoming just that. When one was young, one got all excited over ideas and feelings, then came the lukewarm period, and finally life tasted like...

Where was Muir? She hadn't noticed his leaving. At that moment he brought in some piping hot coffee.

"What do you think you're doing?" she said gruffly. But the hot coffee renewed her. At last she could talk about Marchmont. Then she got up and walked over to the window. The indifferent night lay outside.

Muir brought a second cup of coffee. She wanted to thank him but didn't trust her voice. Too much had happened in just one day.

"I have to go now, Grace. My plane leaves tomorrow."

"I'll come to the airport."

"Please don't. This is not farewell. When may I expect you and Alexander in Broome?"

"As soon as we can. And ... yes ... thanks for everything, Robert."

Muir looked at Grace Rigby, an intense, melancholy look. He felt that she would not bury herself in her sorrow. Later she took her new friend back to the Chevron Hilton in spite of his protests, and drove to Vaucluse under the big stars. She saw light in Alexander's study, and hesitated for a moment. Then she drove home. She was very calm now.

She lay awake for a long time that night and thought of her years with Marchmont. His friendship had been a steadying pole in her life. He hadn't had any extraordinary command of words, but it had been a rich poverty. When it counted he could talk, thunder, and convince. He had wielded the whip of perfection over Alexander's head. He alone had made of his young colleague what he was today. But even Marchmont had been unable to prevent the crises in Alexander's private life. Today Rigby was chasing after two or three birds and therefore caught none. Grace sighed. The hours passed by like scornful kangaroos and disappeared in the thicket of time.

Miss Rigby thought of Robert Muir again. He was chasing nothing and no one. Perhaps that was why Australia gave him everything he wanted of the continent. She knew nothing about his life or his relationship to women. Why had he suddenly saddled her again with the model, Candy? Either he wanted to sleep alone for a change, or play Adam with another Eve. That was his business...

Miss Rigby could see Candy Blyth: beautiful, young, and hungry for life. A little kitten like that had an easier time with men. She herself had always been too energetic, too cool, too critical. And sometimes she had added more acid to the lemons of disappointment. Of course she had never possessed the sensual beauty that electrified or moved a man, and bound him against his will to create a career for a fool. For years she had run up against closed editorial doors and finally pushed them open with great exertion. But sometimes these doors had closed again, and she had been left standing outside. Alex had always had an easier time of it. Already in his youth, so much had come his way—success, women...

Grace Rigby asked herself if she had tried too hard and too often. Would Marchmont have learned to love her if she had been a little more stupid? Or softer? Or more in need of help? No. She could never have brought it off. And so she had had

to look on, outwardly unmoved, at how the door to Marchmont's heart had opened hesitantly years ago on an outing to
Windsor, only to fall shut again soundlessly. She had never
been able to resign herself to it and tried again and again to
push the door open. Marchmont was seventeen years older,
and had once advised her to find someone her own age. She
hadn't had to run after men. Several colleagues had wanted to
marry her, but stubbornly she had compared them to Marchmont. That had been foolish. But she had stuck to her conviction that she and Marchmont would have been a good married
couple, and she had simply never been able to resign herself
to the fact that he thought differently. In the end she had had
to realize that a steady drop of water did not always hollow
out a stone.

She had also tried to force other things with her will. Today,
in her fifties, she knew that it had been wrong. Robert Muir
had become her friend without her having to move a finger.
Wasn't one supposed to fight for the possession of a heart?

She didn't know. She lay on her couch, sleepless, and groped
for solutions. Was she trying too hard again?

It only seemed so. She was on the track of a recognition
and was fortunately too weary to pursue it with her razor-sharp
logic. Just because of that she sensed suddenly the presence
of a providence that unpredictably makes life bearable, even
precious, and refreshes the thirsting spirit in a wonderful fashion: when one door falls shut, another opens.

23

Visions in Darlinghurst

There were no visible signs in Mrs. Doody's boardinghouse that Candy had returned. Molly Fleet, Charlie Rainbow, the Umbrella Uncle, Mrs. Doody and Candy spent their days as they always had done, but they kept inconspicuously out of each other's way. There was a tear in the weave of their everyday life which Mrs. Doody mended as best she could every now and then. She hated any unpleasantness. *She* was the one who might scold, and she scolded enough for all the rest. And she was especially sensitive about Candy. Nobody was allowed to criticize her. Mrs. Doody had forgotten completely that some time ago she had written her niece a rather unfriendly letter. It had bothered her only for a few days.

Sydney had given Mrs. Doody a hard time. She had had to defend herself for years to the best of her ability. But like every good Aussie, she had mastered instinctively the air of self-defense. She had always been sly; now she had also grown hard. Candy, however, was the painful toe that she hid in her shabby slippers. The logics of feelings are scandalously illogical. So Mrs. Doody was insulted when Molly Fleet quite openly disliked her niece. The two girls spoke to each other only when absolutely necessary. Not that Mrs. Doody noticed it, because she did most of the talking. Molly Fleet continued to write love letters for Candy, but the crazy traveling salesman, who had been so avid for them, seemed to have disappeared into thin air. Candy missed neither him nor Trent. She didn't miss any man; she found them all interchangeable.

Aunt Doody, on the other hand, was not only a member of

the clan; she was her mother surrogate. Candy's mother would have criticized her mercilessly and condemned her. *Insight* had not been a success in Kalgoorlie. Mrs. Blyth had looked at her daughter's pictures with horror. The shameless hussy was showing herself to all Australia in a bathing suit! Mrs. Blyth could see Satan behind her daughter's profession. After her husband's death she had grown even more bitter. She wrote to her sister in Sydney that Candace would come to a bad end, and that *she* was not blame.

After this letter Mrs. Doody scolded Molly Fleet and Charlie Rainbow, who threw a sofa cushion at her head and "accidentally" broke the old teapot. That evening Mrs. Doody and Charlie were laughing uproariously in the kitchen. Molly, in her room, heard it and ran out into the street. Candy had gone out with a new admirer. Charlie was so full of gin that Uncle Doody, who could drink gin by the quart, shoved him into his room in a rage. Charlie, who secretly loved the old man, brought him another umbrella. Mr. Doody growled: that was the last thing he needed. His room was full of the damn things! He threw the umbrella on the floor and Charlie saw it roll under the bed. He slunk off sadly, but that evening Uncle Doody hung Charlie's present on a hook with all the other umbrellas. Then Charlie was proud. The threadbare umbrella with the split handle had cost quite a bit. You didn't get anything for nothing in Sydney. Charlie also called the old Irishman "Uncle" and made a table for him, which Mr. Doody accepted graciously. He even went so far as to tell Mrs. Doody that the abo was the best lodger in the whole damn house. The old man couldn't stand Candy, but since he was paying no rent, he said nothing. He wanted to thrash the little whore with Charlie's big umbrella, because Candy ignored him whenever they met, so he didn't greet her either.

And then, one day, he "forgot" one of his umbrellas on the staircase. If Charlie hadn't helped Candy to stumble upstairs— the old man had turned out the light too—she might have broken her neck. Mrs. Doody hurled the umbrella into the old man's room and gave him notice for the hundred and eighty-fifth time. Later they were singing Irish songs to the accompaniment of the radio. Uncle Doody and his umbrellas were part of the inventory.

Sometimes, before an earthquake, a tremor runs through the house. The furniture wobbles, the tea cups clatter, family photographs drop off the wall, and a cold shiver passes through the bodies of the inmates. After that, all is still and everyday life comes into its own again. The archangel's trumpet is silenced by the chatter of the morning hour. People talk about the price of eggs again . . . so soothing . . . and tell each other who got married, is traveling, or has kicked the bucket. The heavy silence of the night is temporarily dispelled and waits for the next opportunity to outwit the day. But the day, with its wonderful immobility, is limited.

The night appears punctually and plagues the day-worshipers with nightmares, visions, wild, suppressed desires, and a lust for revenge which no decent person would let cross the threshold of consciousness. The visions are worst of all. They pour like tidal waves across the sleeper, and when he is drowning, he screams for the lifeboat of day. With the day, routine begins, heaven be praised! With the first cup of coffee the specters of our dreams sink powerlessly into the ocean of forgetfulness.

"Do you know who came to see Candy yesterday, Molly?" asked Mrs. Doody.

"No idea."

"Charles Preston! What nerve!"

"Why?"

"Why? The bastard stole from his Mrs. Moneybags in Hobart and he's been sitting in jail ever since. A fine fellow! And now the stinker wanted to get money out of my Candy again. But this time he's come to the wrong address!"

"I thought she was crazy about him. She ran off to Hobart after him, didn't she?"

"Rubbish! He begged her to come. Candy told me so herself. I threw him out. We don't want anything to do with pimps. Besides we need our dó-ré-mi ourselves."

Mrs. Doody drank her fourth cup of coffee. Candy was still

asleep. She had had bad dreams in the night and screamed aloud. It had been dreadful. She hadn't really been dreaming, she had *seen* it all. She was walking back and forth in front of a big mirror, a silk shawl across her shoulders. She was practicing a pose for the photoboys. The sun shone through the green venetian blinds and suffused her room with a pallid light. It wasn't the room in Darlinghurst at all. She was standing in the ocean in Manly, mirroring herself in the water. Then she could feel somebody coming up behind her. Suddenly it was darkest night, and she couldn't see who it was. She turned around abruptly, and found herself staring into a huge, fathomless eye. It was not an eye. It was the night, which had always been her enemy. No. It was a man. She could sense it. She wanted to run away, but she couldn't. She turned to face the ocean again because then the eye of night would be behind her. She didn't have the shawl around her shoulders any more, only a rope, and the emissary of the night—it was Charles Preston—pulled at the rope until she couldn't breathe. Then she screamed.

"The bastard was going to choke me!" she sobbed, as Mrs. Doody ran into her room.

"Who, my sugar doll?"

"Charles! You shouldn't have thrown him out. I . . . I'm afraid!"

"You must try to go back to sleep, darling."

"I can't. He'll come back!"

"Rubbish! The bastard knows that I'd get the cops." She gave Candy a sleeping pill, and talked the whole thing over with Uncle the next morning. Uncle said he was willing to wallop the wop over the head with one of his umbrellas.

"Do that! You're an angel, Uncle. My doll is so frightened. I could hear her screaming with Charles."

"Have a gin, Lydia."

"Not in the morning," Mrs. Doody said virtuously. "But thanks just the same." She waddled off into the kitchen and drank strong black coffee with Molly Fleet. Candy's hoarse cries had gone right through Mrs. Doody. Such a beautiful young creature shouldn't have to be afraid.

Candy was right back where she had left off. The photoboys and the *Insight* subscribers were all for her again. Candy had always known that there wasn't another model like her in Sydney, but she wished it would never be night. Others wished that the sun might never set, but what good were wishes when you were faced with the dictatorship of the night?

So they lived as they always had. Nobody in the boarding-house sensed the fact that the ground was beginning to tremble under their feet. They couldn't sense it because Mrs. Doody's kitchen table wobbled without any geological assistance. One of these days the building commission would come and test the foundation of the house. That's what they were doing every-where. But no building commission would find out why Mrs. Doody's boardinghouse was trembling, because it was being undermined by hatred.

Molly Fleet from Parramatta hated Candy Blyth.

Candy had always taken everything away from Molly Fleet. First Charles Preston and now Mrs. Doody. They still sat to-gether in the kitchen, and Molly still scrubbed the floor, but it wasn't the same. Mrs. Doody saw and heard no one but Candy. She was too good-natured to give Molly the cold shoul-der, but she didn't need her any more. Since Candy's return, Mrs. Doody was as indifferent to Molly as she had been before Candy left. Molly didn't show that she was hurt, but she was. After her departure from the farm, the boardinghouse had be-come her only home. She had felt safe there. Molly was too young to know that her misfortune was a very general occur-rence. Every day people lose something—house keys or money or—people. If everybody were to sing mournful songs or shed tears about it, the world would be a funeral chorus or a drown-ing planet. Perhaps it would have been preferable for Candy to have hated Molly too. Anything would have been better than the indifference of the Doodys.

Molly could of course have moved, or gone back to her father in Parramatta, but she waited with the stubbornness of youth for Rigby's visit. He had promised her in the Blue Moun-

tains that he would come again to take her for an outing. Molly
always kept her promises, and it didn't occur to her that Rigby
had simply forgotten her. Perhaps not forgotten, but was just
not in a hurry to keep his promise. He was grieving for Marchmont, and there was a lot of work at the office. He spent most
of his weekends with his sister in Manly because his empty
house seemed emptier all the time. Besides, he and Grace
intended to visit Robert Muir in Broome in a few weeks, if
French didn't swallow too much water surfing. The junior
partner often came to Manly now, with Rigby, when Grace
happened to have guests in Sydney. Rigby lived as in a men's
club. Molly couldn't know any of this, but even if she had,
she would have been on the lookout for Rigby's visit.

Gretchen had married and had little time for Molly. Just the
same, she was the only one who hadn't forgotten her, and
occasionally invited her to come over. She had attached her
bakery to the restaurant, and Gretchen's crumb cake was actually the only thing that hadn't changed in Molly's narrow
world.

Gretchen found Molly unusually pale, and urged her to go
to a doctor. But Molly wouldn't hear of it. No doctor could
help her. She had to accept life as it was. Gretchen meant well
as far as Molly was concerned, but she could do very little for
her. Why didn't she go back to her family in Parramatta? If
she couldn't earn as much there as she did in Sydney, she could
work in the brewery, or on the farm. Everything Gretchen
suggested during these coffee klatches was very sensible—
Molly realized that—but she stayed on at Mrs. Doody's. She
dreamt often of the farm, but always with Grandmother Fleet
there, and Stephen doing his accounts on the veranda, and his
dog sitting beside him at the wooden table.

Molly Fleet didn't scream in her dreams, nor did she cry
when she woke up. She had met Stephen's wife at their wedding. Jennifer was a good egg. She had asked Molly repeatedly
to spend all her free time on the farm, just as before. Molly's
room had been fixed up as a nursery, and she was to sleep in
her grandmother's room. But the big, old-fashioned room be-

longed to Grandmother Fleet. Jennifer's lips had tightened when Molly had protested. What nonsense! Old Mrs. Fleet was dead and nothing on the farm belonged to her any more. Jenny's uncle hadn't given them the money because Molly hadn't sold her share of the farm to them. Such stubbornness! Stephen agreed. He had told Molly so. Since then Molly hadn't been to the farm. She only went there in her sleep. There was no end to Grandmother's preserves. Molly ate them every night. The fields had never been so verdant, the hides of the cow so shiny!

Molly helped Charlie Rainbow with his flower boxes. She had to feel something blooming between her fingers and to smell earth even during the day. Charlie Rainbow didn't mind. He respected Miss Fleet and grew miraculous flowers for Candy.

Since Candy had come back to Darlinghurst, Charlie Rainbow hadn't gone walkabout anymore. He waited for her in the evenings as he used to do, and in the morning he tried to catch a glimpse of her when she went out. Unfortunately Miss Blyth often slept so late that Charlie didn't get to work on time, and the harbor boss didn't like that.

Candy found the abo droll. Besides, he was so willing, and everything she asked him to do made him crazily happy. On the day after Charles Preston's visit, Charlie waited for a long time in front of her door. He was bringing her the most beautiful flowers he had ever grown. But what was wrong? When Miss Blyth came out of her room, she looked at him so angrily that he stepped back.

"Get out of my way!" she shrieked.

Wordlessly he held his flowers out to her. "For you, miss!" he wanted to say, but his lips were trembling so, he couldn't get his disobedient tongue to utter a word, and his black eyes clouded over like the night in the bush. Because Miss Blyth, in a fit of rage, tore the flowers out of their box, murdered them by trampling on them, and threw the box down the stairs. "Leave me alone, for God's sake!" she screamed, hoarse with fury. Then she rushed back into her room and slammed the door.

Charlie Rainbow stared after her. Rage sat like a caged animal within the four walls of his soul. Nothing but a muted singsong issued from his throat as he looked at the destruction. He held his kinky head to one side, as if thus he could see the crime in its entirety. His head burned as if the sun had fallen on it.

He didn't go to work but picked up the box with the broken glass cover, the good earth and the crushed flowers in his arms. Uncle Doody had heard the noise and stuck his foxy old head out of his door. "What's the matter, Charlie-boy?" But the abo just stared at him, his lips moving.

"Lydia!" cried Uncle Doody. "Bring Charlie some coffee! The fellow's crook!" Uncle Doody even came down the stairs and took Charlie by the arm gently. "Come, come, young man." He wanted to take the flower box because the abo was swaying like a young tree in a storm. But Charlie howled, tore what was left of his loving gift out of Uncle Doody's hands and ran out of the house.

"He's gone," growled Uncle Doody as Mrs. Doody appeared with the coffee.

"What happened?"

"Ask your dear niece." Uncle Doody's hands were fists in his trouser pockets, and he stumbled, cursing, back to his umbrellas.

Candy listened, yawning, to her aunt's halfhearted lecture. But she was a little sorry that she had been so mean to the poor blackfellow. She had had bad dreams and was scared to death of Charles Preston, and she had to let it out on *someone*, she explained. She would have liked to apologize to Charlie Rainbow, she really would. She even cried a few fat tears. But two days later she had forgotten all about it. After all, she couldn't pour ashes on her head because she'd broken a few flowers.

Three days later Mrs. Doody was standing on her balcony. Wasn't that Charlie Rainbow, sauntering along slowly? "Molly!" she yelled. "Run downstairs! Charlie's standing in front of the door and doesn't want to come in!"

But Charlie wanted to come in. He was only taking a good look at the boardinghouse. As if he didn't know the old decrepit building! Funny fellow.

Candy smiled at him radiantly, and he smiled back. He waited for her in the dark again too. Everything was dinkum again. Mrs. Doody had got excited for nothing, as usual, but she just couldn't stand it when Charlie got hurt in her house! It was his first and only home.

On the following day, a Saturday, Molly Fleet wanted to take a walk through the coffee bars of King's Cross, when suddenly Rigby appeared. *"You!"* Molly stammered. "Is it really you, Mr. Rigby?"

"In the flesh! And the name is Ritter. How are you, young lady? And why so pale? Lovesick?"

At that moment Candy appeared at the top of the stairs, in full regalia. She saw Mr. Ritter and remained standing, rooted to the spot. The fellow looked so much handsomer than she remembered him! "Hey!" she cried cheerily.

"Hey!" cried Rigby, even more cheerily.

He had no idea that Candy was modeling for the magazines again. He never read the stuff. But he hadn't looked at a beautiful girl in weeks, or was it months? Much less taken a bite . . . and now here she was! In his eyes something sparkled that had been snuffed out for a long time, the spark of sex and the arousing of illusions that either die down quickly or start a raging fire.

Molly stood there in her pretty light-blue dress and knew that Mr. Rigby had forgotten her. He was already halfway up the stairs. "Listen to me!" Molly cried out in her despair. "I was the one who wrote the love letters. I . . . I was . . ."

Rigby turned around, surprised. Had the little Fleet girl gone crazy? What letters was she talking about? Of course! Candy's charming letters. Candy laughed shrilly and Rigby had to laugh too. He came down the stairs again and patted Miss Fleet on the shoulder. "Take it easy! You little girls certainly do the craziest things!" Then he ran up the stairs again and disappeared into Candy's room. Later, from behind the curtains, Molly saw them leaving the house, arm-in-arm. It wasn't fair!

Mrs. Doody came home from visiting her friend with the wooden leg and looked for Candy. Then she asked Molly where her sugar doll had gone.

"She's gone out." Molly poured tea and turned her back on Mrs. Doody. She still had on her light-blue dress.

"How's Gretchen?" Mrs. Doody asked, settling down comfortably. "Are they expecting a little one yet?"

"No idea."

"You don't seem to have an idea about anything. Sit down, for heaven's sake! You make me dizzy, running around. Would you like a gin?" Then she gave Molly a sharp look. "What's the matter, child?" she asked, almost gently, but Molly only shook her head like a dummy in the Tunnel of Love at Luna Park.

Night fell over Darlinghurst. Molly Fleet was lying in bed, unable to sleep. Candy had pushed her out of the Tunnel of Love, laughing all the time. It wasn't fair. It would perhaps have been better if Molly had never spent that day with Rigby up in the clouds, weeks ago.

She sighed and took a sleeping pill, which she did rarely, but she had to forget Rigby and Candy. She had always loved the night and wasn't afraid of nightmares. Anything was better than the merciless day.

Charlie Rainbow couldn't sleep either. It looked as if Miss Blyth wasn't coming home at all. That wouldn't do. She had to come back. Charlie wanted her to come back.

He stared into the dark and caught sight of a trail. It led from the boardinghouse in Darlinghurst across the city limits into the bush. Charlie had to follow this trail. Every blackfellow knew how to, just as he understood the language of trees and stones.

What did Charlie want any more in the big city anyway? He couldn't part from the beautiful white bird yet, but one day he would be free. No Candy. No more waiting. He just had to be patient.

He walked up to the little window that had been set into his attic room like a dim eye. He saw lightning shoot through the clouds. In the dream age, when this continent had still belonged to the black man, the spirit of lightning had chased all sinners on land and in the water. They could hide wherever they wanted to: in the ocean, in the bush, in the dust of the plains, behind rocks. The lightning had always struck, burnt, riven, and left them to rot under the blazing sun until nothing was lying around any more but bones. Then the lightning had shot back up into the sky. He who sang the praises of lightning stood in the light of justice.

Charlie Rainbow sang the praises of lightning. He smiled in his sleep. Was he already seeing the new day? He knew that there were three kinds of days: the dead day of yesterday, the everydayness of today, and the unborn day that dispensed the light of justice. Charlie Rainbow waited in ecstatic expectation.

24

Schlesisches Himmelreich in Parramatta

Molly Fleet, faced again with a lonely weekend, decided without any further ado to visit her father in Parramatta. She couldn't stand it anymore, seeing Candy leave the house smiling blissfully. Of course she was meeting Rigby! Molly was positive of it. Actually the only person Candy saw during these weeks was Charles Preston. On his return to Sydney there had been a tearful reconciliation in the Restaurant Rosso. Dear old Raffaele had overflowed with compassion for the prodigal son. Poor Carlo had been an innocent man in jail. Exactly what one could expect from the police. Mr. Rosso's opinion of the police coincided with that of his Australian compatriots. He had received Carlo with open arms—grand opera in King's Cross! Muriel let "Ha, so you're back in Sydney," suffice. She took things and her waiters as they came. She found Charles Preston more sensible than she had ever known him to be. His experiences in Hobart had evidently had a sobering effect on him. And he brought Muriel's bracelet back to her. He had redeemed it from the pawnshop with his uncle's money. Candy, of course, had melted, as Charles had expected. Both of them were sensualists and lived for the moment. That was Italian, and oddly enough, also Australian. Charles's Ligurian imagination had caught the girl from sober Western Australia. His descriptions were palpable; anyone could have grasped them. He painted pictures of his home for Candy. With a gesture he could describe a landscape, light, colors, flowers, fruit, smiling girls with their hair parted like madonnas, hymns in their voices, a café on a piazza, the outlines of a palace ruin in the background. When Candy asked how he could stand it in Australia after that, he replied that his memories sufficed. Australia was the land of the future. Candy asked him how he thought he was going to manage. Charles shrugged, as if he didn't have a care in the world. Something would turn up. He mumbled, *"Da tempo al tempo."* Leave time a little time. He had inherited the motto. At times like these he was a stranger to Candy, just as he had been when they had first met. Now she had the oppressive feeling that Charles Preston's splendid future would take off without her. What she wanted was for him to stay a waiter and marry her! But she didn't dare express such old-fashioned ideas.

Right now, though, the future wasn't raining any Australian pounds. Charles hated to do it but he had to borrow from Candy. It was more practical to have an egg today than a hen tomorrow. Or a shandy with Candy here rather than a case of wine in the clouds.

Charles Preston didn't put in an appearance at the boardinghouse in Darlinghurst again. That vulgar Irish bitch had hurt his feelings. "The first one to leave an argument is the one with breeding," Charles had finally bellowed at her. Then he had slammed the door behind him.

So Molly never found out about the big reconciliation. Candy had apologized to Charles. She didn't know why she had been so horrid to him when she loved him so much! Yes, in her misery over what had taken place in the boardinghouse, she had thrown Charlie Rainbow's flowers downstairs. Charles listened, unmoved. He couldn't be expected to be interested in the abo too!

Only Molly Fleet looked after Charlie Rainbow. He was just as alone as she was. Molly still stood on the veranda, looking for Rigby, but he never came. She didn't khow that Rigby didn't want to see Candy again. She didn't know that being with Candy left him feeling flat. She didn't know anything.

Actually Rigby felt uncomfortable about Molly Fleet. She had looked at him as if he were a ghost when he had come to invite Candy for an outing. Poor young thing! Molly had worshiped him so naively; he really could have been nicer to her. He was always nice to girls when they were nice to him. To make a long story short, he wanted to do something to make Molly happy this weekend. Her youth had done damn little for her. But when he called on Saturday morning to take her for an outing, she wasn't there. Uncle Doody looked at him with ill-concealed disgust. The fellow was too elegant for him. Uncle Doody said he didn't know when Miss Fleet would be back.

Rigby drove to Patrick Trent's house. Klari needed rest in the mountains in Bowral. It seemed to Rigby that lately the Trents weren't as happy as they had been, but he could be mistaken. Anyway, Paddy had time again for his cobber Alex. Everything was a-okay.

At the boardinghouse Rigby had left his regards to Molly Fleet, but Uncle Doody didn't pass them on to her when she came back from Parramatta. He proceeded to hit rock bottom in a miasma of gin and had forgotten his visitor.

Molly expected to find the usual humdrum life at the brewery. Her father had always been grumpy and monosyllabic, and April, with her sour face, used to pore over the accounts like a broody hen on her eggs. For years she had been brooding over nothing but figures. In the evenings Molly and her sister would sit in front of the television while their father, in his room, wondered why his daughters didn't marry. There should be a man in the brewery. He felt his age more all the time, in his legs, at the back of his neck. He hoped Stephen and Jennifer would produce a son who would later remind people that there had been Fleets in Parramatta. He didn't know why the youngest one didn't go out to the farm any more. Mr. Fleet didn't understand his daughters, but he told himself, with some justification, that it wouldn't change anything if he did understand them. It wouldn't bring a son-in-law into the brewery. Lately he had been more friendly to his youngest daughter, since it was evident that April's good looks hadn't done a damn thing for her. She was twenty-seven and souring fast before his very eyes. Nothing he could do about it.

Years ago he had been bitterly disappointed when April's first-rate engagement had been broken off. To this day he didn't know that his youngest daughter, in her childish rage, had written April's fiancé an anonymous letter about April's behavior with the boys. Molly always felt guilty in the brewery. If only she could find a husband somewhere for her sister!

But when Molly arrived at the brewery this time, she noticed a change. April was wearing a green dress and she'd had a permanent. Her red-gold hair was done up high, making her look taller and more elegant. But Mr. Fleet was the greatest surprise of all!

He was in fine spirits, didn't bawl his daughters out, and— wonder of wonders—sat with them for a while in the evening in front of the television set. And on the evening of her arrival, Molly knew why. A European man in the prime of life had been recently employed in the brewery. He appeared for dinner in a neatly pressed sports shirt. His hair was parted with mathematical precision and his tie hung down straight as a dye. He was tall, broad-shouldered, and serious. His slim, well-shaped hands looked as if they were familiar with musical instruments.

He smiled in a friendly fashion, a little unsure, and spoke English correctly with a north-European accent. In short: a new Australian. His name was Kurt Hildebrand, and he came from the Polish city of Wroclaw, which before the war had been the German city of Breslau.

"How do you do?" asked Molly Fleet.

To her astonishment he gave a fairly lengthy account of how he did. He took the conventional greeting at its face value. Where he came from, people really wanted to know how one "did"; otherwise they didn't ask.

The new Aussie didn't seem to notice Molly's birthmark. This was not surprising, because he had eyes for no one but April. She was enthroned on her wicker chair as in her best days, smiling and with artificial poise. She felt attractive because a man's eyes were resting on her. Just the same, the effect was cold and indifferent. She had evidently fled from life for too long.

Did Mr. Hildebrand think this was Australian? He stared at April and kept his thoughts to himself.

Kurt Hildebrand was the first German the Fleets had got to know well. This time Molly stayed a week in Parramatta, and found out in what sinister ways many new Australians had reached this sunny continent. It was as if Mr. Hildebrand had kept his experiences stored up inside him for years. Nobody had asked him how he had happened to come storming into the brewery. Mr. Fleet and April never asked questions. As good Australians they minded their own business. That had been the most difficult hurdle for Kurt Hildebrand. In Breslau, the city where he had spent his early childhood, everybody knew what everybody else did. The capital of Silesia was a big, friendly, small town. But Molly asked questions. She knew how hard it was to live without communicating. And so it all came pouring out. In his excitement, Kurt Hildebrand occasionally lapsed into German.

When Kurt Hildebrand was born in Breslau, Germany in 1935, he was no longer able to grow up among poets and philosophers. The Nazis determined what was to be written and thought. The Hildebrands were well-to-do brewers, and their beer was more important to them than politics. That was why they interrupted with "Hush . . . the little one!" when one of them spoke disparagingly about Adolf Hitler in front of six-year-old Kurt. They had voted Social Democrat until one could no longer do so, and they opposed the new regime, but that didn't prevent the downfall of their world. Anyway, the brewery kept them too busy.

Kurt understood nothing his parents were talking about, nor the grumbling of his grandfather, who came from Upper Silesia. He played with his friends in Park Poludnia, at the time still called Südpark. In the winter the boys went sledding in the nearby Riesengebirge, or Giant Mountains, or in the summer they sailed on the small Oder River boats to friendly restaurants where Hildebrand beer was served together with *Breslauer Korn*, or schnapps.

When Kurt wasn't allowed to join the Hitler Youth movement—this was in 1943, and he was eight years old and a big strong boy—he retired to his room, ashamed, and wept. He lost his school friends, his rollicking self-assurance, and the fun of being a schoolboy. All his older cousins "belonged." Only Kurt was left out because his father was so dumb! He didn't even go to the *Frühschoppen*, his early morning ale at Kempinski's any more. At about this time, Kurt's grandfather died, and Kurt's father said it was the best thing that could have happened to the old man. Then, in his general feeling of world-malaise, he bawled out his son, who was standing there staring at him open-mouthed. His mother said hastily, "Leave the boy alone, Friedrich," and then they all ate *Schlesisches Himmelreich*, an undigestible dish consisting of pickled meat and stewed fruit, served with dumplings, which required a Silesian stomach and enthusiasm. "Go on, child. Eat!" said his mother. Nobody could cook Silesian "heavenly pudding" like Mrs. Hildebrand.

Kurt found it weird that his father had gone for him like that. He had been a peaceful, even timid man, who when he was with his family joked and laughed, but now world events had him by the throat. Kurt couldn't realize yet that in the Hilter era, no one would stay the same. Not even the Hildebrands who lived quietly and minded their own business. When Kurt was sad and silent, he and his mother would play music. Kurt was going to study music, "later." He sang and played the violin, and his mother accompanied him on their fairly decent piano. Mrs. Hildebrand prayed regularly in church for Breslau and for her enemies. As the years went by, Kurt's mother had more and more enemies even though she was an established citizen of Breslau. But his mother's enemies were Nazis, and in her innocence she prayed to God to forgive her for not praying for Gauleiter Hanke, the führer of their district. Gauleiter Hanke had everyone worried to death because he had bellowed at his constituents in January, 1945 that Breslau would never surrender to the Russian pigs. Kurt's father was listening to him over the radio and asked nobody in particular how Gauleiter Hanke could talk such absolute nonsense? The entire structure was crumbling daily and in his opinion the Thousand-Year Reich had been German beer gone flat for quite some time. His fearful wife held her hand in front of his mouth when he uttered such blasphemies. Hadn't Gauleiter Hanke hanged the mayor in public because the latter no longer believed in victory, and in his straightforward, Silesian way hadn't hesitated to say so? What would she and Kurt do if Mr. Hildebrand was hanged? Fortunately Gauleiter Hanke had more important things to do than listen in on what his dissatisfied constituents were saying. He was transforming the old Oder city into a fortress, with the result that the Russians arrived in Breslau a little later and the entire south and west end of the city was destroyed. Gauleiter Hanke didn't wait to witness this. Shortly before the capitulation, he fled.

Before the arrival of the Russians, Mr. Hildebrand drank one strong schnapps after the other because his fear of the future made him feel sick to his stomach, but the wheat of certainty can be just as indigestible as the chaff of doubt. Of course nobody gave a damn anymore whether Kurt had sung the Horst Wessel Song in the Hitler Youth movement, or Schubert or Mahler; whether he fiddled a march or bumbled his way through a Brahms violin concerto. That was life.

The Hildebrands were very much alone, and sat like mice in a trap. Except for the few who felt as they did, they had lost all their former friends, and for their Jewish friends, life had either ended involuntarily and abruptly, or they had saved their skins by emigrating to "wild" countries, where no one read the *Schlesische Zeitung*, or knew anything about the magnificent Breslau Jahrhunderthalle, to say nothing of Kant, Schopenhauer, and *Schlesisches Himmelreich*. In the end even Kurt Hildebrand emigrated to such a country and landed by chance in Australia. His life had always been ruled by chance.

There had been no stability in Germany when he was born. Before the Hitler era, in 1930, the unemployed had fought each other on the streets of Breslau—communists against Nazis and vice versa, Catholics, Protestants, pacifists, and all of them united against the Social Democrats. The Hildebrand family stuck it out for a comparatively long time in postwar Breslau. They opted for Poland because they didn't know where to go, and the occupation troops would probably drink Hildebrand beer. But as Breslau became more and more clearly Wroclaw, father and son no longer knew their way around in their own city. The Jahrhunderthalle was called Hala Ludowa, the honorable department store Wertheim had a name they couldn't pronounce, and what had become of the Café Fahrig, which had had the Breslau intelligentsia, students, artists, to thank for its existence? Ashes to ashes and dust to dust . . .

The Poles began to move in en masse. The schoolchildren learned that Wroclaw had always been Polish, just as Kurt had learned that Breslau had always been German, even though in Upper Silesia, where his grandfather had come from, there had been a lot of Polish names in the registries before 1914. But what were names?

In 1949, Friedrich and Kurt Hildebrand were on the verge of emigrating. Mrs. Hildebrand was dead. She had been hit by a stray bomb shortly before the capitulation. Friedrich Hildebrand said it was a good thing. But Kurt Hildebrand had to bury his father in his homeland too, before he emigrated. Friedrich Hildebrand hadn't felt like going along with things for a long time, and the good Lord, who knew his Silesians, took him before he had to go to a foreign country. Because Friedrich Hildebrand had already looked upon Berliners as foreigners . . .

Kurt Hildebrand now joined these "foreigners." The old saying that every third Berliner came from Breslau finally became true in the post-war era. Kurt took any kind of job he could get in West Berlin. He lived with distant relatives and thought of Silesia as the aborigines think of their dream era. In 1955 he was working in a Berlin brewery. He was twenty, Berlin was grimly divided and not *"gemütlich"* any more. A big wall was rising up all around him, but it wasn't the actual wall of a later day. West Berlin was still feverishly striving for freedom, but Kurt saw the city in the diminishing glass of the homeless. He counted his savings and moved on to Hamburg because it was a port city. This might be the gateway for him to the outside world. He wanted nothing, nothing to remind him of Breslau! In this respect New South Wales was to fulfill his highest expectations.

He was taken on by a German freighter and landed in Sydney. His mates had taught him as much English as he'd need for a start. All of them had done the trip to Melbourne and Sydney several times. A beer brewer couldn't go thirsty in Australia, his new friends told him. Beer was the nectar of the fifth continent.

Many years later, after wandering around taking odd jobs, Kurt read an ad. A Mr. Fleet in Parramatta was looking for an experienced assistant for his brewery. By now Kurt was almost thirty, and he was finding Sydney too restless, too noisy, too grand. When he heard that Parramatta was an old country town he applied for the job. He was an Australian citizen now, and his immigrant's agony had subsided as the years had gone by Hildebrand, like his grandfather and father, was a thorough and fanatically dedicated worker. He was a perfectionist in a modest sphere of action, and suffered the tortures of the damned in a country where "fair enough" was dogma. Kurt also liked to give advice. Nothing was less desired on this continent. But by the time he came to Mr. Fleet's brewery, he had left all the malaise of immigration behind him. He never gave advice anymore, and minded his own business with a heavy heart. He sometimes played the violin, but mostly it was too hot to practice. And somehow or other he missed his mother, the Breslau living room, and *Schlesisches Himmelreich*. He was a lonely man in the prime of life. Occasionally he slept with a girl, but that wasn't what he wanted. In his thick Silesian head he could see a quiet young woman who was there only for him and would give him children. And this young woman could be April Fleet, if she was prepared to meet him halfway.

Whenever Molly Fleet sat on the veranda with Kurt Hildebrand or went for a walk with him beside Parramatta Lake, she brought up the subject of her sister.

"April. What a strange name!" said Kurt. "Where I come from it's the most unpredictable month of the year."

"But my sister isn't unpredictable," said Molly, although she knew better.

"Of course not!" Mr. Hildebrand was shocked. "Miss April is wonderful!" Whereupon Molly took the bull by the horns and took Mr. Hildebrand at his word. She asked why didn't he marry April, since he found her so wonderful?

"Aber Kindl," Mr. Hildebrand lapsed into German. *"Sie nimmt mich doch im Leben nicht! Sie kann doch jeden bekommen!"* He blushed as he translated. "But she'd never take me! She could have anyone she wants!" Molly tried not to laugh. She knew a little more about April's chances.

"Ask April," she said, with Australian straightforwardness.

"What would your father say?" Kurt was on the best of terms with Mr. Fleet, but surely he hadn't been in Parramatta long enough to be a son-in-law.

Molly Fleet could very well imagine her father's satisfaction if at last April made the grade. And with an expert who could later run the brewery when Mr. Fleet, whether he liked it or not, joined his wife and Grandmother Cocker. In short, Molly made it quite clear to Mr. Hildebrand that he would not be unwelcome.

Kurt took a deep breath. April was pretty as a 'picture, and she didn't chatter all day. And she knew a lot about book-keeping. She would give him children. And he'd give her the recipe for *Schesisches Himmelreich*! Now he would really start to save seriously for a good violin and piano. For Kurt Hildebrand, April was the Australia of his dreams. She was the only one who could give him the new home he craved but couldn't build with his two hands. Four hands and two hearts built a home wherever it was to be built . . .

"Does April play the piano?" he asked dreamily.

"Here she comes!" said the youngest one, and disappeared.

Molly Fleet said goodbye to a radiant, engaged couple. April was smiling like a young girl capable of making a solid, warm-hearted, good-looking young man happy. They intended to marry soon, and Molly would come to the wedding. Mr. Fleet had asked, not exactly tactfully, how long April, at twenty-seven, intended to wait before producing a grandson for him. April had laughed out loud; then Mr. Fleet had joined in hesitantly.

When Molly got back to the boardinghouse in Darlinghurst she felt inexplicably depressed. Naturally she had expected no paradise, but the house looked so dark and empty by the light of the street lamp. Charlie Rainbow's boxes of flowers stood on the narrow balcony with its attractive wrought-iron railing, but the flowers were drooping.

Molly Fleet didn't suffer from premonitions. She stood with her two feet planted firmly in harsh reality. But she started even before she heard the wild cry. It came from the entry of the dark house. Was it a cry of triumph or agony? The bulb in the hallway had burnt out. Molly felt her way cautiously up to her room. Then she almost cried out. In front of her door stood a stone figure, black, mute, the arm raised as if to hurl a boomerang. How in God's name had the statue of the black fellow from the Parramatta town hall got here?

But of course it was Charlie Rainbow, and he wasn't about to hurl any boomerang. He was lighting up the stairway with his flashlight. Molly began to laugh. She must have been seeing things because she was so tired.

"Welcome, Miss Molly. Nobody home."

A strip of light shone down from the attic floor. So Uncle Doody was home. "Uncle is always home," said Charlie Rainbow. "Uncle not go-out man. Uncle like Charlie."

He laughed again, very high and shrill, and—it seemed to Molly—crazily. But that was the way the abos laughed, if they laughed at all.

"Good night, Charlie. I'm tired."

"Me too," Charlie Rainbow said softly, and suddenly seemed to shrink before her eyes. His arms dangled like broken pine branches, his muscular body went limp, and he rolled his eyes very slowly. They looked like circling black opals.

"Charlie, are you crook?"

The abo took Molly's hand and shook it wildly, then he lowered his kinky-haired head and doubled up like an opossum in a hollow tree, a trapped animal. Molly had never seen him behave like that, and it frightened her. On the other hand, she felt sorry for him.

"Go to bed, Charlie. Tomorrow everything will be better."

"Tomorrow everything more bad."

How did he know? Molly asked him if he'd like some tea.

"Tea is good," Charlie Rainbow said dreamily. He looked ecstatic, as if he were already gulping down the hot, golden-brown drink. "But my friend fire gone out, Miss Molly. No fire, no tea. Only lemons." Charlie Rainbow laughed shrilly and leapt up to the attic. Molly could hear him singing.

Only Charlie wasn't really singing; rather, it was more as if he were weeping, and every sound seemed to catch in his throat. Then Molly heard him laugh again. She walked into her room and closed the door. It had a lock, but the lock was rusty and the key was lost.

Molly didn't drink any tea either. She lay in bed and couldn't sleep, and tried to figure out how many miles the Silesian heaven in Parramatta was from Mrs. Doody's boardinghouse: exactly fifteen miles.

25

The Smoke Signal

Charlie Rainbow listened. The night had caught his scream in its black cover. He had dreamt of a girl in a bottle tree. She looked like beautiful Candy, held flowers in her hands, and sat naked among the branches. She laughed scornfully and waved to Charlie to climb up to her. The bottle tree got bigger and bigger. It grew up into the clouds, and Candy became more inaccessible all the time. Now she was laughing to rival the cockatoos, was tearing the heads off the flowers and throwing them at Charlie Rainbow's feet. Then Gheeger-Gheeger, the evil storm wind, penetrated Charlie's heart, shook it like a rotten tree until it split and the lotus bird flew out. In his dream Charlie knew it was the lotus bird. It flew around the bottle tree, rumpled Candy's hair, stuck its bill into her face, and beat its wings at her. Candy screamed and fell down. At that moment the lotus bird became Charlie Rainbow again. He climbed down from the bottle tree and twisted the white neck of the girl who had torn the heads off the flowers, and strangled her. And now the storm wind was a prisoner in Charlie's soul. It couldn't howl or rage any more, or shatter the eucalyptus tree or destroy the crows' nests.

Was that a car? Charlie looked cautiously out onto the street. The car raced by. The time hadn't yet come...

There were voices coming from Uncle Doody's room. He was talking to a customer who was just as old and weathered as Uncle Doody. Uncle Doody's cobber wanted a used umbrella for his wife, his sister, and his daughter in the Outback. They could take turns using it. The cobber was trying to get the price down. Uncle Doody shook his long, narrow fox-head. The women could mend the holes, couldn't they? "Get a bloody move on, mate!" Charlie Rainbow heard the old men laughing. They were probably drinking gin. Tonight Charlie didn't want any gin. He wanted nothing to make his eyes bleary. He had to see what happened on the street clearly, and what was passing by in the heavens. Gin was a no-good drink. The liquid fire made the abos merry or furious. But sometimes they needed the liquid fire, just like the white man. When somebody humbled them, for instance, or despised their gifts.

That time when Candy had killed his flowers and thrown his box down the stairs, that was when Charlie had needed the no-good drink. He had never grown any more flowers for Candy, but she didn't seem to miss them. Charlie looked at his watch. Eleven o'clock. He crept down the creaky staircase. She had to come home soon. Lately she had been coming home alone because she didn't want Molly Fleet to see whom she'd been out with. Charlie didn't know with whom she went out in the evening. Candy's men were not like emus who moved together. Charlie only helped Candy humbly up the stairs because the bulb burned so dimly.

Charlie stood in front of the boardinghouse and looked up at the night sky. He laid his kinky head on his right shoulder. He looked as if he were conversing with the stars. The street was empty. At this hour things were lively only in King's Cross. The big stars burned like white fire. Charlie nodded to them. He recognized and understood the ways of the stars, the wallabies, the snakes, lizards, opossums, and the birds in the bush. The only things he didn't understand, although he lived in Sydney, were the habits and the fancies of the white Australians. The hectic city unnerved him and was gradually using up the emotional reserves he had accumulated in childhood. The visual attractions—shop windows, neon lights, white flesh shining through flowered dresses—were all destroying his inherited vision. The technology of everyday life in the city— food in tin cans or in the deep freezer, the shopping for practical things without having to seek them out or fight for them, the baskets and nylon bags made by machine, the electric lighting and the metal birds in the air, the distorted pictures of reality on Mrs. Doody's television screen—all of it frightened and confused him. He was increasingly horrified in the stony lap of a big city that ceaselessly spat out all these surrogates. In the mission, the wonders of a civilization that could be bought with money had already aroused hostile feelings in Charlie Rainbow, isolated him, and made him difficult to handle. In Sydney he experienced the growing social integration of the aborigines and half-breeds with helpless astonishment. He had nothing in common with these young boys and girls who were fighting against the extinction of their race, and were trying, with the help of their white brothers and teachers, to understand the new Australia. For Charlie Rainbow the nature of the bush was and remained the element that gave life. It was fiery warmth and creative darkness. Trees, animals, and plants were his brothers and sisters. His early curiosity to get to know the white world had died within him. Sydney was a sack full of riddles and misunderstandings, and he had to shake off the burden. An evil spirit had found shelter in Miss Candy. He wanted to cast this bundle of vexation into the dust in the street.

When a dingo vexed a blackfellow, he threw his spear at the animal, but you couldn't do that to the city people. You had to strike them in different ways. The thoughts in one's brain had to be as sharp as the stone axe that lifted honey slices out of the hives of wild bees. Charlie had been sharpening his thoughts for many days and nights now. He made various signs with his fingers, and the stars nodded. They understood him.

And the time had come. A veil broke loose from the stars and wafted like a gigantic smokescreen across the night sky. Only Charlie saw it and knew what it meant. The magical knowledge rested in him like the pit in a fleshy fruit. You didn't learn it in the mission and you couldn't read it in a book. The magic of nature was as old as the memory of the black man and as enduring as the stone of antiquity that he wore on his chest, under his checked sport shirt. But the intimacy with living nature was a burden in the age of the machines, and you couldn't shake it off or talk it away or dilute it. Charlie saw the smoke signal and wanted to laugh or cry or scream. But all he did was throw his head far back as if offering his throat to a knife. His wide-open eyes saw pictures in the star smoke. He could see what was happening right now miles away from the boardinghouse. He saw an accident on the street, and a little later he saw a stone frog. Then the smoke signal dissolved in the clouds. The pictures disappeared and the stars gleamed without any magical fire.

Charlie Rainbow was shaking as if he had chills, but he didn't cry out any more. He had seen it all.

Press bulletin, Sydney:

A tragic accident took place last night at eleven o'clock on a side street in Darlinghurst. Miss Candace Blyth, the well-known model, ran straight into a passing car and was seriously injured. She was trying to cross the street where there was no traffic light.

St. Vincent Hospital reports that Miss Blyth is off the critical list, but the doctors can't say anything definite yet about her condition.

The beautiful young victim of our traffic, which becomes more hectic all the time, explained today how it happened. Miss Blyth declares that somebody pushed her from behind just as the car was rushing by.

Mr. Billy Hall, a well-known Sydney industrialist and owner of Holden Cars, described the accident. He was obviously shaken. Police officer E.F. Lewis, who was on duty in the area, questioned everybody standing in the vicinity. Nobody saw anyone who could possibly have pushed Miss Blyth. But everyone saw her rush straight into the car before the driver had a chance to stop. Mr. Hall is not being held responsible. Under the circumstances he will not have to pay damages.

Police officer E.F. Lewis found Miss Blyth's address in her handbag, and saw to it that she was taken straight to the hospital. Mrs. Lydia Doody, who runs a boardinghouse in Darlinghurst and is Candace Blyth's aunt, told us, in tears, that her niece was night blind. This was corroborated by Miss Molly Fleet, Mr. Edward E. Doody—no relative of Mrs. Doody's—and Mr. Charlie Rainbow, all lodgers. Mr. Rainbow also explained that he often helped Miss Blyth up the stairs, and on this tragic evening had been waiting in front of the house for her to return.

The two pictures show the famous model from Kalgoorlie, Western Australia. Like so many young people, Candy Blyth came to Sydney to seek her fortune. *Insight* and the *Australian Teenager's Weekly* were good enough to let us release the pictures which show Candy in all her fresh, blond beauty. We wish the beautiful young model a speedy recovery so that she may continue to enchant her innumerable admirers in magazines and on television.

Before Candy was allowed to leave the hospital, Charlie Rainbow went walkabout again. Everybody was accustomed to his periodic disappearances, and nobody in Mrs. Doody's boardinghouse knew that this time he had gone for good.

There was no more fun for Charlie in Darlinghurst. Mrs. Doody wept and wailed all day, and even Miss Fleet, who had so often been annoyed with Candy, went around looking glum. Umbrella Uncle sat in the kitchen all the time, cursing and scolding, as he tried to cheer up his old friend. Naturally everybody was wondering what Candy would do now. The wounds on her face would heal, but the neurologist had told Mrs. Doody, cautiously, that her niece's spine was badly injured. When Mrs. Doody, in her blackest moments, envisioned Candy ending her days in a wheelchair, Uncle Doody got mad as hell with her. In his own Irish fantasy, he saw the same picture. Both the old people pestered Molly Fleet with questions: Did she think massage might help? She had worked miracles, hadn't she? Anyway, right now Molly was the most important person in the boardinghouse, and she liked that. Mrs. Doody kept urging her to go to the hospital and massage Candy. All she herself could do was pray for the poor thing. But since Mrs. Doody was out of practice in this respect, she doubted that her prayers would be effective. That was why she went to Father O'Brien to get an expert in on it who had better connections "up there."

Charlie Rainbow first visited his friend on the outskirts of the city. He wanted to stay a day with him and then wander off into the bush. Perhaps working with lumber, and as a friend of the plants and the birds, he would one day find his nomadic tribe. Charlie had a good nose for that sort of thing and followed every footprint with instinctive assurance. The melting pot of Sydney had not been able to dilute his visionary core.

Charlie and his cobber laughed and tore around like children. Since there were only two of them, they couldn't perform a *corroboree*, the ceremonial campfire dance, and they no longer knew the ritual songs of their tribe. They had become fence watchers in their big tribe, and could remember only from their earliest childhood that the dancers were painted with white clay, charcoal, red and yellow ocher, and had worn ornaments and feathers on their naked bodies. The echo of hunting songs, war songs, animal, wind, water, and tree songs lived in their souls. In the mission Charlie had learned songs about a foreign savior which had remained incomprehensible. He continued to believe in the spirits of nature.

The life in Mrs. Doody's boardinghouse was already seeping out of his memory. Even his mute inner revolt against police-men, machines, and white wisdom quickly became part of the past. Charlie didn't even thank his cobber for following Candy patiently for so many evenings until at last, with a precisely calculated blow, he had propelled her into the car. There is a certain spot in the back of a human being that hurts so intensely when struck that the person thus hit rushes forward like some-one possessed. Charlie's cobber had acted swiftly, and in the general excitement had been able to get away unnoticed. He had the necessary striking power and presence of mind when in danger, and was a master at disappearing unobtrusively and with lightning speed, just like the humans and animals in the bush. It had not been Charlie's intent to avenge himself per-sonally on Miss Blyth, but she had broken the backs of his flowers, and for him they were living creatures.

Charlie and his cobber laughed and danced in the sunshine. Before Charlie left the shack on the city limits, he planted the flowers of the season and two more fruit trees. The young men threw their painted boomerangs into the sunlit air until the woman called them in to eat.

That was life.

* * *

At last Charlie's cobber went back to work in the harbor, but Charlie didn't go with him. He had seen a smoke signal in the heavens the night before, and packed his bundle. The bundle was important. It was almost a part of himself. In the old days the bush wanderers, the gold prospectors, and the adventurers from Europe had called their bundle "Matilda." During the months of loneliness they had wanted something to hold in their arms, and Matilda circled around with them, was soft and warm, and kept her mouth shut. Charlie's bundle didn't have a name, but contained the obligatory blanket that comforted the body.

Thus in his fatalistic humility he followed the smoke signal. He had been born approximately twenty years earlier under a eucalyptus tree, and under a eucalyptus tree he would one day die. He knew all the colors of light and darkness, and that was good enough for him. He had already forgotten the neon lights in the big city, just as he had forgotten what he and his friend had done to Miss Blyth. For him the reality of Sydney had sunk into the abyss of time passed.

Charlie's sinewy body disappeared soundlessly from the big city. He had been a transient in Sydney, astray in a bush of cement and glass. His cobber watched him go. At first Charlie was still a man with a kinky head of hair and thin arms and legs. Then slowly he became a dancing shadow. When the people in the shack finally sat down to eat, Charlie Rainbow had become a dot in the story of the Australian creation.

26

Waltzing Matilda

Charlie Rainbow was not the only one leaving Sydney at about this time. Two months later Patrick Trent said farewell to the big city that had witnessed his triumphs and defeats for so many years. Trent had put the new villa Rigby had built for him and his second wife up for sale the day before. Like the bushman with his bundle, all Trent wanted to shoulder was his sack of memories. Turning his back on Sydney was not easy. Every city that has held us prisoner for any length of time holds onto some part of us. One goes forth poorer, but one goes forth free!

Trent had always been on good terms with pain; that was why he had hidden it under a barrage of jokes. Pain was part of the natural order of things, and Trent could bear it better when he wasn't holding a woman in his arms, but only "Matilda." In Sydney millions of people were together but alone. As in his youth, Trent wanted to go walkabout.

And now he was sitting with Rigby on the big terrace in Vaucluse for the last time, having to break the news to his friend. He was hesitant, but not from weakness. The truth in his soul made him feel strong. He had lived too long with lies. After a bitter struggle, he had found his way to the core of his soul, to the discreet place where the truth rests in all its strength and glory. "I must talk to you, Alex. My time in Sydney has come to an end."

"I don't believe it, Paddy!"

Rigby had known for years that Paddy was a little crazy. A brooder in his way, like Anne. Wasn't it funny how Rigby always ended up with the brooders? Even funnier how he seemed to like them? "You're joking!" he said, but he knew that Trent was serious. He sat there so quietly. Patrick Trent never bored his cobbers with endless, excited talk, but Rigby felt that there was something special about Trent's silence now. It was stony. What in God's name had happened? Why did his friend want to leave Sydney?

Trent wanted to go back to Queensland, and not even his beloved friend Rigby could do anything to change his mind. Trent drank his beer and assured Alex that nothing would ever change between them. Trent had been moving a lot of his real-estate business to Queensland for years now, and had been in Brisbane noticeably often lately. His partner in Sydney could run the office without him. The business wasn't important anyway, he declared. He had more money and opals than he needed. He had bought a house in Bundaberg on the Burnett River, near his sister, Catherine.

The peaceful city between the sugar cane fields had also appealed to Elizabeth West. Dr. Catherine Trent was a gynecologist there, Rigby suddenly remembered. What the devil was the meaning of it all? Why did Trent want to vegetate in a small city like that? And what did Klari have to say about it? The baby was expected in a few months. Did Trent want to bring up his son in Queensland? Rigby stared at his friend, speechless. But by now Trent had come trundling out of his stony silence and with a heavy appetite was tackling an enormous steak which Rigby's housekeeper had grilled to perfection. (Andrews was giving a final performance. She had found and "trained" a new housekeeper, and Rigby was going to have to make the best of it.)

Trent helped himself to a second serving of fried potatoes, which infuriated Rigby. "Don't eat so many potatoes! You're a regular walrus already!"

Trent laughed. Rigby finished his beer hastily. If Paddy was suffering brain damage because he was about to be a father, his appetite had certainly not been affected. Rigby looked at the deep furrow between Trent's brows, the trace of gray at his temples, and his calm, full face with the shiny dark eyes. He found Paddy unusually pale.

"What does Klari have to say about all this idiocy?" Even Rigby knew that expectant mothers needed restful surroundings. Was she still in Bowral?

"I have sent Klari away," Trent said calmly. "It's all for the best."

Rigby jumped to his feet and knocked over a beer bottle, and scraped the shards together, cursing. "Now I know you've gone crazy!" he mumbled, not looking at Trent. "What do you mean? Is Klari already in Queensland?"

"No," Trent said. "She is in Melbourne, and that's where she's going to stay."

"Patrick! You don't mean it!"

Trent sat quietly, his steak growing cold in front of him. He looked at Rigby with deepest sympathy. Throughout the years Alex had been a true friend, loyal, even patient, and still he had to leave him to his own resources now. He couldn't live in a grave. He saw Candy Blyth once. He had gone to the hospital every day, but she hadn't wanted to see anyone. Poor child! Candy had lived in an artificial world: photographers, the press, television, cosmetics . . . a world with no corner for comfort and no roof for a rainy day. Sensations had been her daily bread. What would she do now? Trent was going to ask Rigby to keep an eye on the unfortunate girl. But Alex had damn little talent as a good samaritan. Trent intended to go to the boardinghouse once more tomorrow morning, and see if he couldn't talk some sense into Candy.

Rigby tore him out of his reflections. He shook Trent's arm brutally. "Wake up, man!" he cried angrily. "You can't send your wife off to Melbourne now. Just between us—it stinks! Say something, Paddy, for God's sake!"

Rigby mopped his brow. Trent began to walk restlessly up and down. "Sit down!" Alex yelled. "You're making me nervous!"

"I'm sorry, Alex."

"What's the meaning of all this nonsense? Did you two have a falling out?"

Trent sat down obediently in "his" chair. It was a very wide wicker armchair that fitted his huge proportions. Even Rigby looked lost in it. "I wonder who'll sit in my chair now," Trent said dreamily.

Rigby poured another beer for Paddy, and moved the cheese nearer. Trent noticed nothing. His dark eyes had grown even darker. He cleared his throat, then he explained the "situation" to Rigby. Even a tragedy became a "situation" in Trent's restraint. An Aussie remained an Aussie.

Trent had come to the end of his explanation, throughout which he had barely raised his voice or changed his expression. The case of Klari Trent was already a thing of the past. Anyway there was no possibility of a future together.

"I'll be damned!" mumbled Rigby. He didn't look at his friend but was watching a harbor ferry. But when Trent referred to his wife as "a poor little thing," Rigby exploded in righteous fury. The woman deserved a good beating, and if Trent wouldn't do it, Alex would be delighted to. Besides . . .

"Please, Alex. Not so loud."

Trent couldn't stand loud voices, whether he was in a "situation" or not. Alex stopped thundering and tried to dissuade him. If Klari wanted to stay with him, in spite of everything, he didn't have to send her away. He had been looking forward to the child, hadn't he?

"You mean well, Alex," Trent said gently, but he was going to abide by his decision. He had recognized it as the right thing to do. He had sent his wife away to where she belonged—to the father of her child.

Rigby never forgot how simply and calmly Trent explained the situation to him. But just that was what had been so eerie. Paddy should have been raging, breaking beer bottles, swearing, and then dreaming up a revenge that would be worth something! In short, he should be doing what Rigby would have done. But Trent had his own methods. Yes . . . he had tried first and foremost to bring some sort of order and decency into his and Klari's life. Were she and the unborn child to live with lies? The child's father was an engineer from Hungary who had a good job in Melbourne. Although Rigby, according to his sister, was as tactful as an elephant, this time he kept his mouth shut and behaved like a gentleman. He had seen Klari Trent several times with a compatriot in the Hungarian restaurant, talking intimately, but he had thought it was just a little paprika flirtation, the kind he himself had sometimes indulged in when Anne was waiting for him in Vaucluse. Nothing serious. And now the compatriot had made Mrs. Trent pregnant, and Paddy had found out. How, when, where?

Rigby never found out. He really didn't want to know. The little kernel of virtue that he was so careful to hide from everyone, stopped him. But if Rigby ever had admired anyone silently, then it was Patrick Trent in his "situation." He was firm, dignified and—goddamn the woman!—compassionate.

But Trent did not want to remain in Sydney.

"I'll visit you often in Queensland," Rigby said gruffly. "If it gets to be too much for you, you can throw me out!"

Before he moved to Queensland, Trent went once more to the boardinghouse in Darlinghurst. But this time too he did not get to see Candy. Finally the Umbrella Uncle appeared.

"What's going to happen now?" Trent asked the old man.

Edward Doody shrugged. Candy's spine was damaged. She sat in the wheelchair Trent had bought for her, and made life difficult for her aunt. "She's never going to get over it," said the old man. Of course he meant his friend, Lydia Doody.

"Please don't send any more money, mister. Mrs. Doody has to spend it all on liquor for the sick sheila." He said it disapprovingly, as if he had never drunk anything stronger than milk in his life. "Do you hear, mister?"

Hoarse, drunken sounds came from Candy's room. Trent recognized her harsh voice. "Waltzing Matilda ... Waltzing Matilda ..." and then silence.

Trent walked slowly up the stairs. As he opened the door to Candy's room cautiously, an empty bottle of gin hit him on the temple. "Out!" screamed the girl in the wheel chair.

"You bitch!" cried Uncle Doody. "I'll give you one on your head!"

He slammed the door and swore every Irish curse in his rich repertoire.

Trent held his handkerchief over his bleeding forehead, and Uncle Doody bandaged it for him. "Here it hails glass," he growled. "The sheila is possessed of the devil. How about an umbrella for the trip, mister?"

But the old Irishman only asked out of habit. He had raised his fox head and was listening. Again maudlin singing, and then a whimpering that died down.

"Waltzing Matilda," the old man murmured grimly. "That's life, mister."

27

A Murder in Sydney

"Please have another piece, Mrs. Doody. You know you love my apple cake."

Gretchen pushed the cake plate across the table, ignoring Mrs. Doody's red-rimmed eyes. Candy had tried to commit suicide and failed. She sat in her wheelchair, her hands tied, and threatened to do it again.

"I'm finished, Gretchen." Like Caesar, Mrs. Doody could do two things at a time: eat cake and cry.

"You mustn't get so excited, Mrs. Doody. Not after your heart attack. Candy will adjust to her condition, you'll see." But Gretchen spoke without conviction. She asked what Molly Fleet was doing.

"She's gone to Parramatta, to her sister's wedding."

"How nice that April got married. It's the only right thing

to do." Gretchen was very happy in her second marriage. Mr. Lange was an excellent restaurateur, and so nice to her children from her first marriage, who needed a father. And that's just what Mr. Lange was. He had always liked young people, and after years of bachelorhood had taken over the duties of a father happily.

"How are Molly and Candy getting along?" Gretchen asked. She knew how difficult Candy was to handle now. Gretchen felt for the girl although she had never liked her, but she wasn't one of the people who were really taking Candy's accident to heart. The kookaburras in King's Cross were sorry for Candy with a shade of malice. Candy hadn't played the game. She had set herself up on a throne between the professional call girls and the more modest prostitutes.

Mrs. Doody took the last piece of apple cake and said that at first Molly had behaved wonderfully to Candy. But now things had changed. "Just think, the other day when Candy called her 'Mole,' Molly went berserk! I don't know why. It was just a joke."

"But it wasn't very nice of Candy."

"Candy was always so good-natured. In the movies she'd cry over people she didn't even know. She has a warm heart. I don't know what got into her. Molly should be more considerate."

Gretchen said nothing. She would have been furious too if someone had reminded her so cruelly of a physical flaw. Mrs. Doody was a good old woman, but she was so crazy about Candy that she was entirely unjust to others.

"Since then they don't speak to each other. I think Molly hates my poor little love." Mrs. Doody began to cry again. "How many eggs did you put in this cake, Gretchen? It really is first-rate. Nice of you to be so good to me. Apple cake always comforts me. But I have to go, child. It's been a real rest. I mean, to talk to a normal person, now that Molly's away. What's going to become of us?"

"Candy should be moved to Kalgoorlie. It's really too much for you, Mrs. Doody, and the doctor said you should avoid excitement."

"What do the doctors know?"

"Why don't you write to Candy's mother? After all, a mother is a mother, especially when things go badly."

"Not my sister! All she does is preach. And she never did love Candy. She was too beautiful. No, no, Gretchen, Candy stays with me, even if it's the death of me!" said Mrs. Doody, proud of her martyrdom. But she truly loved the girl, and nobody else did that. Without her Candy would be utterly abandoned.

"What's Charles Preston doing?" Gretchen asked. "You can trust me to keep my mouth shut, Mrs. Doody."

"I know, Gretchen. You're loyal. The Germans are known for that."

"I was born in Australia," Gretchen said stiffly. "My great-grandfather came from South Germany."

"That's what I mean. If you didn't wage war all the time, you'd be a very nice mob. Hardworking and clean. What was I going to say? Oh yes—Charles Preston, the bastard! Just imagine—he doesn't want to marry Candy now! And after getting all that money out of her! And he was in jail, too. Just like my old man," Mrs. Doody added generously. "I tell Candy all the time: You'll get somebody else when your back's okay. Do you think Candy will ever be able to dance again, I mean, after a while?"

"Let's hope." Gretchen was fighting tears.

"Now don't you cry too." Mrs. Doody blew her nose vigorously. "Oh Gretchen, I can't go on!"

"I'll drive you home, Mrs. Doody."

"But your husband's coming any minute."

"I'll leave a note for him on the kitchen table. My Friedrich will understand."

"Is a little one on the way?"

Gretchen blushed, and Mrs. Doody patted her on the shoulder. "I'm so happy for you! I always hoped Candy and Charles Preston would give me a little one. But now he's through with her, the dog! Those two shout at each other so that the walls shake when he does happen to turn up. Unfortunately she gave him everything that dear, good Mr. Trent put in the bank for her. We have nothing!"

"Everything may still turn out all right, Mrs. Doody. Of course Preston must marry her now. You can't take that much money from a girl and then..."

"You don't know life, Gretchen, even if you are in your middle thirties. I can say that, can't I? You look so much younger. Yes, yes, happiness keeps us young. But we're in a hell of a mess, and nobody helps us out. But I love my Candy, even if I don't get any more money from her." Mrs. Doody wept again, partly for Candy but also because all the money was gone.

"Don't cry, Mrs. Doody. Couldn't you get some money from Albert Ritter?"

"If I only knew where he was! I'd ask him to help us, all right. Candy wrote several times to his cover address, but the letters came back. He doesn't seem to be in New South Wales any more. He's a mean dog too!"

"Can't Molly find out where he is? She went for an outing with him once to the Blue Mountains, if I'm not mistaken."

"Uncle Doody remembered the other day that he came and wanted to take Molly out. But that was long ago. Molly was in Parramatta. Now he's probably over the hills and far away. How are we ever going to get hold of some money?"

"May I lend you a little, Mrs. Doody?"

"I don't take money from my friends. At the most, five pounds, if you can spare it. God bless you! You'll get it back with interest!"

"I don't want any interest, Mrs. Doody." Gretchen blushed as she handed Mrs. Doody a ten-pound note.

"God bless you!" Mrs. Doody said again, pocketing the money hastily. "When you're in trouble you know who your friends are. Mr. Trent was first-rate, but he's in Queensland now. How am I going to get gin for Candy? Uncle Doody gets so mad..."

"He's right. You shouldn't give her any hard liquor. It only excites her."

"But that's all she has!"

Mrs. Doody cried all the way to Darlinghurst and Gretchen watched the traffic. "Do come in just for a minute," Mrs. Doody begged. She dreaded being alone with Candy.

"All right. But just for a minute." Gretchen couldn't leave the miserable, helpless old woman to go into the house alone. It was eerily quiet as the two went upstairs.

"Let me take a look first," murmured Mrs. Doody, sounding almost frightened. "If Candy's going to rage, I won't let you in. Not in your condition."

Gretchen stopped halfway up the stairs. Huffing and puffing, Mrs. Doody reached Candy's door. Gretchen waited. She didn't know why, but she felt uneasy. The old house had such a deserted feeling. Uncle Doody's room was dark. It was six o'clock. That was Mr. Doody's time for a beer in the pub. Gretchen thought of the child she was expecting, and wished she was at home. But Mrs. Doody had looked at her so imploringly. If only Molly were here!

A scream from Candy's room. Gretchen trembled. Who had screamed? Candy or Mrs. Doody? Gretchen walked up to Candy's room. She felt dizzy, and her heart was beating fast. If only Fritz were here! He'd always disapproved of Gretchen's friends at the boardinghouse, but he let her go. Gretchen knocked on the door. No answer. What should she do? She called, "Mrs. Doody! *Mrs. Doody!*" When there was still no answer, she pushed open the door. With all her powers of self-control, she suppressed a scream. Oh God, oh God, oh God! Mrs. Doody lay motionless on the floor. And Candy? Candy, in her wheelchair, had her back turned to Gretchen. All Gretchen saw was her blond hair hanging over the back of the chair. But what was *that*? The end of a nylon stocking hung over the back too. Gretchen walked up to the chair, shivering. Then she screamed.

Candy had been strangled with a nylon stocking.

For one crazy moment, Gretchen wondered if Mrs. Doody had done it in her despair. No, no! She could never have done anything like that. With every ounce of strength, Gretchen forced herself to calm down. She knelt beside her unconscious friend and sprayed some of Candy's cologne on her face. At last Mrs. Doody opened her eyes, and as soon as she returned fully to consciousness, she crossed herself. "Please don't look," she said.

With Gretchen's help, Lydia Doody walked to her room. "Cover her, please," she said hoarsely, tearless. The big, corpulent Irish woman was in such a state of shock, that the tears which usually came so easily, wouldn't flow.

Gretchen touched nothing in Candy's room. She knew from the crime novels she'd read that this was something one shouldn't do. Still trembling she went out into the hall and called the police.

The eerie stillness in the boarding house was soon transformed into an atmosphere of palpable activity. Inspector Cox, Sergeant Cunningham, the coroner, and a photographer appeared and filled every corner of the house with their presence. The police car in front of the door had such magical attraction that the neighbors stood around it as if in front of a popular movie. A young policeman pushed back the sensation-hungry crowd. "Nobody is allowed in!" he cried every now and then. "Go home, mates!"

"What happened?" everyone wanted to know.

The policeman didn't answer. Now the curious were standing a small distance away, talking to each other, pleasantly excited. It was homicide, of course! *Who* had been murdered?

"You can tell me, young man," said a fat, jolly woman. "I deliver Mrs. Doody's groceries."

The young policeman suppressed a smile. He'd rather be playing soccer than disappointing these people. Besides, he didn't know who had been murdered, but he would never have admitted that.

Inspector Cox went through the whole house with his sharp eyes. Nobody was allowed to leave. He wanted to know who lived here. Gretchen, terribly agitated, answered. She was so frightened that she looked guilty, and blushed fiery red at every question. But Inspector Cox, "the best bloodhound between hell and New South Wales" as the press called him, knew faces. After taking Gretchen's name, address, occupation and relationship to Mrs. Doody and Miss Blyth, she was allowed to go home. She was to remain at their disposal, but Inspector Cox could see no reason for her presence now. Sergeant Cunningham accompanied Gretchen to her car, pushing the people in front of the boardinghouse aside with his long arm. "That's the inspector," somebody whispered, and Cunningham didn't object to being taken for Inspector Cox. One had to be satisfied with small honors too.

In the house the inspector was in the parlor which was never used, with its moth-eaten, plush-upholstered furniture. He was looking at the yellowed photographs of Dublin, Candy's best pictures, which were stuck on the wall with thumbtacks, and the tasteless holy figures. The plaster-of-paris Mother of God looked down on Inspector Cox with sympathy. It was going to be a tough job, Cox was thinking. Had Mrs. Doody got rid of the girl like a superfluous piece of furniture? The house stank of decay. But the dead girl must have made a lot of money at her modeling. What had happened to it? With puritanical repugnance, Inspector Cox took in the pink room where Miss Blyth had received her admirers in happier days. He'd find out who had visited the girl.

Mrs. Doody's deposition corroborated what Gretchen had said: Candy had phoned while the two had been drinking tea. Lately Candy had been calling Mrs. Doody all the time. She had evidently found solitude unendurable. Mrs. Doody declared that she couldn't possibly have been eating cake with Gretchen and strangling Candy at the same time! Until now nobody had ever managed to be in two places at the same time, had they? But this shameless policeman seemed to think it was possible! Mrs. Doody's face was red, and she screamed something that wasn't in the book at Inspector Cox, who remained friendly.

"It is not my intention to be insulting, Mrs. Doody. A murder has been committed here. I am only trying to get some useful information from you."

"All of us here, every one of us, is absolutely decent," Mrs. Doody said, a little more subdued now. "We're not going to let the police accuse us of murder. I just want you to know that, sir!"

"Who lives here?"

Mrs. Doody gasped; she saw an insult in even the simplest question.

"Well—who lives here?" Inspector Cox asked, a little sharper now.

"Right now, Miss Fleet and Mr. Edward Doody."

"A relative of yours?"

"I don't know. There are loads of Doodys at home. Possibly he's a relative. What's that got to do with Candy?"

"You have another empty room in the house. Who lived there?"

"You mean the junk room?"

"I mean the room next to Mr. Doody's. There's a bed in it."

"That's where I put my mending, and all my Candy's magazines and bottles of gin, full and empty."

"Who slept in the bed?"

"I'll have to think. Everything's turning around and around in my head!" Mrs. Doody burst into tears and Inspector Cox waited patiently for her to calm down. Finally she said grumpily that a Mr. Heller, an unemployed actor, had slept there. A new Aussie, but not young any more.

"Does Mr. Heller still come here?"

"Why not?" Mrs. Doody was indignant again. "We don't have fleas!"

"When was he here the last time?"

"Yesterday. Around this time he usually has a beer with Mr. Doody at MacQuarie's Chair, the pub around the corner."

"Where does Charlie Rainbow live?"

Mrs. Doody's eyes opened wide. "How do you know that our Charlie . . . have you been snooping around here?"

"Does Mr. Rainbow still live here?"

"Not right now. Charlie always stays a while, then he goes walkabout."

Inspector Cox didn't like people who came and went. He asked where Charlie Rainbow was now.

"No idea! The things you want to know! Our Charlie wouldn't hurt a fly! All he did once was put soap in my jam jar. A dumb young fellow, like a lot of others."

"When is Mr. Doody coming home?"

"Uncle . . . I mean, Edward should be back any minute. He was going to buy me a new fly swatter."

"What does he do for a living?"

"He's old and there's not a lot he can do. Sometimes he sells an old umbrella. He'll be punctual today. We're having goulash for supper. Just a minute, Inspector. I have to put the meat on. Uncle gets mad when it's tough. An old man like that shouldn't get excited."

"We won't be able to spare him a certain amount of excitement today," the inspector said drily. "He can't be that frail. Just a minute, Mrs. Doody. I haven't finished. Sorry about the goulash."

"Then we'll just have to eat later. I can't eat anything anyway."

"Where is Miss Fleet?"

"You mean our Molly? She's gone to a wedding in Parramatta."

"Her wedding?"

"No. She's gone to see her sister get married."

At that moment Uncle Doody and his cobber came marching up to the house, singing happily. They were so drunk they didn't even notice the people in front of the house. But they did notice the policeman, and Uncle Doody asked, not exactly politely, what the hell he was doing there.

"Get in and don't ask stupid questions," said the young policeman, and shoved the two drunks through the door, which he locked immediately.

Uncle Doody's drunken friend was questioned first. He was the old Viennese actor who had emigrated to Sydney shortly before the Second World War, and had lived in Mrs. Doody's boardinghouse for a while. He lived nearby now, and after work in a paper factory, he still conversed with his wife about performances in the Burgtheater and the Josefstadt. He had been at the pub with Mr. Doody. They had forgotten to buy the fly swatter. Mr. Franz Heller told Inspector Cox in his Austrian English that the business about Candy was horrible.

"Why?" asked the inspector.

"*Why?*" The old doctor threw back his white-haired head, the head of a character actor, and got all set for a big scene. "You ask why, Inspector? You don't have a heart? Everybody wants to live. The poor little thing did too. She went through enough with that fellow, a lying bastard, if you ask me!"

"Whom are you talking about?"

"Whom am I talking about?" Mr. Heller liked rhetorical questions. "About the wop, of course. Who else?"

"If you mean an Italian, please say so. And which Italian are you talking about?"

"About Carlo Pressolíni, of course. He works in the Restaurant Rosso in King's Cross and calls himself Charles Preston. A *very* new Australian, if you ask me. My friend Doody tells me that Charles threatened Candy a while ago. I'm not surprised. He's a good cross between Rigoletto and a pimp!"

"In what respect did Mr. Preston threaten the girl?"

"I wasn't there," Mr. Heller said cautiously. "But from what I heard, handsome Carlo wanted to wring the girl's neck. My friend Doody said Mr. Preston was a violent man, like every wop—sorry, Italian—but he couldn't stand her nagging him much longer."

"Why?"

"Candy wanted him to marry her! The good Lord knows he got enough money out of her, the good-for-nothing lout! You know something, Inspector Cox? Carlo reminds me of Liliom."

"Who is Liliom and where does he live?"

"Where does he live? In heaven, that's where he lives! When I played Liliom in the Burgtheater, everybody cried, even the archduchess and the whole audience! Do you know Charles Preston, Inspector?"

Inspector Cox wasn't sitting in Mrs. Doody's parlor to answer questions. A long time ago he had read a file from Hobart on Charles Preston, and at the time had wanted to ask Candy, here in the boardinghouse, if she was missing anything of value. But nobody had been home. Inspector Cox knew a lot more about the boardinghouse than Mr. Heller did. He also intended to investigate Charlie Rainbow's whereabouts. Perhaps the abo had wanted to take revenge on Miss Blyth for some reason or other.

"Did you know Charlie Rainbow, Mr. Heller?"

"The blackfellow? Of course."

"Do you know where he is?"

"*He* didn't do it, Inspector. Charlie used to strew the ground with flowers for Miss Candy to walk on. He worshiped her, like Othello his Desdemona, if you know what I mean."

Inspector Cox wanted to ask another question, but he hadn't counted on a former actor.

"You should have seen me as Othello, Inspector! There wasn't an Othello to equal me. Not even in Vienna. I can show you the reviews. They're a little yellowed from the heat here, but you'd be surprised! When I emigrated to Sydney thirty years ago, because of my Mitzi, I was *the* Othello! People stood in line to see me, Inspector!"

"Do you know where . . ."

"Not a single Aussie knew about my Othello!" Mr. Heller sounded indignant. "And they have blackfellows right here in their own country! It's fantastic! I told my Mitzi. She was with the Vienna opera, and she'd have sung Elsa, and *Die Frau ohne Schatten* for them just like that, if that idiot Hitler hadn't objected to my Mitzi's Jewish grandfather. And her grandfather had the finest, but really the finest fur shop in the Kärtnerstrasse. Do you know what the Kärtnerstrasse in Vienna means?"

"I would like to know what . . ."

"I don't want to seem argumentative, Inspector, but compared to the Kärtnerstrasse, George Street is . . ." The Burgtheater actor sounded condescending. "I'd like to give you some idea, but I simply can't describe it!"

Thank God! thought Inspector Cox. But before he could ask

another question, Mr. Heller informed him that Mitzi's mother, a blond just like Hitler had wanted but never got—the damned vegetarian—that Mitzi's mother, who had been a natural blond like Miss Candy...

"You can tell me all about that another time. A murder has been committed here."

"I know," Mr. Heller said with indifference. "When you think how many talented actors Adolf Hitler..."

"When and where did you see Candy Blyth last?" the Inspector asked patiently. With the new Australians, if one didn't accept their entire private history together with all the rest, one didn't find out anything.

"I saw Candy months ago with Charlie, the blackfellow, at the front door. He used to help her upstairs because she couldn't see in the dark. Strange, the way Charlie Rainbow reminds me of Othello."

"My time is limited, Mr. Heller. I would like to know exactly..."

"Wait just a minute, Inspector. What's the hurry? Try to understand us new Aussies. We find our way into our graves soon enough. You can see that with Candy. I always said to my Mitzi: I don't like the Nazis! I can't stand the sight of those brown shirts any more, and all because of your grandfather. But even the Nazis knew my Othello. You have to grant them that!"

"Thank you, Mr. Heller. That's all I want from you right now. You may go home."

"But I'd like to stay to tea. I'd like to give Madame Doody something else to think about. Mine is a very sociable nature, Inspector. You see, I grew up with the wine. What do you people here in Sydney know about the *Heurigen*? Nothing! Absolutely nothing! *Servus*, Inspector Cox."

Inspector Cox took a deep breath and lit a cigarette. At least he had found out that Charles Preston and the dead girl had been quarreling lately. The blackfellow would be more difficult to find than the waiter in King's Cross, but they would send out another blackfellow after Charlie Rainbow, an abo who worked for the Criminal Investigation Bureau. You never knew...

Sergeant Cunningham brought in Mr. Edward Doody, without his umbrella. Uncle Doody looked as sly and secretive as only an honest man can look when faced with the police. His gin inebriation was almost gone because of the shock, and he was his usual pleasant self. He was holding his cat in his arms and spoke sometimes to it, sometimes to the police fellow. Sergeant Cunningham sat in the back with his notebook. He had taken down Mr. Heller's testimony, Othello included. One never knew if a kernel of important information might not be hidden in the wild underbrush of a witness's garrulousness.

"How long have you known Miss Blyth, Mr. Doody?"

"Be quiet," said Uncle Doody, meaning the cat, which seemed to think it was being interrogated too. "Excuse me please, Inspector. I was speaking to the little beast here. I knew Candy since she came to Sydney."

"Was she a pleasant lodger?"

Uncle Doody looked at the fellow, speechless. "*That* fresh sheila?... Get out of here, you pest!" He threw the cat like a sack in the direction of Sergeant Cunningham, who let the animal out. Now one would at least know to *whom* Mr. Doody was speaking.

"So you didn't like Miss Blyth?"

"Not my type, if you know what I mean."

"I'd like to know what you mean."

"The fellow who did her in did a good deed. She was too dumb to do it herself. Since her accident, as God is my witness, she was a punishment from heaven! She pestered everybody!"

"Whom, for instance?"

"Me, of course. And poor old Lydia, who clung to the little bitch like an ivy vine. Molly Fleet can tell you a thing or two too."

"Weren't the two young girls friends? I mean, two young girls living in the same house. Usually there's a lot of whispering and giggling." Inspector Cox sounded downright jovial, and offered Mr. Doody a cigarette.

"They whispered, all right. But I think Molly hated Candy because of that fellow Ritter."

Inspector Cox listened carefully. There had been no mention of a man called Ritter until now. "When is Miss Fleet coming back?"

"No idea. I'm not waiting around for her. But Molly is a decent girl, not a whore, if you know what I mean."

This time the inspector knew what was meant, and he asked who had visited Candy.

"Well, Albert Ritter, of course, an arrogant fellow with a long nose, if you know what I mean."

"Do you know where Mr. Ritter happens to be now?"

"I imagine the police can find out things like that."

"We're grateful for any help we can get," Inspector Cox said. "Listen, Mr. Doody . . . you seem to be the only intelligent person in this place. You keep your eyes open, don't you?" Uncle Doody nodded, flattered. "Did Mr. Ritter show his face here often after Candy's accident?"

"You don't believe that yourself, Inspector! That client made himself scarce, all right. Of course he's a traveling salesman. They're on the go all the time. Just between us, these slick fellows only want to have a good time with the sheilas. When something goes wrong, they're gone. Am I right?"

"Like the amen in church," said Inspector Cox.

"Ritter was a pretty crazy fellow. He used to sketch Candy, can you imagine? In my day I'd have known something better to do with the sheilas. Candy was pretty, sure, but not my type. I like something round and soft in my arms. But that's quite a while ago."

Uncle Doody smiled at the inspector and the inspector smiled back as he gave Cunningham a sign. The sergeant left, and in a short time found Mr. Ritter's portrait sketches of Candy between some papers and unpaid bills. Tomorrow they would go through the house again with a fine-tooth comb. On the stairs Mrs. Doody asked the sergeant if the police would ever leave them in peace. She didn't feel like eating anything, but it would soon be suppertime. Cunningham grinned and went back to the parlor with Rigby's sketches in his leather briefcase. Uncle Doody hadn't noticed his disappearance and was conversing animatedly with Inspector Cox about Charles Preston, whom he couldn't abide. Apparently Mrs. Doody and Charlie Rainbow were the only two people in the house he liked.

"Was Mr. Preston jealous of Candy's admirers?"

"How should I know? Lately they were fighting like cats and dogs. Charles is a very excitable man, a *very* new Australian. He's been here quite a few years but never seems to learn."

"What did Miss Blyth and Mr. Preston quarrel about?"

"Because suddenly she wanted to marry him. Before that he wasn't good enough for her, but now that she'd been put out of action, she didn't want to let him off the hook. I'm telling you, that fellow can shout! And in tune, like a wop opera."

"Do you think Mr. Preston could be violent?"

"You mean, did he strangle Candy? Out of the question. He hasn't got the guts."

"And Mr. Rainbow?"

Uncle Doody laughed out loud. "Our Charlie is the last one on the track, absolutely! A regular long shot! He was much too good to Candy. If you ask me, then I'd rather bet on Preston." Uncle Doody seemed to be off to the races. "I don't know, though, Inspector . . . no, Preston can't win either. I'd say Ritter was the favorite. Or . . . maybe not."

"Somebody murdered Miss Blyth, didn't they?"

"Sure. But who?"

"We'll find out. And if you should happen to notice anything here, or if Mr. Ritter perhaps comes to pay his respects, please let me know. I know a bright old fellow when I see one, Mr. Doody."

"I do too!" Uncle Doody had chosen not to say a word about Trent.

"You can always get in touch with me at the Criminal Investigation Bureau, or leave a message there for me. And please see to it that everybody in the house is available. That goes for Miss Fleet too, when she gets back."

"She was supposed to come back today." Flattery made Mr. Doody very communicative. Today, the day of the murder, Miss Fleet was supposed to have been back? Interesting . . .

"Does Miss Fleet have a proper profession, or is she a call girl too?"

"In my day, Inspector, there were only bitches or decent girls. I suppose you could call Molly Fleet a decent girl. She's a masseuse, nice, fine figure. I'm telling you, Inspector, that sheila could hold her own with the strongest man!"

Inspector Cox listened silently to the story of Miss Fleet's accomplishments. This young lady would have to be watched; she rated a thorough investigation too. Apparently Albert Ritter had driven both sheilas crazy, and they had probably quarreled over him. And he wondered why one had only to "suppose" that Molly Fleet was a decent girl.

"I guess you'll be questioning the neighbors now?" said Uncle Doody.

"Now I'm going home to Mother's to eat!"

"We're having goulash," said Uncle Doody. "After all, one's got to eat, right, Inspector? I hope it's tender. All in all I'm a lamb, but when it comes to meat like leather, I'm dangerous!"

"I can't imagine that, Mr. Doody."

"Ask Lydia! There've been times when I've thrown my plate at the wall." Uncle Doody laughed and the inspector laughed with him.

"I don't want to hear any complaints, Mr. Doody. By the way, one of my men will be keeping an eye on this house for a while."

"Why? Are we in danger?" The old man looked frightened.

"Just routine. So's you won't be molested by curious people. You can sleep in peace."

Cox nodded amiably and got ready to leave. Sergeant Cunningham was to stay until the body had been removed. The photographer and fingerprint expert had already left. The silence of death sank over the scene of the crime. In the kitchen Mrs. Doody, sobbing, was stirring the goulash and drinking a double gin for support.

The coroner was waiting for Cox in the police car. Cox gave his report through the radio, then he sat back and took a deep breath. "Where to?" asked the driver.

"To the Restaurant Rosso in King's Cross." Cox would have liked to go straight home to his mother—it had not been a joke—but he wanted to take Charles Preston by surprise before the news of the murder reached the restaurant.

"A horrible case," said the pathologist. "My wife often cut pictures of Candy Blyth out of the magazines. The girl had terribly bad luck, wouldn't you say?"

Cox nodded. The coroner said that such a very pretty young girl like Candy probably would have enemies. Men...

"Or women," Cox said drily. He had to think of Molly Fleet again. How strangely the members of the household had spoken about her. They "supposed" she was a decent girl? What did that mean? Hadn't Miss Fleet found a boyfriend after Ritter? *Who* was Ritter? And *where* was he?

"Do you have a suspect?" asked the doctor.

"A suspect?" Inspector Cox raised his eyebrows. "You're joking, doctor! Right now I suspect everybody except Mr. Doody's cat!"

28

The Kookaburras of King's Cross

The kookaburra is a bold, sociable bird which from time to time bursts into shrill laughter that sounds very human.

Inspector Cox spent a long evening among the kookaburras in King's Cross. First he went to the Restaurant Rosso to question Charles Preston. Could he be a serious suspect in Candy's murder? Cox watched the young man sharply and felt that the horror on Charles's face when he was told the news was sincere. The usual hubbub of King's Cross was all around them, but for seconds Charles seemed petrified. The shrill laughter of the sheilas didn't register. Either he was innocent, or he was a superb actor. Then he shrugged his shoulders fatalistically and without any transition whatsoever was again the right hand of Raffaele Rosso.

Cox went on watching him, then called him into the Rossos' private room. His alibi was unassailable. Both Rossos corroborated his statement that he had spent the whole afternoon and evening taking inventory of their stock of wines. He hadn't even gone out to the market. Cox asked if Mr. Rosso had seen Charles all the time. Raffaele said that he had *not* accompanied Charles to a certain place, and asked the inspector, his eyes flashing, if "Carlo" was under suspicion because he had emigrated to Australia from Italy. Mr. Rosso went on to say that he loved Charles like his own son, and if the young man was a murderer, so was he! And were immigrants from Genoa especially suspect?

"Stop talking nonsense, Rosso!" said Cox, more sharply than he had intended. The fat, excitable restaurateur was as deeply insulted over every question as Mrs. Doody. It could drive you frantic! However, Inspector Cox preserved his cool and continued to question Mr. Preston amiably. He was curious: the young man had accepted money from the dead girl for months, and admitted it at once. He had of course given her valuable presents from her own money because this went along with having an affair.

Charles also told the inspector that Candy had loved him madly. Women were happiest when they were making sacrifices for their lovers. After this bit of instruction, Charles, again without any transition, recommended the daily special, and Mr. Rosso brought a fine red wine to the table. "On the house," he declared with dignity.

Of course Charles Preston wasn't exactly at ease. Because of his success with the most beautiful model in Sydney, he now found himself trapped. He managed to look indifferent, but he was upset. Cox came to the conclusion that the two had quarreled constantly, then made up only to become mutually abusive again. Preston declared that after his return from Hobart, Candy had forced money on him. The first thing he had done was look her up, but he had been thrown out. Shortly after that though she had appeared at the Restaurant Rosso and begged him to forgive her. Fair enough.

"And did you forgive her?" asked the inspector, with such casual irony that Preston never noticed it.

"Yes sir!" And he had kept Mrs. Rosso informed regularly about the affair.

"Why?" Cox wanted to know.

"But that's perfectly natural, Inspector. Mrs. Rosso is like a mother to me."

"Isn't she a bit young for that?"

Preston explained that this did not depend on the chronological age but on understanding, and he valued understanding highly. He had saved money and offered to show the inspector his bank book.

"Not necessary." Cox was gradually beginning to see through the facade of this melodramatic passion. Mr. Preston was no paragon of virtue, but by now Cox was almost sure that even when provoked, Charles would not commit murder; he would simply get the hell out of wherever. He was much more sensible and realistic than he pretended to be. His operatic affectations, his excitement over Candy's murder, his despair over the tragic death of youth and beauty, would have prompted a less experienced detective to arrest him. But Cox had more subtle methods. He waited until Preston had finished his solo, then he moved on to the business of the day: Preston's alibi and his plans for the future.

"Did you intend to marry Miss Blyth?" he asked suddenly.

"Certainly not!" Preston replied.

"Why not?"

"I would never have married a model, Inspector. Too spoiled and too unreliable."

"But that didn't prevent you from accepting considerable sums of money from Miss Blyth."

"I came to this country as a penniless immigrant. All the old Australians have too much money, if you ask me. What do you know about what we go through here?"

"Let's stay with the subject, Mr. Preston. Why did you accept money from Miss Blyth? You're a healthy young man who can work."

"She gave it to me. What was I to do? I couldn't possibly have taken Miss Blyth out and given her presents in the style to which she was accustomed. She rode on a high horse. But since then a dozen moons have sunk into the ocean."

"You could have persuaded Miss Blyth to a more modest lifestyle. After all, you were older and more sensible." The latter was added with little conviction.

"*Only* the most expensive things were good enough for her!" said Preston, with an unfeigned bitterness. "The little fool was a public idol! She would order a meal that an Italian family could have lived on for a week! Ask her! Oh . . . In my pain I don't know what I'm saying!"

"Why did you ask the young lady to come to Hobart?"

"I *am* going mad!" Preston ran his fingers wildly through his dark hair. "Believe it or not, Inspector, Miss Blyth followed *me* to Hobart, *not* at my invitation! I'd already had enough of her. Monotonous beauties make me nervous, if you know what I mean."

"I know."

"She wrote to me all the time, rambling nonsensical stuff, if you know what I mean."

"I know."

"I had other interests in Hobart. I had no time for Candy. Ask my relatives in Hobart. The Pressolini garages are famous all over Tasmania. Miss Blyth had the nerve to settle herself down with my relatives, and pursued me! No pride! No dignity! I was Mrs. Pugh's secretary in Hobart."

"I know," said Inspector Cox for the third time. Mr. Preston blushed and mumbled something to the effect that anybody could be unlucky.

"Why did you come back to Sydney, Mr. Preston? Did you want to live at Miss Blyth's expense again after all?"

"The hell I did! Do you think Miss Blyth was the only girl in Sydney? Besides, I wanted to be on my own."

"That's nothing to get excited about, Mr. Preston. I hoped to get some useful information from you that would throw light on Miss Blyth's character and her background. After all, a horrible crime has been committed. I beg you therefore to understand my questions in light of this."

"I know I'm the number one suspect," said Preston, with a trace of vanity. "The lover is always the guilty one. We know that from the movies. I have atoned for my bad luck, sir. Do you think Mr. and Mrs. Rosso would have taken me back if they hadn't known I wanted to start a new life? *Without* Candy! But after her accident, I wanted to comfort her. May I be struck dead if this isn't true!"

"One corpse a day is enough for me."

"Now I'm supposed to be an idiot!" Preston said angrily. "Candy's lover in Broome threw her out."

"And who was that?"

"How do I know? Ask Mrs. Doody."

Later Charles waited on the inspector, excellently, once he wiped the tears from his face. Cox looked at Preston's smooth forehead under his shiny dark hair, his fiery eyes, his soft, sensual mouth, and flat ears, almost too delicate for a man. The outer rim was bent like a question mark. The whole man was an emotional question mark, but he was not a murderer.

Meanwhile the restaurant had filled up. More and more laughing birds appeared. Some sat down at the bar, others at small tables with colored lamps. For the most part the ladies were much younger than their partners.

Charles Preston drew the inspector's attention to several girls who had known Candy. Cox took down their names and addresses because he wanted to question them the next day. "Do you know Miss Fleet?" he asked, so suddenly that Preston started.

"Who doesn't know Molly Fleet? You can't mistake her for any other girl. Not my type, if you want to know. Rough. No soul. But a gorgeous figure. Too energetic for my taste, though. I prefer the clinging vine."

"Where did you meet Miss Fleet?"

"In a small bar. She was all alone. I went out with her once or twice, but I found her creepy, if you know what I mean."

"No, I don't," said Cox.

"And by the way—she hated Candy. It was mutual."

"Why?"

"Well, because of me, of course."

"Of course," said Inspector Cox. "You're damn lucky, my boy, with your alibi."

"A little more Parmesan cheese, Inspector?"

"Yes, please."

"I loved Candy in my way," Preston said dreamily, and poured the inspector a glass of wine. "But I would never have married her."

"Not even after the accident?"

"I want a respectable wife, and children. Candy would never have accepted that. Where do you suppose a woman's understanding is located?"

"No idea."

"In her womb," Charles said dispassionately. "Where I come from we don't strangle young women because we don't want to marry them. Practically speaking, sir, that would make no sense. You either pass the girl on to your best friend or you marry the right girl. Discreetly. I got married last week. Discreetly."

"Why discreetly?"

"I didn't want to break Candy's heart. My young wife is an old Australian, naturally. Fourth generation of innkeepers. In Mittagong. Lovely scenery. Later I'll take over the inn."

"Well, congratulations." Inspector Cox looked at Preston thoughtfully, and Preston must have noticed something in the look because he said hastily that he had told his wife all about his "difficulties" in Hobart. Of course that would remain strictly between them. It was none of his in-laws' business. Moreover, their ancestors had immigrated as convicts, who naturally had been guilty of nothing.

"Here comes my wife!" he cried, his eyes shining. "Excuse

me for a moment, please, Inspector. I'll be right back. I can recommend the pineapple salad highly. Would you like it on ice?"

"That would be fine."

Charles's young wife looked so much like Candy that for a moment Cox was shocked. He had never seen the beautiful model alive, but he imagined that this was what she must have looked like. But Preston's choice was an obviously respectable girl: natural, no makeup, but with very promising hips.

While he ate his pineapple salad—Preston, on his best behavior, had added a shot of maraschine—Cox, in his mind, closed the file on that young man. Mr. Preston must have always known what he really wanted, and that took real talent. The *commedia* with the tragic ending was now part of the gray past.

The wedding breakfast had taken place at the Restaurant Rosso. Good old Raffaele had shed tears of joy and given the young couple a check, and Mrs. Rosso had presented the bride with a dozen Irish linen dishtowels. Yesterday, on the advice of his wife, Charles had quietly broken the news of his marriage to Candy. That was the cause of all the hellish noise Uncle Doody had heard.

Inspector Cox finished his excellent dinner thoughtfully. In answer to his question as to who had visited Candy regularly, Preston had repeatedly mentioned a Mr. Ripper, or Ritter. The same name had come up during the questioning of Mr. Edward Doody. Perhaps a trail led from Miss Fleet to this mysterious traveling salesman? The sketches of Candy showed artistic talent. Why did Preston find Miss Fleet "creepy"? Was she strong enough to have tightened the noose around Candy's throat? Perhaps she had been in Sydney on the afternoon of the murder without anyone in the boardinghouse knowing it? But Cox didn't want to draw any hasty conclusions. Had Miss Blyth been a regular prostitute, or had she chosen the somewhat higher-prestige position of call girl? This seemed more likely in the case of a well-salaried model. But perhaps the beautiful girl had only joined the race as an outsider. The kookaburras of King's Cross ought to know. Nor had anyone mentioned Trent, Candy's former benefactor.

"Candy Blyth *was* an outsider!" Beatrice Fright said contemptuously. There were very few guests in the Greek Bar in King's Cross, and Miss Fright and her friend, Antigone, were drinking the drinks to which Inspector Cox was treating them. They downed them astonishingly fast. "I mean, we girls are friendly and help each other when it's necessary, but Candy Blyth only helped herself." In spite of her name, Miss Fright was a call girl with first-rate addresses in her book. She nudged her friend. "Right, Gonnie?"

Antigone had come to Sydney a few years ago. She was a waitress in a Greek restaurant, and for a small percentage Miss Fright gave her telephone numbers she wasn't using any more. Miss Fright was tall and statuesque, twenty-eight years old, and street-smart. Antigone, from Athens, was shy. She had left her home with her family as a child. Called "Gonnie" in Australia, she was trying to make a living at the oldest profession in the world. Miss Fright's laughter scared her. She towered over the poor little girl from Greece who had to solicit her clients on the street and was often arrested for it. Miss Fright stared at Inspector Cox, her face expressionless. She knew how to handle cops. She had her own apartment in King's Cross and only accepted johns who had been recommended to her. She was born in Sydney, the daughter of a tailor, but needle and thread had proved too boring.

"Candy Blyth was unfriendly," she said contemptuously. Inspector Cox knew Miss Fright, and it was not to her disadvantage that she occasionally helped the police. She knew all the kookaburras in King's Cross, and most of them were afraid of her.

"Do you know a Mr. Ritter?" Cox asked, after the third espresso.

Miss Fright thought hard. "Ritter?" Then she shook her neatly curled head regretfully.

"He was a friend of Miss Blyth's," said the inspector. "Try

to remember." But no, Miss Fright had never heard of a man called Ritter.

"I know him," Antigone said shyly.

"*You*?" Miss Fright was furious, and her pride was hurt. This girl, Antigone, just over with the last boat, with no assurance, only fear, and clumsy at that, knew someone whom she...

"Just a minute, Miss Fright." There was a hunter's gleam in Cox's sharp eyes. "Where did you see Mr. Ritter, miss?"

"In King's Cross," the frail little girl stammered. "He treated me to coffee in my restaurant."

"Where does he live?"

"In Moss Vale. He doesn't come to Sydney often. He's a traveling salesman. He doesn't want anything, just to talk."

"With you?" Miss Fright roared with laughter.

"Please, Miss Fright," Cox said sternly.

"Tell the truth," Miss Fright said, on their way home. "You never saw Ritter in your life!"

"I just wanted to say something too," the little Greek girl said softly. "Nobody in Sydney pays any attention to me."

"Or *is* there a man called Ritter?" Miss Fright sounded threatening.

"I'm sure there is," Gonnie said dreamily. "But I don't know him."

On Preston's advice, Cox questioned one more kookaburra from King's Cross, a streetwalker whom the Three Graces had created in anger. Miss Fletcher had had enough of love, and it showed. Her hair hung like a ragged straw fringe across her forehead—not a windblown hairdo: Miss Fletcher had been shaken by a real storm. "Why should I still go to the hairdresser, Inspector?" she asked aggressively. "What I need for my business is a new face!" And she really laughed like a kookaburra in the bush. She needed a new body too, and certainly a new brassiere. But of what concern was that to the police?

Miss Fletcher had never known such an unpleasant fellow as this Fox or Cox. She was furious over being questioned about Candy Blyth. Of course she knew the model. She would have liked to throw acid at that pretty face because Candy Blyth had looked scornfully right past her in the bars in King's Cross. She had hated Candy, not for professional reasons, but because of the girl's arrogance.

"Can you tell me with whom Miss Blyth went out? We'll be glad to pay for any useful information, Miss Fletcher."

"I don't mind earning an honest penny," said Miss Fletcher. "But I'm not an informer. I haven't sunk that low."

"Come, come, Miss Fletcher. All you'd be doing is your duty as a citizen. This is a case of murder."

"The bitch died none too soon, if you ask me."

"I've been asking you all this time. Cigarette?"

Miss Fletcher looked at the inspector out of her clever, colorless eyes. In her youth they had been blue. "Thanks, I don't smoke." She smoked like a chimney, but she didn't accept cigarettes from cops.

"Do you know a man called Albert Ritter, Miss Fletcher? He's supposed to have been a friend of Miss Blyth's. Also of Miss Fleet's."

Miss Fletcher laughed loudly again. Just like a jackal, thought Cox. "Miss Fleet has no boy friends," she said. "Whoever sold you that story? I'm sorry, Inspector, but I don't know any Mr. Ritter."

Miss Fletcher was speaking the truth; traveling salesman Albert Ritter didn't exist, but she had seen Candy Blyth quite frequently with Alexander Rigby, whose picture had been in all the papers on his fiftieth birthday. Ritter? Rigby? The husband from the elegant eastern suburbs probably called himself Ritter when he went out on the town.

Miss Fletcher could have given the inspector a valuable tip. The more she thought about it the surer she was that Ritter *was* Rigby. But she said nothing. Although Candy had chosen to snub her, the miserable streetwalker behaved according to her professional ethic. Besides, Miss Fletcher came from a family where it was a matter of principle not to speak badly of the dead. And since Miss Fletcher had nothing good to say about Candy Blyth, she was silent.

After having questioned the kookaburras of King's Cross, Cox looked up a painter who lived near Mrs. Doody's boardinghouse. He had been told that Mr. Bolter was a curious loner.

Cox found Bolter in his favorite pub. The painter explained proudly that he had been born in Sydney's Central Station, then he reverted to his favorite topic—the arts. "I practice the art of the impossible," he said. "I would like to give Australia an old soul."

Mr. Cox dealt with the situation with his usual patience, but decided that if Bolter ever had to take the witness stand, the judge would have a heart attack. So he interrupted a lecture on art theory with the question: had Mr. Bolter known Candy Blyth?

"Who didn't know her? But if you think I murdered the sheila, then you're on the wrong track, Inspector. I don't think very highly of the female sex—too little brains and too many dangerous curves."

"Interesting," said Inspector Cox. If Mr. Bolter wasn't interested in women, it didn't mean by a long shot that he wouldn't wring one of their necks in an emergency. Bolter seemed to read the inspector's thoughts because he flung back the hair hanging over his forehead and said gently, "I don't strangle girls, Inspector. Why should I? I wish them all the best. Do you know Plato?"

"Do you know Ritter?"

"Certainly," said the painter. "A splendidly-built example. Not very young any more, but in excellent shape. In his case every muscle is where it should be."

"That sounds good."

"If I am not being inappropriate, I could do with another beer. Thank you very much, Inspector. I saw Ritter often with Candy, in Bondi. His first name is Albert."

Cox asked casually for his present address. "I can't tell you that," said Bolter, slightly piqued. He was always sensitive when a cop asked him for the address of a man. If the Greeks of antiquity had been fascinated by male beauty, why not Mr. Bolter?

The inspector hurriedly changed the subject and asked the painter about his work. He had formulated a plan that could be realized only via the arts. Mr. Bolter painted portraits. That was what Cox had hoped. At last he got the painter to the point where he drew a pencil sketch of Ritter on the back of a menu. Cox stared intently at the portrait, so quickly sketched with a few sure strokes. Where in the world had he seen this sharp profile before? Right now he couldn't place it, damn it! He asked the painter to sign the sketch.

"You're going to keep it?" asked Mr. Bolter, astonished and flattered.

Cox put the sketch in his portfolio and said, smiling, "My first original." Then he ordered another beer and asked the painter if he knew Molly Fleet.

"Indeed I do!" Mr. Bolter said admiringly. "The girl's strong as a horse. She cured my back with her massage. A very efficient young woman. Unfortunately she has no luck with men."

"Too strong?" Inspector Cox smiled. "When did you see her last?"

"Wait a minute. . . . My memory's failing me, and I'm only thirty-five! Funny, I could recite Plato's entire *Symposium* for you . . ."

"Another time, Mr. Bolter. *When* did you see Miss Fleet?"

"If I'm not mistaken—yesterday. That's right, Inspector. I was at the movies and she sat in front of me. You can't mistake her."

"In what movie house?"

"I think it was the Plaza, on George Street."

"Are you sure?"

"I don't keep a record of my amusements, Inspector. The films are mostly for children or minors. Did you see the last film at the Variety, in Pitt Street? What did you think of—"

"Perhaps you saw Miss Fleet at the Variety."

"Of course, Inspector. At the Variety. How did you know? That's quite uncanny."

Inspector Cox did not betray in any way how valuable this

bit of information was to him. He talked for a few minutes more about films, Plato, a new fried-fish place and the Elizabethan theatre. Then he was called to the phone. The report came from Mrs. Doody's boardinghouse. Miss Fleet had just arrived from Parramatta.

"I'll be right there," said Inspector Cox. "She's not to leave the house!" He said a hurried goodbye to Mr. Bolter, who was a little surprised at the abrupt ending of their conversation. You could never trust a cop.

Inspector Cox had been given so many divergent opinions of Molly Fleet that his curiosity was aroused, but she didn't make any extraordinary impression. A strong girl who had not entirely shed the country town she came from. A small waistline, long red-gold hair worn flopping over the left half of her face, and the muscular arms of a masseuse. Had she or hadn't she? Whatever Miss Fleet might be, she was certainly not "creepy." Cox couldn't understand why, except for the mysterious Mr. Ritter, she hadn't found a boy friend. The girl looked decent, neat, and the birthmark on her left cheek might help the woman at the movie box-office to identify her. There were no fingerprints; the murderer had apparently worn gloves. No gloves had been found at the boardinghouse.

Miss Fleet didn't seem to be frightened, nor did she make a sly or false impression. But that didn't have to mean anything. If the painter in Darlinghurst hadn't been mistaken, it would be difficult for Miss Fleet to explain why she had been incognito in Sydney on the afternoon of the murder. Cox was still looking her over. Except for the birthmark, she was pretty. Somehow or other he was touched by the way this lively girl arranged her red-gold hair like a curtain over the left half of her face. After all, she was only twenty-two and wanted to be attractive to men. All her character was in her chin. Miss Fleet could probably be tough, but her lips were shy and inexperienced. In her eyes, however, there was a gleam of rebellion. "I didn't do it!" she said, louder than was necessary.

"Nobody says you did, Miss Fleet."

They were seated opposite each other in Mrs. Doody's parlor.

"Then why are you following me?"

"You go to the movies too often," Cox said gently.

"I hardly ever go! I hate those sloppy love films!"

"What was the last time you went to the movies, Miss Fleet?"

"I don't know. Why?" Miss Fleet sounded hostile.

"I am the one who asks the questions, young lady." Cox's voice was a little sharper, and Molly Fleet noticed it. "You are a qualified masseuse?"

"Yes."

"How long have you been working in Sydney?"

"A little over two years."

Cox leafed through his file. "Why didn't you stay in Parramatta?"

"Nobody there needs me."

A shadow fell across her young face. Miss Fleet's moods changed with baffling speed. A sensitive girl. Cox decided to "gently" force her to tell all she knew.

"Well, naturally, Sydney is more amusing for a young lady. King's Cross, dancing, movies. Oh, I forgot, you don't go to the movies."

"I don't go out very much." Miss Fleet blushed.

"I like it when girls are well-behaved."

Molly looked at Cox almost gratefully. The young thing was evidently not spoiled. "I guess Miss Blyth was always on the go."

"Before the accident, every evening. That's the way models live."

"Did you like her?"

"She was a lot of fun," Miss Fleet said cautiously. "I mean, before the accident."

"And after that?"

"She wasn't funny anymore." Miss Fleet's tone made it quite clear that she had never heard such foolish questions. "You can figure that out for yourself."

"There are supposed to be people who become pleasanter through misfortune."

"Well, Candy wasn't one of them. May I go now?"

"What's your hurry?"

"I've got a lot of things to attend to. I'm going back to Parramatta tomorrow."

"Have you a certain reason?"

"My father doesn't want me to go on living in this house."

"You're of age, aren't you?"

"I don't want to either."

"Why?"

"Well, you can imagine why."

"I have no intention of thinking for you, Miss Fleet. I want to know why you intend to leave again so soon."

"I want to. That's all."

"That is not all by any means, young lady. Nobody leaves this house without police permission."

"I have to treat my patients. To do that I have to leave the house."

"Wasn't it your intention to leave tomorrow? How many patients do you think you can massage between midnight and dawn?"

"If you won't let me go back to Parramatta, I would like to spend my time usefully. What's wrong with that?"

"Nothing. Can't you make yourself useful here?"

"I could help Mrs. Doody, of course," Molly said sullenly. "She does nothing but cry."

"Which is understandable, since her niece was so violently murdered."

"I imagine with a stocking it doesn't hurt," said Molly.

"How do you know that, Miss Fleet?" The inspector was looking at Molly strangely. A shiver ran down her spine.

"I didn't say I knew it. I said I imagined it."

"Why do you think so?"

"I saw something like it in a movie. The girl was killed immediately. She didn't even scream."

"Didn't you just say you don't go to the movies?"

"On that day I did."

"Aha! On that day you did." There was a hideous pause—

at least it seemed hideous to Molly. Cox suddenly stepped up so close to her that she shrank from him. His eyes were boring holes in her face. She closed her eyes.

"Why are you afraid to look at me?"

"I am *not* afraid." Molly opened her eyes. "I'm tired. That's why I closed my eyes."

"Tired of lying? Let me tell you something, Miss Fleet: if you go on like this, you'll lie your head and neck off. I'm just warning you because I'm good-natured."

Sergeant Cunningham, who was taking it all down, looked up. Things were looking up.

"I don't lie. Lying is a sin."

"Do you consider murder commendable when it doesn't hurt?"

"I have no experience in that respect."

"Perhaps you massaged Miss Blyth a little too vigorously. Nobody was home yesterday between five and seven."

"How do you know that?"

"Here *I* am the one who asks the questions. And if I don't get some sensible answers out of you soon, you'll be sorry. You are far too stubborn, Miss Fleet." Cox pounded on the table with his fist so that the holy figures wobbled.

"Why are you so furious with me? *I* didn't do it!"

"Then who did?"

"I don't know." There were tears in Molly's voice, but she controlled them. "I've only just arrived in Sydney."

"Are you sure?"

"Of course I'm sure!"

"Well, you seem to be asking for it, Miss Fleet, You arrived in Sydney yesterday, the day of the murder."

Molly stared at him, horrified. Something was very wrong here. She was trembling from head to toe.

"Why did you come back to Sydney yesterday? Put your cards on the table, you stupid little thing. At least assure yourself of mitigating circumstances."

"I didn't do it! Please, please believe me!"

"Why did you come back secretly?"

"That's my private business, Inspector. Really it is."

"If you want to go on living your private life, I advise you to tell me the truth. It's your only chance."

Molly was silent. Then she said haltingly that her presence in Sydney had nothing to do with the murder. Inspector Cox ignored this as utter nonsense.

"Were you at the Variety movie house yesterday afternoon?"

"For a little while."

"Why did you leave earlier? To visit Miss Blyth?"

"No!" Molly screamed.

"Please keep your voice down. You could wake the dead." Cox cleared his throat. It hadn't been a very good way to put it. Sergeant Cunningham suppressed a grin.

"For the last time—where were you yesterday between five and seven?"

"If I tell you, I'll involve somebody else..."

"You'd better worry about involving yourself! In a murder case, it's every man for himself. Don't you know that? So— where were you?"

Molly closed her lips firmly.

"I'll wait exactly two minutes because you're so young and silly." Suddenly Inspector Cox sounded quite friendly. He looked at Mrs. Doody's wall clock. "One more minute, Miss Fleet. After which I shall arrest you for suspicion of murder."

Miss Fleet let out a shrill cry and made for the door. The inspector caught her in his arms. "And attempt to escape." He nodded to the sergeant, who wrote it down. "You're making life very hard for yourself, Miss Fleet."

Cox pushed the trembling girl down onto the plush sofa. Molly looked as if she were about to faint. The sergeant got water from the kitchen and splashed some in Molly's face.

Mrs. Doody was playing patience and heard Molly's scream. She stuck her head in the door. "What are you doing to our Molly?" she asked harshly.

"Nobody is to come in here! Miss Fleet and I are talking." Cox closed the door in Mrs. Doody's face. Since the key was missing, Sergeant Cunningham planted himself against it. More effective than a key. Nothing less than an earthquake could have shaken him.

Inspector Cox's success lay in lightninglike changes of method. Like the winds of Sydney, he was sometimes gentle, sometimes rough. Instead of arresting Molly Fleet, he asked some more questions, quietly. The young girl was scared to death. He intended to calm her before playing his trump card. He asked Molly about her home in Parramatta, and offered her a cigarette. His favorite aunt lived in Parramatta too. As Molly, with the optimism of youth, gradually began to forget the danger of her situation, Inspector Cox asked suddenly why she had spent the night in a hotel.

"I wanted to make saying goodbye to Mrs. Doody as short as possible. She would have spent the whole night begging me to stay, and I'd have given in."

"Do you have such a soft heart?"

"When people are good to me—yes."

The inspector was silent. For a moment he looked at Molly Fleet with true human interest. He even found himself wishing that this nice young girl were innocent. She was so different from the kookaburras of King's Cross, damn it! She looked so *clean*. She was living in the wrong surroundings. She should marry, have children, and be happy. That was what she was cut out for.

"So where were you late yesterday afternoon?"

It turned out that Miss Fleet had been with Albert Ritter after massaging Miss Rigby. Of course Cox knew the editor-in-chief of *Insight*. He would have the time checked.

"Do you massage Miss Rigby regularly?"

"From time to time. She's very busy."

"What did you do after the massage?"

"I visited Albert Ritter."

"Did you massage him?"

Molly blushed. "Of course not!" she said stiffly. "He's in great shape."

"How do you know that?"

"You can see that he is," said Miss Fleet, and suppressed a smile.

"What did you want from Mr. Ritter?"

At last Cox could see the light at the end of the tunnel, but he didn't betray it. Miss Fleet was calmer now and had revealed her secret quite easily.

"I wanted money from him."

The inspector's sympathy was quickly dispelled. This young woman was quite evidently pulling his leg by seeming so innocent. So she indulged in a little blackmail too. Things were getting better and better.

"Do you blackmail Mr. Ritter often?"

Molly blushed purple with indignation. "I never blackmailed him!" she said vehemently. "What do you take me for?"

"Nothing bad."

"I wanted the money for Candy." Now there were tears in her eyes. "We weren't speaking to each other any more, and Candy was so horrid to me after the accident, but I did feel sorry for her. Such a stupid girl! What was she going to do? We didn't have any money."

"But you earn quite a bit, Miss Fleet. If you felt so strongly for your friend that you were ready to blackmail strange men for her sake, why didn't you contribute something yourself?"

"I have to save. I'm all alone in the world. Besides..." Molly hesitated.

"What were you going to say?"

"Mr. Ritter is not a stranger. I know him very well."

"You like him?"

"That's *my* business." Again Molly blushed.

"Not any more, Miss Fleet. I am interested in Mr. Ritter. I am interested in everybody who ever came to this house. So— do you like this man?"

"Not at all!" Molly said harshly. "Once I thought he was wonderful, but he is sly and disloyal, and only sees things superficially."

"Most men do. Is that all you have to say against your Ritter?"

"He is *not* my Ritter! He was Candy's man. He had plenty of fun with the poor thing. I felt he should help her now. I told him not to be such a pig!"

"Are you always so polite when you want something from a man? Did Mr. Ritter give you the money?"

"He did not!" Miss Fleet said scornfully. "He just led us by the nose!"

"Who do you mean by 'us?'"

"Candy and me. Once he took me for an outing in his car, and then it was all over. And he had promised . . ." Now Molly was sobbing.

"Why didn't he give you the money? Doesn't he have any?"

"He's stinking rich!" Miss Fleet's outburst left nothing to the imagination. "But he said he had enough of being black-mailed, and there was the door!"

"Enough of being blackmailed? Had Mrs. Doody asked him for money?"

"She doesn't know his address. He's no dope!"

"How do you happen to know his address?"

"I massaged his wife for a while, and saw his picture in her room. The bastard looked so elegant!"

"Is that so?" said Cox. In spite of her abusive language, Miss Fleet quite obviously was infatuated with this mysterious Mr. Ritter. But he wouldn't be mysterious much longer.

"Then what blackmailing was Mr. Ritter referring to?"

"Candy's. All the time after the accident."

"Did she have his address?" Cox had heard from all sides that Ritter was constantly on the road, and nobody knew where he lived.

"I gave Candy his address after the accident. The letters she wrote to his cover address kept coming back."

"So you betrayed Mr. Ritter to the Doodys. Do you think that was a very noble thing to do, Miss Fleet?"

"I meant well. The dog could have done something for us, once," Molly said stubbornly.

There was an uncomfortable pause. Then the inspector asked for Mr. Ritter's address.

Molly paled. She said she couldn't give the police his address because it would have dreadful consequences.

"Now don't get brazen!" Cox thundered suddenly. He jumped up and stared piercingly at the petrified girl. Then he said with frightening calm, "The case is fairly clear, Miss Fleet. You planned the murder together with Mr. Ritter, and you crept into this house yesterday afternoon. You are completely under the influence of this man. You should be ashamed of yourself, a girl from a respectable family!"

Molly stared at Cox, so flabbergasted that he began to wonder if his theory was right. "I didn't do it!" she sobbed, and wiped her tears away like a child. "I am not . . . under the influence of this man. I *have* no man."

"And I am supposed to believe that?"

The young girl looked at him in despair from behind the curtain of her hair. Cox understood. She had a complex about her birthmark. But that didn't concern him now. All cats were gray in the dark.

"Ritter is *not* a murderer!" The words burst from Molly Fleet.

"Do you want to teach me my business? How do you know that?"

"He was at home at the time of the murder, and I was with him."

"How long?"

"I don't know. Until he said, 'There's the door!'"

Molly found the inspector's silence more frightening than his questioning. "May I go now?" she asked shyly.

"I'm afraid you must give me a few more minutes of your time. Now listen to me carefully, Miss Fleet. If you lie to me *now*, it will cost you your head! *Where does Mr. Ritter live?*"

Molly was so horrified that all the color drained from her face. Only her left cheek burned a fiery red. "No . . ." she whispered.

"His address!"

Molly looked at Cox like a trapped animal, but her mind began to work feverishly. She could not saddle herself with a murder rap for Rigby's sake. He had to understand that. "Albert Ritter is not his real name."

"So who is he? This man here?"

Inspector Cox held out Bolter's sketch. It was his trump card. Rigby was so clearly recognizable on the sketch that Molly felt dizzy. She grasped her head with her slim, strong hands.

"Headache?" asked the inspector. "That's what I'd have in your place. That is he, isn't it?"

Molly nodded, stupefied. The police in the house were more terrible than in a film. They knew everything and then some . . .

"*Who is this man?*" asked Cox.

"You know who he is."

"I want to hear it from you!"

"Alexander Rigby from Vaucluse," Miss Fleet said tonelessly.

This time Cox knew that Molly Fleet wasn't lying. Of course! The long narrow nose with its arrogant hook, the cool, scornful expression—that was Alexander Rigby as he and his sister Shirley had seen him on his fiftieth birthday in Manly. How could he have missed it?

He pushed a few loose papers across the table and told the young girl, "Sign your statement, please. But first read everything through carefully. It's in your interest, Miss Fleet."

Molly began to read, Cox watching her all the time. "I made one mistake," she murmured, sounding thoroughly intimidated.

"In what connection?"

"I didn't go to see Mr. Ritter until eight o'clock. He didn't have time before that."

"What did you do after you massaged Miss Rigby?"

"I . . . I ate dinner in a restaurant."

"Where?"

Molly mentioned a place in Pitt Street and Sergeant Cox entered it on the report. Cox asked what Molly had done after eating.

"I told you. I went to see Mr. Rigby at eight o'clock. Then I went back to my hotel and cried."

"Why?"

"I just cried," said Miss Fleet. "Because it's all so terrible."

"You're young. If you've been telling the truth, and I'll soon find out if you have, you have your whole life ahead of you."

"It's always the same."

"Nonsense! Come along, Miss Fleet."

"Where to?" Molly asked, startled.

"Come on, come on! Get a bloody move on!"

He grabbed Molly by the shoulders and shoved her through the door. As they drove through King's Cross in his police car, it seemed to Molly as if all the kookaburras were laughing at her . . .

29

The First Mrs. Rigby

Inspector Cox took Molly Fleet to the restaurant and the Variety movie house for identification purposes, and had inquiries made as to whether the girl had visited Miss Rigby at the time stated. Molly seemed to have a perfect alibi. What Inspector Cox had to do now was find out what Alexander Rigby had been doing on the day of the murder between five and seven. And the inspector would try to cast more light on the relationship between Molly Fleet and the architect. The whole thing gave him a funny feeling. Had the two hired a third person to commit the crime? In spite of her reticence on the subject, there was no doubt in the inspector's mind that Miss Fleet hated Candy.

Rigby's jewel ushered him onto the terrace. One might as well have a beautiful view if one was to be molested by the police. Mrs. Andrews had said farewell to her family a few days before, and returned to Vaucluse. She had come to the conclusion that she would rather be vexed by Rigby than by her son-in-law. With Rigby she at least knew where she was at. Naturally he hadn't asked her why she had come crawling back, and in this case the indifference of the Aussies was a boon. Rigby sent the housekeeper Mrs. Andrews had "trained" to Elizabeth West Grierson in Brisbane. That lady could write novels, but as a cook her husband found her too inexperienced.

Rigby had not rolled out the red carpet for Mrs. Andrews's return, but he usually ate at home, and that came perilously close to a declaration of love. Moreover, the second Mrs. Rigby was apparently gone for good. No more letters from London. On one occasion, when Mrs. Andrews mentioned it, Rigby slammed the door in her face, polite as ever. But he seemed pleased that she had come back because he slammed doors a little more gently. And yesterday he had put a box of chocolates in her room. That was after she had cooked chicken in wine. The way to Rigby's heart had always been through his stomach. She was evidently the only woman who had ever grasped this simple truth. She wondered if the first Mrs. Rigby had cooked, but Mrs. Andrews was careful never to ask the boss any questions about his wives.

Inspector Cox was told that Mr. Rigby would not be coming home today. It was his intention to spend the weekend in Manly, and he would proceed straight there from the office. "We are not murderers," Mrs. Andrews declared.

She reacted to every question as if it were a personal insult. She sat in her big chair on the terrace and drank coffee. She did offer her archenemy a cup; she knew how to behave. "There's no poison in it today," she said, and was surprised when Cox laughed. He was wondering if Mrs. Andrews would be the third Mrs. Rigby. She looked so pleased with herself.

"Were you employed in this house while the second Mrs. Rigby was living here?"

Mrs. Andrews laughed long and dramatically. "I came to this house quite a bit earlier than the second Mrs. Rigby," she said with poorly disguised scorn. "One might say that the second Mrs. Rigby was a transient, passing through Sydney. I became Mr. Rigby's housekeeper just after he lost his first wife under very tragic circumstances."

"Was that a long time ago?"

The inspector knew exactly when it had happened, but he had the feeling that Mrs. Andrews knew a lot that hadn't been entered in the files.

"Poor Mr. Rigby was thirty-five years old at the time and inconsolable, naturally."

"Naturally," said Inspector Cox.

"I did my best to distract him."

"Did you succeed, Mrs. Andrews?"

"Sometimes I made him laugh, and that was something, considering how unhappy he was. Of course he inherited an enormous fortune, and that *can* be a comfort. Unfortunately I wasn't in very good spirits myself, since I had had to leave my beautiful homeland, penniless, and had only been in Sydney a short time."

"Did you come from Poland or from Greece?"

"From *Hungary*!" Mrs. Andrews said sternly. "Budapest. One of the great cultural centers of the world. Perhaps you have heard about it?"

"Plenty!" Cox said drily. "Today you can stretch culture like a rubber band. Why did you leave Hungary?"

"For political reasons. And what do you know about that over here?"

"We hear enough from our new Australians. You're not exactly reticent."

"I have lived in Sydney for fifteen years and remained a stranger," Mrs. Andrews said grimly, and poured her third cup of coffee. "I came to this young country as a pilgrim. I wanted to kiss the very earth. I wanted to worship, Inspector. But I soon gave up."

"Why do you suppose that was, Mrs. Andrews?" Cox was amused.

"It was not my fault. I soon noticed that the primitive materialism that rules this country was murdering my soul."

"I wouldn't come to a murderous conclusion so fast." The inspector was smiling. "Your coffee is first-rate, Mrs. Andrews."

Rigby's jewel relaxed and offered the inspector a second cup. "What do you want from Mr. Rigby?" she asked suspiciously.

"Some routine questions. I've just come from his sister."

This bit of information seemed to calm Mrs. Andrews. "Miss Rigby is a real lady," she said. "But she can give you a hard time. Too little heart. She was here for dinner yesterday and she spoke about the tragic murder so icily. *I* didn't close my eyes for two nights!"

"Were you a friend of Miss Blyth's?"

"*I*? A friend of *hers*? You must be joking, sir! I don't associate with whores. I am accustomed to quite different social contacts at home."

"So why couldn't you sleep?"

"Because of Alex—I mean, Mr. Rigby." Mrs. Andrews coughed. "The news upset him terribly."

"How did he find out?"

"From the paper. Like all of us. We don't have any courier service between Vaucluse and the boardinghouse in Darlinghurst, if that's what you mean."

"I don't mean anything, Mrs. Andrews. I'm just asking if you can give me any useful information about Miss Blyth."

"Mr. Rigby knew her," Mrs. Andrews said, mollified. "Not that I spy on him, but I had the opportunity of seeing my boss with her in Bondi. I swim there occasionally. The beach is for everybody, no?"

"This is a free country. I swim there too, when I have the time."

"Molly Fleet does too," Mrs. Andrews said thoughtfully. "She sometimes massaged the second Mrs. Rigby. What nerve that girl has! Just imagine—she came here to see Mr. Rigby on the day of the murder. I wasn't listening, but I happened to overhear their conversation as I was about to serve some refreshments. Mr. Rigby was so enraged that I stopped with the drinks in front of the door, I was trembling so."

"It isn't easy to work for a choleric man." The inspector sounded sympathetic.

"He wouldn't behave like that with *me*. But I must say, I read his every wish."

"That is remarkable. But Miss Fleet apparently doesn't know how to handle Mr. Rigby."

"He threw her out! He yelled something about not letting himself be bled white, and that he'd wring anybody's neck who tried it again. He didn't mean it literally, Inspector."

"Let's hope not, for his sake." The inspector laughed, and even Mrs. Andrews managed a bitter-sweet smile.

"I watch over Mr. Rigby, Inspector. Barking dogs don't bite. But right now he's so nervous that I speak to him as little as possible."

"Is he working very hard?"

"Yes. That on top of everything else. Since this murder he had been beside himself. Unfortunately when Mr. Rigby is upset it is very hard on those around him. He raves! When the first Mrs. Rigby came to such a tragic end, they say he actually flogged himself."

"You're joking, Mrs. Andrews!"

"I'm not. All Sydney knows it. It only goes to show that the first Mrs. Rigby was just as unable to get along with him as the second one."

"I thought you didn't know the first Mrs. Rigby?"

"I knew her like my own pocket. All Sydney said at the time that my boss pushed her over the cliff. She was always overdressed and drunk. He couldn't get a housekeeper after that, although the police couldn't pin anything on him. Of course he would never have done such a thing!"

"Did Mr. Rigby tell you all this himself?"

"Of course not! The subject is taboo in this house. Miss Rigby prepared me for the gossip before I took on the job. The first Mrs. Rigby must have driven him crazy. Miss West, the writer, said so once."

"To you?"

"To Miss Rigby, of course. The ladies were waiting here for Alex—I mean, Mr. Rigby, and I was serving tea. I heard excited voices, so I waited discreetly until Miss West had calmed down. Authors are always ridiculously excited. Of course Miss West was madly in love with my boss, but it didn't get her anywhere."

"You have such interesting things to tell, Mrs. Andrews. I could listen to you for hours, but I'm taking up too much of your time."

"I am hungry for conversation, Inspector! Right now Mr. Rigby is a regular Trappist. Do help yourself to the apple strudel."

"Did you bake it?... It's wonderful!"

"A recipe from home. Forgive me if I say that we new Aussies understand a little more about the art of cooking than you natives. Steak—morning, noon, and night. No true culinary culture! But the beer in Sydney is really good."

"It doesn't have to be baked," said Cox. "I would be very grateful for the recipe for that apple strudel when I come the next time. I'll try to explain to my mother how it should taste."

"I'm honored, Inspector! It would make me very happy. If I may say so, you aren't like a policeman at all!"

"Policemen like to eat well too. So don't forget, next time..."

Mrs. Andrews beamed. But then it occurred to her that the inspector, albeit most pleasantly, had announced a second visit. She said Mr. Rigby couldn't tell the inspector anything more than she had already told him. Frankly, Cox was afraid that Rigby would have much less to say. He calmed Mrs. Andrews, assuring her it would be an absolutely routine visit. He simply had to question everyone who had known Miss Blyth.

"But I have strict instructions not to let anyone see Mr. Rigby," said Mrs. Andrews. "As I just tried to explain... it's his nerves. Unfortunately he's a pretty wild fellow by nature, and when he speaks softly, he's dangerous. The second Mrs. Rigby used to tremble before him. On the other hand, Mr. Rigby can be a darling, as trusting as a little boy. Especially when he has enjoyed his food."

Cox digested this bit of information. He offered Mrs. Andrews a cigarette. "Things can't have been easy for you after the death of the first Mrs. Rigby."

"I didn't come to Sydney to lead an easy life, Inspector. By coming to this innocent continent I saved myself and my daughter. Believe me, from the very first day I had the patience of a saint where Mr. Rigby was concerned, although he hurt my feelings daily. I told myself he didn't know any better."

"But he makes a highly intelligent impression. Or am I wrong?"

"Too intelligent sometimes, Inspector. There are times when I find him downright eerie!"

"Why?"

"He can hear the grass growing. But the murder in Darlinghurst he did *not* anticipate. Nor could he sense the fact that the first Mrs. Rigby was going to fall over the cliff. The poor old thing was nearsighted, but she wouldn't wear glasses, out of pure vanity, because she wanted to look young."

"Who told you that?"

"Miss Rigby. It was a terribly tragedy. When his wife fell into the abyss, Mr. Rigby was just unpacking the picnic basket."

"So I suppose that was the end of the picnic."

"Oh, *he* can always eat!" Mrs. Andrews said good-naturedly. She must have been nurturing a morbid jealousy of the first Mrs. Rigby throughout all these years, thought Cox. "If I were to be quite frank with you, Inspector . . . but no. No. I've already said too much."

"Not at all," said Inspector Cox cheerily, and he meant it. "As I just said, I could listen to you for hours. I have seldom come across such perspicacity combined with tact. So—what were you going to say?"

"Well . . . that it was a blessing for Mr. Rigby that the old woman bowed out. Life with her must have been hell."

"Did Miss Rigby tell you that too?"

"Not she! She's too much of a hypocrite to speak that frankly. Quite by chance I found a letter from Mr. Rigby's first wife in his desk. The stupid woman was threatening to sue him for assault!"

"How could Mr. Rigby leave a letter like that lying around?"

"He leaves everything lying around! In this respect he's a real Aussie. I'm sorry, Inspector! At home we hid threatening letters like that in a metal box and wore the key around our necks."

"A very good safety measure."

"That was before the communist regime. After that no one wrote letters any more."

"Did the first Mrs. Rigby write anything else?"

"She wrote that she had no intention of letting him wring her neck. Have you ever heard anything like that?"

"No."

"And she wasn't going to throw her money at him anymore, either!"

"Did she have money to throw?"

"Did she ever! She was the widow of a very wealthy sheep farmer in New South Wales. If I may draw a comparison with antiquity—I studied literature and philosophy in Paris—the first Mrs. Rigby owned the Golden Fleece!"

"Nice for Mr. Rigby."

"Later, Inspector. Later. Alex—I mean, Mr. Rigby at once offered me a generous salary. After the death of the first Mrs. Rigby he could afford to. The second Mrs. Rigby owned no more than the dress she had on!"

"Did the second Mrs. Rigby want a lot of money too?"

"That woman?" Mrs. Andrews said scornfully. "That sleepy-head was even too lazy to spend money! We're happy to be rid of her at last, after seven years."

"I can imagine that."

"To be honest, I have never seen such blackmail letters as Miss Candy wrote after her accident."

"Did Mr. Rigby let you read the letters?"

"I found them on the floor, all crumpled up and torn. I mean the first letters. Suddenly, two weeks before the murder, Mr. Rigby locked them up. I don't know why."

"We can ask him," the inspector suggested.

"Not I! I don't want him to wring my neck. Figuratively speaking, of course."

"Of course, Mrs. Andrews."

"I did happen to read the last letter before the murder. Quite by chance. Believe me, I only did so because I was so terribly worried about Alex . . . I mean, Mr. Rigby. He left the letter lying on the breakfast table because he was called to the phone. I was just bringing in his ham and eggs and there . . ."

"Very understandable, Mrs. Andrews. You were worried. . . ."

"My blood turned to ice in my veins. How much longer was my boss going to be blackmailed like this? The young woman— I mean Candy—couldn't make any more money. . . ."

"But why did Mr. Rigby pay up? It's not exactly like him, is it?"

"Not exactly," said Mrs. Andrews hesitantly. "Listen to me, Inspector. My Mr. Rigby wouldn't have given that little gold digger another penny if she hadn't threatened that she . . ." Mrs. Andrews looked out into the garden and stopped, petrified. "Excuse me, Inspector. I have to go to my kitchen."

"But I thought Mr. Rigby had gone to Manly!"

"Here he comes!" Mrs. Andrews stood poised for flight. "He is *so* unpredictable. He's just putting the car in the garage."

Inspector Cox had already noticed Rigby's arrival out of the corner of his eyes. What had Candy Blyth threatened? And what lay behind that threat?

"If you want to see a picture of the first Mrs. Rigby, Inspector, I put the painting of her in the flowered hat in our spare room, beside the bureau of the second Mrs. Rigby." After which words, she disappeared.

Rigby took the terrace steps three at a time. He looked at Cox, his eyes narrowed. "Good evening, Inspector. I was expecting you. What would you like to know?"

30

Rigby's Monologue

When I saw Inspector Cox sitting on the terrace with Andrews, I knew at once what game he was playing. The fellow's a regular fox! Andrews was red as a beet and took herself to the kitchen on the double. The cop stayed for supper, naturally. That's one of our customs when we have agreeable visitors.

"I just want to ask some routine questions, Mr. Rigby."

I'm sure that's all you want to do, I thought. Funny, but my various wives always reproached me for a lack of tact, when actually I am plentifully endowed with it. For instance, I sensed for years that the thing with Flora would come to a bad end. She just giggled too much. I also could feel how Anne and I were slowly slipping into a fallow season: she became more silent all the time. And I felt—godammit—that Andrews, with the best intentions, had just dug my grave; why else would Cox be grinning at me with such satisfaction? The only sure thing in life is that one day we're going to lose it. While Cox asked me his routine questions, smiling amiably, I knew that I was being grilled alive. But I'm tough, and decided not to make it easy for him. He has a nice curly head of hair and I am sure he is a model son and brother. Yes, there sat Cox, smiling apologetically because he had to bother me with this nuisance of a murder case. He merely wanted to find out if I'd wrung Candy's neck or only provided the nylon stocking! Idiot that I am, I gave her a dozen pairs after the accident. Of course I admitted it at once. I even added that girls can never have enough stockings.

"But it was one stocking too many," Cox replied, and I

didn't contradict him. Still, I hadn't given Miss Blyth the stockings to strangle her, and I made that point quite clear. Cox was waiting for my confession and I was waiting for my steak.

The inspector gradually turned the conversation to the time of the murder, and "for routine reasons," asked where I had spent the hours between five and seven. I had gone for a walk. That's always the worst possible alibi, but that was his problem.

Had anyone seen me on my walk? Yes—at least three hundred drivers. Not all at once, naturally! Cox reddened, either with pleasure over my innocence or fury over my sass. Who can tell? I used to wander through Sydney regularly with Marchmont, frequently between five and seven. We saw the city as it had been and as it was going to be. I saw skyscrapers in the sky and Stan explained the Victorians to me. In short, I went for a walk this time too.

French had accompanied me for a while, but I didn't want to drag Robbie into this interview with the inspector, and get him into trouble with the police just as innocently as Andrews had managed to. The young man is shaping up splendidly, and is thoroughly decent. Interested in nothing but sports and architecture. So . . . I said I had gone out by my soul-searching self, and shall inform French to this effect tomorrow.

"What did Miss Fleet want from you?"

Cox had already questioned Molly Fleet. I had that from Grace. Grace doesn't like the whole business. She keeps thinking of the scandal over Flora. Who can blame her? Over the cheese I became aware of the fact that Andrews must have told some wild tales about my first wife. I had to admire the way Cox led the conversation to the subject of kookaburras, and tried to get out of me what role I had played in Flora's death in the Blue Mountains. This was where my appetite came in again. I can't deny that I ate three-quarters of the contents of the picnic basket at the scene of the disaster. The shock hit me in the stomach. Already at the time the police had seen my appetite as a symptom of hard-boiled criminality, whereas I couldn't see what cold pork could possibly have to do with murder! And now I noticed that Inspector Cox would also have found it more sympathetic if the picnic basket had arrived at headquarters untouched. Naturally Cox had already been through all the files on *that* case. I was certain that he had not enjoyed reading that even the chief of police hadn't been able to pin anything on me. To this day I am sure that it was my sister who scared the living daylights out of them.

Cox asked if I had visited Candy frequently after the accident. To his disappointment, I had to say no. I had had enough of that sheila's sparkling conversation long ago. I had felt sorry for her, but it wasn't my fault that she'd run into a car. One thing though I couldn't know was that after the accident, this little gold digger from Kalgoorlie intended to live off me for the rest of her life. Of course the inspector had harried Molly Fleet until she had admitted her visit to me. Ethical motives had prompted Molly to mobilize the blackmail effort. She had suddenly and unexpectedly developed such compassion for Candy that she had given the girl my address. Noble as I am, I might have gone on paying for a while if Candy hadn't behaved so shamelessly. I don't let dolls like that touch upon my marriage.

I showed Inspector Cox the last letter. I prefer to put my cards on the table as long as it doesn't cost me my neck. Cox read it with rather flattering interest and remarked that under these circumstances, Candy's death must have been very convenient. I wasn't dumb enough to deny it. Then Inspector Cox thanked me for a delightful evening, and left.

I watched him go and didn't feel good about it. Andrews removed the dishes without saying a word. I asked her what she had told the inspector, and she said, "Nothing." Just what I thought. The people who mean as well by me as Mary Andrews are of necessity my ruination.

"I hope the inspector doesn't come back," she said.

"If we didn't have that to hope for, I'd be a goner," I told her. "Don't rattle the dishes so, Mary. I have a splitting headache."

Later she came over to the couch I was lying on and sobbed.

She said that she had committed the murder so that the black-mailing bitch would finally leave me in peace. I asked her where she'd got hold of this information, although I knew she'd been going through my correspondence for years. Then I told the poor thing to go to bed.

The fallow season began for me after the death of my first wife, with a vast emptiness. Socially they had buried me. Only Marchmont, John Darling, and of course Paddy Trent had stuck to me although they must have had their own doubts about my innocence.

This time things are different. The *saison morte* comes at a wildly busy time. We are planning extensive projects at the office and the inspector and I are going steady in Vaucluse. He usually arrives before me. Instinct or coincidence? Cox is a most genial, patient man and I'm sure it often pays off. And he argues elegantly, I have to grant him that. A new generation I suppose, with a new technique. They are big on psychology and don't stumble around like our grandfathers. But psychiatric tact is lost on me, and Cox is much too cunning not to become gradually more pointed. I don't have much patience, but I've got to be patient this time or he'll nab me. I imagine Andrews had told him that I can be very unpleasant, and reports of my beating up Flora are in the file. Cox will soon know the story of my past by heart. Now he only asks questions in an effort to somehow, sometime, trip me up. I have to be damned careful not to lose track of my surroundings and let Cox catch me in his web.

Grace has written to Robert Muir. I wish he'd invite me to Japan now. But Cox would justifiably see my departure as a flight attempt. His reply to any request of this kind would be to remain at his disposal until the murder is solved. I hate superfluous questions just as I hate questions that are asked just to lure me out of my lair. Flora used to drive me crazy like that. She would constantly ask me if I still loved her, when she knew all the time that I'd never gone that far astray. At the beginning, giggling behind the bar in Pitt Street, she had been very sympathetic. I called her "Kookaburra," and the name stuck.

During these last days I get the feeling that somebody is trying to throttle me from behind with a nylon stocking. I may not be as emotional or sensitive as some of the ladies I know, but I don't have to ask Cox whether I am now seriously a suspect. Like everyone else in Sydney, I read the papers, and what they print daily is as repugnant to me as it must be to the inspector. The voice of the scandal sheets gets louder and louder: Are the police asleep? How much longer are the honest citizens of Sydney to be exposed without protection to the "nylon murderer"? And is a certain inspector, known as the sharpest bloodhound between hell and New South Wales, now herding sheep in the meadows? I can imagine how delighted Cox and his chief must be when they read these daily questions. I can hear the chief mumbling, "Get a bloody move on, Cox!"

Cox simply has to come up with an arrest soon, if only for the sake of his reputation. I told him everything I know. It may not be much, but everything depends on how you approach the material. To be blackmailed for life is not a pleasant prospect, and the inspector had read black on white that this was just what Miss Blyth intended to do. Why hadn't I torn up the letter? he asked, almost compassionately. I told him I hadn't come down with the last shower. When Miss Blyth suddenly and unexpectedly departed this life, it had been my intention to sue her. After that Cox didn't appear for days. By then he had recovered from the blow, and the day before yesterday he had everything he needed.

A Mrs. Evans, who delivers Mrs. Doody's groceries, had reported something, not for the express purpose of breaking my neck, but because all the women in Darlinghurst, and all the kookaburras in King's Cross, were in a state of panic thanks to the nonsense printed in the papers. They feared the unknown murderer. Mrs. Evans had rummaged around in her memory. At the time of the murder she had seen "a very tall man" enter Mrs. Doody's boardinghouse. She had just delivered flour, sugar, and tea, and had brought something extra for Candy to enjoy. The door to the boardinghouse was always ajar so that the neighbors could look in on the girl when nobody else was there. That was on the day of the murder. Mrs. Evans had found only Candy at home. When she was back in her shop, she happened to look out the door and saw this "very tall man" coming out of the boarding house. Cox must have shown her my picture and the dumb creature had nodded.

The stupid thing is that I actually was at the boardinghouse on the afternoon of the murder, since in that morning's mail I had received Candy's most despicable letter. I spent a few minutes with her, long enough to tell her off and to warn her that I would sue if she didn't stop. Whether the inspector wants to believe it or not, at 5:05 Candy was still very much alive. She hurled abuses at me, and I wondered where the little angel-face could have picked up such obscene language. Flora's insults were bouquets in comparison.

After my visit to Candy, I was so furious that I went back to the office and tried to calm myself with work. Robbie French was still there, and that's when we went for a walk together. He noticed that I was enraged about something, and after a while let me go on alone. I had told Molly Fleet to come and see me after supper because she insisted she had to speak to me.

Since I had not done Miss Blyth in, I didn't see why I should attract more suspicion by admitting that I had been at the boardinghouse that afternoon. My common sense told me that Cox would never have let that sort of an incident pass. How could he? I wouldn't have believed it myself. Nobody in the world believes coincidences like that. That's why mystery writers have such a hard time with the reviewers. Yet things like that happen more frequently than we realize, and break a lot of people's necks.

And how had Candy known my wife's London address? Molly told me without batting an eyelash. In her natural friendliness, Anne had sent Molly Fleet a card from London. Candy had seen the address while Molly was out working. It would therefore have been quite simple for Candy to inform my wife that I was still fooling around with little girls. And I'd only been out once with the little bitch after her return from Broome. But Anne would never have believed it. In short—I felt that I had gradually shelled out enough for that bit of fun. But Mrs. Evans remembered . . . damn her!

Inspector Cox appeared secretly, silently, and softly as I—assisted by Robbie French—was instructing our second generation of would-be architects in Vaucluse, in the art of modern architecture. We had just tacked a plan on the wall when Cox appeared with Sergeant Cunningham. I saw at once that Cox had found out everything, and was perfectly calm. We can only live one life and die only one death. I don't know who strangled the girl, but I know whoever it is is going to laugh himself silly.

Cox proceeded according to regulations. He called me out of the room and told me he had a warrant for my arrest, and that I was accused of murdering Miss Blyth. He said, "I must warn you that anything you may say from now on will be put on record and can be used as proof against you."

I asked the young man to be less formal, and with as much respect as he had coming to him, told him he had come to the wrong address. But the inspector was there officially, and this time there was no cozy supper on the terrace. Fortunately it was Andrews's day off, so I was spared a Hungarian rhapsody.

"Get a bloody move on, Inspector!" I said amiably. "Unfortunately I don't have much time this evening. We're working in here with our young ones."

In the meantime French had appeared and was staring at the two cops, speechless. "Go on working, Robbie," I told him. "You're going to laugh but I'm being accused of murder."

French turned pale. Now he'll have to find the partner I've been painting on the office wall since Marchmont's death. Good thing our senior partner is sleeping where no one can wake him.

Meanwhile Robbie had found his voice again and was asking the inspector if he had gone mad.

"I would advise you to express yourself more cautiously, young man," said Inspector Cox.

"Alex!" Robbie yelled. *"Say something!"*

"Draw up plans for a new jail," I told him. "The one we have now has no style, and oh yes, one more thing, Robbie. Call Jimmy."

James Battleship was my lawyer. Robbie nodded. His eyes were rounder than ever with astonishment. I patted him on the shoulder. "Do a good job, partner."

Robbie's face trembled and he looked away. "Let's go," said Cox, at just the right moment.

I've been locked up now for four days, and it seems like four years. I'm tough by nature, but right now I can't see how I'm possibly going to stick this out for a lifetime. I'm trained to be free. Even marriage seemed a robbery of freedom.

My lawyer is persuasive. He really knows his business. He got me out of the mess that time with Flora; he didn't waste any time today either. First he brought regards from Grace and Robert Muir, who is keeping Grace company right now. Good for Grace!

Jimmy said, "You have a lot of things going for you. The girl tried to commit suicide once. And she certainly was blackmailing you. Thank God you saved the letters. I've told Howard everything."

Howard Clifford is Sydney's top defense counsel, and always works with Jimmy. The fact that Jimmy was already mentioning Clifford now, at the beginning, didn't sound promising. But Jimmy said at once that we'd swing it. No doubt about that. Naturally he would like to know...

"I didn't do it, Jimmy. I just tried to bring the stupid girl to her senses on the wrong day. And that's my funeral, mate. Who's going to believe me?"

"I am," said Jimmy Battleship.

"Good of you."

My headache was coming back. There wasn't a trace of the murderer, and Jimmy found this a handicap too. Both of u knew that Cox was a decent human being and had to be totally convinced of my guilt or he wouldn't have arrested me. Everything spoke against me, just as in the first scandal. But the thing with Flora had been much more complicated. I had not been as innocent as I was this time. It's quite possible that old guilt feelings can take one by the throat. Anything is possible in this lousy world. I thought of some cases where people had sat under lock and key for years before the murderer, shocked out of his complacency for God-knows-what reasons, confessed his guilt. But until then...

Jimmy got up. "Cox is still searching."

"Glad to hear that." I sounded hoarse.

"Chin up, Alex!"

"Tell Grace she's not to write to my wife about any of this nonsense. Anne hates scandal. How is Grace taking it?"

"Very well, to all appearances. Robert Muir is a great help."

Jimmy had to go. He could simply walk out into freedom. I had never given a thought to what a great thing that was. I mean, you open the door, nobody stops you ... Jimmy waved, as if we were at Central Station, but my train was on a dead-end track. My old cobber looked tired.

"Don't take it to heart," I said. "I'm not worth it."

"Rubbish!" said Jimmy.

I asked him what he was going to do over the weekend. I wanted things to go on as normally as possible. Jimmy was going out to Manly, to see Grace.

"Why don't you go dancing?"

Jimmy said I should let him do what he wanted with his weekend. Then he told me that Bertie Dobson had been to see Grace and prescribed sleeping pills.

"Is she taking them?"

"You know your sister."

I could see Grace tossing the sleeping pills into the Pacific. Too bad. It wouldn't do her any harm to have a good sleep before the big show in court. I hoped that my case would not be tried too soon. It would be better if all of them had a chance to forget me a little, so that I would be little more than a vague abstraction. With negative signs, naturally. Would they take down the plaque on our house in Parramatta? The one they'd put up for my fiftieth birthday? It only went to show how embarrassingly premature honors can be. On my fiftieth birthday everybody thought I'd march into eternity crowned with laurels. Perhaps I was the only one who knew at the time that I'd only be playing for a few more seasons. I asked Jimmy how Andrews was taking it.

"She's very silent these days. Too silent. Robbie French looks in on her sometimes after office hours. So do Grace and Bertie Dobson." And John Darling had flown back to Sydney from a research trip. Together with Muir, they had descended upon Cox. John is busily married now and spends his free time working for the benefit of our primitive Australians, but he's always there when you need him.

"Any other guests at the Rigbys'?"

"Paddy Trent, of course. He arrived from Brisbane yesterday. He's in Betty West's room."

It was all properly set up as for a funeral, but my cobbers were first-rate. As private detectives, however, they'd hardly manage to compete with Inspector Cox. A dead race.

"Be careful what you say at the hearing," Jimmy warned. "It's your turn in three days."

"I'll tell them where to get off, you can depend on that!"

"And that's just what you're not going to do," said Jimmy, in his stiffest manner. "Whatever you keep to yourself can't be held against you, my boy."

I asked him if I should fall on my knees and thank them for pinning a murder rap on me. I could feel the blood rush to my head. My heart was pounding, and there was the taste of ashes in my mouth.

"I'm telling you one thing, Jimmy—nothing in the world can stop me from..." I was trying to swallow.

"Take it easy, Alex, I'll think up something. And don't forget our Clifford. He's not exactly a beginner."

I was holding my head in my hands. Jimmy asked if I wanted something to drink. I said there was time for that after the verdict. Then I apologized, and he mumbled that it was okay. After that I asked him to leave me alone. He cleaned his owlish glasses and injected one of his famous, carefully measured pauses, which gave his clients a chance to calm down. Finally he said that I must not give up now. It would all be cleared up in the end.

"I hope I live to see it," I said. "Hmm . . . thanks a lot for everything."

Jimmy didn't like to hear anything like that, so I hastily asked him to pass on my best regards to the mob. "You're unlucky with your friends, Jimmy. But this is the last time you'll have to worry about me. I can imagine how they're all slandering me again."

"All Sydney is in an uproar, Alex. The Architects Club is going to get in touch with someone in the upper echelons tomorrow."

"Murder is murder, Jimmy. You should know that. I suppose the yacht-club flag is flying at half mast."

"I'll come again soon." Jimmy nodded encouragingly, and was gone.

Perhaps it wouldn't be such a bad idea to try prayer. But I'm so out of practice that whatever I have to offer is not going to impress anyone in heaven.

I don't know when I first wished Flora dead. A death wish develops slowly, like a cancer. Then suddenly death is unavoidable and there is no cure any more. The desire to be free gnaws, eats you up, and you become morally emaciated. As I lie here listening to the limping footsteps of justice, the past, with flowered hats and shrill laughter, rises up to meet me. I never knew whether Flora was laughing at me when she giggled like a kookaburra, but one day I knew, and began planning her death. Now she is avenged. Her shrill laughter fills my cell day and night. You can't take any pills for that.

I was thirty at the time; Flora was forty-five. Of course I married her for her money. I needed it. I wanted a brilliant career, and I was honest and stupid enough to tell Flora. She couldn't possibly think—or so I believed in my innocence— that a young man of thirty, healthy and virile, would love a shopworn bar girl with a double chin and red veins in her face. I don't know what goes on in the minds of these over-the-hill women, but Flora certainly overestimated her charms. She really believed in true love, right on up—or down, rather— to the grave. I don't know where she picked up this romantic nonsense. Before she married her rich sheep farmer and nursed him to his death, she was a jolly bar girl who knew her way around Sydney. Perhaps the romantic side of her arrived with menopause. She was in sexual purgatory when I turned up. She was, as I already mentioned, forty-five, a dangerous age. It cast a shadow on our marriage. My situation became increasingly precarious. Maybe I *am* a bastard. I probably am. But gradually it became too much for me when Flora told my friends she was keeping her money under lock and key because I was too extravagant.

In a very short time she had turned my house in Vaucluse, which I had built with her money, into a jolly men's bar. What could I do about it? I was a bad-tempered guest in my own house, and sat around with John Darling or Marchmont. Trent hadn't arrived in Sydney yet, and because I was bored I had a little affair with Celia Coleman, his future wife. Flora was idiotically jealous. When we met good old Paddy Trent at the Colemans for the first time, I decided to hand Celia over to him because she wasn't worth Flora's outbursts of jealousy. Paddy fell in love with Celia right away. I wouldn't have advised him to marry an old bat. The first time I met Trent at the Coleman house I found him extraordinary. Flora hated him. Once she told him never to come to the house again. I'm sure that had never happened to him before. But he had come to see Flora and advise her to be a little more cautious with me.

That was the time I used to beat her up when she was fresh, but one thing must be said for her—she could be pretty abusive herself. Once I came to the office with a black eye, and had to tell Stan Marchmont I'd run into an open door . . . not that Marchmont believed me. When he narrowed his eyes and said nothing, I knew he knew.

Once when Flora was left an invalid on the battlefield—she had hurled obscenities at me which no gentleman would repeat—she ran away. Grace brought her back. Grace behaved wonderfully, although she didn't approve of my behavior. Flora told her at the office that I had tried to strangle her that night. All I did was press a little harder than usual—that was all.

After she came back, things were better for a while. Then she boiled over again, and all Sydney was beginning to laugh at me. Since I wasn't sleeping with her any more—I'm much too normal to love and beat up the same person—Flora told my cobbers I couldn't get it up anymore. She didn't express herself in that civilized a fashion, and the mob at the yacht club must have laughed themselves sick when "Auntie" served them the details of her past and present from behind the bar in Vaucluse.

So that's the way we lived.

When strangers thought she was my mother, I was to blame. Once I took a kitchen towel and wiped the bright red rouge off her face and made a mess of her stiff curls. I resented the fact that she awoke sadistic instincts in me. It was a monstrous relationship. When I saw her motionless bird-eyes staring at me, when she wanted me to embrace her, the very idea made me shudder . . . I asked myself sometimes how she could imagine that even a bastard like me could function under such conditions.

I suggested a divorce. She could get the hell out of my life with her money, her profanity, and her varicose veins. All she did was laugh shrilly. Kookaburra! I was ashamed. Not only was she a dead weight, not only was she devouring my virility, but she was making the name of Rigby a joke in Sydney. She slept with anyone who had the stomach for it, and handed out gifts—gold cuff links or checks. Dr. Dobson gave her tranquilizers. She threw them away. One day I found on my place at the breakfast table some quack nostrum intended to restore male potency. She stared at me, hard and sly, and laughed. I laughed too, but I saw red. That was the morning I decided on the outing to the Blue Mountains. I only had to wait for the appropriate time.

* * *

One day I stopped up my ears with plugs because Flora was making so much noise. That night she came to my room. "Be good to Auntie, and good things will come your way," she gurgled. I threw her out, and she screamed that I'd regret it.

Jimmy Battleship had spoken to her several times and explained that I was willing to take all the blame, but Flora told him everything was all right. I was just overworked. She was older and felt responsible for me. Why on earth should we get a divorce? Flora suggested I should go live somewhere else if I wanted to. She was sure I'd soon come back to the fleshpots of Vaucluse. I went to see Jimmy again. "Try a little harder," was his advice. "Perhaps if you're friendly, things will get better."

"Perhaps," I said, not meaning it. Jimmy gave me a sharp look, but he didn't say anything.

That night I went to Flora. It was the shabbiest thing I've ever done in my life. But I had to make up with her or she wouldn't come to the Blue Mountains with me. She was horribly grateful, and I felt . . . Forget it, Alex!

"Now everything's going to be all right," she sobbed. For the first time in years I felt sorry for her. The old thing was starved for affection. I had embraced her, so I loved her. All that was needed was for her to take out her checkbook . . .

Things became worse. I could never repeat the performance; I could feel that in my bones. All I could do was ski out into the Pacific as far as I could and let the ocean wash over me. But I wanted to build, and Marchmont said I was getting better all the time.

She didn't let me work. She came between me and my vision with her aging doll's face, her unbridled temper, her insatiable need for a quarrel, a beating, a drink. I hardly ever spoke to her. She didn't seem to care. I slept with her, so nothing was wrong. A fat old lady in the hay. And I was a searcher for beauty, and a bastard.

We drove off, and Flora told dirty jokes. She was wearing high-heeled shoes, one of her flowered hats, and no glasses

She giggled, and I felt feeble. Godammit! I felt sorry for the old fool. But I had to keep my cool. In those five years she had finished me off, I mean as a man. I never looked at a girl any more. I was afraid. Once I'd spoken to old Dr. Dobson. I told him about a "friend," but Bertie's old man knew whom I was talking about. So there was something like psychic impotence! Damn, damn...In our office in George Street I locked myself in the john and wept. The last time I had wept was when Mother had died and Grace told me. I was still in short pants at the time. I wished Mother were still in Parramatta and not in heaven...

We had taken a picnic basket with us to the Blue Mountains, and wanted to have our lunch on the plateau facing the Three Sisters. How it happened, I don't know, but before I had finished unpacking the basket we were engaged in the most violent quarrel of the season. Flora shouted her usual obscenities and I reacted for a while with silence. Only when she screamed that I had come to her one night only to "milk" her financially afterwards, I walked up to her slowly. She must have seen something in my eyes—Flora was no fool—because she cried out. We were all alone. It was still too early for tourists. I came closer, slowly, slowly, and she shrank back, farther and farther, in her high-heeled shoes and deadly fear, and with her nearsightedness. She stepped back until she was standing at the edge of the cliff.

When I saw it, I stretched out my arm to pull her back. You can imagine pushing someone down into the abyss as much as you want, until the moment for such a gesture arrives. Then things look quite different.

Flora misunderstood my gesture. She had always misunderstood me. "Don't touch me, you pig! Help!" she screamed, and tripped backwards, over the edge.

It all happened in seconds. Words are lame, just like justice.

So here I am, a sitting duck because for five long years I murdered Flora Pratt in my mind. That is the truth, even if Inspector Cox won't accept it. It's a true black comedy. Perhaps Candy Blyth's murderer will one day also atone for a murder he didn't commit. I wonder if Cox will interrogate him...

31

A Good Crime

Inspector Cox was waiting for a telephone call that didn't come. In spite of his patience, he was nervous. Rigby's hearing was scheduled for the day after tomorrow. Cox was still brooding about the murder in Darlinghurst, although with Mrs. Evans's testimony Rigby's guilt seemed established. He had admitted everything except the murder.

Cox had done everything his experience and conscience demanded. The Evans witness had been confronted with six men, Rigby among them, and with the assurance of a sleepwalker, she had walked straight up to Rigby and declared this was the man who had entered the boardinghouse shortly after five. Rigby must have done it. All the other suspects had watertight alibis. The inspector had also carefully gone through the file on Flora Rigby (Accidental Death) once more because he was looking for character information, and had gained the impression that Rigby certainly was capable of a violent act if sufficiently provoked.

Why couldn't the inspector reconcile himself to the facts? Certainly not because Alexander Rigby was well-placed socially, with a whole collection of status symbols and a villa in Vaucluse. Where murderers were concerned, Cox was democratic. For him a blackfellow who hurled a boomerang was just as important as Alexander Rigby, who had done so much for Sydney and could afford the best lawyers. Naturally Charlie Rainbow, if they ever found him, would have a good lawyer allocated to him by the court, but Rigby, Battleship, and Clifford were a formidable trio. Not that this was worrying Cox. All he cared about was seeing justice done.

Rigby couldn't be freed on bail because he was accused of murder. Why did Inspector Cox stay in his office after hours, waiting for a phone call? He was looking for some material that would possibly provide some psychological proof of Rigby's guilt. Only once in his career had Cox felt like this after an arrest, and then too he had silently, secretly taken all possible measures to find the murderer. And in the end had found him. That had been years ago, and now...

He had asked the Evans woman three times if she had noticed any other persons on the day of the murder. After the witness had assured him for the third time that the only person she had seen coming out of the house was Rigby, instinct and experience gave the inspector an idea.

He turned this idea around and around in his mind like something priceless, then he detailed Inspector Carmody—one of his most conscientious men—to watch the boardinghouse. Carmody was wearing civilian clothes and looked like any other fellow lounging around between the boardinghouse and the pub. The instinct that gave Cox the reputation of being the sharpest bloodhound between hell and New South Wales, now told him what instruction to give to Inspector Carmody. The inhabitants of Mrs. Doody's boardinghouse were to enjoy a feeling of security. It was now a house like any other in Darlinghurst. Mrs. Doody, Molly Fleet, Umbrella Uncle, Candy's mother, Catherine Blyth, who was staying there temporarily, were to live as they always had. Gretchen came to see them, Mrs. Doody wept every now and then, Uncle Doody drank his beer and bitters with old Heller from next door—the actor was a steady guest at the house again. Mrs. Evans delivered flour, crackers, and salt, and Candy's tragic end wasn't mentioned. Molly Fleet came home tired from work at night, and Mrs. Blyth preached morality to her as she had done years ago—without success—to her own daughter, Candace. The murderer, Cox decided, had to be one of these people—with the exception of Mrs. Blyth who had come from Kalgoorlie—if Rigby, all the evidence against him notwithstanding, had not committed the crime.

Cox got up and locked the file on the first Mrs. Rigby in his desk. He looked at his watch: six-thirty. He turned to go. Another day . . . nothing. Just then the phone rang. Inspector Carmody reported what Cox had been waiting for day and night. Carmody had quite possibly found nothing but a clue; however, it had to be followed up at once with great caution.

One of Mrs. Doody's lodgers had brought a trunk into the house and removed Charlie Rainbow's flower boxes from the balcony. Who was leaving? And why had the boxes been taken away? Molly Fleet had continued to care for them; there seemed to be no reason to remove them unless . . . they held evidence of some kind.

"Shall I detain the person?" asked Inspector Carmody. Names were never mentioned over the phone.

"No. Just keep an eye on whoever it is. I'll be right over. Well done, young man!"

Mrs. Blyth opened the door to the inspector. A trunk stood in the hall, and turned out to be hers, and had journeyed from Kalgoorlie to Sydney with her. But Cox wasn't disappointed. There had to be a second trunk in the house—but where?

Cox looked at the hard, sharp face of Candy's mother, her sparse gray hair, and bitter mouth. The tall, thin woman was dressed in black and looked like a threatening exclamation mark. Of course she was unfriendly; she hated the police, just like every old Aussie did. "I am Mrs. Blyth," she told Inspector Cox. They were seated in the parlor. "I came to my daughter's funeral. I hope I won't be strangled before I leave here."

Mrs. Blyth seemed to be under the impression that her family was going to be exterminated. The inspector murmured a few words to reassure her. The police were keeping an eye on—

"They should have kept an eye on the house earlier! What are we paying taxes for when we don't get any protection? I was always against my daughter living in Sydney. Sodom and Gomorrah! A snake pit, if you ask me!"

"Why didn't you use your authority earlier?"

Mrs. Blyth's expression hardened. "I was through with Candace when she went off with some stranger or other. She had nothing but fun in her head. People like that are doomed." Inspector Cox found Mrs. Blyth deplorably heartless. "Our bread at home was too dry for my daughter," she mumbled. The inspector was silent. For the first time he could imagine why the beautiful young girl had yearned for love, luxury, and recognition.

It was very quiet in Mrs. Doody's parlor. There was an odor of hell, self-justification, and mothballs—the latter from Mrs. Blyth's dress. She had worn it last at her husband's funeral. "Candace was like her father," she said, disparagingly. "No sense of duty. No sense of decency. No faith."

The madonna above Mrs. Blyth's head frowned, or so it seemed to the inspector. "So I have to reconcile myself to *this* blow too," Mrs. Blyth said grimly. "The potter forms the clay and breaks it according to his will."

"How long are you going to stay in Sydney, Mrs. Blyth?"

"Until my sister has packed her few belongings. Lydia Doody is terribly slow." Mrs. Blyth sounded as if she were talking about someone she had only just met.

Mrs. Doody appeared with tea and greeted Inspector Cox like an old friend. Mrs. Blyth didn't approve, that much was obvious. Lydia was simpleminded. She ought to be careful that this fox with the curly hair didn't arrest all of them for some reason or other. Mrs. Blyth, who not only had a sharp tongue but also a keen mind, was telling herself correctly that the inspector had come for a purpose.

"I hear you are leaving Sydney, Mrs. Doody," Cox said in a friendly tone.

"Is there anything wrong with that, Inspector?" Candy's aunt asked tearfully. She had lost a lot of weight, and her love of chatter had run out of her like sawdust out of a broken doll.

"I have nothing to say against it, Mrs. Doody. Why should I?"

"You never know with the police," Mrs. Doody said. "Will they hang Candy's murderer? Or don't they hang people any more in this country? Another cup of tea, Inspector?"

"Thank you, Mrs. Doody. You look exhausted. You should see a doctor."

"My sister will recover in Kalgoorlie. The police visits have taken it out of her." Mrs. Blyth stood up. She didn't like the sharp way the inspector was looking at her. "Now don't talk nonsense," she told her younger sister, and left the room without so much as a nod to the inspector.

"My sister is so upset about Candy's death," Mrs. Doody murmured apologetically. "She loved her above everything else. Catherine has a fine character, even if she doesn't show it."

"Do you really want to leave Sydney, Mrs. Doody?"

"I don't know." She had grown very red and was trembling. "My sister says I should keep my mouth shut when the police question me. Excuse me, please."

"But we're old friends, Mrs. Doody. This is just a little private visit. I wanted to ask how Miss Fleet was feeling. All of you have hard days behind you."

Mrs. Doody nodded and wiped the tears from her eyes. "I always fussed so over the poor child. Perhaps that's not the right love. My sister says I spoiled her. She knows better. And then . . . I really don't like to talk about it . . ."

"You can tell *me*, Mrs. Doody."

"My sister will be angry if she finds out."

"She won't find out. What's troubling you?"

"You won't tell anyone?"

"Not a soul."

"I mean, I can't stop reproaching myself. I let Candy give me so much of her hard-earned money, and bought gin for Uncle with it."

"You mean Edward Doody?"

"That's what I said. Uncle. He's such a wreck, and the gin is all he has."

"What's wrong with Mr. Doody?"

"It's his heart. The doctor's been here twice. Since the dreadful thing happened to Candy, it's terrible. He shouts out loud in the night."

"Does Mr. Doody want to go to Kalgoorlie with you?"

"I don't know. But my sister won't have him."

"Why not?"

"She says she'll let no drunkard into her house. She's probably right, but we're all so fond of Uncle Doody. I can't imagine life without him."

"Where is he planning to go?"

"I don't know. He came here from the bush. He always says this is his only home. But my sister says that's no concern of mine. She's praying for Uncle Doody, and that's good enough. She's very religious, even if she doesn't express it very nicely. But Uncle Doody says the Bible words stink in her mouth. The two just don't like each other. Uncle is funny too. He's only all right with me and Charlie Rainbow."

"Is Mr. Doody home?"

"Don't go up to see him, Inspector. He's . . . he's a bit tipsy right now. The pain . . ."

"If I remember correctly, Mr. Doody was not one of Miss Blyth's admirers."

"You mustn't pay any attention to him. Our Molly says nobody can talk as much nonsense as Uncle Doody."

"When is Miss Fleet coming home?"

"Not at all today."

"Where is she?"

"At Gretchen's. Gretchen Lange from the bakery. Oh heavenly day! We must go! We were supposed to go over there, my sister and I."

"Don't let me stop you, Mrs. Doody."

Cox waited until both ladies were gone. This suited him fine. Carmody was waiting downstairs.

Cox knocked on Mr. Doody's door. When he got no answer, he pushed it open. Uncle was lying on his bed, a half-empty bottle on the floor beside him. "What do *you* want here?" he growled.

"Just saying hello." The inspector walked slowly into the room. He could see nothing unusual. The umbrellas were hanging from the ceiling as always. Uncle's eyes fluttered as he watched the inspector. "What are you looking for?" he asked.

"Nothing. Or do you have something stashed away?"

"Only a corpse in the closet."

The inspector laughed and walked over to the closet. Mr. Doody jumped up and planted himself, swaying a little, in front of the piece of furniture. "Hands off!" he cried. "I'll teach you a thing or two, Inspector. You're trespassing!"

The inspector pushed the old man aside. "I want to see your corpse in the closet."

He lugged a heavy trunk out of the closet. In the far corner stood two flower boxes. "Are you planting flowers in your closet?" he asked.

"I cut the flowers for Mrs. Doody. She's a good egg."

"But the boxes are going to dirty your things."

"I've packed them."

"Where are you going?"

"Somewhere."

"When?"

"Don't know."

"But you've packed everything."

"Just in case."

"And what do you mean by that?"

"Don't you speak English? Leave me alone! You have your murderer, and we can do what we like. This is a free country."

"How do you know I have my murderer?"

"From the papers. How's he doing?"

"I don't know. Do you?"

The old man stared at the cop. A wild light flickered in his gin-dimmed eyes. "Don't joke with a sick old man," he mumbled.

"When did you buy this trunk?"

"Yesterday."

"Not today?"

"Not today!" shouted Mr. Doody. "And now you'd bloody well better leave me alone!"

"As soon as you tell me where this trunk was until this afternoon."

Edward Doody had turned pale. So the cops had been watching him. He explained that he'd taken the trunk to be repaired. He named a shop in Surry Hills. Later it turned out that no such shop existed.

"I can't buy myself stinking elegant luggage like that murderer, Rigby."

The inspector lifted the trunk with one hand, shook it, and put it down again. "Unpack it, Mr. Doody," he said.

"I'm an old man! I just packed the bloody thing! I can't stoop that much. Leave me alone. My train leaves in an hour."

The inspector ignored this surprising information. "I can wait," he said, his voice dangerously quiet. "Get going, Doody! Or do you want me to help?"

The atmosphere in the narrow room had changed considerably. Cox could sense danger. The old man drew a knife out of one of his umbrellas and threw it, uncertainly, in the direction of the inspector. Cox ducked. "What's the meaning of this?" he asked casually, and laid the bush knife on the table.

"You're to leave us alone!" Mr. Doody drank the rest of the gin and hurled the bottle against the wall. Then he teetered to the trunk and unlocked it. He threw the contents at Cox's feet, with the exception of the newspaper at the bottom. Cox picked up the dented old trunk and shook it.

"If you damage my trunk, I'll sue!"

"You won't need your trunk any more," the inspector said, almost regretfully. He had removed the newspaper and was holding up a pair of gloves, dirty with earth. The gloves seemed to have a life of their own as he dangled them in front of the eyes of the old man. They looked like the hands of a man who had slung a nylon stocking around a girl's neck. "Why did you keep them?" asked the inspector.

"I don't know."

But Uncle knew very well. The gloves reminded him of what he had done for Lydia Doody. He hadn't been able to watch her any longer fluttering around the moody, sick girl, and the end of all jollity and comfort that was a part of Mrs. Doody, like the creaky doors in her house, the visits of the neighbors, her greed for money, but above all—her warmth.

For Uncle Doody, Lydia was daughter, friend, his host in this small piece of homeland. By all the saints she had deserved something better than to be tortured by Candy! Finally Uncle Doody had had enough. With his scant contact with reality he had formulated his plan in his gin-besotted brain.

"It was a good crime!" he said loudly and rebelliously.

Cox was looking out the window. He didn't even turn around to see if Doody was going to throw something at him again. He knew he was safe. He said quietly that there were no good crimes, and murder was a mortal sin. Had Uncle Doody forgotten?

Uncle rubbed his dim eyes. Then he laid a dirty hand over his heart. He didn't have much more time; he knew that just as well as the jackass doctors in Macquarie Street. His heart was acting so strangely lately, ever since he had planned the murder. It hadn't been easy. The cop at the window was not to think it had. Uncle Doody had grown up with a thorough knowledge of the register of sins, and at home he had knelt like a lamb to take the sacraments. He thanked God for the gift of his life, and now he owed him his death.

So he had crept around Candy for days like a bushman hunting a bird. He had waited and waited and listened patiently to what Candy had to say. He couldn't bring it off right away. That was to be expected. He'd stood several times behind Candy's chair. At first he'd been overwhelmed by a sort of horror, although his life had always been rough. Three years once for just a minor theft. But when Mrs. Doody had had her heart attack because Candy was driving her crazy . . . that was when Uncle Doody had bought the gloves, or rather exchanged them for an umbrella. Then he had crossed himself and sworn a little and prayed a little because one couldn't be sure what the saints would think of a good crime. Uncle Doody knew of course that God's mills ground slowly, but for him it had all been too slowly. And when things had been very bad at the boardinghouse, he'd looked at the gloves—God forgive him— and was really happy that Mrs. Doody would soon be relieved. He hadn't wished Candy any bad luck. No, her accident had upset him terribly. The poor thing hadn't been equal to it. But when she had giggled and said that now Aunt Doody would never be rid of her, not in her whole life, that was when Uncle Doody had put on the gloves. The sheila was so drunk, she was half asleep, half awake, and it had all happened fast. A clean ending and a good crime.

But it couldn't have been all that good because when it was over he didn't feel calm and happy as he had thought he would. Even so, he had put the gloves away in a safe place. Without the owner noticing it, he had hidden them in an old chest in the pub. Uncle Doody had seen Rigby leave, then he had gone to Candy's room. Yes, yes, that's how it had been. Then out of the house and to the pub! And Mrs. Evans paid no attention to him because she knew that Uncle Doody went to the pub late every afternoon. The person you see all the time becomes invisible! And that was why Inspector Cox had continued to have the house watched.

Uncle Doody had been terribly shocked when Rigby was arrested, but in his simple mind he had manufactured a wonderful theory: the cops couldn't do anything to Rigby because he *wasn't* the murderer. After all, Uncle knew who the murderer was! So he kept his mouth shut. Rigby was safe. They'd have to let him go soon, obviously! Uncle had been waiting daily for it to happen. After Rigby's arrest—and what a noise the press made about it!—Uncle had got the gloves from the pub, and at night had buried them in Charlie Rainbow's flower boxes. He remembered it exactly. There was no moon, and he had found it difficult to part with them. And that the gloves would get dirty had bothered him too. They'd been as good as new. He didn't know why, but somehow they fascinated him. And that was why he had put the flower boxes in his wardrobe. The gloves had to go with him on his wanderings. In his tipsy mind he decided that one day, when his lousy life on earth was over, he would show them when he got "up there." The gloves had freed Lydia Doody, and he was ready to take the blame. He was quite happy that the cop—a nice fellow, but not very smart—had tracked him down. Now he had come to the end of the line. And when, behind the cop's broad back, he took a secret look at his life—what had there been to it? A lot of violence, cursing, ugliness, a while in the slammer, wandering through the bush, and a few hearty Irish songs. Fair enough...

Inspector Cox looked down at the dreary street. And behind him was the old fellow with his "good crime," and Cox had to arrest him as the law demanded. And he would never have nabbed the old man if the sight of the gloves hadn't thrown him. Sometimes the inspector found his job damn difficult— good and evil got so mixed up. They weren't as cleanly separated as in the law books, and they sometimes made the people Cox had to arrest ridiculously lovable...

Edward Doody ran his fingers through his rumpled hair and coughed discreetly. The cop was standing in front of the window as if rooted to the spot. What was the matter with him? Uncle was feeling fine now. All he needed was a small room, only a corner, really, of this vast land, and a cell was a small room. Much better for Lydia to move to Kalgoorlie. She'd have peace and quiet now. In a short while she'd be laughing and chattering again, and would grow fat and be content. Mr. Muir had sent Mrs. Doody a nice sum of money after Candy's death. Decent of him. But the most important thing was that Mr. Doody would be sitting in the right compartment when the saints came marching in.

He walked up to the window and tapped the cop gently on the shoulder. "Hey, Inspector! Get a bloody move on!"

When Rigby was called to the warden's office, he had just made out his will. In spite of her orneriness, Anne was to get most of what he had because he didn't want her to spend the rest of her life working in a stuffy London office. Grace and his cobbers should get their share too. Paddy Trent had turned his new house in Queensland into a children's home for aboriginal children, but white orphans were accepted happily too. Perhaps Paddy and John Darling could use the house in Vaucluse for the same purpose. As for himself, he'd rot here, since Cox had decided he was guilty.

Tomorrow was the interrogation. He'd been in jail a week now. What did the warden want from him? A new house? Marchmont, Rigby & French had built him one five years ago, in Mosman Bay.

The warden explained that Inspector Cox had something to tell him. Aha! The fellow was there again too! Rigby stood and waited expectantly undaunted. But he was pale and he was frowning. He had lowered his head like a bull about to charge, his eyes were wild and half closed.

"We are dropping charges against you," Inspector Cox said formally. Rigby asked why the sudden change of mind. Then he pressed his lips together tightly again.

"As a result of new information and events, we are withdrawing all charges."

"If you'd listened to me in the first place, things would have been easier for you, Inspector."

Cox didn't move. The warden drummed on his desk with his fingers. Rigby hated it. Flora had sometimes drummed with her fingers ... For a second Rigby looked the warden in the eye and had the strange feeling that Cox had personally saved his life, even if he chose to hide behind all this official nonsense. But he might be wrong ...

"Shall I get you a taxi, Alexander?" asked the warden. They were both members of the yacht club and knew each other well.

"Not a bad idea, Gerald," Rigby replied casually. "And thanks for everything."

The warden had already picked up the receiver. Cox mumbled, "Are we friends again?"

Rigby was silent. It was none of the cop's business that he had spent the week in this stable working on the case of Flora Pratt. He looked past Cox and murmured, "I'll see what I can do, Inspector."

Rigby drove straight to Vaucluse. He didn't want to speak to his sister or his good friends now. Tomorrow. Or the day after tomorrow. First he had to give the Harbour Bridge a nod

and smell the evening meadows. He had to look at the illuminated shoreline and the moon over Sydney, New South Wales.

Tomorrow, after sunrise, he would drive to Parramatta and
stand firmly in front of the Rigby house. He had to tell Adam,
Colin and Jonathan Rigby that he was in the running again.
He had to sweat the five days of solitary confinement out of
his system, the vision of the trial with himself in the dock
between the protectors of the law. He didn't want to see the
court wigs any more, hear Clifford's defense, which he had
constantly corrected in his mind while waiting, or remember
the faces of the jury and all the enemies who could at last do
him in. One doesn't go unpunished for living for years in circles
where embarrassing situations were handled with kid gloves . . .

Rigby knew that he would never have been dragged into this
mess if Anne hadn't sent him that friendly farewell letter, and
what was more—if Anne hadn't received that anonymous letter
on his fiftieth birthday, which had precipitated her flight. Who
the hell had hated him so much as to want to destroy his
marriage? *Who*? He would never know. Candy Blyth had not
been as naive as everyone had thought. No one can be a professional gold digger without cunning. She had been smart enough
to play the beautiful dumb blond. After his fiftieth birthday
she had recognized the picture in the paper and had followed
him one day to Vaucluse. It hadn't been necessary for Molly
Fleet to reveal who Ritter was. The only thing Candy had
found out from Molly during the last weeks of her life was
Anne's London address. From Molly's mail.

Perhaps it was a good thing that Candy had taken her wretched
secret into eternity. It was certainly good for Mrs. Doody, and
Rigby could do without enlightenment. He had been too in-
considerate of Anne. If one was too thick-skinned, did one get
a good beating at the apex of one's life? Rigby realized that
he was brooding. But first he wanted to celebrate his return to
life in profound stillness. In old Parramatta, where his ancestors
had lived and built.

32

Meeting in Parramatta

Molly Fleet went back to Parramatta. The dissolution in Darlinghurst, the police interrogations, Rigby's release from prison—a real press feast, that one—and Uncle Doody's silent departure had all been too much for her. Now she was the fifth wheel on the wagon again. In family relationships nothing changed. Wars came and went, a murder in Sydney became a media event, buildings rose into the sky—in Parramatta none of it meant anything. Molly had only a few clients, and they demanded cheaper prices because they'd always known young Molly Fleet. One day she'd go back to Sydney. There was nothing for her here in Parramatta. The young married couples were self-sufficient and satisfied with their futures. Molly saw her father only in the evenings, and he hadn't grown any pleasanter. Nobody could get out of him whether he was happy to have his youngest daughter back. For Molly, life stood still.

After the recent happenings in Sydney, this was at first quite pleasant, but gradually she became restless. She tried to find some warmth and recognition with her family, but they treated her with amiable indifference. So she helped in the brewery and with the bookkeeping. But in the long run that wasn't the right work for a young girl. Not even the cows on the farm were her faithful companions any more. She decided she had been in the city too long. Or had the cow, Lily, belonged to her childhood? Stephen was living happily on the farm with his wife, and soon his children would be running around.

Molly was sitting on the shore of Parramatta Lake one Sunday, staring into the water, when somebody cried, "Hello!" It was Inspector Cox with his curly hair and sharp eyes. "Do you want to arrest me again?" Molly asked harshly.

"Have you done anything wrong?"

"What are you doing in Parramatta?"

"I'm visiting my aunt. How are you, Miss Fleet?"

"What do you care?"

Molly covered her left cheek with her glossy hair, and the gesture touched Cox, as it had done before. He sat down beside Molly and offered her a cigarette. "It's nice and quiet here," he said, and sighed.

Molly stared at him, astounded. He didn't look at all dangerous, but younger, and *different*. If he hadn't once frightened Molly almost to death, she would even have found him nice. He *was* nice, but she wouldn't admit that to herself.

"What are you doing here, Miss Fleet?"

"Helping in the brewery. I had more to do in Sydney."

"And more going for you, of course. Why don't you go back? A smart girl like you who has learned a trade shouldn't be stagnating here."

"My father wants me to stay."

"That isn't true." But it sounded friendly. "You can't put anything like that over on me, Molly Fleet." He laughed, and patted her on the shoulder.

"Don't touch me!"

Her hostility surprised him. But he had treated her roughly while she was under suspicion. What a damned business it had been! How could he make it clear to the girl that he meant well? She needed a friend, and here he was. He simply hadn't been able to forget her. And now she was refractory and unapproachable. He looked at her profile. Her lips were trembling like a child's.

"You're not happy here, are you?"

He said it so gently, that Molly looked up. "I'm very happy here," she said stubbornly.

"Nonsense! Tell me, would you come back to Sydney if you had somewhere to stay?"

"I have nowhere to stay."

"That's where you're wrong." The inspector sounded quite cheerful. "There's a very nice room free in our house. My sister got married last week. Right now everybody's marrying."

"Here too," Miss Fleet said thoughtfully. "You should see April."

"Who is April?"

"My sister. She married Kurt."

"And who is Kurt?"

"Kurt Hildebrand, and he has her eating out of his hand."

"That's the way it should be." Cox winked at her, and suddenly Molly had to laugh.

"April used to be a beast, but now she's fine."

"That's what marriage does. Don't you want to get married?" Molly's face darkened. "Can't you take a bit of fun?"

"Not about marriage," Molly said gruffly. "I know I'll never find a husband."

"Why don't you get a second opinion on that?"

Molly laughed bitterly, the way a young creature shouldn't have to laugh. Cox gently stroked her hair from her left cheek. She pushed him away angrily, tears in her eyes. "Get out of here!" she screamed.

"There, there," Cox murmured soothingly. The stupid little thing thought that because of her birthmark, she couldn't please a man!

"Listen to me, Miss Fleet. You had a devilishly hard time in Sydney these last weeks. And I . . . I mean . . ." Inspector Cox had never been at a loss for words before.

"Do you mean that you were perfectly horrid to me?"

"Something like that," Cox said stiffly. Damn it! All he'd done was his duty. After explaining that to Molly, he asked her if she'd like to stay with his mother. Mrs. Cox could do with some massage; she often had a backache. Or Molly could stay with friends of his, if his presence disturbed her.

"You're away most of the time," she said with her usual candor.

"That's right." Cox tried not to smile. "And by the way, I've made inquiries at two hospitals. You can get steady work there. A young woman like you is always needed in a big city like Sydney."

Molly was watching the horrid cop, mouth agape. She was speechless. Cox was the first man who had ever given her a thought and wanted to help her. "Whatever makes you . . ." She couldn't go on.

"Makes me what?"

"Want to help me?" she asked, her voice hoarse. "What concern is it of yours how I live?"

Cox didn't reply. When he had first seen Molly in Mrs. Doody's boardinghouse—young, alert, strong—he had known that the girl from Parramatta didn't belong in these surroundings. Dust, flies, moth-eaten plush, moral lethargy, and obvious neglect everywhere. And the room of the dead model! Cox could still see the hideous pink lampshades and silk coverlets, and smell the stagnant atmosphere of perfume, sugar daddies, and pathetic Hollywood fantasies. He had felt somehow responsible for Molly Fleet then, even though he hadn't realized it at the time, and had wished he could shepherd this stray lamb from New South Wales to a good herd. Molly knew hardly anything about everyday life in Sydney.

His mother was perfectly agreeable to taking in the young lodger. "Do you intend to marry her?" she had asked, smiling, but her son laughed, and shook his head. Who would marry a cop? He was rarely home, and when he did come home, he was too tired for talk or love. All he wanted to do then was eat and sleep, and what young woman would like that? But he wanted Molly Fleet to be treated well for a change, and his mother would soon talk her out of this *idée fixe* she had about her birthmark. Or he would, if Molly learned to trust him. "Think it over," he told her. "We'd like to have you with us."

"And I'd love it!" she cried impulsively. "It's damn good o you, Inspector. But what if your mother can't stand the sigh of me?"

"Don't be foolish, Molly!"

"What do *you* know about things like that?" Molly crie passionately. "You're a handsome man. Plenty of girls mus

be running after you. Here they used to call me 'Mole'!" Now
she was sobbing.

Cox cleared his throat. He realized suddenly what this girl
must have suffered. He spoke soothingly to her, but she shook
off his arm. "You're only saying that to be nice."

"I'm not famous for being the nicest fellow around," said
Cox. "But a pretty, smart girl like you shouldn't be so vain."

"You think I'm *pretty*?"

"You heard me," Cox said drily.

"And you're not saying all this because you feel sorry for
me?"

"Any more foolish questions?"

He smiled. Molly smiled back shyly. "What are you doing
tonight?" she asked.

"Nothing."

"Will you come to us for a beer? But it's hopelessly boring
at our house."

"Thank you, Miss Fleet. I'd like to meet your family."

"As I said, only Kurt is nice."

"I can hardly wait to meet this miracle of manhood. But
right now I prefer you."

He looked at her and she blushed. Dear heaven, how innocent the girl had remained despite Mrs. Doody's gin house!

"Why are you staring at me like that?" Molly stammered.
"What do you want to know now?"

"Nothing, pet," said Inspector Cox. As happened so often—
one look and he knew what he wanted to know.

"We're having steak tonight," Molly Fleet said after a pause.

"Great. By the way, can you cook?"

"Of course I can cook! Grandmother Fleet taught me on the
farm. But I'm not very experienced."

"Maybe it'll be good enough for me. If you like you can
call me Curl."

"Come on!" cried Molly, jumping to her feet. "Let's run all
he way to the brewery. Whoever gets there first wins!"

"You've won already. I'm an old man of thirty-seven."

Molly laughed and started off, but Cox was used to a chase.

He was waiting for her, calm and relaxed, in front of the brewery, which he had taken a look at earlier.

"Phew!" gasped Molly. "I can't keep up with you. For an old man you run first-rate. Nobody's ever beat me."

"High time somebody did."

Just then Mr. Fleet came out of the brewery and looked over the young man who was joking with his youngest. He didn't seem pleased about it.

"This is my father," Molly murmured apologetically.

"And who is *he*?" asked Mr. Fleet.

"A friend of mine from Sydney."

"A friend of *yours*?" Mr. Fleet's eyebrows went up.

Cox gave his name. Fortunately Mr. Fleet understood it. He read the papers too, and would rather not have trouble with a cop. "How about a beer?" he asked the tall man with the sharp, light eyes. "And it doesn't have to be just one, mister."

"Thank you very much," said Inspector Cox. "When it comes to beer, I can take a lot."

"In other respects too," Molly said sassily. "You're a tough guy!"

"Who says so, Miss Fleet?"

"I do!"

"Well, then it must be true," the inspector said thoughtfully. "Mr. Fleet, your daughter can hear the grass growing."

That night Molly tried to recall her life in Sydney. Had she really lived at Mrs. Doody's or had it all been a bad dream? In her childhood on the farm she had taken reality like a bull by the horns. She'd learned that from Grandmother Fleet and Stephen. Did a lot of people in Sydney live like Candy and the Doodys? The inspector was different.

Molly couldn't make up her mind to accept his offer. She didn't want to say thank you, and that was odd. Her father had always said that in the end nobody got along with his youngest daughter. After all, he knew her; when she was at home she was sullen. She was sure that secretly Cox didn't think she was exactly something to show off. He probably had a lot of pretty sheilas on tap. When he laughed he looked extraordinarily young, and he could run like a weasel. Why had he offered her a room in his house?

That evening they had taken a walk by the sea, and he had said she had landed in a wrong corner of Sydney. Then he had pushed the hair away from her face again, and had stroked her red cheek gently. She had wanted to run away, but Cox had assured her that a real man saw beneath the facade. The main thing was for the heart to be in the right place. And besides, Molly was a very good-looking young lady. But . . . he hadn't kissed her. When things got serious he was just like other men.

Molly stared into the dark. Cox felt sorry for her because she didn't have a boy friend, and because he was a good human being. But she had to stay and rot in Parramatta because she had no intention of being a burden to anyone. And anyway, there was no real difference. At home her days were just as uneventful as they had been in Sydney. They came and went like the clouds in the sky of New South Wales.

After three horrid months, Molly couldn't stand it any longer. She wrote to Cox and asked him if he still knew who she was, and whether she could still come.

She took the Vynyard bus and drove over the Harbour Bridge to Lane Cove. The inspector was waiting outside the garden gate. He had come home from headquarters a little earlier. It was a beautiful, roomy house and the garden was gorgeous.

"Why didn't you come sooner, Miss Fleet?"

"I thought you might have regretted it."

"We've been expecting you for quite a while. But I couldn't exactly come crawling to you on my knees, could I?"

The very idea was so funny that Molly burst out laughing. "I'm so happy," was all she could say. "The garden is enchanting."

"Just like the residents. We hope you will feel at home with us. Next week I shall introduce you at the hospitals. Until then you can work on Mother's back if you like."

"What's wrong with her?"

"My mother was a member of the police force in New South Wales for years. She was on duty in all kinds of weather. She gave it up when Shirley and I were born."

Inspector Cox smiled as he thought how Police Sergeant Edith Roberts had developed into a very contented Mrs. Cox. Lillian Armfield, the first woman police officer in New South Wales in the year 1915, who had hunted down criminals fearlessly with her male colleagues, had inspired young Edith Roberts. A few weeks ago Miss Rigby had asked the inspector's mother for an autobiographical sketch for *Insight*. When Inspector Cox had interviewed Miss Rigby for the first time, in spite of the embarrassing situation, Miss Rigby had found out that he was the son of Edith Roberts-Cox, who today was helping to train the new female recruits. Cox had admired Miss Rigby at the time. She had guts. Rigby, too, had behaved damn well.

"Was your father a cop too?" Molly asked shyly.

"Naturally. It's hereditary."

"Is your mother very strict?"

"What makes you think so?"

"I mean . . . because . . . after all, she had to arrest girls."

"That was a long time ago. Besides, at home we don't bite."

He led Molly through the garden. "If I get to be too much for you," she said fearfully, "you must throw me out. Father always said nobody could put up with me for long."

"Mother says that about me too. Parents always think like that."

"I won't be home much anyway," Molly said consolingly.

"Neither will I. You see, we were made for each other. Mother isn't around much either."

Molly swallowed hard. At last she managed to say, "There's something I must make clear, Mr. Cox."

"Now what?"

They had remained standing under a blossoming magnolia tree, and Molly's excitement was written all over her face. "Don't look at me like that!" she said.

"I've got to look somewhere, don't I? So . . . what is it?"

"I'll go for a walk or stay in my room when . . . when your girlfriend comes to see you."

"My *what*?"

"Surely you have a pretty sheila you go out with. I mean when you have time."

"When I have time I swim or sleep. I warned you in Parramatta: hands off the cops. They're a crashing bore."

"I find you terribly interesting, Mr. Cox."

"Well that's fine. And you can call me Curl."

"Thank you, Mr. Cox. I don't know why you're so nice to me."

"I don't know either."

"I really have nothing to offer, I mean as far as conversation is concerned."

"I enjoy talking to you very much when you're not being foolish."

"The men I knew in Sydney were quite different."

"How many were there?"

"I didn't have a boy friend, you know that. I only knew Candy's men." Molly hesitated. "I'm really not a very nice girl, Mr. Cox. I used to write Candy's love letters to Mr. Rigby for her."

"What do you know about love?"

"I go to the movies."

"Oh yes, I forgot—the movies." Miss Fleet's visit to the movies on the day of the murder had been a sticky wicket in the interrogation. "If you don't want to get out of practice, why don't you write me a love letter?"

"You?"

"Why not? I like to read that sort of thing. After all, I'm a man."

"Well, sure. But you're so experienced. You'd laugh yourself silly over my nonsense."

"Or weep. You're not nearly as naive as you pretend to be, Molly Fleet. Well, if you don't want to write me a love letter, you could whisper something nice in my ear."

"I'm not that sort of person," Molly replied. "Besides, I respect you much too much."

"That's what an old man likes to hear."

"But you're not *that* old, Mr. Cox. You can run like a fox. I mean, you're a little old only compared with me, right? But that's no reason..." Molly hesitated, embarrassed. The inspector was looking at her so strangely again.

"What were you going to say?"

"Nothing," Molly stammered.

"Don't worry. I'll find out. But it would be nice if you could trust me a little more. Every now and then you're going to need some good advice, child. You're too green for a city like Sydney."

"I have *loads* of experience." Molly sounded hurt.

"I found you in one hell of a mess, young lady. How did you ever get into Mrs. Doody's gin house?"

"I saw the sign: Room to Let. I didn't know anybody in Sydney, and I didn't want to sit around at home all the time." Cox said nothing. "My friend Gretchen even told me—that was before Candy was... was murdered—that I could have a room in her house."

"So why didn't you go there? Mrs. Lange is a very respectable woman."

"Gretchen's husband wouldn't have liked it, I'm sure. Now they have an adorable baby."

"Do you like children?"

"I love them!" Molly cried ecstatically. "I'd like to work with sick children. Gretchen said I could give their little son a bath occasionally. Isn't that wonderful?"

"If you like children so much, you're going to have to put up with a husband." Inspector Cox was amused.

"I wouldn't mind marrying." Molly was silent suddenly. When one got married, one knew where one belonged. Then she said aloud, "But most men are false."

"I shall examine your future husband with a magnifying glass," said the inspector, "or you'll get into a mess again. You know nothing about men, Molly Fleet."

"What I know is quite enough."

"It will do you no harm to learn a little more. And if you get into a jam again, just call on me."

"You . . . you're too good to me. I'm not used to it."

Cox was silent again. This young sheila was very different from the chattering, fast-moving kookaburras of King's Cross, whom she probably admired and envied. But in spite of her misadventures in Darlinghurst, she had remained true to herself. She had probably thought everybody in Sydney lived like the Doodys. How could she know that this city had room for thousands of individual ways of life, and offered a wealth of human experience. Molly had grown up in a country town and on a farm, and had been transplanted in foreign soil. But she had great reserves of strength, and a stubborn innocence. She brought with her to the big city an aura of the quietude in Parramatta, wild bush flowers, and the old Australian sense of moderation.

"May I plant some more flowers?" she asked hesitantly. "I always had a flower garden on the farm."

"Of course you may," said Inspector Cox. "But not right now. Mother is expecting us for tea." He gave Molly Fleet a friendly shove. "Hey, young lady! Get a bloody move on!"

33

On Harbour Bridge

Rigby drove back to Vaucluse in the late afternoon. He had attended a conference outside the city, and was looking forward to his dinner. Bertie Dobson had insisted that after her heart attack, Rigby's jewel should enjoy some peace and quiet with her family. Rigby thought that with Andrews's move there would be an end to the family's peace and quiet, but he had agreed. Andrews was a good egg, but she had participated far too much in his life. Once in a while he had even gotten the impression that she would have liked to be the third Mrs. Rigby, and was just biding her time. If so, she had backed the wrong horse. To begin with, he was still married to Anne, which Andrews liked to ignore, and he had had enough of marriage. Andrews had trained a young woman before she left. She wasn't much of a cook, but in his fallow season he had learned a thing or two: if necessary he could eat simply.

He stopped with a swarm of other cars before Harbour Bridge and looked at the lively world on the water and greeted the harbor. He had jumped from the ocean of error onto land. The triumphant arch of the bridge swung across the just and the unjust. He had managed to come through once more. Now all he had to do was free himself from the jail within him, and that was not easy. For that he would have needed Anne, but that chapter was over. All he knew was that he had been an idiot. He had thought love lasted forever. The truth of the matter was, one experienced it only for a short time. He watched the ferries and boats. They came and went, as Anne had come and gone. If he had known then what he knew now, he would have held onto her with both hands. Too late! Anne had written him a letter. She was sorry that he was in trouble again and hoped things would turn out all right. He had torn it to pieces after they had let him out. When he recalled how Miss Rigby and his cobbers had practically devoured him with their joy, he could climb the walls over Anne's cool reaction to the mess. But he forgot his anger because he had big plans and was a man, not a self-pitying infant.

He was still waiting before the bridge. The afternoon sun illuminated the magnificent shoreline and the high-rise houses. The light, the breadth, the mute experience of the stone … Rigby's life had remained fragmented, with no solid foundation. Why was he such a bungler in love? He could plan and build, he knew the laws of measurement and the balance between material and motion. Probably the building of emotion needed a solid foundation too. In his fallow season, Rigby had balanced his books, and had found out why he had still gone running after little girls in his mature years. After his experience with Flora Pratt he had had to prove his virility over and over again. His humiliation had provoked his need for female admiration. Did this happen to other men too?

He sat behind the wheel, motionless. The still poetry of the Harbour Bridge melted away in the harshness of his thoughts. Damn it all! There came a time when a man simply had to stop behaving like a fool! He had to strive for bold thinking, clear action, and loyalty in his feelings. In short, the dignity of age had to conquer the enchanting foolishness of youth. And that was that!

The Harbour Bridge opened up and Rigby drove back to Vaucluse.

He had put the car in the garage and was standing in the garden. Everything was blooming and greening innocently, and with brilliant superfluity. This earth did not produce a lean harvest.

A blond young woman in a white dress came down the terrace steps and walked up to Rigby. He stood rooted to the spot. "I don't believe it!" His heart was beating fast and the blood rushed to his head. Then Anne was in his arms. He kissed her and she responded to his kisses. At last Rigby pushed her away and looked at her. She was unbelievably beautiful, and more alive than he had ever seen her. For a moment he stood absolutely still, then a strange sound issued from his throat and he stretched his powerful arms high. He looked as if he were trying to grasp the evening sun with both hands. He was victorious. He had not crept down into the misty underworld, like Orpheus, to retrieve his wife. Eurydice had come back to this Australian earth of her own free will. But would she stay? Would she never look back?

Rigby's arms sank to his sides. The ecstatic moment was over. If Anne was only passing through, she could take the next plane back to London. He didn't want to look for only one day at what he had lost. If Anne left him again now he would live like a half-dead fish in a dried-up ocean, waiting under a merciless sun for the flood that never came—a dumb, shrinking, wriggling fish. That he would have to hate what he loved, and in spite of his unfaithfulness, had always loved—that would be the sickness of his old age and finally his death. Still, the only thing that could be of any use to him now was the truth. The moment of perception on Harbour Bridge could only be a new beginning if there was to be clarity between him and Anne.

He looked silently at her fine features, her soft blond hair, her pastel beauty. But she had turned pale suddenly, like a dying woman, who still felt his kisses but was inexorably bidding him farewell. He smiled coldly.

"Don't you want me?" she asked.

"Only under certain conditions."

"And what do you mean by that?"

"I mean that I'm not going to let you make a fool of me!" Rigby cried in very unphilosophical fury. There was no resemblance any more between him and the serene man on Harbour Bridge. But Anne had balanced her books in her fallow season too, and learned a thing or two about marriage. After much soul-searching she had recognized that her frigidity could only make a man like Rigby more difficult. She had had too little patience with him and had wanted to transform him into a tamed domestic animal. She sensed now that Rigby could even be domestic if one didn't force him. He had loved her at first, perhaps he loved her still. His kisses had spoken their own language. What was more—after family life on Avenue Road Anne found it most agreeable for someone to be excited over her.

"I don't know what you're talking about, Alex," she said casually.

"There's nothing new about that! I mean—if you're only passing through, you can swim right off again!"

"On my first visit to Sydney I stayed seven years."

"Why did you come? Have you quarreled with your dear mother?"

"Nobody can quarrel with my dear mother. She didn't even notice that I was back."

"If you've come to console me over my second scandal, you've come a day late, as usual. I'm feeling fine. Every goddamned day!"

"Stop swearing," the second Mrs. Rigby said sternly. "I've come back and that's all."

"Why?"

Anne stood on tiptoe so that she could look into his eyes. "Can't you imagine why?"

"I never imagine anything," Rigby growled, but he felt appeased.

"Seriously, Alex," said the second Mrs. Rigby, "without you it was even worse."

After thinking it over for a moment, Rigby found this was fair enough. He laid his arm across Anne's shoulder, and they went into the house.